THE IDEA HAD BEEN SO BRILLIANT. . . .

Monique's glance fell on the radiant faces of the three brides smiling out at her from the open pages of the magazine, faces that had haunted her since she'd found the first copies of the June issue in a box beside her desk.

Grief tore through her. Oh God, only three of us. There were supposed to have been four—Evie, Teri, Ana, and herself. Her heart cried out for the one who was missing.

This had all been her idea. Four stunning brides, the weddings of the year, showcased in dazzling style. *Save the magazine, save my ass, make Richard happy.*

But for one of them the dream had turned into a nightmare. *You never know what life will spring on you,* Monique thought, sinking into her chair as the rain pelted more fiercely against the window. *You just never know. Not one of us could have guessed what would happen.*

She hadn't, that long-ago dawn when she'd first conceived the plan for salvaging the magazine, her job, and her future with Richard. Her brilliant plan. She'd had no idea what she was getting all of them into. . . .

Something Borrowed, Something Blue

JILLIAN KARR

BANTAM BOOKS
New York London Toronto Sydney Auckland

This edition contains the complete text
of the original hardcover edition.
NOT ONE WORD HAS BEEN OMITTED.

SOMETHING BORROWED, SOMETHING BLUE

A Bantam Fanfare Book / published in association
with Doubleday

PUBLISHING HISTORY
Doubleday hardcover edition / November 1993
Bantam paperback edition / June 1994

FANFARE and the portrayal of a boxed "ff" are trademarks of
Bantam Books,
a division of Bantam Doubleday Dell Publishing Group, Inc.

ISBN 0-553-29990-5

Published simultaneously in the United States and Canada

PRINTED IN THE UNITED STATES OF AMERICA
RAD   0 9 8 7 6 5 4 3 2 1

For Larry, Lawrence, Mitchel, Rachel, and Steven
(Not to mention Buster and Scamper)
With love

ACKNOWLEDGMENTS

A special heartfelt thank-you to all the following people for their advice and help during the research and writing of this book:

Mary Cybulski; Myrna and Ken Dosie; Marge Kasparian; Ilene and David Katz; Judy Katz; Dr. Marty Levinson, Chairman of Pediatrics, Sinai Hospital, Detroit; Joanne and Edward Rodzik; Dr. Clifford Saper, Beth Israel Hospital, Boston; Alice Sieloff, publisher, and the staff of *Detroit Metropolitan Woman*; Doris and Jay Silcox and family; Sandra Sonnino; Robin Terebelo; and to everyone involved in the production of *Used People*—especially Beeban Kidron, director; Scott Mansfield, extras casting, Toronto; Peggy Rajski, producer; Arthur Rowsell, wardrobe supervisor, Toronto; and John Tintori, editor.

Something Borrowed, Something Blue

Prologue

The intercom buzzed, braying intrusively into the early morning silence of the office.

Standing by the window, looking down at the sea of umbrellas bobbing far below, Monique D'Arcy took another sip of her coffee, ignoring the insistent drone, her secretary's attempt to draw her into the formal start of this workday. Not yet, Linda. The Sinutab hasn't kicked in. What the hell could be so important at seven-thirty in the morning?

She closed her eyes and pressed the coffee mug into the hollow between her brows, letting the warmth seep into her aching sinuses. The intercom buzzed on, relentless, five staccato blasts that reverberated through Monique's head like a jackhammer.

"Dammit."

She tossed the fat, just-published June issue of *Perfect Bride* and a stack of next month's galleys aside to unearth the intercom buried somewhere on her marble desk. She pressed the button resignedly. "You win, Linda. What's up?"

"Hurricane warning."

"*What?*" Monique spun back toward the window

and scanned the dull pewter skyline marred with rain clouds. Manhattan was getting soaked in a May downpour and her window shimmered with delicate crystal droplets, but no wind buffeted the panes. "Linda, what are you talking . . ."

"Shanna Ives," Linda hissed. "She's on her way up. Thought you'd like to know."

"Shit." Adrenaline pumped into her brain, surging past the sinus headache as Monique dove into her fight or flee mode. She started pacing, her Maud Frizon heels digging into the plush vanilla carpet. Shanna was the last person in the world she wanted to tangle with this morning. She was still trying to come to grips with the June issue, with all that had happened. As she set the mug down amid the organized clutter of her desk, she realized her hands were shaking. Get a grip. Don't let that bitch get the better of you. *Oh, God, this is the last thing I need today.*

Her glance fell on the radiant faces of the three brides smiling out at her from the open pages of the magazine, faces that had haunted her since she'd found the first copies of the June issue in a box beside her desk a scant half hour earlier.

Grief tore at her. Oh, God, only three of us. There were supposed to have been four. There *should* have been four. Her heart cried out for the one who was missing.

This had all been her idea. Four stunning brides, the weddings of the year, showcased in dazzling style. Save the magazine, save my ass, make Richard happy. All of us famed celebrities—except for one.

Teri. She smiled, thinking of the first time she'd met the pretty little manicurist who'd been so peculiarly reluctant at first to be thrust into the limelight. Most women dreamed of the Cinderella chance she'd been offered, yet Teri had recoiled from it. *But I made it impossible for her to refuse. I never guessed where it would lead, or what it would do to her life.*

And Ana, Hollywood's darling, with that riot of red curls framing a delicate face, exuding sexy abandon. Monique had found Ana perhaps the most vulnerable and private of them all. *Poor, beautiful Ana, with her sad, ugly secrets—I never dreamed anyone could have as much to hide as I do.*

And then there was Eve—lovely, tigerish Eve, Monique's closest friend in the world, the once-lanky, unsure teenage beauty she had discovered and catapulted to international supermodel fame. *All I asked was one little favor* . . .

And me, Monique reflected with a bittersweet smile, staring at her own glamorous image alongside the other two brides. Unconsciously, she twisted the two-and-a-half-carat diamond on her finger. Monique D'Arcy, the Comtesse de Chevalier. *If only they knew the truth.*

Shanna Ives would be bursting through her door any minute, breathing fire. But Monique couldn't stop thinking about the three women whose lives had become so bound up with her own during the past months. Teri, Ana, Eve—all on the brink of living happily ever after with the men they loved . . .

For one of them the dream had turned into a nightmare. *You never know what life will spring on you,* Monique thought, sinking into her chair as the rain pelted more fiercely against the window. *You just never know. Not one of us could have guessed what would happen.*

She hadn't, that long-ago dawn when she'd first conceived the plan for salvaging the magazine, her job, and her future with Richard. Her brilliant plan. She'd had no idea of what she was getting all of them into. . . .

Chapter One

Eve balanced her spike-heeled shoes and leather tote in the crook of her arm and fumbled impatiently through her handbag for the apartment keys. One more minute and she could peel off these panty hose. She couldn't wait to get out of her dress, her bra, her makeup—and into a steaming tub. She fished out a lipstick and two tampons before finally snaring her crystal heart key ring from the depths of the bag. When the door latch clicked open and she stepped onto the cold rose marble tile, she breathed a sigh of pure bliss to be home at last.

She'd been on the run since six A.M., first with a shoot that had lasted ten hours, and then dinner with her agent, Natalie Royce, and the Estēe Lauder people. Her body was crying out for sleep.

The familiar, reassuring beep of the security system greeted her like an old friend. She nearly tripped over Ragamuffin as she dumped her gear and scurried to press the buttons, silencing the electronic welcome.

"Good to see you too, baby. And how was *your* day?" she grinned wryly as the midnight-black cat with the crooked tail whisked past her without a backward glance and leapt onto the settee beneath the living room window.

She followed Ragamuffin across the softly lit apartment, knelt down beside the cream satin settee, and stroked the tiny cat's sleek back. "Oh, why can't you be a dog? A dog would lick my face, fetch my slippers, and at *least* say hello when I walk in the door. You—you're a little ingrate."

She pressed a quick, weary kiss on the top of Ragamuffin's head and stood up to peel off her panty hose.

"Don't try to tell me how exhausting *your* day was. Nothing could beat mine."

Ragamuffin yawned, and curled into a tighter ball.

Eve chuckled, remembering how little and helpless the cat had seemed the chilly spring day she had found her while on her daily jog through Central Park. Eve had nearly stumbled over the tiny creature curled on the path, intently licking her broken tail. The injury was fresh; Eve could still see crusts of blood. She'd scooped the scrawny kitten into her arms and jogged her straight home. A little peroxide on the tail, a little milk, and half of Eve's tuna sandwich, and Ragamuffin had settled in good as new on the soft throw pillow nestled before the fireplace. Since then, she'd never so much as sniffed a thank-you, but Eve spoiled her rotten just the same. *We're alike,* Eve frequently reminded Nico, who hated cats. *Both of us are survivors—stubborn, sensible females who happen to share a passion for soft satin pillows, tuna fish sandwiches—and you.* It was true, Ragamuffin followed Nico about like a lovesick fan, rubbing her silky back against his leg, purring whenever he entered the room. The more he ignored her, the more she swooned.

But then, I've never met a female who didn't swoon over Nico, Eve thought, yawning, as she tossed her panty hose over the back of the sofa and then padded barefoot into the bedroom.

No message from Nico. Damn, she really wanted

to tell him about the new Estée Lauder contract Natalie had outlined for her tonight. She glanced at the ormolu clock on her bedside table and did a quick mental calculation of London time. It was still an hour or more before dawn would bathe the River Thames in pale mist. Well, the news would have to wait until morning. If she didn't get her weary body into bed soon, she'd be comatose on her already aching feet.

A thud echoed through the penthouse. Eve froze. A tentacle of fear constricted her heart. Cautiously she edged to the door and peered out, then laughed at her own jumpiness. Ragamuffin had knocked her appointment book off the coffee table and now stood over it, pawing the pages.

"Troublemaker! I bet you wouldn't even meow if someone *was* hiding in here!" she scolded. She rescued the book and on second thought double-checked the burglar alarm. Everything was fine. After all, Clara had called the security company last week after the letter had come, and had upgraded the system—just in case.

And anyway, she told herself, returning to the rose and cream bedroom, he was probably just some harmless nut case who would never be heard from again.

Eve unzipped the clingy gold lamé sheath and snaked it to the floor. As she bent to pick it up, her eyes locked on a beautifully wrapped package nestled among the brushes and crystal perfume bottles on her dressing table. It was unmistakably a wedding present, swathed in silver and white doves and thick satin ribbon.

"Nana!" Eve exclaimed as she recognized the familiar script on the card. "What could this possibly be?" She tore off the paper and opened the box, her exhaustion momentarily forgotten.

She caught her breath as she saw the magnificent tablecloth of ivory Finnish lace tucked between protective layers of white tissue. Eve stroked the delicate stitching with reverence. "Oh, Nana, your heirloom tablecloth," she whispered, and for a moment tears blurred her eyes.

An instant later she was on the phone to Minneapolis. There was no way she would wake Nana. Liina Hämeläinen never went to bed before watching *Nightline*.

"Nana, I don't know what to say." Eve brushed away a tear and smiled, picturing her stately, silver-haired grandmother propped in bed with a crossword puzzle on her lap and her Nikes perched alongside her exercise bike. "It's gorgeous. You know how much I've always loved it."

"Evie Bettina, you enjoy it for many, many years. I know it'll be in good hands."

"It will, Nana."

Her grandmother chuckled. "You know, I've always meant it to be yours. I never saw anyone's eyes shine the way yours did when you used to help me set the table each Thanksgiving. Margo, she never noticed anything but her books—but you, you're as sentimental as I am and you always appreciated the few things of beauty we had. Of course, now that you're a rich and famous model, you can afford to buy whatever you want, but I still knew you would like to have my heirloom cloth."

"I'll treasure it, Nana. So will Nico. And I promise you, when the time comes, I'll pass it along to someone who will love it as much as we do."

She'd have to tell Nico about the tablecloth in the morning, she thought as she tumbled into the satin-sheeted featherbed a short time later. Darkness cloaked the room as she switched off the night-light. Ragamuffin leapt onto the bed and burrowed into Nico's pillow with a sharp meow.

"You miss him too, don't you, baby?" Eve smiled as she curled on her side. Her eyes closed. She was fast asleep before Ragamuffin could purr an answer.

．　　　．　　　．　　　．

Someone was in the apartment.

The unmistakable creep of cautious footsteps woke Eve.

"Nico? What is it, darling?"

Silence, except for Ragamuffin purring on the pillow beside her. Then she remembered. Nico wasn't there. He was still in London.

Then who . . .

She sat upright in the bed, fear punching into her gut.

Oh, God, it's him. He's going to kill me.

She heard it again, the barest whisper of movement. She strained to see through the thick darkness but was unable to discern anything beyond the green quartz crystals of her bedside clock that read 2:30 A.M. She groped along the wall next to her pillow for the panic button on the security panel. Her movements seemed excruciatingly slow and her trembling fingers couldn't find the panel. Oh, God, where is it? Please, please . . .

Bile rose in her throat. Panicking, she swung her hand in a wider arc, toppling the African violet. It fell to the carpeted floor with a thud. She heard a soft laugh.

Then she saw him, a shadow sliding silently toward the bed.

Eve screamed, her voice piercing the night. Over and over she screamed.

Terror paralyzed her, freezing the blood in her veins, choking the breath from her. He came closer. She tried to jump up from the bed, but her leaden body refused to respond. She was helpless, immobile. And then he was upon her. As he grabbed her hair she saw the glint of the knife slicing toward her face. . . .

．　　　．　　　．　　　．

"No!"

Eve sat up, her breath coming in tortured rasps. All around her was darkness and silence. The apartment was empty. She listened, hearing only the sound of her own labored breathing.

She was alone. Nico was in London, Clara was at her sister's, and there was no one there. No one.

It had been a nightmare, nothing more.

Still, she sat there on the pillow-strewn bed, shivering, afraid, her palms slick with sweat, her nightgown stuck to her clammy skin.

Oh, God, would she ever be free of this fear?

There had been only one letter, she reminded herself. One. Probably a prank.

So why couldn't she believe that?

She fell back against the pillows and glanced at the clock beside the lush African violet. Four A.M. And she hadn't gone to bed until one.

Yesterday had been such a grueling day that she'd been sure she'd sleep like a baby. The shoot had been an eternity of wet hair and icy, damp bathing suits interspersed with brief respites of heated bathrobes and gulps of hot coffee. Never had she worked with such a bear of a photographer, an up-and-coming jackass who had reduced one of the girls to tears and taken so long to set up his lighting that it had been after seven when they'd finally finished. Every muscle had ached by then and all she'd wanted was to retreat to the solitude of home for a long soak in the tub and the warmth of her down comforter.

But her agent had hosted a dinner meeting, and she'd had to go and play supermodel. All through dinner she'd relished the prospect of getting home, getting comfortable, and sleeping until ten, so she'd be relaxed and ready for her *Esquire* interview the next day. Now here she was, wide awake at four A.M., spooked, shivering, and wishing like hell Nico were there.

She rubbed her bleary eyes. Only a nightmare. But

it had been so real. Damn her all-too-vivid imagination. Why couldn't she be more like Margo? Even as a little kid her composed, ivory-blond sister had scoffed at the boogeyman. Margo, so analytical and logical, had never been susceptible to slumber-party horror stories. Instead, she had gleefully recounted in grisly detail the tales of ax murderers and ghostly visitors to Eve, preying upon her little sister's gullibility. Terrified, Eve had lain awake through countless nights, listening to every creaky floorboard in that tiny tract house in Duluth.

I've got to stop this, or else I'm going to lose my mind. If Nico were here, I'd feel safe. He's always made me feel safe.

The very first time she'd met him he rescued her. Attending a rock concert in Lisbon, Eve had been caught up in the surge of a crowd gone wild. Trapped in the stampede, separated from her escort and certain she'd be trampled, she twisted and turned, strangling in the press of bodies, but found no crevice for escape. Suddenly, out of nowhere, a strong arm encircled her waist and dragged her from the bedlam. Moments later she was in a sleek silver sports car beside the most handsome man she had ever seen.

Nico Caesarone was six feet tall, with silky black hair and bedroom eyes the color of the Mediterranean. She'd learned later he was one of the top race car drivers in the world. He took her to a tiny sidewalk café, ordered thick peasant soup with crusty bread and dry red wine, and sang snatches of bawdy Italian love songs to her in an off-key baritone until she giggled away the last remnants of the ordeal she'd just been through.

She fell in love with him that very night.

Nico. She could almost smell the exotic, musky scent of him, could almost see his lean, sensuous face and feel his kiss. If only he were there with her now. With his strong arms around her, her head nestled against the dark, matted hair of his chest, she always felt protected. Or at least she had until the letter had come.

She hadn't told Nico about the letter. She hadn't told anyone. She'd simply torn it up and thrown it away as if that would make her fear disappear.

It hadn't.

Instead, the terse message wrapped around the tiny scrap of fabric had haunted her with its sinister warning.

Maybe I should go to London. A few days with Nico right now will be heaven. Except for the interview, my schedule is clear until Monday—I can catch the Concorde tonight and surprise him. . . .

The sudden jangling of the phone made her jump.

"Eve, I know it's disgustingly early, but I really need to talk to you." Monique sounded urgent, but regal as always. "I waited as long as I could before I phoned. . . ."

Eve glanced at the clock. Six-fifteen. Shit, she'd been lying here scared out of her mind for more than two hours.

"What's up?"

"I can't explain it all on the phone, but believe me, you'll want in on this. How soon can you get here?"

It was a longtime habit. When Monique D'Arcy, now the editor of *Perfect Bride* magazine, called, Eve still jumped. Twenty minutes later Eve dashed out the door into the fresh pastel pinkness of the morning, adroitly sidestepping an early morning jogger.

"Your taxi's double-parked, Miss Hamel. Let me get the door for you."

She nodded absently as Eddie, three steps ahead of her, swung the cab door open with a flourish worthy of a royal footman.

"You look very pretty for so early in the morning, Miss Hamel," the middle-aged Jamaican doorman said. "Very pretty."

"Thanks, Eddie," Eve said. Sure, pretty. No sleep,

no coffee, no makeup. She hadn't even taken time to put on lipstick.

No matter how many covers she'd done for *Vogue*, she still thought of herself as that gangly teenage wall-flower who'd desperately wanted to be pretty like her sister. She'd hated herself because she wasn't five inches shorter and somebody's girlfriend. All those years of being nobody while Margo was the golden girl, so lovely, so smart, so popular. And then suddenly, the summer before her senior year, it had been as if a fairy godmother waved a magic wand over her head and answered her prayers.

Eve gave herself a shake as the taxi maneuvered along Central Park West toward the Dakota, dodging potholes. She wished she'd had time for a cup of coffee, she reflected, her shoulders settling back between the broken springs that poked through the faded green upholstery. But Monique had sounded so insistent, she'd only taken time to throw on her sweats and Nikes, scrunch her hair into a ponytail, and stuff a bagel into her pocket.

What a night. She dug the bagel out of her pocket and broke off a chunk. She had to get out of New York. At least she'd be able to sleep in London, with Nico beside her. Maybe, for just a few days, she could forget about that damned letter.

As the cab slammed against the curb at One West Seventy-second Street, Eve was almost smiling, picturing Nico's face when he came into the darkened suite at the Savoy to find her in his bed, wearing nothing but her engagement ring, a dab of perfume, and a wicked smile.

Perfect.

"Just say you'll do it, Evie B! *Promise* me you'll do it."

Monique grabbed her hands and pulled her into the spacious, sunlit apartment. Eve stared in surprise.

The usually immaculate red and charcoal rooms that mirrored Monique D'Arcy's own unique drama and charm looked like a landfill. The Oriental rug was strewn with crumpled balls of paper, coffee cups and candy wrappers littered the onyx cocktail table, and crystal ashtrays overflowed with cigarette butts. The place reeked of stale smoke and overheated coffee. The October sunlight pouring in through the expansive windows highlighted the unkempt appearance of this usually spectacular apartment.

"Watch your step. Don't slip on the midnight oil." Monique waved an airy hand at the mess. "Annette will be here in an hour to deal with all this, but in the meantime, I hope you haven't eaten. I've got breakfast waiting for us in the dining room—coffee, strawberries, and the most yummy orange-nut muffins. I've been up working all night and I can't even think straight without some carbohydrates."

This has to work, Monique thought as she flung open the French doors onto the terrace, allowing a reviving breeze to sweep the stale air from the apartment. She then led the way into the dining room, her pedicured bare feet skimming the pickled-oak floor. She slipped into a high-back Oriental chair, adjusted the belt of her peach satin robe, and poured steaming coffee from the silver pot into Eve's Limoges cup.

The sunlight slanting through the dining room windows warmed Monique's icy hands.

Last night, when Richard had left for the coast, she had been nearly overwhelmed with despair. He'd been pissed as hell about the board of directors' reaction to the slipping circulation figures. She needed something big, something dramatic and flashy, and she needed it fast.

Every time she thought of the grim set of Richard's face, the disappointment reflected in his eyes, she was filled with panic. She was desperate to do something so brilliant, so dynamic, he would know he'd made the right decision in naming her editor-in-chief in Shanna's stead.

She'd stayed up all night—God, what a night. Pacing, groping, her mind racing in a frenzy fueled by cigarettes and caffeine, she'd crafted and discarded one idea after another until finally at five in the morning she'd hit on it.

It had to work. How could it not? Every instinct told her that this particular blend of glamour and romance would captivate not only subscribers and brides-to-be all over the country, but every woman who'd ever dreamed of a fairy-tale wedding. If anything would punch up *Perfect Bride*'s stodgy image and catapult it into the ranks of the hip and sophisticated, this would.

"Okay, you win." Eve took a sip of coffee and regarded Monique curiously. "I'm dying to know. What exactly is it you want me to do?"

As always, Monique looked exactly like what she was: a native-born French comtesse and the epitome of beauty and glamour. But this morning, beneath her carefully applied makeup and sleek sweep of shoulder-length ebony hair, her gray eyes were bloodshot and underscored with dark circles, and her skin was pale despite the rosy dusting of blush.

"I'm planning something fantastic for *Perfect Bride*," Monique said, lifting one expressive black brow. Her eyes shone with excitement as she leaned forward. "And you, my love, are going to be the main attraction."

"Don't tell me you want me hawking magazines outside of Saks," she warned, smearing a muffin with orange marmalade and silently promising herself to run an extra three miles to offset the indulgence.

"That's Plan B." Monique exhaled her rich, throaty laugh, but Eve thought her face looked pinched as she compulsively reached for another cigarette. "Plan A is somewhat more exciting. And glamorous. Think about it: What do you and Nico, me and Richard, and Ana

Cates and that gorgeous Senator Farrell have in common?"

"We're all being investigated by the IRS?"

"Bite your tongue. Okay, seriously."

"We're all getting married," Eve said warily, beginning to suspect where this was headed.

Monique nodded, her smile widening. "Exactly."

"And you want us featured in *Perfect Bride*?"

"Not just featured—spotlighted. Can't you just see
it on the newsstands? Eve, it'll sell more copies than
Madonna's *Sex*. Guaranteed." Monique took a few
swallows of coffee. *Easy*, she cautioned herself. *Don't
oversell*. "Every woman's fantasy will be captured right
there in the June issue," she said, and suddenly the
words began tumbling out. "Fame, fortune, true love.
Three beautiful brides, three hunky grooms, exquisite
clothes, and a honeymoon in Maui to die for. Plus, the
surefire hook—the Cinderella girl."

That was the coup de grâce.

Monique's gray eyes sparkled as they locked with
Eve's across the table. "Are you ready for this? I am
going to choose some lucky Cinderella from the audience of the *Oprah Winfrey Show* to share the limelight
with us."

Monique watched Eve's aquamarine eyes light
with surprise, and she went on without missing a beat.
"She'll win a free honeymoon, an all-expense-paid wedding, plus get to keep all the clothes worn in the shoot
—gowns, peignoirs, bikinis, sportswear—all shot on location in Maui. We'll do wedding, boudoir, and beach
shots on the island, and maybe I can even talk Richard
into doing some shots on his yacht. Just picture it, Evie
—three celebrity couples and one ordinary bride and
groom splashed all over the pages of *Perfect Bride*. So,"
she finished. "Will you do it?"

Monique held her breath. Eve certainly looked in-
trigued, but she guessed Nico might be a sticking point.
Monique said a little prayer and busied herself refilling

their Limoges cups. Her hands were shaking, whether from nerves or lack of sleep she wasn't sure. Once she got past Eve and Nico, she still had to convince Ana Cates and Senator Farrell. But she'd cross that bridge when she came to it.

"Evie, you know it's going to be fabulous," she pressed on. "I'm sure I can get Antonio to do the shoot." She was trying as hard as she could to exude confidence, for if there was one thing she knew, it was that if you acted like you knew what you were doing, people believed you actually did. She realized she was twisting the ends of her hair around her finger, a nervous habit she'd been trying for years to break. She reached for another cigarette and lit it with slow deliberation.

A police siren screaming far below blared into the silence of the apartment. Eve forced down the last bite of her muffin. She sensed this was important to Monique, maybe even more important than Monique was admitting, but she hadn't counted on Nico being dragged into whatever business they chose to do together. The comtesse was not one of Nico's favorite people, not since she'd interrupted one of their early secluded weekends in Milan, pressing Eve to fill in at the last minute for a model who'd been hospitalized with bulimia. Nico, possessive by nature, had resented the intrusion into his time alone with Eve. To this day the mention of Monique's name triggered a mutter of colorful Italian curses.

"Of course I'd love to do it," Eve said carefully, "but I can't speak for Nico. You know his endorsement contracts are very strict."

"Oh, come on, let him throw his weight around."

"It's just that he's still working with his designers on that new car. . . ."

"But you'll ask him."

Again that urgency behind Monique's exuberant sales pitch. Why was this so important to Monique?

She was usually so smooth and high-powered, but to-day there was a desperate edge beneath the dynamic veneer.

This was more than just another high-concept idea. This really mattered. Maybe the magazine was in trouble. If so, Eve knew Monique would rather swallow cyanide than divulge it.

Rich, exotic, and driven, Monique D'Arcy was a born executive with meticulous taste and habits and a genius for manipulation. She was always in control of everyone and everything around her. *And lucky for me that she is,* Eve reflected, thinking back seven years to the terrified, willowy seventeen-year-old who'd first tip-toed into the D'Arcy Modeling Agency with a scrap-book of photos clutched under one trembling arm. Monique had taken one look at the trembling innocent with the rattling kneecaps and had eased her into a chair.

"You're my Wilhelmina, Cheryl Tiegs, and Elle MacPherson all rolled into one," she'd breathed. "Your face was sculpted by God with the express purpose of delighting the camera. Darling, you've come to exactly the right place."

And then I dropped my scrapbook onto that lus-cious alabaster carpeting, pages flying everywhere. Monique had laughed, the sound echoing off the beige suede walls of her corner suite. "Darling, don't look so scared. You're about to become the most famous model in the world. Guaranteed. All of your dreams are going to come true—even those you haven't dreamt yet."

She'd made good on her word. Eve would never forget how the irrepressible comtesse had pressured *Sports Illustrated* into featuring an untried, unknown model in their legendary swimsuit edition, relentlessly pushing to ensure that her ingenue was given the most provocative bikinis and sexiest backdrops for her smashing debut.

It had been a brilliant ploy, and a fabulously successful one, catapulting Eve into instantaneous super-stardom. That had been the beginning for Eve, a stunning debut that had been followed up quickly with an *Elle* cover and a *Vogue* pictorial that had taken Europe by storm. And she owed it all to Monique. Not only had Monique helped Eve survive those first mind-boggling months of overwhelming success, but she'd become more of a sister and confidante than Margo had ever been, a guardian angel protecting her from the circling vultures ready to gobble up naive little girls from Minnesota.

Through all their years of friendship, she'd never seen Monique vulnerable, but she knew her well enough to recognize that there was something damn close to it beneath all this hype. She took a deep breath.

"Yes, I'll ask Nico. As a matter of fact, I'll ask him tonight." She smiled suddenly, thinking of her little surprise. She drained the last of her orange juice and added slowly, "I can guarantee you he'll be in a good mood, but beyond that, we'll have to check with the lawyers."

"I knew I could count on you. This will be *dynamite*."

Monique fought against the urge to close her eyes for a moment. She knew she needed sleep, but even after Eve left, she would not let herself succumb. Sleep would just have to wait. First she needed to reel in her other big catch.

She reached for the phone, stifling a yawn. "Shit, not yet. Not until I've pinned down Ana Cates."

Lying on the red silk settee, waiting for Ana Cates to return her phone call, Monique's mind drifted back to the first time she'd met Eve. She herself had been the one to transform that unsure but exquisite seventeen-year-old ingenue with the cascading honey-blond hair

and hopeful aquamarine eyes into the elegant sophisticate known throughout the world as Evie B. *And I can
transform* Perfect Bride *in exactly the same way. I've
never failed at anything and I'm not going to let myself
fail at this. Shanna Ives is just waiting for me to drop
the ball, and I'll be damned if I will.*

But deep inside, a tiny voice reminded her that
Shanna had humiliated her once before.

But this is going to work, she told herself. *It damn
well better work.*

After all, Ana Cates was the hottest young star in
Hollywood, and every weekly tabloid sold out any edition that spewed forth even the minutest details of her
whirlwind romance with the dashing senator from
Rhode Island.

And Eve, a superstar in her own right, was engaged
to marry heartthrob European race car champion Nico
Caesarone—what bride in the country wouldn't want to
look like Evie B on her wedding day?

And she herself was no slouch either. She'd made
her mark in both fashion and publishing—running her
own top modeling agency, discovering and representing
beauties all over the world and catapulting them to
stardom. And Richard—well, Richard was Richard,
Monique thought wryly. Not only did he own control-
ling interest in so many companies that he employed
ten executive vice presidents just to keep track of them,
but Richard Ives was handsome, witty, and one of the
most powerful, magnetic men in America.

And he's all mine, she thought with pride at how
very far she had come.

She glanced about the cluttered living room and
winced, grateful that Annette would be there in an
hour to restore order. Poor Eve had tried so hard to
disguise her shock at seeing the state of the apartment.
*If it had been anyone else, I'd have been too embar-
rassed to let them in, but no one else would have rushed
over at that ungodly hour.*

Eve's friendship was a bonus Monique had never expected. *She knows more about me than anyone else except maybe Richard,* Monique mused. *I wonder what she'd say—what they'd both say—if they knew the whole story.*

For all they knew, the Comtesse Monique Lisette de Chevalier had grown up enveloped in incredible wealth and luxury, until her playboy father gambled away all of his fortune in Monte Carlo and then ran off with a Greek shipping heiress, leaving his twelve-year-old daughter and his beautiful wife, Mireille, penniless and alone. Monique and her mother had arrived in the United States with only their pride and their title to sustain them, but the exquisite Comtesse de Chevalier had quickly recouped by marrying a Texas oil millionaire. Monique, however, hating her stepfather, had proclaimed herself wary of entrusting her heart or her future to any man's control, and had been determined to make her own fortune, one no one could take away from her.

She had succeeded brilliantly, according to all accounts, first as a buyer for Saks, then as a consultant to Edith Head, and later as a fashion editor at *Glamour* and then managing editor of *Seventeen.* Eventually she had struck off on her own, building an elite stable of the world's most sought-after models—the legendary D'Arcy Modeling Agency. Now she had taken on a new challenge, abdicating her post as president of the agency to helm foundering *Perfect Bride,* owned by her very own fiancé.

Sounds good to me, Monique thought, stretching languorously on the settee. A little fact, a little fiction. *So I fudged some of the details. Like my mother being the Comtesse de Chevalier instead of being her seamstress.* What would Richard say, she wondered, if he ever found out how much I hate Shanna, and why?

Shanna Mulgrew Ives was a part of her past, a part she wouldn't forget, not until she'd settled the score.

The ringing of the phone jarred Monique from her reverie. She stared at it, praying it was Ana Cates, and praying Ana would say yes.

Please, God, let her say yes.

"Eve bambina, for God's sake, where are you? You're my one ray of sunshine in all this damned foggy drizzle. I miss you," Nico murmured, his voice purring sensuously from the answering machine. "I miss your eyes looking into mine when we wake in the morning. I miss your lips, the taste of you. I miss your . . . agh! Where could you be so early? Never mind, I will call you after my dinner meeting. And bambina—*please* be there."

Caught between a laugh and a groan, Eve clicked off the machine. If only Nico were there with her instead of an ocean away. The raspy purr of his voice was driving her crazy. Even from another continent he could seduce her. Her delicious, romantic Italian. She pictured him making the call, dark and brawny and wild, his white silk shirt-sleeves rolled up to his elbows and his hands raking through his hair in frustration as he paced back and forth. Nico had the body of a Greek god, the soul of a poet, and the hands of Svengali. Even now her body was responding to him, desire aching through her.

I miss you too, sweetheart.

Propping her flight confirmation for the Concorde on her dressing table alongside the crystal perfume bottles, brushes, and creams, she stripped off her clothes and mentally packed her suitcase. She padded naked across the lush carpeting to the glass-doored sun room, where a jungle of dieffenbachia and philodendrons nestled in their Chinese porcelain pots. Slipping into the steaming tub, she blasted the jets full strength and gave a sigh of pure pleasure. Tiny drops of mist lightly stung her face. Eve felt all remnants of tension melting away into the swirling water.

In the bright light of day, her nighttime fears seemed absurd. She leaned over, reaching for the thick lace-trimmed towel—and froze.

The green envelope was nearly concealed by the fronds of the dieffenbachia. But it was there, tucked among the leaves, marked with the unmistakable penmanship she had seen once before.

She sat on the edge of the tub. He had been here —maybe he was still here.

She screamed.

Clara ran in from the kitchen, eyes wide, her flour-dusted hands gripping her apron.

"Call the police," Eve gasped, clutching the towel to her with shaking hands. "Someone's been in the apartment. Oh, God, he might still be here."

White-faced, Clara went to the bedroom phone. Eve stared at the envelope, fighting back nausea. Part of her wanted to tear it into little pieces and throw it away without reading it, but the other part of her needed to know. Filled with dread, she tore into the flap. As she pulled out the single sheet of lined green paper, a scrap of gold lamé fabric drifted onto her lap.

"Oh, God, not again."

The green paper seemed to burn right through her icy fingers. He wasn't going away. He was drawing closer.

What was she going to do?

Chapter Two

GEORGETOWN

Anastasia gave a gasp of pleasure and shuddered all over as John slowly nibbled his way from the titian tendrils clinging to her damp nape down the gentle slope of her spine to kiss the twin dimples nestled above her buttocks. She rolled over, sensing his imminent need, and pulled him down to her. She wrapped her legs around him and closed her eyes, concentrating on every sensation as their lips clung together and she tasted the Dom Pérignon still lingering on his full lower lip.

"Ana, you witch, I'm supposed to be debating on the Floor right now," he breathed huskily in her ear. His blue-gray eyes glinted as he traced the hollow beneath her cheekbone with his mouth, following the delicate bone structure of her oval face to the pulse beating rapidly in her throat.

"Who's stopping you, Senator?" she murmured. She slid her lips down to his taut nipples, eliciting a moan of pure delight.

Sunlight splashed through the French doors of Senator John Farrell's bedroom, bathing the lovers on the deep pile rug in a golden glow, and setting Ana's hair afire.

The tousled charcoal satin sheets on the four-poster were strewn with crushed rose petals. Two champagne glasses still glistening with pale amber droplets sat on the nightstand. Ana's perfume mingled with the scent of the crushed blossoms to create a heady fragrance that was the perfect backdrop, she thought, for the sweetness of their lovemaking. Her green eyes flew open as John entered her, and she clasped him to her, trying to lose herself in the sizzling heat that radiated from his sinewy body.

Perspiration filmed John's cleanly chiseled face. "Don't stop, Johnny, don't stop, don't stop, Oh, God, don't stop. . . ."

The world should have melted away, leaving only the two of them entwined in a paradise of perfect passion. But it didn't.

It never did, Ana thought despondently, struggling to hide her disappointment as his climax came with a shuddering outpouring of tension, and still her body refused to ignite. Next time, she thought, squeezing her eyes shut tight to press back the tears.

"Can I stop now?" John laughed, and licked the rosy tip of each of her nipples, then rolled aside and gathered her into his arms.

"Hmmm?" Ana murmured, feigning a dreamy haze. She felt on edge, unsated, and unable to let him know.

John searched her face. "Angel, are you all right? Did you enjoy it?"

"It was wonderful." Her lips curved in the famous Ana Cates smile that lit up screens all over the world. Reaching up mischievously, she tousled his hair, then delicately slid her fingers down his neck, across his tautly muscled back, her smile deepening.

But for just a moment John caught a glimpse of the bleakness behind those incredible green eyes.

He didn't understand her. She was the sexiest woman he'd ever met, and she loved him, God knew she loved him, but there was always a small part of Ana that seemed held in reserve. Sometimes when they made love, or when he held her, she seemed a thousand miles away.

When he'd first encountered her at the AIDS Awareness Telethon in Los Angeles a little over a year ago, he'd expected a shallow little sexpot. Instead, he found a warm, caring young woman with a great deal of poise and practical good sense.

"Senator," she said backstage, holding out her hand to him, and smiling with genuine warmth, "I saw you speak about your national health plan on *Good Morning America,* and I just want to say that I admire your views. But don't you think you should join forces with the Democrats just this once? Their proposal has some points yours is lacking. I mean," she added hastily, blushing at his startled expression, "yours could adopt the best of both, and become even stronger. Or is that conflict of interest or something?"

John grinned. He had to fight to keep his eyes from dropping down to the lush cleavage revealed by her amber sequined gown, but by some miracle he managed to do it. "It isn't, Miss Cates. You should know, though, that the day I need to borrow from the Democrats is the day alligators fly. Don't tell me you're one of them—you look far too bright for that."

She had stared at him through those marvelous eyes of hers, eyes that seemed to sparkle in the backstage dimness with a vibrant green fire, and she said slowly, silkily, with just the hint of an edge to her voice, "Well, as a matter of fact, yes, I am one, so perhaps you shouldn't be seen speaking to me. . . ."

"On the contrary."

"Or listening to me . . ."

"I'd be honored to . . ."

"Or taking me seriously . . ."

"Miss Cates, I plan to convert you."

"Senator?"

"Over dinner. Tonight. Spago's, after the show?"

"Senator," Ana had murmured sweetly, looking up at him from beneath sweeping lashes, "I'd be glad to join you for dinner, but as for converting me, well, I'm afraid that could happen only when alligators fly."

She'd been razor-sharp, bright, and completely feminine. John was instantly fascinated. Watching her mingling in the wings with the children suffering from AIDS, giving them teddy bears and autographs and hugs, chatting with the ease of a breezy teenager come to baby-sit, he'd been impressed by the light and warmth that followed wherever she went.

And later that night, over dinner, he'd perceptively tuned in to the mixed signals she gave out: beneath the coolly sophisticated, glib façade, he saw with blinding clarity the fragile, vulnerable creature burning within. She was half angel, he'd realized, half hellion. Physically, she'd reminded him of pictures he'd seen of a young Brigitte Bardot, with something innocent yet wild about her, with that same irresistible saucy sexiness glowing in her face. But Ana Cates was much more than an alluring sex goddess, more even than a gifted actress. She was forthright, genuine. So giving, and so desperately needy.

"An actress," his mother had sniffed when he'd told her he was bringing Ana home for Thanksgiving dinner. "Oh, John, how could you? She'll bring you nothing but trouble."

But Ana brought him happiness. His career, his firm belief in his own ability to change the world for the better, and Ana—those were the things that made him feel happy, powerful, complete. He didn't give a damn if marrying an actress was a politically risky thing to do. He'd make it work, he'd make it all work—and he'd make Ana as happy as he was.

"I wish I could stay," he said regretfully, dropping a kiss on the top of her head.

"Me too. We could order lunch. Right now I'd kill for a chicken sandwich."

"There's roast beef in the fridge. Will that do? Sorry I can't join you, but I've really got to go. If this abortion bill doesn't pass the Senate, I'm screwed."

"I've already seen to that, Johnny."

He chuckled. "And very nicely, thank you. But I'm talking about the bigshots back home. My reelection coffers will be running on empty unless Jeffrey Tobes III and William Gordon see that I can get the job done."

"Of course you can get the job done. There's nobody more committed and persuasive than you in the Senate. They don't call you Home Run Jack for nothing."

He laughed again, a deep, resonant laugh that echoed across the high-beamed ceiling. "Well, I'm batting a thousand with you, angel. Too bad you vote in California and not Rhode Island. And don't tell me you wouldn't split your ticket then."

He kissed her once more, deeply, satisfyingly, before dashing into the shower. Ana heard him whistling as he turned the shower massage full blast.

She heard birds singing outside the French doors as she lay a few minutes longer, luxuriating in the softness of the carpet beneath her naked back. Happy, she really was happy. Johnny was her rock, the anchor that held her in place. He was her safe harbor.

The last thing she wanted to do was to fly back to L.A. tonight. She knew Arnie would put up a hell of a fight when she told him she hated the script he was so positive would pull in her second Oscar. She could hear him already: "If it's good enough for De Niro, why isn't it good enough for you? The chemistry between you two will burn up the screen like nothing since *Body Heat*. Ana baby, you'd have to be out of your fucking mind to turn down this role."

But her mind was made up. She didn't want to play

a hooker, one with a heart of gold or any other kind—
and Oscar or no Oscar, she wasn't going to do it. Screw
Arnie. *He needs me a hell of a lot more than I need him,*
she thought, sitting up and brushing the tumble of curls
from her eyes. *I told him up front that I make all the
final decisions on which role to take, but he has a real
problem with knowing when to back off.* If he didn't
start catching on, she'd just have to find herself a new
agent.

It would be a shame, since Arnie had been with
her since her second major film role, a small but juicy
part playing Paul Newman's schizophrenic daughter in
Abraham's Journey. He'd been the one to convince
Tylo Miller to let her read for the role of Phoebe in
Comes a Stranger, for which she had won the Best
Supporting Actress Oscar. After that her career took off
like a roman candle. *But I'm the one who ultimately
chose to play Phoebe, and I'm the one who followed it
up with Cameron in* Chimes. *I haven't made a mistake
yet.* She seemed to have a sixth sense about which roles
were right for her, which films would best showcase her
talents. Arnie might be good, but she trusted herself far
more than she'd ever trust him, far more than she'd
ever trust anyone.

This time alone with John was a blessed respite
from her work schedule, from Arnie, and from all the
endless details to be ironed out for her July fourth wedding. Her head spun just thinking about everything she
still had to coordinate. Order flowers from Eleganza, a
menu consultation with Wolfgang, a fitting for her dress
next week—and Angelina could be such a pain—as well
as the nightmare of seating arrangements for her Hollywood friends and Johnny's Capitol Hill colleagues. And
then there was the posthoneymoon Washington reception which she hadn't even begun to plan. Some things
she couldn't delegate, not even to Louise, who was the
best secretary money could buy.

She wanted the reception to be perfect, to reflect her perfect new life as Mrs. John Farrell.

Her marriage to Johnny would be the ultimate frosting on the cake, Ana thought as she got to her feet and did a few ballet stretches. She pulled John's crimson silk dressing robe from the armoire and slipped it on, loving the feel of the silk against her skin, the vibrant scent of Johnny wrapped tightly around her. Every time she felt herself embroiled in the pressure cooker of her life, she made it a point to remind herself how far she had come, and that these "problems" were merely the trappings of her hard-won success.

At twenty-seven years of age, Ana Cates had reached a pinnacle that few actresses ever achieved. She was an alabaster-skinned beauty with full, pouty lips and smoldering green eyes that could sear right through a man to his soul. The camera adored her and so did everyone who watched her up on the screen. Reviewers claimed she possessed a uniquely arresting combination of saucy sensuousness and fragile beauty. On-screen she displayed a natural gift for winning the hearts of her audiences, bringing a special luminosity and poignancy to each of her roles. Something about her made people care.

But Ana knew the image she projected was merely a fantasy created by her fans. Her life had been a bitch, and she'd gotten where she was today only by sheer will, guts, and determination.

There had, of course, been an element of luck involved. Without it she'd still be an extra waiting in block-long lines for a chance to graduate from background-crowd scenes to on-camera crosses, praying someone would remember her and give her a shot at a speaking role. But she'd also paid her dues working so damn hard for so many unbearably long, boring hours that she was going to relish every hard-earned moment of stardom.

The only thing she didn't like about her life was the

paparazzi hounding her mercilessly day and night. But as for the rest of it, she loved it, she loved it all. She loved her gorgeous Beverly Hills stucco with the pool and curving gardens, her white Mercedes convertible with the emerald-green leather interior custom-dyed to match her eyes, and above all the clothes, the glittering, sexy, knock-'em-dead clothes, the kind of clothes she'd only dreamed about as a kid back in Buck Hollow, Tennessee. It had taken her eight months of intensive tutoring with a dialect coach to lose that damning drawl, eight months of skipped lunches, dime-store makeup, and begging for extra shifts waiting tables at LuLu's Garden Café. But she'd done it, she'd lost the drawl and with it the last traces of the dirt-poor runaway who'd hit town with nine dollars and twenty-seven cents left in her purse. She'd made it to the top and she planned to stay there, with Johnny right at her side.

Johnny—he was the sweetest blessing of them all. Johnny loved her, he truly loved her. No man had ever loved her before. Not her father, not Eric, not any of the wild crowd she used to run with in high school. But now she had Johnny, the most decent and wonderful man she'd ever imagined.

She strode to the mirror and studied her reflection, the tangle of titian curls haloing her face, the eyes searching for something within her soul. But that sad part of her, the scared and wounded part, was hidden deep, and the armor of toughness she had built around her was equally invisible. No matter what she felt inside, what horrors she had lived through, the face that peered back at her in the mirror remained a face vibrant with beauty, verve, and down-home straight-talking intelligence.

Deliberately, she turned away from the mirror, away from the image that revealed so little.

"I thought you had a plane to catch, lazybones," John teased, towel-drying his hair as he emerged from the bathroom. "Why didn't you join me in the shower?"

"You've had enough excitement for one day." Ana ducked as he tossed the towel at her. "Besides, I didn't feel like dressing yet. I want to delay jumping back on the roller coaster as long as possible."

John pulled on his briefs. What a gorgeous body he has, Ana thought, mesmerized by the ripple of muscles across his lean stomach. He could have been a movie star instead of a senator.

John caught her staring and grinned. "Should I take these off again?" he offered.

She tossed the towel back at him. "Don't tempt

bowl. "Little did he realize I don't let anybody make decisions for me."

"Including your future husband?" He slipped his arms into his gray Armani jacket and grinned at her.

"You've got it, Senator." She threw a grape at him and laughed. "But since this *is* a democracy, I'll occasionally let you have veto power. Which reminds me," she added, sitting up and suddenly growing serious. "How do you vote on that *Perfect Bride* proposition Monique D'Arcy wants us to do? I really should get back to her."

Fully dressed, John came toward her and pulled her to her feet. Her body nestled into his powerful six-foot-two-inch frame as though it had always belonged there. Ana was enveloped by his strong arms and the scent of Lagerfeld. "Is this one of those things I get veto power over?"

"Um-hmm."

John toyed with the satiny curls falling across her forehead. "I'll talk it over with Eliot tonight, but I'm sure he'll think it's a good idea. *Perfect Bride*, perfect couple, soon-to-be perfect presidential candidate. And future First Lady," he added, kissing the tip of her nose. "If my campaign manager votes yes, I'll vote yes."

"Good." She cupped his face in her hands and kissed him on the mouth. "I'll call Monique tonight after I hear from you. She'll be thrilled. And I think it'll be fun."

"Fun is what we did here today. Now it's back to work. Time to change floors. This one won't be nearly as exciting."

"I'll call you as soon as I get home to find out how it went."

Suddenly she threw her arms around his neck, reluctant to let him go. "Home Run Jack, I'm going to miss you like hell."

The kiss was hard and hungry, each of them trying

when they made love as when they kissed. It was the one thing she couldn't help holding back from him and from herself. She needed more time, she told herself, moving to the window, leaning her cheek against the cool pane. When the pressures of the wedding were behind her, she'd learn to let go, to let Johnny love her, to let herself respond. Once or twice she'd toyed with the idea of seeing a therapist, but wouldn't that be a joke? She could see the tabloids now: ANA CATES, THE SIZZLER OF THE BIG SCREEN, FIZZLES IN BED. No, she'd overcome this on her own, just as she'd overcome everything else.

She watched Johnny stride to the car, so tall, so self-assured, so keenly aware of his own self-worth and power. Maybe that came from the kind of life John had always led: privileged, wealthy, growing up in the East. He was the cherished eldest son of an old, prominent came president. He firmly believed that both things would come to pass.

That's something the two of us have in common, Ana reflected as she headed into the bathroom. *For all the differences in our backgrounds—we both know exactly what we want, and what we need to do to get it.*

Later, as she stared out the window in the first-class section of the 747, she thought about what very different worlds they came from. In contrast to his upbringing, her own childhood had been sordid and miserable. Thank God she'd left all that ugliness behind and could almost pretend it had happened to someone else. The old Ana, the teenage runaway who'd been waylaid in hell, was buried deep in the past. Now she was Anastasia Cates, Hollywood's darling, and John Farrell's love.

The blond stewardess paused beside her and proffered a bottle of Bordeaux. "May I refill your glass, Miss Cates?"

"I'd love some, thanks." As Ana held out the goblet, her five-carat diamond engagement ring twinkled in the reflection of the crystal. The middle-aged businessman across the aisle, probably a Fortune 500 CEO, unabashedly ogled her as he capped and uncapped his black and gold Mont Blanc pen.

"I just loved *Comes a Stranger*," the stewardess told her. "I cried my way through it. I knew you were a shoo-in for that Oscar."

Ana thanked her, autographed the airline magazine, and at last leaned back in her seat, slowly savoring the wine.

Across the aisle, the businessman, overhearing their conversation, replayed his own recollections of *Comes a Stranger*, in particular the scene where a nearly naked Ana Cates seduced her costar illuminated only by the dying embers of a beachside campfire.

He played a mind game, only this time he was the seducer, slowly peeling off each layer of her clothing, unwrapping her like a priceless gift. First he untied her gold corded sash, then unbuttoned the olive green silk shirt and tossed it aside. He'd have bet his Jag she was wearing nothing but a black lace teddy underneath. The black suede skirt would come next, the softly draped folds falling like a whisper around her ankles, leaving her only in that delicious teddy, sheer black stockings, and gold-trimmed black suede boots. Sweat broke out on his brow. He felt himself growing hard.

Ana sipped her wine, aware that the businessman was still staring at her. She felt herself flushing, and smoothed her skirt with nervous fingers. She was beginning to feel uncomfortable. People always stared at her, but not quite in that way. It reminded her of the past, and the past was dead. Dead and buried.

She turned and faced him head-on. Her eyes glittered like jade daggers. "Would you like me to hike my skirt higher? Would that give you a better view?"

He turned as red as his bloody Mary. A steward handing a pillow to the passenger behind Ana stifled a laugh. Ana let her gaze burn challengingly into the businessman's perspiring face for a moment longer, then summoned the steward to her side.

"Do these seats come equipped with ejection buttons?" she asked in a clearly audible tone.

The steward struggled to maintain his composure. "No, I'm sorry, Miss Cates, they do not."

"Too bad."

"Is there anything else I can do for you?" he inquired.

"I think that 'gentleman' over there could use a bucket of cold water. On the rocks."

The businessman stood up and hurried toward the lavatory. The steward shot him a scornful look.

"Sorry, Miss Cates. I guess it takes all kinds."

"I guess it does."

One more jerk put in his place, Ana thought with grim satisfaction. She'd made a vow to herself never to let anyone make her feel cheap again. She took another sip of wine to calm her racing heart, and fixed her attention on the expanse of clouds outside her window, billowing like the skirt of her Katsura wedding gown. She forced herself to think of the wedding, of the future, of Johnny—and of the way *he* looked at her.

She grew calmer, and closed her eyes. The past *was* dead, she reminded herself.

No one would ever have to know.

She reached over to the olive leather satchel on the seat beside her and retrieved the latest issue of *Variety*. Flipping idly through the pages, she read about the rumored shake-up at Fox, and studied the rave review of Beeban Kidron's new film, making a mental note to herself to alert Arnie of her interest in working with this director. By the time she reached the classifieds she was ready for a second glass of wine. Suddenly she froze with shock, her fingers clenching the pages. She stared in disbelief at the five-inch ad in block letters.

CANDY MONROE—I MISS YOU. WILL BE IN TOUCH. DADDY.

It couldn't be. Ana blinked in confusion. The words were still there, jumping off the page, taunting her. Her stomach rolled with nausea. She felt as if all the oxygen had been sucked out of the cabin. She couldn't breathe.

Candy Monroe. The pages slipped from her numb fingers. It had been years since she'd been called by that name.

Only one man could have placed this ad.

But he was dead, she told herself dazedly. She knew he was dead.

She had killed him herself.

Chapter Three

"Hope I'm not too early, Teri," Mrs. Warnler called out from the beauty shop doorway. She stamped the slush off her boots and peeled off her snow-crusted red wool parka.

Teri deftly stroked Robin Red polish on Mrs. Jensen's oval-filed nails and replied without glancing up. "Actually, it'll work out great for me. You're my last appointment, and if I finish up early I'll have a chance to go over my notes once more before my final tonight."

Mrs. Jensen peered out through her wisps of graying bangs at the dark-haired, olive-skinned young manicurist. She raised her thinly penciled eyebrows. *What was it with these young girls today? So much studying. Such hard work. And for such a pretty girl.* With her jet-black hair, worn simply and to her shoulders, her heart-shaped face beneath a delicate widow's peak, and those doe-shaped brown eyes, Teri Mathews could have been a model for *Seventeen* or *Glamour* or one of those other dog-eared magazines Hilda kept neatly stacked next to the coffeepot. Mrs. Jensen had told Teri so time and again, but the girl just laughed, accentuating those pretty dimples of hers. *She looks a little tired today though,* Mrs. Jensen reflected critically. There were circles under her eyes—*I'll bet she was up all night studying.* Even her bright pink crew-neck sweater with the little jewel-eyed elephant pinned beneath the right shoulder, and her short denim skirt did nothing to spark the perkiness that usually characterized Teri Mathews. *She's a sweet girl. Now, that skinny Josie, over there with that electrified mop of bleached perm straggling down her back, and the Trident bubble gum constantly cracking away, now, she has a mouth on her. And probably a few miles too. But Teri is a little doll. She belongs home baking cookies and bouncing a sweet little baby on her knee,* Mrs. Jensen thought. *Well, I'm sure once she marries that nice boy, Brian, it will happen soon enough.*

"Is the semester over already?" Mrs. Jensen inquired as Teri dabbed top coat onto her crimson nails. "So are you graduating now?"

Teri shook her head and met the older woman's quizzical look with a wry smile. "I wish," Teri sighed. "I'll graduate in June and then I'm looking at two more years until I get my master's degree."

Mrs. Warnler sank into a worn green vinyl chair beside Teri's workstand and lit a cigarette. Melting slush dripped from her boots, forming a small gray puddle at her feet. "Bet you'll never make it."

She winked at Mrs. Jensen, who smiled knowingly.

Teri glanced up then, looking from one to the other of them. "Says who?"

Mrs. Warnler beamed at her. "Says me. You're getting married to that handsome boy, aren't you? I predict you'll have a baby and forget all about night school."

Here we go again. Teri smiled patiently, capping the polish and pushing back her chair. "Brian *wants* me to be a social worker, Mrs. Warnler. We've talked about it many times. We both agreed to wait for children until

I can establish a part-time practice. After all"—she gazed straightfaced at Mrs. Jensen, who was now smiling widely—"I've had plenty of on-the-job counseling training working here for five years. Right, Josie?" she called to the beautician mixing a perm solution at the sink.

"Yeah, we get all kinds. And all kinds of stories. The only thing we're missing here is the couch."

Teri tucked a loose strand of hair behind her ear as Mrs. Warnler and Mrs. Jensen traded chairs. "Passion Pink again?" she asked, scooting her chair forward once more, her fingers already on the bottle.

"How about something brighter? It's so dreary out. I hate November. Now, if I was in Hawaii, I wouldn't hate it so much."

Teri massaged cuticle remover into Mrs. Warnler's nail beds. "You and me both," she said in her pleasantly low-pitched voice. An image of white sand beaches and turquoise ocean dotted with surfers floated into her mind. She and Brian had talked about going to Hawaii for their honeymoon, but had decided it was too expensive. He and his dad were buying a new trimmer for the tool and die shop, and her tuition was going up next semester. Toronto was as close to Hawaii as they would get for a while. Especially if they scraped up enough money for a down payment on that bungalow in Plymouth. *Every tip will count,* she thought bleakly as she watched Mrs. Jensen amble toward the front of the shop, forgetting once again to tip her.

"By the way, Teri," Josie called out from her work station where she was rolling a perm, "Mrs. Salinski left your tip with me yesterday when you went out for lunch. Remind me to give it to you."

"Oh!" Mrs. Jensen stopped short and hurried back toward Teri, holding her open brown handbag out at her. "I almost forgot. Take a dollar, honey. Right there in the side pocket. I'll see you next week same time."

"Thank you, Mrs. Jensen." *Thank you, Josie,* Teri

thought, shooting her friend a grateful look. Josie met her eyes in the mirror and grinned.

Teri tried to concentrate on Mrs. Warnler's prattle about her grandchildren, but her mind kept drifting to the final exam looming before her. She was more nervous about it than she cared to admit. She had to do well, she couldn't afford any setbacks. Her life and Brian's had been carefully planned out for the next two years, starting with their wedding in May. It was all drafted out as methodically as the neatly written entries for each day and hour were logged in the Hair and Now appointment book. Finish school, get her MSW at Wayne State, buy a house, and set up a private practice counseling dysfunctional families—all before their second wedding anniversary. And Brian was hoping to bring in enough additional business to start a second shift at the tool and die shop. That would be tough, but she knew it would mean a lot to them if he could swing it. No, there was no time for setbacks or failures or babies, not for a while. As long as she had a plan and stuck to it, Teri felt as if her little universe was in order. It was the small glitches in life that scared her, wreaking havoc with her sense of security. And so Teri meticulously strove to keep her little world intact. It drove Brian crazy, she knew, because he tackled life like a star quarterback, charging, dodging, maneuvering, confident in his strategy and in his abilities to win on the field. Teri, on the other hand, wrote her game plan in permanent marker, and once the ink was dry it was as official as a final score. But Brian humored her, and between Teri's lists and schedules and Brian's calm good sense, they were on the right track, she could feel it. Every day closer to the wedding she grew more confident of the future.

At three-thirty Teri put her nail files in the disinfectant-filled tumbler, packed her polishes away, and lifted her fleece-lined denim jacket from the metal coat hook in the back room.

"Not so fast, kiddo." Josie, grinning, blocked her path as Teri started toward the front of the little shop. *Here it comes*, Teri thought, a smile spreading across her heart-shaped face. *They didn't forget after all.* But her smile froze as Josie dangled a dollar bill before her nose. "Mrs. Salinski's tip. You almost forgot it."

"Oh. Thanks."

"Good luck on your final."

"Thanks, Josie. I'll be glad when it's over."

"You and Brian going to celebrate?"

For a moment Teri brightened. "Celebrate?"

"The end of finals. Hey, what's wrong with you today? You're halfway to Nebraska."

"I didn't get much sleep last night. Brian had to go to Indiana on business and he won't be home until tomorrow. Since I can never sleep well without him there anyway, I stayed up studying till almost four."

"You'll make up for it tonight. Just snooze your little heart away once that final's over."

Yes, Teri thought as she walked out into the snowy November drizzle. The wind whipped the freezing droplets at her face, stinging her cheeks and driving her ungloved hands deep into her pile-lined pockets. *I'll snooze all right. Straight through my birthday.* She had thought that at least Josie would remember. Last year, Josie and Marie had brought in a Baskin-Robbins ice cream cake, and the whole shop, even Hilda, the owner, had sung "Happy Birthday" so loudly, people had looked in from the bus stop outside on the street. Well, she'd just treat herself to a Sander's hot fudge sundae after the final, then go home, put on the soundtrack from *Les Miz,* wrap herself up in an afghan, and unwind with a glass of white zinfandel until Brian called. He'd remember.

Teri whizzed through the essay questions in less than an hour. That late-night review had crystallized some important theories in her mind, and the answers flowed freely from her brain to the Bic pen skimming rapidly along the lines in her blue book. She felt a sense of triumph when she finally set the pen down.

The sleety drizzle had stopped and it was clear and dark when she finally headed toward her little, used Volvo in the parking structure. As she buckled her seat belt, Teri realized she was famished. *Next stop, Sander's. Happy birthday to me.*

The apartment hallway was lit only by a small, flickering bulb when an hour later she trudged up the salted cement stairs. Brian would probably call right after eleven, when the rates went down. Maybe she'd have time to take a hot bath with that zinfandel and then wrap herself in a pair of his flannel pajamas before his call. As she let herself in, the lonely darkness rose up to meet her. Sighing, she fumbled for the light switch.

Then everything happened at once. The light came on and she blinked in confusion as twenty voices screamed "Surprise!"

"Oh, my God!" Teri's hands flew to her mouth. "I don't believe it!"

Red, purple, yellow, and green balloons cascaded through the air as Josie, Marie, Hilda, Brian's sister Tina, and her other friends leapt forward around the sofa, laughing and cheering to draw her into the festively decorated apartment. There were banners and streamers across every doorway, and a giant cake studded with twenty-six yellow candles festooned the walnut coffee table.

Tina snapped a picture of Teri's stunned face, the Beatles' "Birthday" blared from the stereo, and Josie yelled, "Pizza will be here in twenty minutes!"

"Or we get three dollars off," Marie chuckled.

Teri, recovering from her astonishment, grabbed Josie by her bony shoulders, laughing. "You remembered!"

Josie kissed her on the cheek, smelling of wine and creme rinse. "We've been planning this for weeks! You should have seen the look on your face. I almost bust a gut!"

Then Tina, Brian's eighteen-year-old sister, thrust a card into Teri's hand. "Brian's going to call around eleven, but he said to give you this."

The next few hours were a blur of pizza, chocolate cake, presents, and laughter. Teri took Brian's phone call in the privacy of their bedroom, with the beat of "Born in the USA" reverberating through the walls.

"Sounds like you've got one wild party going on there. Hope you're not doing anything I wouldn't do, babe."

She wanted to kiss him right through the phone.

"Oh, Brian, it's great. I wish you could be here. . . ."

"Me too, but I'm stuck in Indiana till the day after tomorrow. I hate missing your birthday. I'm going to make it up to you, Teri. I'll never be away from you again on your birthday."

"Promise?"

"Scout's honor."

"But you said you weren't a scout."

"Picky, picky."

She grinned, and glanced at the framed photograph on her oak-veneered nightstand. It was a photograph of the two of them. At six feet two, Brian was a good eight inches taller than she was, with a lanky, muscular build, sandy hair the texture of satin and eyes the color of hazelnuts deeply set within an angular, good-humored face. He was handsome enough to pose for a Budweiser ad, and hunky enough to give Billy Ray Cyrus a run for his money. Brian, however, was more interested in playing pool and shooting baskets at the park than trying on clothes. In fact, he still wore the pair of faded Guess jeans on weekends that he was wearing the night Teri first met him on a blind date.

"Have you opened my card yet?" Brian asked. Teri could barely hear him because someone—Marie?—

screamed with laughter. She pressed the phone tighter against her ear.

"Not yet. Should I open it now?"

"After we hang up. Then go back to your party. And remember, I love you. Happy birthday, babe."

She clutched the phone, suddenly reluctant to let him go. "I love you too, Bri. Hurry home, it's cold here without you."

"It's cold there anyway," he teased. "It's November, and it's Michigan, remember?"

"But when I'm in your arms it's always July."

He laughed. "Well, in that case, I'll just have to set off some fireworks when I get back. Scout's honor."

Teri stood motionless for a moment after she hung up the phone. She was so lucky to have Brian. And lucky to have friends like Josie and Marie. She hadn't been forgotten after all. There were people who cared about her, and that was pretty remarkable since Teri Mathews had existed only for the past ten years.

Brian's card, showing a baby elephant saying: "ME forget YOUR birthday?" made her laugh. She turned it over and found scrawled on the back in Brian's nearly illegible handwriting the words:

> IOU—Dear Teri, I owe you one hell of a dinner at the Old Parthenon. We'll hit Greektown when I get back—shish kebab, moussaka, baklava, the works. Love you, babe. Bri.

She sat down on the bed, staring at the letters "IOU."

Unbidden, a scene from her ninth birthday sprang into her mind:

Her father, handing her a pink-flowered card with a balloon in the center. "IOU two tickets for opening day at Comiskey Park," it had read. She had been thrilled. A chance to be alone with her father, without competing for his attention with six younger brothers and sisters, had been the best present she could imag-

ine. And the White Sox! She'd known every player on the team, every position, every batting average. She was her father's daughter. It was her dream come true. On the April day when he fulfilled the IOU, her mother packed them a box lunch of tuna fish sandwiches and Fritos. At the stadium Daddy bought her a pack of hot-roasted peanuts from the mustachioed vendor boisterously soliciting customers from behind his steaming pushcart. Later Daddy helped her keep score. Someone spilled Coke on her new canvas sneakers during the seventh inning stretch, but she hadn't cared. The White Sox won that day, and Daddy bought her a pennant to celebrate. A perfect day.

Teri blinked, realizing that there were tears on Brian's card. *Even Bri doesn't know the truth,* she thought heavily. She set the card down on the floral chintz bedspread and pushed away the memories. There was no Daddy anymore, no family, no going back. That little girl was gone, erased as if she had never existed. Now there was only Teri Mathews, future bride of Brian Michaelson.

There could be no past. Teri knew that. There was only the future. And as she brushed the tears aside and composed herself to return to the party, she thanked God with all her heart that she had one.

"Rise and shine, Mathews. This party ain't over yet."

Teri was jarred awake by Josie and Marie tearing the sea-blue blankets and flannel sheets away from her sweatshirt-clad body. Suddenly, a blast of cold air chilled her naked legs.

"Go away!" she complained, trying to shake the grogginess from her head.

She yanked the covers back again, but Josie pulled her out of the double bed. Josie and Marie, who had spent the night in sleeping bags on the floor, had already showered and dressed, Teri noted.

"We let you sleep until the last minute in honor of your birthday, but there are places to go and people to see," Marie chirped at her from behind her fuchsia-rimmed glasses.

"My birthday ended yesterday, guys." Teri yawned.

"But not the celebration," Josie said, pushing her toward the bathroom. "Hurry up and shower, we'll pick your clothes out—and breakfast is on the table."

No sooner had Teri turned on the shower than Josie and Marie flew into frantic motion. While Josie plucked a red turtleneck sweater and black wool slacks from the crowded little closet beside the bathroom, Marie dashed into the kitchen and pulled out slices of cold pizza. She set them on white and blue Corelle plates, beside leftover wedges of birthday cake, and poured orange juice into tall tumblers.

By the time Teri entered the kitchen, the smell of coffee convinced her it was really morning, though her watch read five forty-five.

"Five forty-five! I don't have to be at work until ten!"

"You don't have to be at work at all. Hilda rescheduled all your appointments. You're free, girlfriend."

"What are you up to?" It usually took Teri three cups of coffee to wake up in the morning, but now she was alert as she stared warily at her two friends, both of whom looked particularly well put together today. Josie's usually wild mane was tamed with a huge tortoiseshell barrette, and Marie's brown hair was fashioned in a French braid with a purple ribbon that matched her gold-buttoned blouse.

"Wear those gold hoop earrings Brian gave you last Christmas," Marie suggested. "And put on a little more eye shadow."

"Where are we going?"

Josie grinned. "I know you hate surprises, Miss Planner, but you're going to love this one. Now, hurry *up.*"

When Josie's '88 Century pulled onto the Metro Airport exit ramp an hour later, Teri's mouth fell open.

"Wait, wait," Marie laughed. "Don't even try to guess."

These guys are crazy—but this is kind of fun, Teri admitted to herself, though she still felt eager to know what was in store for her. *Maybe Brian is right and I should go with the flow more than I do. Relax, enjoy yourself. They've obviously gone to a lot of trouble,* she thought, feeling a rush of affection for her friends. *But where were they taking her and when would she be back?* As they dashed toward the check-in counter, she thought: *My God, we're actually getting on a plane! I didn't even bring a change of underwear!*

Her tan shoulder bag slammed against her hip as she raced hand in hand alongside Josie and Marie toward Gate 4. Breathless, Josie handed the boarding passes to the stoop-shouldered gate attendant posted outside the jetway.

"*Now* will you tell me where we're going?" Teri pleaded, sending her friends a beseeching glance.

The middle-aged gate attendant took pity on her, boredom vanishing as he gazed down into her luminous brown eyes. "Better keep that coat buttoned up, miss, because you're headed for the Windy City."

Teri stopped short. Josie yanked her arm. "Come on, you're holding up the line."

Chicago. *No.* Marie and Josie excitedly drew her along into the plane, but their words were gibberish to Teri, and she felt as if she were moving in slow motion as she allowed herself to be led up the aisle to the window seat.

Suddenly, Josie's voice penetrated her daze. "Oh, Marie, I can't stand it anymore. Let's just tell her."

Marie's face flushed with excitement. "We've got tickets for the *Oprah Winfrey Show* that's being taped this morning," she announced triumphantly. "It's all about weddings, and there's going to be a fashion show and an editor from *Perfect Bride* magazine. Then we have reservations at Due's for lunch—their deep-dish pizza is fantastic—and then we'll shop till we drop. My cousin works at a discount bridal shop on Wabash, and she's picked out the most gorgeous dresses for you to try on! But there's one last surprise you'll have to wait to see."

Teri swallowed hard. "I'm not sure I can handle any more surprises," she said hollowly. Marie, misinterpreting her dazed expression as one of stunned delight, squeezed her arm.

"Ever been to Chicago?" she asked, securing her safety belt.

"No."

Liar. Teri's palms began to sweat. As the plane soared off the runway, her mind whirled. *I swore I'd never go back. How could I ever let them trap me into something like this? But now there's nothing I can do about it,* she despaired. *There's nothing I can do.*

Forty-five minutes later, Teri had disembarked the plane and was following her friends toward the sea of faces in the airport lounge. Suddenly, one face came into focus. *Brian.* She hurtled into his arms so urgently he almost dropped the bouquet of roses he held. "Whoa, babe"—he kissed her, laughing—"take it easy. I'm not going anywhere."

"You'd better not."

Brian's strong arms tightened around her. "Hey, you okay?"

She wasn't. But she had to pretend that she was as excited and happy as they all hoped she would be. "I'm great," she murmured, managing a forced smile. All the while she clung to him, fearing her knees would give way if she let go. "You've all outdone yourselves. This is the most unforgettable birthday I've ever had."

She was still trembling when they all took their seats in the tenth row of the audience on the set of the *Oprah Winfrey Show.* Television. She was in Chicago, on television.

lly, her black
he red turtle-
. Her hands
her shoulder
e absorbed in

't be noticed,
her life could
en years. *Oh,
en.*

r theme song
d in an exqui-
udience with
dience today?
ell, ladies and
lo we have a

d in exquisite
edecked run-
ce. Monique

D'Arcy, the editor-in-chief of *Perfect Bride* magazine, provided sparkling commentary and hit it off with Oprah, the two of them exchanging easy banter about the pleasures and pitfalls of planning the perfect wedding. Monique D'Arcy was a tall brunette beauty whose curvaceous figure was flattered by the clingy pink sandwashed silk suit she wore, accented only by a long strand of pearls and a huge Tiffany diamond ring on her finger that flashed in the studio lights. Teri barely heard Monique's quips, and her introduction to the random drawing about to take place. Vaguely, she realized it was something about a magazine issue devoted to celebrity brides, something about Ana Cates and that famous model, Eve Hamel—and something about one lucky audience member getting the opportunity of a lifetime.

"Teri Mathews!"

Someone had called her name.

"Teri Mathews of Livonia, Michigan," Oprah exclaimed. "Where are you? Stand up, you lucky girl!"

Oprah? Oprah was calling my name?

Then Brian was on his feet, clapping, and Oprah ran with her microphone into the audience, straight toward Teri.

This couldn't be happening.

"Teri, come on, it's you!" Josie screamed, jumping up and slapping her on the back so forcefully, she almost fell forward. "Hurry! Go up there!"

"They're waiting for you!" Marie added.

Brian pulled her to her feet, kissed her, and pushed her into Oprah's welcoming arms.

Teri couldn't breathe. She couldn't think, couldn't even run. Panic surged through her.

No, no, no, no, Teri screamed silently. Her quiet new life, her carefully cultivated anonymity, had been blown to smithereens. Oprah Winfrey was talking to her—and she was on national television.

.R

ne would recognize

y the beautiful doe
at haunted him ev-
ll these years.
elieve it. There she
l, but utterly beauti-

earthy beauty that
t teenager. Outside,
nountaintops. Inside
d face blanched pale

ank her through the

e had changed her
able to find her. Teri
Well, Gina, you're a

arching, he'd finally

unning away.

Chapter Four

Eve ushered Maxine Goodman into the living room and invited her to take a seat in one of the vanilla suede chairs. She was surprised by the woman's petiteness. She had expected the director of New York's premiere security firm to cut an imposing figure, but in her navy suit and poppy-colored scarf and earrings, Maxine Goodman looked as warm and friendly as an elementary-school teacher. She had short, curly brown hair, a slim build that nevertheless projected wiry strength, and piercing amber eyes in a pleasant, freckled face. As Maxine settled back against the cushions, Eve guessed her to be about forty.

"I'm glad you were available on such short notice, Ms. Goodman. Coffee?" Eve offered.

"No, thanks. And please call me Maxine—we'll be seeing a lot of each other until this matter is resolved, so we may as well be informal."

Eve liked the way she spoke: direct, assured, her voice exuding a calm strength that Eve found reassuring. She was glad she'd followed Natalie's recommendation.

According to Natalie, half the celebrities in Hollywood and New York had Maxine Goodman's Champion Security on retainer. Her reputation among the rich and frightened was sterling. Maxine's thirteen years as a crack homicide detective on the NYPD had stood her in good stead when she decided to open her own security firm in Manhattan five years ago. Not only did she employ retired Secret Service agents as bodyguards for her elite clientele, she also surrounded herself with the finest detectives and lab technicians, and had direct hookup with the most advanced computers and crime labs in the country. As her reputation grew, she opened a West Coast branch to service the growing demand from celebrities in L.A. and Las Vegas. But it was Maxine Goodman herself who helmed both operations and whose personal prowess was legend. She was known for her brilliant investigative mind, and her keen sense of logic, combined with intuition and a relentless passion for her work. Celebrities gladly paid her stiff monthly fees, and slept soundly at night.

"Do you mind if I tape our interview?" Maxine asked, making a notation in the small leather notebook on her lap. "Sometimes small words and details can prove significant, and this way my secretary can transcribe the entire conversation into your file." Eve nodded her assent, and Maxine reached into her burgundy leather briefcase. She set the minirecorder on the glass coffee table and pressed the record button. "Okay, tell me about these letters you've been receiving."

Eve realized that Maxine Goodman was subtly scrutinizing both her and the black and cream drama of the apartment. She sensed they were sizing up each other, and that somehow, immediately, both felt comfortable with the fit. She glanced down at her hands, then thought back over the past three unsettling weeks.

"The first one came September twenty-eighth. It was a Wednesday," Eve began. "It was in a lime-green envelope, the same as the second one, which came last week as I was leaving for London. And"—Eve involuntarily shuddered—"both of them contained a scrap of fabric snipped from something I'd been wearing a day or two before the letters arrived."

Maxine pursed her lips. "May I see the letters?"

"I have only one—the second one. I tore the first one up. Pretty stupid, right?" Eve shook her head, grimacing. "I still can't believe this is real. At first I thought it was just some sick, stupid joke."

"That's a very normal reaction, Eve—may I call you that? Here, put these gloves on in case there's still a clear fingerprint."

Eve nodded, drew on the thin cotton gloves, and moved to the ivory writing desk beneath the expansive window overlooking Central Park. She unlocked the center drawer and gingerly withdrew the lime-green envelope. It was incredible to think that here in her own lovely sunlit apartment, with its plush carpeting, ebony silk crepe settees, and the enormous pink granite fireplace, surrounded by all the things she loved: the crystal ballerina sculpture Nico had given her for her birthday, the Degas she had bought herself after her twenty-fifth *Vogue* cover, the hand-crocheted ecru afghan her mother had sent during Eve's first winter alone in New York, even here she was not safe from the intrusion of some unseen menace. She was glad to hand the envelope over to Maxine. She never wanted to touch it again.

Maxine had already donned a second pair of gloves. "I know the entire postal system has handled the envelope, but has anyone besides you touched the letter?"

"No."

"Good. I'll need to get your fingerprints for comparison purposes."

The scrap of gold lamé fabric glistened in the sunlight as Maxine removed it along with the single sheet of lined green paper. Her eyes narrowed as she read the tight black script.

*Pretty clothes for a pretty girl. I wonder
how you look without your pretty clothes. One
day I'll find out. Billy Shears.*

Maxine stared hard at the tiny, neat letters of that signature. Billy Shears. A punster. There was a distinctive double curlique on the *y* that Maxine zeroed in on immediately. And something else—the name was familiar, jarring. She couldn't quite place it. But she'd have bet that three-carat sapphire on Eve Hamel's finger that Ronson would find it in the computer.

"Was the first one signed the same way?"

"Yes, Billy Shears. And I remember the double curlique on the *y.*"

"Tell me what the message said in that one, as best as you can remember." Maxine watched Eve's face closely.

"I remember perfectly. The words are burned into my mind." Eve paced to the settee, where Ragamuffin was basking in the sun. She picked up the cat and cradled him against her shoulder. Ragamuffin's rough tongue scraped her cheek. "It said: *I bet you're as hot in bed as you are in this dress. One day I'll find out.*"

Silence fell in the room except for the purring of the cat and the faint whir of the tape recorder. Eve returned to her flowered armchair opposite the security specialist. "I think what really spooks me is that he could get this close to me, close enough to actually cut off part of my clothing, and I never noticed."

"Sometimes these individuals can be extremely clever—brilliant, even. I'm not trying to scare you, Eve, but that is partially what makes them so dangerous." Maxine saw the fear darken Eve's eyes to a stormy sapphire. She went on quickly. "I'm not telling you that this particular individual is violent. I don't know that yet, and neither do you, so please don't be overly alarmed. It could be that he's merely getting his kicks out of frightening you. Some people derive pleasure from psychological power over celebrities—they feel like they're having a relationship with you, an interaction, and often that excitement alone is enough to satisfy them."

"But not always," Eve pointed out. Ragamuffin, bored with being petted, jumped off her lap and scooted back to the sun-warmed settee. Eve brushed Ragamuffin's stray dark hairs from her cream silk sweater and leggings. She stared expectantly at the other woman.

"Not always." Maxine agreed equably. She met Eve's troubled gaze with a calm, even one. "Some of these individuals do act out their violent fantasies. But we don't know enough yet about this particular person to make any reliable predictions. We don't even know for certain if we're dealing with a male or a female. But we will." She smiled reassuringly, yet Eve saw the steely coolness in her eyes just behind the smile. For the first time since she'd returned from being with Nico in London, she felt in control. By enlisting the services of Champion Security, she had taken a step to combat her unseen tormentor, the first step toward winning this match of nerves. And Maxine Goodman would be her gladiator.

"Have Ronson run a comparison of any prints found on the stationery," Maxine said into the recorder. For the next half hour Maxine took detailed notes on Eve's daily routine and everybody in it, the name of her employees, the cleaner she frequented and the boutiques where she had purchased the two damaged dresses. She also examined both gowns, the gold lamé and the blue taffeta, and asked for a detailed itinerary of Eve's schedule the days she had worn both gowns. She would run a security check on all the people Eve had regularly come in contact with, from the doorman outside her apartment to the makeup and wardrobe assistants on her shoots.

Maxine called her office and ordered round-the-

clock bodyguards who would be posted outside Eve's
building, instantly accessible at the touch of a beeper.
One or more would follow Eve throughout the day,
but, Maxine assured her, they would be discreet. She
would not even be aware of their presence unless she
needed them.

The bodyguards, Tom Swanson and Joe
Tamburelli, arrived before Maxine concluded the interview. Eve smiled to herself as she shook hands with
each of them. She'd been expecting hulking bodybuild-
ers in too-tight business suits, but was surprised to see
that these two attractive men in blazers and slacks
looked normal and unthreatening.

Tom Swanson, who looked to be about thirty-five,
was tall with wide shoulders and a muscular build. He
had a shock of blond hair and an easy grin. Joe
Tamburelli, in his twenties, had straight black hair, cool
gray eyes, and a big dimple peeking through the five
o'clock shadow on his chin. He looked like he spent
plenty of time in the gym.

Eve studied their faces so that she could instantly
pick them out of a crowd. She wondered grimly what
other face she had skimmed over recently, a face be-
longing to the person who called himself Billy Shears.

By the time Maxine left and the bodyguards had
taken up their posts, Eve was exhausted but felt far
more secure than she had since the first letter had intruded upon her peace. Maxine's final words on parting
had been: "Don't let this interfere with your life. I
know that's easier said than done, but in the high per-
centage of cases, these offenders never turn violent.
We'll know more about this Billy Shears in a few days
when the background checks are completed and the
lab results come in. In the meantime, I'm leaving you
in good hands. Swanson and Tamburelli are two of my
best. And should you get another letter, don't open it.
Call me immediately."

She sounds so confident, Eve thought as she

opened the refrigerator and reached for a diet soda. *Maybe they can catch this creep before I need to tell Nico anything about this. The last thing he needs is a break in his concentration when he's careening at 130 miles an hour on a winding racetrack. With any luck this will even be over before he gets back to New York.*

Ten days later, just as Eve was dashing out the door to meet Nico's plane, her mother called from Duluth with the news that Margo was in New York to address a medical convention.

Eve swallowed back the sarcastic "So what?" that sprang to her lips.

"That's nice, Mom."

She closed her eyes and grimaced, bracing herself for what she knew would come next.

"She's staying at the Pierre," her mother said carefully. "I thought it might be nice if you two got together for dinner."

Nice? More like torture.

Eve was resigned to her mother's attempts to play peacemaker between her daughters. Elizabeth Hämeläinen had always tried to downplay her husband's favoritism toward Margo, whom he'd dubbed "the pretty one, the smart one," the golden girl with the dimpled smile who was double-promoted from the third grade to the fifth and voted class president all through high school. Eve had been "the quiet one," the gangly athlete who tagged along like an afterthought when he played catch with his boys. Despite the track trophies that lined her bookshelf, she'd always felt like a second-class citizen in her father's house. And Margo had liked it that way.

Throughout Eve's adolescence, Elizabeth had been aware of the girls' strained relationship, and had encouraged Eve to try to step out of Margo's shadow. But the friction had dramatically intensified after Eve's startling success. Now Eve and Margo rarely spoke, and saw each other only when family circumstances brought them together.

"Mom," Eve said as patiently as she could, "if Margo wanted to see me, don't you think she would have called?" She glanced at her watch. Fifty minutes until the plane landed.

When she heard her mother sigh, Eve's heart sank. This sounded like the beginning of a lecture.

"Sweetheart, I know it's difficult, but sometimes you have to be the one to make the first move." Elizabeth's voice was soft yet firm. "You're getting married soon. Before you know it, you'll have a family of your own, and I know you'll want your own children to be close."

Eve heard the quiet emotion behind her mother's words. She remembered how many times her mother had held her in her arms and soothed away her hurts.

"You've always been close to your brothers, but Margo is the only sister you have. I'm not asking you to choose her for your maid of honor, but wouldn't it be wonderful if you two could become friends before the wedding?"

Eve couldn't imagine ever being friends with Margo, but if it meant this much to her mother, she knew she had to make an effort.

"I'll call her tonight," she promised without enthusiasm. "Nico is just getting back from London—he's probably circling Kennedy right now—so I'd better run, Mom, but I'll see if we can't all have dinner together."

Nico drained his brandy and tapped at his watch. "If you don't hurry, bambina, your sister will be dining alone."

Eve was securing her diamond-encrusted, oblong earrings in place before the mirror. Nico tightened the knot on the silk tie that echoed the sea-green of his eyes and stood up to button the black European-cut suit that emphasized his perfect physique. As Eve made a move toward the closet, he impatiently raked a hand through his hair. "I'm warning you—if you dare take your clothes off one more time, I'll toss you back in bed and the doctor will have to wait till breakfast to meet her future brother-in-law."

"She can wait until the wedding as far as I'm concerned," Eve bit out as she scrutinized herself, frowning into the mirror. She'd already discarded two outfits, and she wasn't crazy about this one either, but Nico had been dressed for an hour and would explode with exasperation if she changed her mind one more time.

This would have to do. She wore an ice-blue silk sheath with a multicolored crystal beaded jacket, a simple silver bracelet, and cobalt spike heels. Her honey-colored hair was swept up at the crown in a loose halo that allowed fat tendrils to casually frame her face. More lipstick, Eve decided, and applied it with shaking fingers.

Scared of my own sister, she thought disgustedly. But it wasn't really Margo she was afraid of, it was that voice inside herself telling her she wasn't good enough, pretty enough, smart enough. Not when Margo was in the same room.

She stole a look at Nico in the mirror, wondering how he would respond to Margo. Would she dazzle him with her brilliance and charm? *Will I fade into the wallpaper once she starts to talk?* She knew she was being ridiculous. Nico loved her and thought she was beautiful. Not even Margo could dim the love that shone in his eyes.

"Ready," she announced as Nico came up from behind and slipped his arms around her waist. He smelled deliciously of Paco Rabanne as he kissed her neck.

"You're sure?"

"Sure as I'll ever be. Let's get this over with."

He turned her to face him and tilted her chin up until their eyes met. "You don't like this sister of yours very much, do you, bambina?" he asked gently.

"She doesn't like me."

"And you said she was highly intelligent. I think she must be *pazza*—crazy."

Eve laughed and touched his cheek. "I love you."

"I worship you." Nico kissed her so thoroughly that she knew he had obliterated all traces of her lipstick. But when she tried to dash back to the mirror to add more, he dragged her relentlessly toward the door.

"Do it in the car," he ordered her. He paused only long enough for her to snatch up her beaded handbag before pulling her firmly out the door.

Chapter Five

Eve spotted Margo on the secluded banquette even before the maître d' led the way through a fairyland of candlelit tables. *Make the best of it*, she told herself. She fixed a vivid smile on her face, only vaguely aware of all the heads swerving her way as she strolled before Nico through the ornately appointed dining room.

Above the glitter of crystal and china, beyond the pastel shimmer of baby orchids clustered in a Baccarat vase, her sister sat at the pink linen-draped table, a vision of chic in off-the-shoulder black suede. Her short silver-blond hair glimmered in the candlelight. Her jewelry was minimal—a silver bracelet, a ruby ring, and antique marcasite earrings set with onyx and rubies winking at her ears. It was so like Margo to appear utterly cool, understated, and reserved.

"I hope you don't mind—I started without you." She waved her hand airily at the open bottle of Dom Pérignon nestled beside the table. Her glass was half empty, and the ashtray before her was full. "Don't tell me you still change your clothes ten times before you finally walk out the door, Evie," Margo chided, her opal eyes lit with amusement. "Our dad used to go crazy waiting for her," she told Nico with a dazzling smile.

"And you were always the first one to park yourself at the dinner table," Eve retorted. To Nico she added, "After I had helped Mom set it, of course."

To herself she thought, *And you always claimed the chair next to Dad's, while I was stuck between Rob and Derek. That was your way of ensuring that in all the clamor around the kitchen table you'd get Dad's ear.*

Dad. He was at the center of all of her conflicts with Margo for as long as she could remember. Eve had always longed to captivate his attention the way Margo had. A stoic and reserved Scandinavian who worked long shifts in the distillery, Edward Hämeläinen had bestowed all the warmth he could eke out of his soul on his eldest daughter. Eve had never seen him bestow such affection on anyone else, not even her mother.

With the rest of them he was distantly benevolent, a man more given to arm's-length smiles than bear hugs. But with Margo he'd been positively effusive. He'd revered her brilliance and displayed all of her report cards and honors on the living room mantel. On the day Eve took first place in the state track finals her mother and brothers had been cheering in the stands, but Dad had instead decided to pick up a double shift at the plant in order to help pay for Margo's graduation party.

And the last time she'd been home, Eve had bitterly noted that the gilt-framed *Vogue* cover she'd sent him for his birthday was perched on her mother's bric-a-brac shelf in the kitchen, while a laminated journal article of Margo's got top billing in the living room.

Some things will never change, Eve thought as she

brushed her lips across her sister's proffered cheek and properly introduced her to Nico.

"So you're the famous Caesarone," Margo commented with a coolly appraising stare as Eve and Nico slid across the pearl-gray leather banquette. A waiter whisked two more flutes onto the table, and filled them with champagne. Margo took a drag on her cigarette. "I saw you race in Spain last year, but little did I know at the time we were going to be related."

"Luckily I didn't need your services, *Dottoressa,* after Gilbeaut took the front end off my car." Nico slanted his potent smile at the slender woman with the slightly uptilted chin and the sensuous opal eyes glittering with intelligence.

Margo leaned back in her seat and expelled a stream of smoke. "I don't know what my baby sister has told you about me, but I'm *not* that kind of doctor."

Eve's fingers tightened on the fragile stem of the glass. It always surprised her how superior Margo could sound with so little effort, but her sister's haughty tone appeared to have no effect on Nico. His eyes merely glinted with amusement, and he took Eve's hand and kissed it.

"Eve has told me a *great deal* about you, *Dottoressa* Hämeläinen, and I can see that all of it is true."

Eve's fingers curled around his warm, strong ones. Her gaze roamed the room. It could be anyone in this room, she thought trying not to shiver. She reached for her champagne. Anyone. A waiter, a patron, a busboy. Would she ever again be able to set foot in public without feeling stalked? Which nameless, faceless person was watching and tormenting her, perhaps planning to hurt her?

Three tables away she spotted Tamburelli's now-familiar face poring over a menu, his presence confirming the chilling reality of her situation.

"How long do you plan on staying in New York?"

Margo answered, reaching for another cigarette.

Nico watched her light up. "*Dottoressa*, I find it rather surprising that you smoke. You must be the only doctor left in New York who hasn't dropped this so unhealthy habit."

"What can I say? It's one of my weaknesses." Margo sighed, shrugging her shoulders above the revealing suede dress. "That, and my fascination for European men. A fascination that my baby sister obviously shares." She met his gaze with an unabashed stare, all icy-blond beauty and frost-laden sophistication shot through with pure sexual challenge.

Eve caught her breath. Leave it to Margo to flirt

Throughout the meal, Eve tried to keep up a pleasant stream of conversation. Margo, true to form, used every opportunity to highlight the importance of her own endeavors in contrast to her sister's transient celebrity.

"By the time dessert arrived, I was ready to glop the chocolate mousse in her face," Eve confessed later to Nico as she coiled her legs around his waist in the steaming-hot tub.

Chuckling, he slid her closer and scooped up a handful of bubbles which he flourished before her. "And I was ready to fling the whipped cream right up her snooty nose, especially when she said that models didn't have to worry their pretty heads about anything but mascara and cellulite. *Merda.*"

Playfully, he smeared the bubbles across Eve's rosy nipples, which hardened beneath his touch.

"If this *was* whipped cream, I'd lick it off," Nico teased. He caught her earlobe gently between his teeth, his breath warm against her damp skin, making her gasp. She fondled him beneath the swirling water.

"Did you think she was pretty?"

Nico's mouth trailed kisses along her sculptured cheek until he reached her parted lips. "If you like dry little ice princesses with nicotine breath," he whispered huskily. "Personally, I like my women hot and wet."

Eve closed her eyes. "She was flirting with you."

"All women flirt with me, bambina."

Then Nico hoisted her onto his waiting erection. He tangled his hands in the wet strands of her hair and plunged his tongue into her mouth. Eve trembled and clutched his muscular back as she rocked in rhythm to his movements. *"Carissima,"* Nico panted. He thrust inside her again and again, until she forgot about Margo, Tamburelli, and everything else.

.   .   .

He lit the candles. Ten of them, one by one. Slowly, reverently, he blew out the match. In the flickering shadows, his obsidian eyes glittered. He stared, transfixed, at the magazine pages adorning the four walls like a giant, glossy jigsaw puzzle.

"You're so beautiful," he whispered. He had cut away all the background from the covers and ads, leaving only Eve sculpted before him, smiling, laughing, flirting.

"You looked so beautiful tonight. I loved your dress. See?"

He held up a small square of ice-blue silk.

"This one is almost as sexy as the gold lamé. It's so soft, like you. Do you know I nearly spoke to you tonight? But I changed my mind. I decided to wait until we can be alone together. I'm almost ready, Eve, almost ready. . . ."

He laid the square of fabric in the center of the small table ringed with candles. To the right of it he placed the tiny surgical scissors. From the drawer he brought out a single sheet of lined green paper and a matching envelope and set them down within the circle of glowing candle flame.

"I know you've been lonely waiting to hear from me, my darling. But Billy hasn't forgotten you. I could never forget you. Never. And I won't let anything keep us apart. We're going to be together one day very soon, darling, very soon. I'll see to everything. It will be perfect—like you."

Dreamily, he wrote the letter. Then he blew out the candles and traveled the room with measured steps, his hands outstretched, tracing the glossy pictures plastered seamlessly over every inch of the walls as if he were reading braille. Love and a frenzied excitement rose within him. At last he sank down into his mother's bentwood rocking chair. Breathing shallowly, he touched himself, tentatively at first. His strokes gained momentum with the rocking of the chair. He was gasping as the chair scraped rhythmically against the threadbare carpet—gasping as he croaked out, "Eve . . . Eve . . . Eve."

Soon, he promised himself much later when he woke. He had to kill her very, very soon.

Chapter Six

The next morning Eve and Nico took a cab to the Hilton, where Mimi Cohn, the stylist from *Perfect Bride*, had transformed two adjoining suites into mirrored dressing rooms lined wall to wall with racks of prospective wardrobes for the Maui shoot. Gowns, swimsuits, tuxedos, peignoirs, and sportswear were crammed on racks in various sections of the room, with accompanying boxes of accessories piled high. The sofas were strewn with straw hats, sunglasses, tennis racquets, and sandals, and the cocktail table sparkled with faux jewels, wedding veils, and scuba gear. Mimi, a skinny dynamo in cropped black hair and jeweled eyeglasses, orchestrated her two assistants' flurried activity with a conductor's zeal. She waved to Eve and Nico as they entered the suite, and hooked a plastic bag filled with sunglasses and pink neon earrings onto a hanger with a pink and orange metallic bikini. "Monique, they're here," she sang out as an assistant handed her a pair of sandals to complete the ensemble.

Eve drew Nico through the maze of clothes and people toward Monique, who was deep in conversation with a pretty, young brunette and a tall, lanky man in jeans and a white T-shirt.

"Eve! I'm so glad you're here in time to meet Teri and Brian!" Monique embraced Eve excitedly. "Nico love, you're going to slay every woman in America in the swim trunks we picked out for you. They don't leave much to the imagination, but I know you're just the man to pull it off."

"Just so I don't have to pull *them* off," Nico retorted. Monique kissed him effusively on both cheeks. "Not to worry. This isn't *Playgirl*. We're strictly PG-13."

"Then why did I feel like one of their centerfolds when you put me in that leopard-print thing?" the man in the T-shirt shot out with a grin.

Monique chuckled. "Your mother will love it, Brian, don't worry."

Eve extended her hand to Teri. "Hi, I'm Eve Hamel—and this is my fiancé, Nico Caesarone."

"This is absolutely the last thing I ever thought I'd be doing," Teri murmured with a quick, shy smile. "Everything's happened so quickly since the *Oprah Winfrey Show*. Ms. D'Arcy just kind of swept us into all this, and she insists everything will be fine."

"Oh, it will be," Eve assured her. "You're very pretty, and you'll have a couple of pros to show you the ropes. You'll surprise yourself, it'll be just fine."

Monique put her arm across Teri's shoulders. "More than fine, sweetie. You and Brian will be great. You have no idea how relieved I was when I picked you two from that audience. I kept having nightmares that my Cinderella couple would be straight out of *American Gothic* or else an overweight, overage frump with spiked orange hair and a biker boyfriend."

Over the laughter, Monique told Teri, "You'll need to come back for a final fitting right before Christmas. My secretary, Linda, will send you a schedule and your plane tickets. Meanwhile, enjoy *Phantom* tonight—we got you the best seats in the house. Before you know it, we'll be partying in Maui." She winked at Brian. "I bet you do a mean hula."

"My Irish jig is better. Come up to Kelly's Bar for St. Patrick's Day and you can judge for yourself."

As Monique walked Teri and Brian to the door of the suite, Nico surveyed the confusion of clothes, accessories, and assistants all around. "I can't believe I ever let you talk me into this," he groused, rolling his eyes. "That woman reminds me of a snake charmer I once knew."

"Oh, come on. I want to see you in that swimsuit Monique mentioned." Eve punched him playfully in the stomach.

Monique swooped down on them again. "We're going to have to fly to L.A. and Washington with a ton of this stuff for Ana Cates and Senator Farrell to go through. Neither one could get away, and we couldn't wait any longer for their schedules to clear. Deadlines. Deadlines. Tell me what you thought of Teri and Brian."

"She's adorable," Eve replied, "but she seems terribly nervous. Stage fright?"

"I don't know. I think it's more than that, but damned if I know what. I had to practically twist her arm to get her to sign the contract and releases after the Oprah show. Brian, at least, is getting a huge kick out of the whole thing."

"I hate to interrupt this important tête-à-tête," Nico said, "but if you'll point me in the direction of that bathing suit, we can get this show on the road, as you say in America. I'm meeting a sponsor for lunch in one hour and twenty minutes, so if you want my body, Comtesse, use it and be done."

"The king has spoken," Monique stage-whispered to Eve. "Mimi," she called out. The stylist came running. "Show Mr. Caesarone the tentative wardrobe we've selected. Carla"—she signaled to the chunky redhead labeling the fresh polaroids of Teri and Brian in their wardrobes—"bring Miss Hamel that beaded dinner dress I want her to wear on the yacht, and find those Adolfo shoes I set aside earlier. I think they're behind the beach bags."

Monique grabbed Eve's hand as she headed toward the dressing area. "By the way, did I thank you for getting Nico to do this?" she asked in a low tone. "Richard and I are both convinced this is going to be the best issue ever. We're going to have a blast on the yacht—guaranteed." Her eyes sparkled knowingly. "It won't be nearly as bad as Nico is expecting. I mean, how bad can Maui be?"

Eve thought of twelve-hour days in the tropical sun, interminable waiting at Antonio's whim, and only God knowing how the weather would cooperate. How bad, indeed? Eve smiled wryly. But all she said was "It'll be a blast."

The phone rang just as Eve slipped behind the dressing curtain. "It's Richard," Mimi announced, holding the receiver out toward Monique.

"Well? How's it going?" Richard's voice on the phone was brusque.

Monique surveyed the busy room. "Great. You ought to see how that darling couple from Michigan looks all decked out. This is going to be such a smash."

"Good—it had better be. I knew you'd come up with a winner. Look, I just called to tell you there's a fire I have to put out down in Atlanta. I'm at the airport now."

"What's wrong?"

"There's a rumor that Sullivan's negotiating with the Turner people. I can't afford to lose him right now."

Monique closed her eyes. Richard sounded so calm, but she knew he would go crazy if he lost Sullivan. "Promise him whatever you have to and then some," she urged. "Do you think you'll be back in time for the stockholder's meeting tomorrow, or should I cover for you?"

"It's not until three—I'll give it a hell of a shot. Sorry about dinner tonight, Mo. You'll cancel with Mamma Leone's?"

"No problem, darling. As a matter of fact, it'll give me a chance to proof the layouts for the January issue. I'll probably just pick up some Chinese on my way home."

"There's my boarding call. Love you, Mo."

Monique disconnected and immediately punched in a set of numbers. She caught sight of Nico in the mirror, magnificently bronze and muscled, flexing his glutes as Mimi handed him a glass of Bordeaux. *I knew that tush would look sensational in that skimpy little suit,* she thought triumphantly. And Nico, for all his attitude, was enjoying himself hugely as he flirted with Mimi and Carla, and basked in the splendor of his own reflection.

A familiar voice answered the phone in Connecticut. Monique spoke quickly as Eve came out of the dressing area and pinched Nico's ass.

"I'll be there tonight," Monique said quietly into the phone. "For dinner. And this time I can stay late."

Maxine Goodman looked up as Ronson burst into the quiet of her office and dumped a manila folder onto her oak desk. "Your hunch was right as usual. But you're not going to like what we uncovered about this Billy Shears."

She looked at the craggy face of the tall black detective who folded himself into the tan tweed chair opposite her, then focused on the thick file labeled Hamel. She pulled out the shiny fax papers and scanned them, her pulse quickening.

"Shit."

"Deep shit."

Maxine swiveled in her seat and reached for the phone. "Better get this over with," she muttered, her mind racing with plans. Strategies and counterstrategies clicked rapid-fire through her mind as she entered Eve Hamel's phone number. "Shit."

Eve's body glistened with a faint sheen as she curled the five-pound weight toward her shoulder. Ragamuffin watched from his customary spot on the settee. Two more sets to go and she could shower and head out to Natalie's office. There was a troublesome clause in the Estée Lauder contracts that Natalie wanted to explain in person. Eve was determined to get all the glitches ironed out and settled quickly. She really wanted this five-year deal. It would take her nicely through her thirtieth birthday. The cold facts that every model lived with were weighing more on her every day. She wasn't getting any younger—fresher faces and more nubile bodies were clamoring for their turn in the spotlight. This campaign would spell security even if she never worked again.

Security. Financial security and personal security—that's all she wanted. She slung the towel around her neck and wiped the sweat from her forehead. There had been no letters from Billy Shears for nearly two weeks. No word from Maxine either. But as far as Eve was concerned, no news was good news.

She was in the kitchen popping the lid on a diet Coke when the phone rang.

"Eve," Maxine's voice leapt across the line, calm as always, but with an undercurrent of urgency. "This is Maxine Goodman."

"You've found something out, haven't you?"

"Yes, we need to meet."

"Fine. But first tell me what's going on."

There was a pause at the other end of the line.

"I really think it's preferable that we talk in person," Maxine replied.

Eve set the can down on the Formica countertop. "I'm not going to fall apart, Maxine. Tell me."

She heard the investigator sigh. "All right. The news about Billy Shears isn't good. It seems you're not the first woman he's stalked."

Oh, God. Eve closed her eyes. "Go on."

Maxine's voice was brisk now, businesslike. "Very well. But I think you'd better sit down."

Chapter Seven

Indian summer was her favorite season, Monique decided as her foot caressed the accelerator and the red Porsche snaked its way through the winding drive leading up to the estate. Hickory and birch trees flanked the roadside, their leaves aflame with autumn hues. The sloping wooded hillsides were dusted with crisping scarlet and amber leaves, a sea of gorgeous color beneath the lilac sky. It would be dark in another hour, and the glorious rare warmth of this November day would vanish with the rising of the moon, but for now it was perfect, and Monique relished the last rays of the sun, the vivid sights and smells of the Connecticut autumn.

As always, she smiled to herself when she caught sight of the palatial estate crowning the hillside ahead. It was lovely—graceful and regal with its fluted white columns and haloing spires and the formal gardens zigzagging down toward the stream. Twisted vines of dark green ivy hugged the gleaming white granite walls of the three-story mansion she had bought and paid for lock, stock, and barrel only four years after opening the agency. It was a fitting country residence for a comtesse. Every square foot of it gave her pleasure, from the polished expanse of blue and white marble floors to the majesty of the oak-carved staircase, from the huge flagstone fireplaces in each of the seven bedrooms to the sweeping view of laurel-dotted hills and thick forest intersected by the glimmering stream that meandered past the gazebo.

She rounded the final bend and noted in surprise the blue pickup truck piled high with lumber blocking the side drive. Who in the world? she thought, pulling the key from the ignition and heading toward the sound of hammering. She wasn't aware of any repair work needed on the property, and certainly hadn't ordered any. Monique skirted the stone-bordered beds of purple chrysanthemums and stalked around the reflecting pool and birdbath at the rear of the house.

The hammering had ceased. But the sight of four-by-fours jutting up from the low brick walls enclosing the terrace stopped her cold.

"What the hell?"

A Mets baseball cap shot up from behind the low wall. Beneath the visor she saw steel-blue eyes in a tanned, rugged face.

"Who the hell are you?" Monique demanded. "And what do you think you're doing to my house?"

"You must be the daughter." The man set down his hammer and stood up to his full height. He squinted at her through the setting rays of the sun. He was tall, Monique noticed. A good six foot four of solid, rough-hewn muscle—not the kind that came from a gym, but the weathered kind that came from sweat, hard work, sun, and open air. She was able to get a good look at him since he was barechested.

He wiped his grime-streaked palms on his beige cutoff jeans, and leapt down from the terrace to face her. He stuck out his hand. "I'm Pete Lambert. Your mother—"

"I don't care if you're Bozo the Clown. What the hell are you doing to my house?"

His eyes narrowed. He dropped his hand. "Your mother didn't tell me you were high-strung." He regarded Monique with the infuriating tolerance of a man trying to talk sense to a spoiled, petulant child. "It looks like she didn't tell you about our little project either."

"Our little project? *What* little project?" Monique stared at him. He was quite something, she thought, trying to avoid getting sidetracked by his sheer masculine beauty. His shoulders were wide and had been bronzed a deep copper shade by the sun, his chest rippled with muscles above a lean, sinewy waist. She caught a glimpse of thick blond hair beneath the Mets cap, a shade darker than the sun-bleached hair glistening on his chest. She felt a little breathless.

"Look, let's start at the beginning." She pulled off her sunglasses and regarded him coolly. "I'm the Comtesse D'Arcy, and this is my house," she said, mimicking his own attitude, addressing him like a very small, very stupid child. "And I don't recall hiring Pete Lambert or anybody else to do a single thing to it. Your turn."

He grinned. A comtesse. *Is that your delicate way of telling me I should kiss your feet?* he wondered, gazing down at her with amusement. He'd met a lot of smart, beautiful women in his day, but none as vibrant and sexy as this one. She shone like a jewel in her sapphire jump suit. The soft V-neck and clingy sueded silk revealed the full lushness of her breasts and accentuated her slim waist. What a knockout, Pete thought. One thousand volts of electricity. Those crystal eyes of hers alone could light up the night sky.

"You already know who I am," he retorted, deliberately keeping his voice lazy to infuriate her. "I've been renovating the Parker place next door. It's been quite a job. I met your mom and Dorothy a couple weeks ago while they were out for a walk. Your mom's a very sweet lady, Comtesse."

And I'm not, Mr. Lambert? Is that what you're implying? Monique's gaze hardened. She wouldn't have been able to buy all of this for her mother if she'd spent her time being sweet.

"Cut to the chase, Mr. Lambert. You still haven't explained what you're doing here."

"She didn't mention you were so impatient either," he mused aloud. "Hmm, high-strung *and* impatient. I bet you need to take a lot of Valium, lady, to get to sleep at night."

"My sleeping habits are none of your business."

But I wish they were, Pete thought, unable to keep from wondering if she would be as feisty in bed as she was standing there with her hands on her hips and those cool gray eyes of hers sparking.

"You've got a point," he conceded unexpectedly. "I apologize."

Before Monique could object further to the way his eyes were running over her in that appreciative manner, Dorothy's voice broke the tension.

"You *are* here, Miss D'Arcy. I thought I heard a car." She came out through the French doors and picked her way carefully across the terrace strewn with cut lumber and nails. She was a tall, sturdy woman of about fifty with salt and pepper hair cropped short in a wash-and-wear style that suited her crisp personality. She wore a smidgen of coral lipstick, a starched white uniform consisting of shirt and pants with spotless Nikes, and a cotton ball soaked with Jungle Gardenia always nestled in the cup of her minimizer bra.

"Do you like your surprise?" Dorothy smiled expectantly. "Your *maman* knows how much you love sitting out here, watching the sky and the trees and all, and she thought this way you can enjoy it all year long. Mr. Lambert is glassing it in all the way around—even the ceiling—to make it like a Florida room. You'll be able to watch the deer drink from the stream, the snow falling, all those things you enjoy so much." She beamed at Monique, but as she read the stoniness in her young employer's gaze, the smile faded from her lined face. "It is all right, isn't it, Ms. D'Arcy? Your mother thought you'd be so thrilled."

Monique hiked the gold strap of her handbag higher on her shoulder. "I am, Dorothy, it's a wonderful idea. It's just that—well, Mr. Lambert took me by surprise."

"Oh, I see. So, you've met, then, have you?" Dorothy's gaze shifted anxiously back and forth between the two of them.

Pete gave a short laugh. "More like collided, you might say."

Monique regarded him icily. Arrogant son of a bitch, all mouth and muscles. And the brains of a moose, no doubt. She said, "I hope you're not charging me overtime, Mr. Lambert. It seems to me that working hours have ended."

"Yep, time for us dumb working stiffs to be moseying on down to the corner bar for a brewskie or two. Maybe I can even round up some other lugheads for a belching contest," he drawled, those glinting blue eyes alight with mockery.

Monique spun on her heel. "Don't let me keep you." She stalked up the steps to the terrace in the swinging, confident stride she had perfected at the age of fifteen, but her imperious exit was marred when she tripped over the hammer and stubbed her toe into the four-by-four lying in front of her.

"Son of a bitch," she screeched before swallowing back a second string of curses. To her fury, she heard Pete Lambert chuckle behind her. Damn that man to hell.

"Oh, Ms. D'Arcy, are you all right?" Dorothy asked anxiously, dashing up toward the house.

"Never better," Monique bit out. She limped inside, disappearing without a backward glance.

"Klutzy too," Pete remarked under his breath as Dorothy shot him a bemused look.

"I really thought she'd love the idea," Dorothy mumbled, adjusting her tortoiseshell glasses on her slightly crooked nose. She shook her head. "Don't mind Ms. D'Arcy's temper. She's used to running things, you see. But my, she's a fine, lovely girl. I never saw anyone who takes such good care of her *maman*. You'll see what I mean, Mr. Lambert, once you get to know her better."

Know her better? Pete mused. *I'd rather paint every square inch of trim with my tongue.*

"See you tomorrow, Dorothy," he called, packing away his tools and covering the lumber with a tarp. The sun had waned to a pale lemon glimmer above the mauve horizon, and the air was growing chilly, almost as chilly as Ms. High-and-Mighty D'Arcy herself. A woman like that could probably freeze a guy's dick off, he decided, shaking his head as he tossed the heavy toolbox into the pickup. This was one job he intended to finish as quickly as possible.

Monique was still steamed as she hobbled across the hall to her mother's sitting room at the front of the house. *Maman* was in her wheelchair, listening to Luciano Pavarotti arias with her eyes closed. Her eyes flew open as Monique came in and flung herself into the flowered Queen Anne chair. Monique yanked off her shoe and rubbed her bruised toe, swearing under her breath.

"What's wrong, *ma petite*?" Mireille D'Arcy asked, her soft voice still faintly tinged with the French accent she'd never lost even after more than thirty years in America. She regarded her daughter with dismay. "You've hurt your foot?"

"My pride," Monique grated. "*Maman,* why didn't you tell me you hired that obnoxious man?"

"What obnoxious man?"

"Pete Lambert!"

Mireille cocked her one good eyebrow. At sixty-two, she was a frail, petite posy of a woman, still beautiful despite the stroke that had weakened the muscles on one side of her face and body and robbed her of her mobility.

Though the right side of her face was slack, she nevertheless maintained her immaculate grooming. Each morning Dorothy helped her apply foundation, rouge, and mascara, darkening her thin lips with poppy color, and bringing out the fire in her black eyes. Her lustrous dark hair was hennaed with auburn to cover the gray. Though bound to her wheelchair, she kept a trim figure, and diligently worked at the physical therapy that helped preserve her remaining muscle tone. She preferred bright colors and tailored clothes, so Monique saw to it that her mother's closet was always full of the beautiful softly cut silk jackets, wool slacks, and high-necked classic blouses Mireille loved. Today she looked especially chic in a jade blouse, black and jade herringbone jacket with pearl buttons, and dark slacks, a double strand of pearls looped at her throat. Her good hand went to her throat now and twisted at the necklace.

"You saw the terrace?" Mireille looked dismayed. "I wanted to show you myself."

"I went around back when I saw the pickup and heard all that racket! *Maman,* it's a lovely surprise, but why did you have to hire that man? He's a jerk."

"Pete? No, no, he's charming. And so good-looking."

Monique rolled her eyes. "If you like the caveman type, *Maman.*"

Mireille regarded her quizzically. "What in the world happened between the two of you?"

"Let's just say we got off on the wrong foot," Monique muttered, massaging her sore toe. She kicked off her other shoe and walked across the Dhurrie rug to press a kiss to her mother's soft, powdered cheek. "I'm sorry. You were so sweet to think of enclosing the terrace. It's a terrific idea and I'm sorry to be such a grouch. But I wasn't expecting to run into Mr. Macho."

Mireille shook her head. "Pete is anything but that. He's a dear. Do you know that he brings me a little something almost every day? Fresh pastries, flowers, sometimes a book he's especially enjoyed."

"You mean he can read?" Monique gasped in mock amazement.

The diminutive woman laughed and patted her daughter's cheek with a delicate blue-veined hand. "Monique, don't be impossible. He can read, he can build, he can even cook. Last Tuesday when Sophie had the night off, he whipped up a ratatouille that was out of this world."

"You're kidding." Monique shook her head trying to picture the lean, mean building machine wearing an apron.

Peering down at her swelling foot, she resolved to stay clear of the kitchen if he was prone to leaving butcher knives and meat cleavers strewn around as casually as he did hammers and four-by-fours.

"*Maman,* just how well do you know this man?"

"Dorothy and I met him while we were out walking one day—you know that little path that winds down to the Parker place? We were following it to the bridge and we saw him working on the roof. He's done wonders on that old house. You wouldn't recognize it, Monique."

"So just like that you hired him?"

"More or less. We just sort of fell into the habit of visiting each day. He stopped by with his lunch once and we sat out on the terrace. I started telling him about that being your favorite part of the house. . . ."

"And he just *happened* to suggest enclosing it. The man's an opportunist, *Maman*."

"No, no. It was all my idea. Monique, you've always been so suspicious of people." Sadness crept over Mireille's face, accompanied by an inward pang of regret. "I suppose it's to be expected. I wish you could have had a different kind of childhood, *petite*, but . . ."

Monique knelt down beside her and took her hand. "*Maman*, we've had a good life—*built* a good life," she whispered. "Let's not think back."

"But sometimes I wish I could have given you a happy, carefree girlhood. Monique, you do so much for me, more than I've ever been able to do for you."

Monique's eyes glistened suddenly with unshed tears. "Shh. *Maman*, my greatest pleasure comes from being able to do things for you. You always worked so hard to support us without ever once complaining. It must have taken such courage to bring me to America and make a life for us all by yourself."

Mireille clutched her fingers, a reminiscent smile softening the lines in her face. "Even then you were a handful."

Before Monique could reply, they heard Dorothy's Nikes squeaking across the marble-tiled hall.

"Is it safe to come in?" the nurse inquired from the doorway. "I brought an ice pack for your foot, Ms. D'Arcy. That was quite a smack you gave it."

"Thanks, Dorothy, but as long as I don't have to put my shoes on for a while, I'll be fine. Dinner ready?"

"Anytime. Sophie said the gumbo is hot and spicy, just the way you like it."

Mireille glanced up at her daughter as Dorothy unlocked the brake of the wheelchair and steered it toward the door. "It's too bad Richard couldn't drive out with you. We haven't seen him in quite a while."

Maman, so tactful, Monique thought. She knew her mother wondered why Richard never accompanied her on her weekly visits. But she was too considerate to probe.

"He had to fly to Atlanta this afternoon." Monique fell silent as she followed along to the dining room. "He'll drive out with me sometime soon, I'm sure."

But she knew in her heart it wasn't true. In the eighteen months since she and Richard had been together, he'd come out to the country house only twice —once at Christmas, and again to formally announce their engagement.

Richard tried hard to act comfortable around Mireille, but Monique knew it was difficult for him to handle her mother's infirmity. He had told her once about his grandfather's long, torturous bout with cancer and how helpless he had felt as a fourteen-year-old, watching the robust man who had taken him fishing and skiing shrink to a feeble skeleton unable even to speak his own name. To this day, Richard couldn't cope with sickness, his own or someone else's.

So Monique made countless excuses to her mother, and drove out alone once a week, more often when Richard was traveling. She understood Richard's feelings, but she often wished the two people she loved most in the world could get to know each other in the same way that she knew each of them.

She suppressed a wistful sigh as she slipped into her customary place at the head of the table, her mother and Dorothy seated at her left. The spicy fragrance of the gumbo filled the twenty-foot dining room with a tantalizing aroma. Monique looked around her with pleasure. The table was set with an oyster damask cloth she had selected herself from a shop in Ireland, and the gold-rimmed china embossed with a white swan had been imported from England. A matching swan vase filled with velvety yellow roses sat between tall gold candlesticks, their amber tapers already flickering in the saffron-and-gold-papered room.

"Will you and Richard be joining us for Thanksgiving dinner?" Mireille persisted, looking hopefully at her daughter as Dorothy filled the crystal goblets with Chardonnay.

Monique bit her lip. She carefully ladled gumbo into her mother's bowl, choosing her words deliberately. "Sorry, *Maman*, I just found out—we'll be in Maui then, scouting locations for the June issue. Shooting starts January second. You remember I told you about the special issue I'm doing?"

"She remembers," Dorothy piped in. "She watches that Oprah tape all the time."

Mireille forced a smile. But beneath the gentle curve of her lips, Monique saw the quick flicker of disappointment. "I'm sorry, *Maman*. I'll come for Christmas, I promise."

"Oh, that's all right. Don't you worry about us. Maybe we'll invite Pete Lambert for Thanksgiving dinner. I don't think he has any family around here." The very thought of Pete Lambert seemed to cheer her up. She smiled at Monique again, this time with genuine interest. "Now, *ma petite*, tell me about *Perfect Bride*. How is that June issue coming along? Have you met Ana Cates yet?"

"Not yet, but I've talked to her on the phone. She gave me a list of stipulations as long as a cat's tail."

Dorothy leaned forward, always eager for the inside scoop. "Like what?"

"She absolutely doesn't want John Farrell shot in a bathing suit. No boudoir shots of the two of them, though Ana said she'll pose in lingerie or a swimsuit as long as she has full approval of each and every garment in advance. And she wants their work schedule limited to ten hours each day. Period. A tough cookie—not much like her image. But she was sweet as sugar once she knew she was getting her way."

"I read in the tabloids that Senator Farrell nixed her latest movie deal because he didn't think the part

suited the image of a future First Lady," Dorothy offered, her spoon paused in midair.

Monique's brows shot up in amusement. "Based
on my conversations with her, no one makes decisions
for that lady except Ana Cates herself."

Monique had found that she liked the actress's direct, no-nonsense approach. Ana hadn't whined, she
hadn't cajoled, manipulated, or commanded. She had
just stated with a flat, firm politeness the terms of her
participation.

Monique had even heard something of herself in
the actress's crisp tones as they'd discussed the various
details. *Ana Cates likes being in control as much as I
do,* she'd reflected.

Richard was exactly the same way, a control freak
of the highest order. So far it had worked out. So far
their respective territories hadn't overlapped. But that
was one of the reasons they had each kept their own
apartment up until now. Monique was afraid of what
would happen after the wedding when they moved in
together. But one way or another they'd have to make
it work. After eighteen months—ten of which he had
been married to Shanna—it was time, time to make a
home together, not in either of their apartments, but a
fresh start in a place all their own. A place, Monique
thought, warm and earthy enough where they could
someday raise children.

They'd chosen a penthouse in the Osborne, and
Monique had begun decorating it with the eclectic
drama that was her signature, tempered by the En-
glish-manor formality Richard favored. A self-made
man born to a middle-class family in Upstate New
York, Richard liked to surround himself with reminders
of his success. He preferred overstuffed leather sofas
studded with brass, crimson velvet draperies, and
paintings of English hunt scenes to the contemporary
or art deco styles Monique loved. So far she'd managed
to blend their disparate tastes—the apartment was a

smashing combination of drama and understatement, bright color and subdued texture, sophistication and old world charm.

Later, after she and her mother had enjoyed coffee in the sitting room and Dorothy had taken Mireille up to bed, Monique threw a log in the fireplace and plopped down on the rug to watch the flames. Her thoughts were still on Richard.

The rich smell of the burning wood reminded her of the pungent aroma of his pipe tobacco, taking her back to the first time she'd met him. The attraction had sprung up between them before she even knew he was married to Shanna Mulgrew.

I wanted him before I knew about her, she reminded herself.

Finding out about Shanna had only made her want him more.

na Trump's parties. It was a
lete with strolling mariachi
ded with huge overstuffed
veritable jungle of tropical
. The air was clogged with
pungent aroma of Jamaican
sauce. Monique had wan-
to escape the din of voices
ibbean band. The throbbing
the drunken laughter kept
ccelerating pounding in her

with a bemused smile as Monique joined him at the wrought iron balcony.

"Sinus headaches and sambas don't mix well. Mind if I join you?"

"By all means."

Monique pressed her hands to her temples, drawing in deep breaths of the fresh air. When she opened her eyes, he was studying her, his gaze flickering over the jet-black halter sheath shimmering with sequins that flowed down her body like cooling lava. Strands of rhinestones swinging from her ears flashed moonlight back into his eyes. She studied him right back.

He was in his late forties, she guessed, judging by the hint of gray frosting his temples. Monique admired the strong jaw outlined in the shadows, the air of command he wore as confidently as his exquisitely cut tuxedo. He looked rich, powerful, and very sure of himself.

"Would you like me to get you some aspirin?" he asked. He tamped tobacco from the bowl of his pipe into the stone urn beside him.

"No. I'll be fine in a minute."

He tucked the pipe into his pocket and stepped closer. He smelled of tobacco, fine leather, and some exotic spice she couldn't place. Looking up into his face, Monique felt the electricity between them.

When he reached up to cup the nape of her neck, pushing aside the escaped tendrils of her upswept hair, she tensed, suddenly wondering what he had in mind.

"Sometimes this helps," he murmured. He began sensuously kneading his fingers over the taut muscles of her neck. Involuntarily, she shivered, unsure if she was hot or cold, if she was responding to the chill air or the warm fingers soothing the throbbing tension from her neck.

"Better?"

"Mmm-hmm." Monique leaned back against his massaging fingers for just a moment, then stiffened and

ay. "Thank you. I'm feeling

you're going?" he asked as
he French doors. His voice
oothing as those magical fin-
npkin already? It's nowhere

m, a handsome, self-assured
ook of playful challenge. She
curve her lips. "Time to slip
m afraid. These glass slippers
it."

down as she'd known they
atively along the sleek shim-
the glittering Louis Jourdan
help with that too," he said
ve scare us up some mice and
? They brew a mean cappuc-
caffeine, a little conversation.
ff. I'll even massage your feet

"

princess deserves."
Close enough. Actually, I'm
Comtesse de Chevalier. And

asure, Comtesse."
ment she had realized that this
a her on a darkened balcony
isband.
ne whistled through her like a
Billionaire tycoon. Head of a
ment empire. He could buy
ngland. He had corporate of-
nd he was married to her only

puccino?" He hadn't let go of her hand. He still held it, and tucked it into the crook of his arm as he led her back toward the blare of Caribbean music.

And she allowed herself to be led, her mind racing, churning with a jumble of emotions. Shanna Mulgrew aside—she was drawn to this man. She would follow for now, and see where it led her.

The logs crackled in the fireplace, and Monique reached for the chocolate liqueur on the low coffee table. It ran down her throat, warm and tingling. Warm and tingling. That's how she'd felt after that first night meeting Richard. And where had it led her? To a new job, a new home, and a new husband.

A smile played about her lips as the wind outside hurled leaves against the windows, and she heard Dorothy's quiet footsteps pattering down the hall above. Warmed by the liqueur and the fire, she felt deeply satisfied with her life. That first night she'd had no thoughts of replacing Shanna Mulgrew Ives in either the bedroom or the boardroom. She wasn't sure exactly when it had become a deliberate goal. She knew only that she'd been magnetically attracted to Richard from the first and he to her, and somewhere along the line her feelings for Richard and her desire for revenge against Shanna had become inextricably linked.

She and Richard were a matched set. They were both driven, energetic dynamos. The fusion of their personalities, of their lust and passion for life and power, had been too intense for either of them to resist. Six months after that first night, Richard had asked Shanna for a divorce and moved into his own apartment. Later, after some very messy divorce proceedings, he had removed her from her position as editor-in-chief of *Perfect Bride* and installed Monique in her place.

Delicious, Monique decided, and she wasn't thinking anymore about the liqueur. Oh, yes, she had relished every sweet moment of dear Shanna's fall. She had taken away her job, her husband, and her damned smirky confidence. But the final blow was yet to come. Monique's wedding day to Richard would mark the crowning pinnacle of her triumph over Shanna Mulgrew. What a perfect revenge. It would almost make up for what Shanna had done, for the suffering she had caused so long ago.

Another sip of the liqueur, and Monique's thoughts drifted back, back even further than her meeting with Richard, back to the first time she met Shanna Mulgrew Ives.

"Where are those gowns?"

Mireille D'Arcy quailed before the white-hot fury in Shanna Mulgrew's face.

"I asked you a question, you idiot. Mrs. Emerson is waiting. Where are her gowns?"

"I have not seen them, Miss Mulgrew." Fear thickened Mireille's French accent, further infuriating the other woman, who had to struggle to make out the words. "Please, have you asked Della? Maybe she—"

"Your name is on the ticket." Shanna flung the yellow card in Mireille's face. "You were supposed to have them finished by *today*. Mrs. Emerson is leaving for Europe in the morning and I gave her my personal guarantee that these gowns would be ready."

Shaken, Mireille stared into the blazing toffee-colored eyes of the department head. Shanna Mulgrew was only twenty-five, but she had already moved into the ranks of management at Bonwit Teller. Tall, thin as a model, with thick, tawny-blond hair styled in the wildly fashionable Farrah cut, she possessed a flair and a brittle self-assurance that expressed itself in her chicly put together clothes and aggressive stride. Beneath her heavily mascaraed lids, her eyes were deep-set and shrewd, missing nothing that went on within her little realm. With her upturned nose and small bow mouth, she looked more like a country-club princess than a driven career woman, but Shanna had self-centered ambition coursing coldly through her veins—a quietly ferocious drive to get somewhere, be somebody, that wouldn't allow anyone to stand in her way.

But she wasn't quiet today. She was exploding with anger and frustration, all of it directed at the diminutive French seamstress before her.

Mireille thought desperately back, trying to remember if she had ever seen the gowns in question. When she cast a frightened look at the angry Chanel-suited matron fuming at the sales counter, her stomach churned. She glanced helplessly at the young salesgirl hovering at Shanna's elbow. "Miss Dunbar, what color were the gowns—"

"I don't *believe* you," Shanna snarled. "I never saw such incompetence in my life." She whirled on the salesgirl and thrust the yellow ticket into her hands. "Miss Dunbar, find these gowns. Now." She stalked back to her customer, somehow managing to mask her fury with a veneer of reassuring composure. "Mrs. Emerson, I apologize for this inexcusable inconvenience. I assure you that I'll get to the bottom of this myself and I'll have the dresses delivered to you by five o'clock this afternoon. I give you my personal guarantee on it."

Mrs. Emerson glared at her. "Based on the service you've given me so far, I won't hold my breath. However, if I don't have those dresses by five o'clock, you have my personal guarantee that your manager—no—the president of the company—will hear about it," she warned.

Mireille retreated to the rack of completed garments hanging outside the alterations department with Carrie Dunbar following worriedly at her heels. "Mireille, I think she assigned those gowns to Della," Carrie whispered. "Look at the date on this ticket. Isn't that the week Monique came down with chicken pox? You weren't even here."

Mireille ceased her frantic search through racks of neatly bagged pantsuits, ankle-length dirndl skirts, and long chiffon evening gowns. Today had begun so brightly, with Monique kissing her and bringing her French toast in bed in honor of her birthday. But Mireille's happiness had vanished with the eruption of this crisis. Deep in her heart she feared the outcome was inevitable.

She faced Carrie, her shoulders slumped, her face desolate. "It doesn't matter," she said quietly. "She's going to fire me anyway."

Mireille had worried for months that something like this would happen—ever since she had worked late one night and accidently overheard Shanna and Wayne Kingsford, the head buyer for men's ready-to-wear, making dinner plans. Neither of them had known she was within earshot in her little cubicle, working on Mrs. Delancy's dinner suit.

Wayne Kingsford was married, Mireille knew, with a pregnant wife and two little kids. But his conversation with Shanna had left no doubt that this was to be a romantic evening. And from some of the pauses Mireille overheard as she sewed, there had been much more than conversation going on.

Mireille had worked quietly, hoping that Shanna would leave without discovering her. It was no concern of hers what Shanna Mulgrew did. *Who am I to judge?* she thought with a rueful shrug of her shoulders. Still, it would be mortifying for both of them if Shanna knew she'd had an audience during her secret tête-à-tête. But as luck would have it, Shanna had left her raincoat on a hook in the alterations department. Mireille would never forget the expression on her face when she passed Mireille's cubicle and saw her sitting there.

"What are you still doing here? We closed fifteen minutes ago."

"Finishing up some work, Miss Mulgrew. I don't like to stop in the middle of the hem. The stitching is never the same if you set it down. Joe Nestor usually lets me out the back door when I stay late." Mireille knew she was chattering from nervousness. She tried to keep her voice even and her eyes downcast, but she could feel Shanna's tension as the department head glared at her for a long moment.

"I never realized we had such devoted employees," Shanna bit out. A fine film of perspiration beaded her upper lip. "In the future, Mireille, kindly inform me if you're too slow to finish your work during regular hours." She grabbed her raincoat and swept out without a backward glance, but from that moment on, Mireille sensed her hostility and tried to stay out of her way. She knew Shanna thought she had blabbed the gossip all over the store. But Mireille told no one. She was a proud woman, one who treasured her own privacy and would never consider invading someone else's. It would be beneath her.

"That bitch—she's just been waiting for an excuse to get rid of you," Carrie groaned, clenching the yellow ticket tightly in her hand. "She's been all over your case for months now, God knows why. You should have heard how pissed off she was when you missed work to nurse Monique."

Mireille sank wearily into a folding chair. "I knew that would make her angry, but she was so sick, my little girl. Such a high fever—the doctor said it's much worse when older children get chicken pox. And my poor Monique was covered from head to toe. How could I have left her?" she whispered.

There was no time for Carrie to reply. They both froze as Shanna burst into the alterations department. "Mireille, I want you out of here. Now. Carrie, why aren't you looking for those dresses? Can't anyone do anything around here except for me?"

Carrie watched the color ebb from Mireille's thin

face. "Miss Mulgrew," Carrie began desperately. "There's been a mistake. Mireille wasn't even here two weeks ago when Mrs. Emerson bought those dresses. That's when her daughter had the chicken pox. I think—"

"I don't pay you to think. Go find those dresses before you find yourself standing in the unemployment line right behind your friend."

Mireille put her hand on Carrie's arm. "Go," she urged, her eyes huge and sorrowful in her pasty face.

As Carrie fled, Mireille rose. "Please, Miss Mulgrew." Mireille forced herself to sound as humble as she could, thinking of Monique at home, of the rent that was due next week, of the doctor's bills she had yet to pay. "Please, I can't lose my job." She spread her hands in a delicate Gallic gesture of supplication. "I wasn't even here when the work on those dresses was assigned. This is the first I've heard of it. You must believe me. And you know there has never been a complaint about my work. In fact, many regular customers specifically request me."

"Well, they won't anymore," Shanna retorted coldly. She turned on her heel. "You can pick up your last check at the end of the week." And she was gone in a cloud of Charlie perfume, her platform shoes stomping the tiled floor as she headed toward the racks of after-five dresses in search of an additional salesclerk to help hunt down the missing gowns.

Mireille heard the languid notes of Elton John's "Goodbye Yellow Brick Road" floating from the stereo as she let herself into the tiny walkup apartment a short time later. She fought back tears, dreading the moments ahead. She mustn't cry in front of Monique. She had to be strong.

The windows were open, but the meager breeze barely stirred the flowered curtains, much less moved the stifling August air through the cramped quarters Mireille had tried to make cheerful and homey. She had sewn new chintz slipcovers for the second-hand sofa she'd bought from the Salvation Army. The white macramé wallhanging threaded with pink and yellow beads which Monique had made her for Christmas hung beside the bookcase painted pale lemon. Its shelves were filled with a few precious books and a profusion of green plants and scented candles.

Though earth tones were all the rage, she and Monique had carefully painted the gold-toned refrigerator and stove a sparkling white, then splashed their domain with airy pastels to visually enlarge it. They had only a living room, a kitchen, and one bedroom to share, but they had made it charming and inviting with throw pillows, mirrors, and a fluffy white hand-hooked rug on the scrubbed floor.

Monique sat in the kitchen at the maple table, hunched over her algebra book. She was still trying to catch up from the week of missed school. So intently was she concentrating that she hadn't heard her mother's key in the door. Mireille paused for a moment, studying her daughter's serious face. Monique was beautiful, she thought with pride. Even the fading chicken-pox scabs dotting her face and neck couldn't detract from the charm of her exotically shaped eyes and delicately sculpted profile. Her dark hair was cut in a shag, partially hiding the fourteen-year-old features that seemed to be changing daily from those of a child to a blossoming woman.

Mireille delayed a moment longer from facing her daughter with the catastrophe that had befallen her. She sucked in her breath and glanced around at the spotless kitchen. Every day, never fail, Monique saw to it that all the breakfast dishes were washed, dried, and put away before she left for school. When Mireille returned from work at the end of each day, she found the floor immaculately swept, the sink scrubbed, even the dishtowel neatly snared into the lip of the silverware drawer to hang dry. Monique must have also folded and put away the laundry when she came home, Mireille noticed, for the basket she'd left this morning in the corner of the living room was gone.

Such a good girl, Mireille thought, love welling up in her chest so tight it hurt. I can't bear upsetting her.

Mireille sighed, unable to contain her distress. Monique's head jerked up. *"Maman,* why are you home so early? You're not sick?" She shoved back her chair and hurried across the kitchen with the coltish gait of adolescence.

Mireille could only shake her head, not yet trusting her voice to speak. She sank onto the sofa and slipped off her shoes, trying to keep her emotions under control. She didn't want to frighten Monique.

"Maman." Monique's voice rose in alarm. Her mother's usually creamy skin had an ashen tint to it that made her complexion appear almost green. No light shone from her usually vibrant eyes. What could have happened?

"Please, *ma petite,* turn off the music. I have to talk to you."

Half an hour later Monique was standing before the imposing grandeur of Bonwit Teller. She had to do this. She couldn't let *Maman* lose her job, especially not today, *Maman's* birthday. She wasn't afraid of Shanna Mulgrew, or anybody else, she told herself, flipping her hair behind her ears. This store was like a second home to her. She and Mireille came here one Saturday each month to drink in the loveliness of the clothes, the jewelry displayed in the long glass cases, the designer shoes and rich leather handbags, and to explore the enchanted aisles that intoxicated them with perfume and makeup. They would thread their way slowly through the various departments, savoring everything.

Mireille would study the fashions that caught Monique's eye and later at home show her painstakingly how to duplicate them with similar fabrics purchased at J. C. Penney. Under her mother's tutelage, Monique developed an eye for fine clothing and she delighted in the array of smart suits, dresses, and pants outfits that *Maman* often brought home to work on at night.

Today, however, the euphoria she usually felt upon entering this glittering paradise was nowhere to be found. Putting her hand to the brass handle, she caught a glimpse of herself in the sparkling glass doors, thin and long-legged in her Chinese-red minidress. She took a deep breath, thought of her mother pacing the floor at home, and pushed through the massive double doors.

You can do this, she told herself as she wove her way past the fragrance counters toward the escalator. You can explain to Miss Mulgrew that it wasn't *Maman*'s fault.

Monique had never met the dreaded Shanna Mulgrew, but she'd overheard *Maman*'s friend Della fretting about their boss's incessant demands and harsh temper. Yet *Maman* never complained. Monique knew that her mother wanted to protect her from worrying about such things. They had enough to worry about already. It was hard just keeping up with the monthly bills, not to mention the piano lessons that *Maman* insisted she continue each week.

Monique tried her best to help out by baby-sitting for the Scaparelli kids and by running errands for old Mrs. Devane, who had trouble getting up and down the stairs. She knew they couldn't afford to lose even one week of her mother's paycheck. Besides, *Maman* liked her job, Shanna Mulgrew or no. She was the best seamstress at Bonwit's, and the customers loved her precise work. They favored her European tailoring and the standard of excellence to which she held herself. Mireille D'Arcy was a proud woman and would never turn in anything but her best work, work far more elegant than any run off by machine.

Miss Mulgrew is probably already regretting firing her, Monique thought as she rode the escalator up to the second floor. Despite her determination, her hands were sweaty. They slipped as she clutched the handrail. *Miss Mulgrew has probably found the dresses, the problem is solved, and she's had a chance to think things over.*

Everything will be fine, Monique told herself.

Maman had begged her not to go, but she had gone anyway. How could she not plead her mother's case? Monique thought of all the sacrifices *Maman* had made for her. She thought of the surprise party planned for her mother tonight and how it would all be spoiled if *Maman* didn't get her job back. She couldn't let *Maman*'s birthday be ruined.

Mireille D'Arcy had had a difficult life. Born in a small village in France and orphaned at an early age, she had toiled in a convent for many years, sewing vestments for the priests, embroidering altar cloths, and mending habits for the nuns. Monique couldn't imagine anything more boring than that. Mireille had eventually escaped the tedium of the convent, married, and gone to work for the wealthy Comte and Comtesse de Chevalier. As their personal seamstress, she had fared well. Her fine needlework caught the eye of their friends, who secretly kept Mireille busy sewing well into the night. For a time she had been happy. Her dream had always been to emigrate to America and someday open her own European tailoring shop. She'd saved every sou, and within another year or two might have been able to comfortably make the journey. But the untimely death of the Chevaliers in a car crash forced her to make the move sooner than she had planned.

Monique never knew her father—he had died when she was still an infant. But her mother told her he was a kind and gentle man, very handsome but very poor. Monique wondered about him sometimes, wondered what their lives would have been like had he not died, but she was so used to life with only the two of them that she could scarcely imagine any other way. It was *Maman* who had supported her from the very beginning, never complaining, never doubting, trying always to shield Monique from worries no matter how precarious their financial situation.

And now it was her turn to protect her mother.

She stepped off the escalator with resolve quickening her stride. When she reached the alterations department where her mother worked, she recognized Carrie Dunbar, whom she'd met one Saturday. "Miss Dunbar, can you tell me where I can find Miss Mulgrew?"

It seemed to Monique that Carrie Dunbar's enormous blue eyes grew even larger within her round, pretty face. "Oh, I don't think you'd want to get within ten feet of her, Monique. She's in a terrible mood. We still haven't found those dresses."

"Where is she?"

Carrie pointed to the sales desk, where a tense-looking blonde was poring over a stack of receipts. "But honey . . ."

Monique didn't wait to hear the rest of the sentence. Straightening her spine and walking with measured steps, she approached the woman stabbing her pencil eraser quickly through the receipts. Monique cleared her throat.

"Yes," Shanna said, "can I help you?"

"Miss Mulgrew?"

Shanna's toffee-colored eyes narrowed. She tossed the pencil onto the pile of receipts and straightened as she regarded the dark-haired teenager before her.

Shanna was tall, slim, and fashionable in her sleeveless A-line dress of pristine white linen. She wore a gold chain to match the dangling discs at her ears and a Longines watch studded with pavé diamonds. Her nails were brightly polished, and each pinky nail sported a tiny floral decal.

She deserves to be old and ugly, Monique thought as she returned Shanna's cold stare. There was no denying the sleek attractiveness of the woman before her. But she's wearing way too much perfume, Monique decided triumphantly. Fortified by this flaw, she plunged ahead.

"I'm Monique D'Arcy, Mireille's daughter, and I'd like to talk to you about my mother."

Shanna gave an exasperated groan. She picked up her pencil and returned her attention to the stack of receipts. "There is nothing to talk about."

"But please, Miss Mulgrew, you don't understand. My mother needs this job. She didn't do anything wrong. Somebody made a mistake, but it wasn't my mother. You have to give her another chance."

"I don't *have* to do anything."

With a sinking heart, Monique read the chilly disdain in the woman's eyes. Shanna Mulgrew was looking her over as if she were a bug. She has no feelings, Monique realized. She doesn't care about me or *Maman.* Monique fought the panic building inside her. She had to make Shanna care. "But Miss Mulgrew, my mother works so hard. This job means everything to her. She even brings her work home at night."

Shanna's head snapped up. "Does she?"

Monique paused, wondering why Shanna was looking at her that way, suddenly scrutinizing her dress with such keen interest. "Where did you get that?" the department head asked sharply. Monique glanced down.

"My mother made it for me."

"You're lying. That dress is for sale right over there. It costs one hundred seventy-five dollars. Now, tell me, how could you possibly afford to pay for it?"

"I am not lying." Monique's cheeks flamed as red as her dress. "My mother made it. She copied it. There's nothing wrong with that, is there?"

"Not if it's the truth."

Monique desperately tried to turn the subject back to salvaging her mother's job.

"I'm sure my mother's customers have told you what fine work she does."

"Then she shouldn't have any trouble finding employment elsewhere, should she?"

Monique felt herself growing cold all over. Despite the air-conditioning, her armpits were sticky with sweat. She placed her hands on the counter and leaned forward, hating this woman for reducing her to begging. "But she loves *this* job, Miss Mulgrew. Please give her another chance. She's only two years away from qualifying for her pension—she'd have to start all over someplace else."

Shanna gathered up her papers and turned away. "That's not my problem, now, is it? My problem is Mrs. Emerson and those dresses I guaranteed her would be ready today—dresses we can't seem to find."

Monique ran after her as Shanna stalked away. From the corner of her eye she saw Carrie Dunbar watching sympathetically. "But Miss Mulgrew, it isn't *fair.* . . ."

Shanna's eyes flashed with pure venom. "I've already wasted enough time on you and that idiotic mother of yours. I suggest you leave before I have to call for security. Do you hear me, you stupid little jerk? *Get out of my store.*"

People were staring. Monique was frozen in shock. Then Shanna was gone, leaving a nauseating trail of perfume behind her. Tears pricked Monique's eyes. "That stinking, rotten bitch," she whispered. "Who does she think she is?"

Somehow Monique made her way out of the store and into the steamy New York street.

Later that night she struggled to keep a smile on her face as, one by one, her neighbors pulled their chairs around the festively decorated kitchen table.

Mireille pondered the blazing candles on the chocolate cake, seemingly hypnotized by the tiny flickers of light.

"Make a wish, *Maman*," Monique urged, circling an arm around her mother's thin shoulders.

Mrs. Scaparelli tucked a napkin in the neck of Joey's striped T-shirt and said, "Don't tell anyone your wish, or it won't come true."

Just as Mireille blew out the candles and fixed a smile of forced gaiety on her face, a sharp knock sounded at the door.

"But who can that be? Are you expecting someone else?" Old Mrs. Devane glanced around the room. They were all there, Ida Scaparelli and her two roughhousing kids, Joey and little Eva, Mrs. Witkowski, as usual fidgeting with her hearing aid, even Mr. Gummer, the building super and his wife, who'd brought a gallon of Neapolitan ice cream for the occasion.

Monique peered out the peephole and made out two uniformed policemen.

"Evening, miss. We'd like to speak with Muriel Darcy. Is she at home?" The older officer, a burly man with glinting red hair beneath his cap, misread her mother's name from a formal-looking paper.

Monique's heart leapt into her throat as she stepped into the narrow hallway and partially closed the door. "Yes? What is it?"

"We need to ask Mrs. Darcy a few questions. Is she at home?"

"Yes, but we're having a little birthday party for her. Can you come back tomorrow?"

They couldn't, and Monique was forced to call her mother into the hall. Monique was conscious of the curiosity and concern of their friends inside as the policemen questioned Mireille about the missing dresses, and informed her that they had a search warrant. As Mireille slumped back against the wall Monique clutched her arm. All the color had drained from

Maman's face, but Monique's cheeks were red hot with fury.

How could anyone believe *Maman* would steal? Even Shanna Mulgrew can't believe that, can she? But she obviously did.

By the time the officers had systematically rifled through the closets and dresser drawers—even looking under the beds—the guests had filed out in embarrassment and Mireille's humiliation was complete. At last they were alone together in the apartment. Half-eaten cake and melted ice cream puddled on the table amid torn streamers and silent party blowers. Monique threw her arms around her mother, unable to contain her tears another moment.

"I hate Shanna Mulgrew! I could kill her for this!"

"Hush, *ma petite*." Mireille smoothed her daughter's hair back from her tear-washed face and held her close. "It doesn't matter."

But Monique knew it did matter. Her mother prized her dignity and her privacy, and both had been unjustly invaded. For all her efforts to appear calm, Mireille was deeply shaken. She looked ill, her skin grayer than wet cement.

Monique was overcome with hatred. How could anyone be so cruel?

Later that night Monique awakened from a fitful sleep to find herself alone in the hot, airless bedroom. She turned over. Her mother's bed was empty and no light shone from the bathroom. She crept out of bed and tiptoed to the door. As she paused uncertainly, she heard a muffled sound like a cat whimpering in pain. Her mother rocked before the open window, her arms clasped around herself as she wept.

Monique bit back a sob. She threw herself back into her bed and buried her face in the pillow. She sobbed torturously, torn apart with grief for her mother's pain. When at last she dried her cheeks on the edge of her pillowcase and hugged her knees in the darkness, Monique made a silent vow.

She'd make Shanna Mulgrew pay for what she'd done. Somehow, some way, she'd get that heartless bitch and get her good.

Monique drained the last of her liqueur, savoring the sweet, dark droplets almost as much as she savored her victory over Shanna. Of course Shanna had no idea that the woman who had bedazzled her husband and taken over her job had once stood before her as a desperate teenager in a copied Chinese-red minidress, a girl frantic to protect her mother but unable to do so. Well, she was able to protect Mireille now. Shanna would never know that the "stupid little jerk" she had so cruelly dismissed twenty years before was the cause of her downfall.

If living well is the best revenge, Maman *and I have both evened up the score,* Monique reflected with satisfaction early the next morning as she drove back to the city. A tangerine glow bathed the milky morning sky as she headed onto the Merritt Parkway, flipping a Mariah Carey CD into the player.

If today's board meeting went according to plan, and her final budget for the June issue was approved, she'd be home free. Unless a hurricane blasted through Maui or John Farrell had second thoughts and backed out at the last moment—or unless her little manicurist, Teri, turned out to be an ax murderer or something—Monique was almost certain she would pull this off. The circulation figures had to jump and jump high though, or the board would want her blood. If sales didn't soar, Drew McArthur, the president of the publications division, would force her resignation and then campaign to have Shanna reinstated before the ink on Monique's final paycheck could dry.

I'll kill her first, Monique swore as rush hour traffic

forced her to slow to a crawl. The throbbing in her toe each time she pressed on the brake brought back the annoying memory of Pete Lambert's smirk. It was sweet of *Maman* to be enclosing the terrace for her. Too bad she hadn't hired a professional contractor instead of that macho pea-brain. Monique wondered how he could stay in business if he went around insulting his customers. But she couldn't deny that for all of his attitude, Pete Lambert had seemed like a man who knew exactly what he was doing.

We'll see, she thought. If he screwed up this job, she'd see him in court. Otherwise, she didn't care if she never saw him again.

Chapter Nine

"Picture's up, everybody!"

The director's command cracked down Rodeo Drive like the snap of a whip, sending the actors scurrying back to their starting positions on the cordoned-off street. Perched atop the dolly, the director, Jim Koslow, barked at the first A.D. to quiet the extras.

"No voices, I don't want to hear voices. Gary, for God's sake, tell them only to mouth their words, and not to scrape their feet on the sidewalk."

"Quiet on the set!" Gary bellowed, and sputtered rapid-fire orders to the second A.D.s through his walkie-talkie.

Ana closed her eyes while Molly layered more powder across her lids and darkened her lipstick. Then the set was cleared and the cry "Rolling!" reverberated up and down the Beverly Hills street.

"Scene thirty-four, take seven—marker!" The clapper-board snapped like a crocodile's jaws in front of the lens. Ana's whole visage changed as she melted back into her role as Vicki, the psychic young artist who suspects her lover is trying to kill her. For the next few moments she abandoned herself to the scene with complete concentration.

It was a pivotal moment in the film. Vicki had just stumbled upon her lover and another woman kissing in a café, and was now trying to slip away undetected.

"And cut." Jim strode past the sound tech and assistant directors to Ana's side. "Lovely, Ana, that was just lovely." He waited just a beat, smiling encouragingly at her, then continued as she knew he would. "I'd like you to try it again, this time with a little more devastation at that pause—right before those two extras start to cross. Let us in. You've got to let us see the depth of the betrayal."

"Okay, got it."

Ana knew he was right. She'd felt at low power on that last take. Leave it to Jim to zero in on the exact spot where she needed to dig deeper. Jim Koslow had directed her in *Comes a Stranger,* and had pulled more out of her than she'd known she had in her. Tall and balding, endlessly chewing bubble gum, he was the kind of director actors trusted. He didn't yell, didn't curse or scowl, just kept asking for more until he got what he wanted.

Ana lowered the sunglasses from the top of her head so that they shaded her eyes. "Don't you think I should pull these down before I get into the car?"

Jim agreed. "Nice touch. That'll leave them wondering what Vicki is thinking at that point. Try it, Ana." He squeezed her shoulder. "Ready?"

Ana nodded and readjusted the sunglasses on top of her head. It was supposed to be a hot day in July, but actually a rare November chill was whipping through the city, and she was shivering in her gauzy wrap skirt of bright fuchsia with its midriff-baring top. The silver earrings were too heavy for her delicate lobes and pulled painfully. But she tried not to think about her discomfort, only about Vicki and her devastation in this scene.

Forty minutes and five takes later Jim yelled, "Cut —that's a print, folks!" and they broke for lunch. Crossing the set on her way to her honeywagon, Ana passed Debbie, the third assistant director, sitting cross-legged on a bench, eating pasta salad and thumbing through *Variety*.

Ana grimaced. She'd scanned the *Variety* classifieds regularly but no other message had yet followed that first cryptic ad she'd spotted on the plane.

Still, sooner or later there was bound to be another one. Now that she knew Eric was alive and had begun some twisted game, she was convinced he wouldn't stop until he'd played out his hand.

Eric, alive. She clambered into the honeywagon and closed the door, then reached into the tiny refrigerator for a can of orange juice and the croissant with turkey and honey mustard she'd brought from home. At this point she didn't know how much trouble Eric meant to cause her, but the private investigator she'd hired after the *Variety* ad had surfaced confirmed her suspicion that in the nearly seven years since she'd seen him, he hadn't changed one iota.

She remembered those first weeks and months after she'd thought she'd killed him. At first she'd cowered every time someone knocked at her door, terrified that they'd come to throw her in jail. Even after a year had passed and she realized that no one had connected her to what had happened, she suffered from nightmares and sleepless nights, the constant replaying in her mind of those awful, indescribable moments in the car.

And after all that, she hadn't even managed to kill the bastard.

Ana sank onto her cot and bit into the turkey without tasting it. Her relief at knowing she wasn't a murderess had been immediately overshadowed by dread as she faced the spector of Eric creeping back into her life.

He was living in L.A. now, Harry Damone's report had stated, renting a scummy one-bedroom in a building on Western in old Hollywood. Still making porn films, still dealing drugs.

She shuddered, thinking back to that nightmare time in her life when she'd been about as miserable as a human being could be. The ugly memories were as vivid as welts despite the passage of seven healing years. No matter what it took, she intended to keep Eric Gunn out of her life.

Her appetite gone, she threw the half-eaten turkey sandwich into the trash can, then restlessly prowled the cramped confines of the trailer. She couldn't stop thinking about what a field day the tabloid reporters would have once they got wind of Eric and the things he could hold over her head. John's career, as well as hers, would go up in smoke.

She glanced at her watch, relieved to see it was time to report back to makeup. The afternoon's work would help take her mind off Eric. She started for the door, then paused to drain the last of her juice.

Ana prided herself on always being punctual. No one would ever accuse her of not being a professional. She set down the empty can and squared her shoulders, deliberately shutting out all thoughts of Eric. She would use the time walking back to the set to immerse herself in the vulnerable and complex role she was portraying. As she opened the door and squinted into the glare of afternoon sunlight, a delivery man on the steps thrust a foil-wrapped bottle at her.

"For you, Miss Cates. Enjoy."

Ana stepped backward into the honeywagon to read the card dangling from a gold cord around the bottle's neck.

From Jim, she thought. Sending gifts already? He must be pretty confident we're going to wrap the film this weekend. But there was no writing on the card, only a smiley face drawn in pencil.

The bottle felt oddly light. She shook it and heard a slight rattling. Ana bit her lip as she ripped the blue foil away. There was no label and no liquid, only a sheet of folded white paper swimming in air.

Ana sucked in her breath.

Eric. Good old Eric. Still as good at games as he ever was.

Fucking bastard. She glared at the bottle, wishing she could smash it against his skull. He probably guzzled it dry before he sent it, sniggering all the while. Ana yanked a towel from the counter, wrapped it around the bottle, and carefully tapped it against the table edge. Shit, the damn thing won't break. She tried again, tapping harder. This time the glass gave way, splintering into fragments. She peeled back the towel to allow the note to fall out along with tiny shards of glass. Swearing, she managed to extract the handwritten note without cutting herself and held it up between fingers that were remarkably steady despite the pounding of her heart.

> *Something borrowed, something blue,*
> *Someone's going to tell on you.*
> *Something old, something knew,*
> *Something naughty,*
> *Shame on you.*

There was no signature, but Ana didn't need one. She stared at the paper, reading the lines over and over. At last she let out her breath in a long hiss.

No, you don't. You *bastard.* I won't let you get away with it.

She tore into her handbag for her small eelskin address book. Then she picked up the portable phone and punched in Harry Damone's office number.

The private investigator answered on the first ring.

"Harry? Ana Cates. I just received a special delivery from that old friend you found for me recently. I'd like to send him a particularly fitting thank-you, one he won't forget."

"That can be arranged, Miss Cates."

Damone sounded like Robert Mitchum on the phone. He was quite different in person. Ana had first engaged his services three years ago, after her first major part. She'd hired him to find her mother. He had—at the Shady Meadow Cemetery where she was buried. Two years after walking out on her family she had walked out in front of an eighteen-wheeler on a dark country road.

As she considered what she was about to propose, Ana felt immense satisfaction. "Come by tonight so that we can hammer out the details. I have something really memorable in mind, so it may take one or two of your delivery boys to help with this one."

"Gotcha. I know just the guys. They specialize in overnight deliveries, if you're talking quick service."

"Not too quick. I want to make sure the message isn't garbled."

Damone laughed. "How's about eight o'clock?"

"I'll see you then." She switched off the phone, reminding herself to stay calm. Eric could scare her only if she let him.

As she refolded the note and stuffed it into her handbag, Molly knocked at the open door.

The makeup girl stared at the broken glass littering the table and floor. "Oh, my God! Miss Cates, what happened?"

Ana schooled her face into an expression of nonchalance. She stooped and picked up a long, jagged shard of glass. "It's nothing. I dropped a bottle. Careful where you step. Oh, shit!"

"You're hurt." Concern flashed across Molly's face. She reached instantly for the phone. "Hal, we need a first aid kit and someone to clean up a bit of broken glass in Miss Cates's honeywagon."

"It's okay. All I need is a Band-Aid." Ana pressed a clean towel to the small cut on her finger. "Come on, let's go. We'll get it on the set."

Gary stuck his head in the door. "Problem? Jim's pacing, Ana, and you know what that means."

Shit. That fucking bastard made me late, Ana thought as she stepped over the broken glass toward the door.

Gary's gaze took in the broken glass on the floor and the blood seeping from Ana's finger. "Hey, you're hurt. Let me see that. What the hell happened?"

"Nothing that's going to affect our insurance rates." Ana joked as Gary helped her down the metal steps of the trailer and unhooked his walkie-talkie.

"Ana's had a slight accident," Gary snapped into the unit. "Nothing major. We'll be on the set in five."

Suddenly, she was surrounded by people. Molly clattered down the trailer steps, Debbie sprinted toward them clutching a first aid kit. "All I need is a Band-Aid," Ana insisted.

"Gimme your hand." Gary carefully inspected the cut while Molly hovered nearby holding out a bottle of Bactine. "How the hell did you manage to do this?" He doused her finger with the antiseptic, careful not to splash any on her costume. There weren't many stars he could talk to that way, but Ana was different. There wasn't an ounce of prima donna in her. She was a thorough professional who mingled easily with the cast and crew, yet still took time to sign autographs for the extras. But once the cameras began to roll, she became singularly focused, zeroing in on her character like a Patriot missile targeting a Scud.

"Clean-up crew is on the way," Debbie panted, and turned to Molly. "What happened?"

"I just broke a goddamn bottle," Ana exploded.

"Why is everyone making such a big deal out of this?" As Gary, Molly, and Debbie stared at her, she caught herself. "Sorry, guys. I guess I'm getting paranoid about the tabloids. They could get wind of a little accident like this and the next thing you know we'll be reading headlines about Ana Cates being drunk in the middle of the afternoon or trying to slash her wrists." Gary had finished wrapping the Band-Aid around her finger. She regarded it with raised brows and nudged the first A.D. with her shoulder. "Continuity's going to love me for this. How are they going to explain a Band-Aid in one scene and not in the others?"

"Not our problem, babe." Gary grinned at her as the four of them sprinted toward the set. "Least you didn't break your arm."

As Ana reached the cordoned-off street Jim was scowling at his watch. He didn't smile as she wiggled her bandaged finger in the air and called, "Sorry."

"Listen up, everybody," Jim announced. He popped a piece of gum into his mouth. "There's no way we're gonna wrap this weekend—too many delays. After today, we'll break until Monday and see how it goes. Gary will get you Monday's call sheets before the end of the day."

Lovely, she thought as she darted past the staring extras and took up her position at the curb. Thank you, Eric. She smoothed her gauze skirt and pulled down on the sides of her halter top.

Eric Gunn is *not* going to disrupt my life or my career—or Johnny's, she vowed. Whatever it takes, I'll shove that snake back under his rock for good. He might have slimed out temporarily, but he'll crawl back and stay put or be squashed like a worm.

Yes, whatever it takes, Ana thought as Molly dashed up and smoothed the powder-laden puff over her nose and forehead. Estelle fluffed her hair and let loose a wallop of spray as the script supervisor checked his notes and handed her the sunglasses. "They were on your head in the last scene."

Ana nodded. She tried to focus her thoughts on Vicki. Eric will be taken care of, she told herself. One way or another—and good riddance. Just so long as none of the slimy mess oozes back on me.

Chapter Ten

Turkey tetrazzini and salad in fridge. Miss Louise left facks on your desk about wedding magazine lady. Sen. Farrell called, also Monike Darsey. (twice—will call in a.m.) See you Monday.   *Graciella*

Ana tore the scribbled note off the kitchen cupboard, shaking her head. She'd have to speak to Graciella again about taping these damned messages on the clear glass panes of the maple cupboards. That's what refrigerators are for, she mumbled to herself as she crumpled the note and tossed it in the trash compactor. Turkey. If she had another bite of anything turkey today, she'd barf. But the salad sounded perfect.

They'd wrapped for the day an hour before, and Harry Damone was due at her doorstep any minute. Drained after more than fifty takes, Ana had barely paused to let Molly reclaim her false eyelashes before she'd slipped out of her costume and into the waiting studio limo, wanting only a quick shower and light dinner at home. It had been a relief to change into purple sweats and Nikes, scoop her hair into a ponytail, and scrub the makeup from her face. If she was quick, she'd manage to scarf down some dinner before Harry Damone arrived.

She was famished, she realized, her stomach growling as she caught sight of the cellophane-wrapped pita bread beside the bananas on the counter. *Pita with Graciella's artichoke butter would be wonderful with the salad,* she thought. She reached for a dinner plate, wincing as her bandaged finger closed over the edge of the heavy peach-colored stoneware.

Eric still had the power to hurt her. But not for long. She'd had enough, enough pain for a lifetime.

Her thoughts raced ahead to the meeting with Harry Damone. She'd have to make it clear that she didn't want Eric killed or maimed, only roughed up enough to scare the shit out of him, to convince him that there was no future in trying to blackmail her. She was stronger than he was now, and she wouldn't even have to scrape a knuckle to cause him more pain than he could imagine.

When he understands that, he'll slither quietly away. Ana was certain of it. He might be vicious, vindictive, and vengeful, but he wasn't stupid.

It was when she was pulling out the salad from the crisper that she spotted the bowl of spaghetti on the middle shelf. The moment her eyes locked on the thick red meat sauce clumped atop the twisted strands of pasta, the familiar feeling of nausea clogged her throat. *Graciella knows I hate spaghetti. She must have fixed this for Louise,* she thought, slamming the refrigerator. She leaned against the cool white door and closed her eyes, trying to block out the image of hundreds of limp strands of airborne spaghetti—gummy and dripping with curds of red-sauced meat—flying full force through the air, spraying, splatting, spoiling everything. . . .

And her father's voice, raw with liquor, screaming at her the last words she had ever heard him say: "You can't do anything right around here, you worthless stupid little snot. All gussied up like a bridesmaid, are you? Well, little girlie, looks like you just better think again. You ain't goin' nowhere!"

The memories flooded back, sucking her down like an undertow. Ana was no longer in her spotless, southwestern-styled kitchen with its curving bar of aqua-veined agate, its huge stone hearth and the bright jungle of potted cacti and geraniums spiking upward toward the skylight. Instead, she was back in the dingy eight-by-eight-foot kitchen of her youth with the green linoleum floor that looked grimy no matter how hard she scrubbed, the chipped enamel stove, and the folding chairs set around a wobbly wooden table. She was back in Tennessee, back in the house her mother had fled from when Ana was ten. The house her father ruled with a bottle and a bellow, and which her grandmother had tried desperately to make into a home.

She could see it all. The worn eyelet curtains on windows sealed shut by years of yellow paint, the television set that transported her each week into the worlds of *Dynasty* and *Dallas*—worlds of powerful women and seductive men, worlds of wealth and glamour light-years removed from the small town of Buck Hollow.

The threadbare rag rug in the dining room was the only thing of her mother's left, that and the simmering frustration and anger that seemed to pervade the crumbling five-room house.

Once again she could breathe in the scent of the magnolia trees flanking the high school that last spring, inhale the musky sweat of Buddy Crocker mingled with his Aqua Velva aftershave, smell the exhaust fumes belching from the ancient school bus.

"Hey, Ana, wait on up—you got a cigarette?" Buddy hollered across the school parking lot as Ana hitched her scruffed vinyl shoulder bag and hurried toward the bus. Buddy sprang up the steps behind her, shifting his books and brushing the long, greasy hair off his forehead.

"You boys know there ain't no smoking on my bus," Mrs. Hewitt bellowed, closing the doors with a grunt.

A chorus of voices hooted down the aisle, and Buddy grinned at Dennis and Jesse laughing like hyenas in the back of the bus.

Ana slipped him a pack of Kents as they flopped into their customary seats across from Dennis and Jesse, with Shirleen and Bobbie Sue slumped right in front of them. Buddy passed the pack around and lit up surreptitiously, cracking the window and grinning as Mrs. Hewitt called, "Nothin' funny goin' on back there, is it?"

" 'Course not, ma'am. We're just doin' our homework," Dennis sang out. He pretended to rake a hand through his shoulder-length russet hair, flipping the bird at the heavyset bus driver. Ana guffawed and Buddy pulled her onto his lap, nuzzling her neck and trying to slide his hand up her short black skirt as the bus jostled them down the country road.

"Yeah," Buddy chuckled in her ear, "I like doin' this kind of homework. You're my favorite subject, baby."

Ana smiled. Here in Buddy's lap she felt sexy, grown-up, and desirable. She kissed him so noisily that Shirleen and Bobbie Sue turned around and giggled.

"Jesse, did you get your brother to buy us those six-packs for tonight?" Bobbie Sue's high-pitched voice chirped over the rumble of the bus. She leaned into the aisle, fluttering her white-blond lashes and blowing smoke rings toward the boys.

"You bet your sweet ass, darlin'." Jesse was shorter than the other boys, but had a huskier build and an ever-present five o'clock shadow. He reached out and yanked Bobbie Sue into his lap. "Party starts at eight at the Dairy Queen."

Shirleen was watching jealously as Buddy tussled

with Ana in the backseat. "I saw Mr. Touchdown talking to you today, sugar," she drawled with a wink at Bobbie Sue. "You invitin' *him* to the party?"

Buddy sat up. He stared at Ana through suddenly suspicious brown eyes. His reaction was akin to that of a young wolf who hears the howl of another male in the woods. He tossed his cigarette down and crushed it into the floor with the toe of his boot.

Buddy Crocker had the wiry build and heavy-lashed eyes of a young James Dean. Not exactly handsome, he nevertheless possessed a rough, cock-sure charm that had a lot to do with the arrogant gleam in his eye and the defiant set of his shoulders. The way he held his cigarette, the way he looked out at the world from those coffee-dark go-to-hell eyes, touched a chord in Ana. A chord of rebellion. Like Buddy, she sizzled with the desire to thumb her nose at the world.

"Whoa, now, baby doll." He grasped Ana's chin and tilted it, forcing her to meet his eyes. "What're you doin' talking to that jerk? You fixin' to try out for cheerleader?"

Ana tossed off a laugh, shrugged, and shot Shirleen a furious look. "Don't be an asshole, Buddy." She put her arms around Buddy's neck and nestled against him. He continued to study her warily.

"He just wanted to ask me when that chemistry report was due. He missed class today, that's all." She met his gaze head-on, and smiled coyly in her best imitation of Erica Kane, hoping she was as good an actress as Susan Lucci.

"You sure it was old man Wilcox who put y'all in the same group?" Buddy asked suspiciously. "Or did Roy Cody fix it that way 'cuz he's got the hots for you?"

"If I was you, boy, I'd kick his ass," Jesse told Buddy, reaching for another cigarette.

Ana's heartbeat quickened in alarm. She slid her hand along Buddy's chin, tracing his stubbled jawline with a tapered finger. The smoky shadows in his eyes seemed to glow more intensely at her touch, and she felt a surge of relief at the power of her feminine wiles. "Buddy honey, don't be a bigger fool than you already are," she murmured sweetly. "Everybody knows that I'm your girl."

"Just so long as you don't forget it." Roughly, he grabbed a handful of her thick, burnished hair and pulled her head down. He kissed her hard, his teeth nipping into her bottom lip, his hands groping possessively down her buttocks.

Ana writhed against him, triumphant. She scraped her fingernails across his back, digging into the hollows of his shoulder blades. She knew Buddy was trying to prove something here, and she was perfectly ready to help him do it, but a small secret part of her kept wondering all the while Buddy kissed and pawed and grunted, what it would be like to be kissed by Roy Cody. The strapping blond quarterback would never fit into her crowd—or she into his. She was known at school as one of the wild kids, the kids who drove too fast, drank too much, and flirted with drugs, who cruised the Sonic drive-in and the Dairy Queen every Saturday night, roaring up and down the strip, honking, waving, and making out while the car radios blasted anything but country. Roy Cody was Mr. All-American, with a football scholarship and law career ahead of him, an uptown address in a stately old Victorian home on Main Street, and a straight-A average.

Ana pulled Bs without studying. She knew she was smart, but she didn't have time to study, not when she had to keep the house clean, cook her father's meals, and party with Buddy every night. It was knowing she was Buddy's girl that kept her going when her father started in on her. She'd tune out her father and think about Buddy. About how proud she was to be his girl. Ana liked being stared at as they swaggered through the halls, hearing the whispers, seeing the looks. It almost made her feel like a celebrity. She knew that those girls who whispered about her in the john, who told stories about her and Buddy making out behind the lockers by day, and at night along the dark back roads, were just horny, jealous prudes too scared and prissy to get any action themselves.

Buddy cared about her, he was tough and cute, and he paid attention to her. Her father sure as hell didn't —the only thing he cared about was his Budweiser, his bowling ball, and the latest waitress to jiggle her hooters in his face down at J.T.'s Bar.

The only time Ana had seen him sober in the past two years was at her grammaw's funeral. At least he'd had the decency to wait until after the last shovelful of dirt had been tossed on his mother's coffin before starting on a bender that had lasted for three days.

When Buddy drank, it was different. He didn't throw things or yell and cry like her old man did. He got horny and cracked jokes, and when he pulled her down on top of him in the backseat of the car and kissed her, his hands sweaty and urgent as they slid up and down her body, she could almost forget the dismal house across from the railroad tracks where drunken curses peppered the air and rage hung like a cloud of hornets ready to swarm down without warning. And yet, this afternoon, when Roy Cody had stammered out an invitation for a movie date to see *St. Elmo's Fire*, something in her blossomed like a flower in sunlight. She never thought anyone like Roy would consider dating her, but he blushed so adorably that his freckles popped to the surface. Roy Cody. What would he want with hell-raisin' Ana Cates from the wrong side of town?

But the funny thing was, Ana thought as the bus lumbered up her street, Roy didn't look down on her like some of the other straight kids did. And when her arm had brushed his while they'd worked on the chemistry report in the library, she had felt something like electricity charging through her. But she was Buddy's girl, she told herself. Buddy was her type. His father had worked in the same auto repair shop as hers for the past eight years, bowled in the same bowling alley, drank the same beer. His mother wasn't dead, but she might as well have been. Ana had often seen the same bleak look in her eyes as she'd seen in her own mother's before she'd escaped. She and Buddy, Shirleen, Bobbie Sue, Jesse, Dennis, and the rest all shared the same world. A world louder, dirtier, and emptier than the realm inhabited by the uptown jocks and princesses of Davison High. She was definitely no princess, so why would a drop-dead handsome jock like Roy Cody want to go out with her?

For my bod, Ana concluded with a bitter twist of her mouth as the bus lurched to a stop at her corner. Well, she'd find out soon enough. She just hoped Buddy didn't find out she and Roy Cody had a date for Friday night.

"See you at eight," Shirleen called through the grime-streaked window as Ana and Buddy headed down the pebble-studded asphalt arm in arm. They disappeared beneath the dipping branches of the weeping willows as dust kicked up by the retreating bus swirled in a hazy cloud. Buddy walked with Ana until they reached the edge of the dense woods flanking Ana's yard.

"Wear somethin' real pretty tonight, you hear?" Buddy called as Ana trudged up her front steps.

"Don't I always?" she called back.

To her surprise, her father was snoring away on the sofa, newspapers spread across his stomach and beer cans littering the coffee table. A hoarse snore stuck in his throat as the screen door banged behind her and he lurched up, eyes bulging.

"Daddy! What are you doing home so early? Are you sick?"

"Yeah, I'm sick. Sick and tired of bein' jacked around by that friggin' SOB Dixon."

"What happened this time, Daddy?" Ana cautiously moved into the room and cleared a space on the coffee table for her books. Her father didn't look too drunk yet. He must have slept it off, she concluded, relaxing her guard slightly.

Warren Cates was an ox of a man, well over six feet tall, with fists the size of half-gallon moonshine jugs. He'd done some boxing before his hitch in the marines, and he still had the burly frame and surprising agility of a trained fighter. The crooked nose that squatted on his face like a sweet potato and the scar under his left eye attested to the fact that Warren Cates had taken his licks, but he'd told Ana time and again that no one had ever KO'd him, not once, and he'd always given as good as he got. Even when his target was a woman, Ana had often reflected to herself, for she dimly remembered the black eyes and mysterious bruises her mother had worn.

Strangely enough, he'd never struck Ana with those fists. When he was in a roaring rage he screamed and threw things—once an open can of beer and once the living room lamp—but mostly he tore into her with words, cutting, belittling words that left her in no doubt about how worthless she was.

She was biding her time. Only one more year until graduation, and then she was getting out of Yuck Buck Hollow for good. She planned to live in a big city and get a proper job, maybe work as a bank teller or a bookkeeper. She had a head for numbers—hadn't her math teacher told her she should try business school after graduation? With a steady job, maybe she could even save enough to take night courses at a business college.

No matter what Daddy said, she knew she was smart. Her grades proved it and her grammaw had made her believe she could really be somebody. Of course Buddy didn't know about her plans. He'd laugh and say she was dreaming. But Grammaw had said that if you held on to your dreams and worked hard to make them come true, anything was possible.

Her father groaned, yawned, and popped the top of another beer can as Ana gathered up the empties. "Dixon sent everyone but Ellis home early. Said things're slow and there ain't enough work for all of us to just be sittin' around like maggot-covered roadkill. Shit. Now, you tell me how I'm supposed to make a goddamn living?" He swilled down the warm liquid and his heavy-lidded tobacco-colored eyes narrowed. "Shit. This tastes like cat piss. Girlie, go get me a cold one and turn on the TV—gotta be a ball game on here somewhere."

I am getting out of here, Ana vowed to herself. She fled into the kitchen, sickened by her father's beer belly and the bristly two-day stubble fringing his massive jaw, by his greasy crew cut and the permanently embedded filth beneath his ragged fingernails. She hated this house, hated sitting down to dinner with him and listening to his belches and grumbles. But most of all she hated him for driving her mother away and doing his damnedest to make her feel like dirt.

Yep. I'm getting out of here, Ana promised herself as she opened the refrigerator and rooted out a Budweiser. And no one's going to stop me—not Daddy, not Buddy, not even Roy Cody. The minute I get my hands on that diploma, I'm leaving this shithole behind.

But three weeks later Ana was having second thoughts. Roy Cody had called her every day and taken her out the past two weekends. Suddenly, things were different.

She no longer rode the bus with Buddy, Shirleen, and the others. Now Roy Cody drove her home in his J2000 with the sunroof open to the balmy spring breeze and the scent of magnolias floating between them. He'd asked her to the prom and she was going. They were double-dating with Cindi Jo Harris and Al Whitcomb, both student council hotshots. Kids who'd never spoken to her before were now greeting her in the hallways and inviting her to parties.

She felt bad about Buddy and wished they could still be friends, but Buddy wouldn't even talk to her. None of them would. They treated her as though she were invisible. It didn't bother her that Shirleen oozed all over Buddy like sap stuck to a tree. But it did bother her that Buddy's eyes which once had glowed hotly into hers now stared icily right through her. That was the hardest thing to take.

But she didn't want to go back. Roy listened to her. He made her feel as if all her dreams were within reach. He saw something in her, something other than her tits and her dimples, something she could barely recognize in herself. She felt special, smart, and pretty and hopeful—alluring in a way that had nothing to do with groping and grunting in the backseat of a car. When she kissed Roy she felt cherished and beautiful. Buck Hollow was no longer a dreary prison, but a fairyland of promise. Ana felt like Sleeping Beauty awakened by her prince's kiss and the prom would be the magical grand ball, the most memorable night of her life.

Roy's sister, Ashleigh, had even helped her get an after-school job car-hopping at the Sonic. Ana figured that with the money she was earning she would have enough by the first week of June to pay for the prom dress she'd put in layaway.

The instant she'd laid eyes on the dress, she'd known she had to have it. It was a mouth-watering confection of creamy white satin and Chantilly lace highlighted by a pearl-trimmed sweetheart neckline that swept over her shoulders and dipped nearly to her waist in back. Ashleigh had shown her how to pile her hair on top of her head and had suggested long dangly crystal earrings. Ana couldn't afford to buy the earrings, but she would be perfectly content with the tiny pearl studs her grammaw had left her along with the matching teardrop necklace. It was the only real jewelry Ana possessed, and she would be proud to wear it when she swept into the prom on Roy's arm, as elegant and glamorous as a movie star.

On the Friday of the prom Ana rushed out of school and slid into the bucket seat beside Roy, feeling as if she would burst with anticipation.

"Ashleigh told me you've picked out some pretty dress," Roy commented as he pulled out of the parking lot onto Grainger Road. He turned his head quickly and shot her a teasing smile. "Just remember who your date is when all the guys zero in on the most gorgeous girl in the room."

"Who my date is . . . who my date is . . ." Ana repeated, feigning bafflement. Then she laughed aloud, exulting in the joy of being with him, in the joy of being alive. She had a million things to do when she reached home: bathe, wash her hair, fix dinner for Daddy—she was far too excited to even think of eating anything herself. Tonight was going to be perfect, she knew it. Things were changing for her, her life was suddenly brighter than it had ever been. For the first time since grammaw died, she felt that someone actually loved her. The way Roy looked at her, talked to her, and treated her in front of his friends convinced her that his feelings were genuine. Tonight he'll tell me he loves me, I know it, she thought as the J2000 eased up the gravel drive to her house.

"See you tonight, Ana." Roy tugged her back as she started to open the car door. He leaned over the gearshift on the floor, his muscular body seeming to fill the small car as he caught her chin in his hand. Roy was strong, probably nearly as strong as her father, but his touch was gentle. His lake-blue eyes gleamed into hers, mirroring the same eager happiness that soared through her. "Thank God Wilcox made us lab partners," he whispered. His familiar lopsided smile, the one that made his eyes crinkle sexily at the corners, leapt out to warm her all over. "Otherwise, I might never have gotten to know the greatest girl in the school."

He kissed her gently at first, then the kiss deepened. Ana clutched his muscular shoulders, her heart racing. A flush swept over her cheeks and neck as Roy's tongue played with hers. He loves me, she thought.

Roy was breathing hard. Ana could barely breathe at all. When his hand moved to her breast beneath her Harley T-shirt, her nipples hardened.

Suddenly a childish voice yelled out: "Race you to the garbage can!"

Jerking backward, Ana saw eight-year-old Willie Fenton and his best friend Tyler Moss roller-skating past at breakneck speed. "Damned brats," she gasped. "They scared the hell out of me."

"Me too." Roy laughed, but she could see he was embarrassed too. "Guess I'd better go on down and get my tux. Hate to leave, but tonight I promise you, Ana, there won't be any interruptions."

Ana stood a moment on the wooden porch until the blue car disappeared around the corner. No interruptions. An entire evening together. She could still feel the heat of his hand on her breast, smell the clean, woodsy scent of him that was as natural and enticing as his easy grin. Roy and Ana, she thought dreamily, turning toward the house at last. Roy and Ana Cody.

Has a nice ring to it, she thought, swinging through the back door. *Mrs. Roy Cody*.

The next few hours dissolved into a blur of feverish activity. She prepared her daddy's favorite meal, spaghetti with meat sauce, and while the sauce was simmering on the stove she dashed uptown to the florist to pick up Roy's boutonniere. When she tucked it in the refrigerator and pulled out a head of lettuce for her daddy's salad, her mind was drifting ahead to the moment she would pin the crisp white carnation on Roy's lapel. With a silly grin on her face she set the table and folded her father's socks. In the ten minutes it took for the spaghetti to cook, she soaked in the tub, treating herself to a bubble bath and scrubbing her hair with honey-scented shampoo.

By six-fifteen Ana stood before the bathroom mirror, clasping the teardrop necklace around her throat. She had brushed her long, coppery hair until it sparked flames even beneath the dim bathroom bulb. She piled it high, securing the curls with hairspray and fine hairpins, and then pulled down several casual tendrils for that flirty look she'd studied in *Seventeen* magazine. From the little jewelry box inside the medicine cabinet she took her grammaw's earrings and carefully slipped them into place. The last touch was a splash of perfume behind her knees, behind each ear, and deep in the crevice between her breasts. Resist me, Roy Cody, if you can, she challenged.

She studied the alluring woman who smiled back at her from the mirror, that glamorous creature in the floaty white dress and brand-new heels. She stepped back and swiveled from side to side, loving the way the lacy poufed skirt billowed suggestively about her legs, the way the satiny bodice hugged her waist and emphasized the fullness of her breasts. She swept on a second coat of mascara, dropped her lipstick into her purse, then waltzed into the living room to await Roy's arrival.

Ana glanced at the kitchen clock visible through the archway. Her timing was perfect. Roy should be there in less than ten minutes. Her heart began racing as she imagined the expression on his face when he saw her.

Just then she heard the screech of tires over gravel and peered out to see her daddy's Ford pickup splaying pebbles as it gunned up the driveway. Oh, God, is he plastered already? she thought in dismay, thankful that his dinner was ready. At least he couldn't bitch at her about that. The covered spaghetti platter was waiting on the kitchen table alongside the salad bowl and a steaming dish of green beans and bacon. Ana hurried into the kitchen and scooped a cold beer from the refrigerator. She was carrying it to the table as her father slammed through the screen door and stopped short at the sight of her. He filled the front doorway, his shoulders bulging beneath his grease-stained workshirt.

"Where the hell d'ya think you're goin', little girl?"

Oh, God, he was drunk, shit-faced drunk. Ana swallowed. She had hoped to introduce Roy to her father tonight for the first time, but now she'd have to run outside before he came to the door. She took a step backward, listening for the sound of Roy's car, and said as pleasantly as she could manage: "Tonight's the prom, Daddy. You remember. Roy Cody? Do you like my dress?" She pivoted, holding out the skirt for effect, but her hopeful smile died as her father looked her over with growing contempt.

"Where the hell's the top half of it? You look like a goddamn slut! You ain't settin' one foot outside this here door until you put on somethin' decent, you hear me?"

Put on something decent? Like what, Ana wanted to scream at him, like my blue jeans or that old plaid skirt I wear to church? She clenched her hands and held her ground. "Daddy, please calm down. Everyone wears dresses like this. C'mon, your dinner is all ready. I kept it nice and hot for you."

His massive arms churned the air as he staggered toward her. "You 'spect me to eat alone?" he roared.

"Daddy, just this once. It's a special night," Ana pleaded, thinking of all the nights she'd eaten alone while he was off at J.T.'s. The ugly glint in his eye frightened her. This was no ordinary drunk. This was one of his mean drunks, the kind she dreaded. Oh, God, no. Please, not tonight of all nights. Where was Roy? she thought desperately, stealing a glance out the kitchen window. If I don't get out of here soon,

Daddy's only going to get worse. "Daddy, just look. I
made your favorite, spaghetti," Ana coaxed, lifting the
cover off the platter, hoping the steaming aroma of
basil-laced tomato and garlic would entice him to sit
down at the table.

At that moment she heard a car turn into the driveway, and glancing out the window caught sight of Roy,
glossily handsome in his white tuxedo, shifting the
sports car into park. Her heart stopped as she glimpsed
Cindi Jo Harris and Al Whitcomb snuggled in the backseat—Cindi Jo wearing a sparkly red dress and Al
sporting a matching red carnation on his lapel.

"I won't be late, Daddy," she promised hurriedly,
holding her breath. The last thing she wanted was for
anyone in that car to see him in this condition. She
snatched up her purse and made a grab for Roy's
boutonniere, but in Ana's haste her elbow hit the can of
beer and sent it skimming off the table, the contents
bubbling across the linoleum. She gasped and looked
up, staring across the living room as Roy knocked at the
open screen door.

He was incredibly handsome, his broad shoulders
accentuated by the elegant cut of the tuxedo, a clear
plastic box holding an orchid corsage tucked under his
long arm. Her daddy was too drunk, too single-minded
in his fury to notice him, but Ana's eyes were dismayed
as they met Roy's through the archway. Then Warren
Cates's roar drowned out all hope of avoiding a scene.

"Look what you've done, you clumsy idiot!" A purple rage suffused his face, spreading upward from his
thick neck, staining his clenched jaw, exploding in his
eyes.

"Daddy, please, I'll clean it up. . . ." Ana tried
desperately, starting to edge toward the living room to
explain to Roy that she'd be out in just a minute, but
her father slammed his fist on the table, rattling the
plates.

"You can't do nothin' right around here, you worthless stupid little snot!" He leaned toward her, filling the gap between them with his beer breath. His veins bulged with the rage beating in them. Spittle foamed at the corners of his lips. "All gussied up like a brides-maid, are you?" he sneered. "Well, little girlie, looks like you just better think again. You ain't goin' no-where!"

His massive fist scooped up the platter of spaghetti and hurled it before any of them knew what was hap-pening. Ana watched, feeling as if everything were playing in slow motion. The heaping platter sailed like a Frisbee toward her. It splattered across the Chantilly lace skirt, dumping its steaming contents upon the deli-cate fabric. Ana gasped in pain and shock as burning sauce penetrated to her thighs. She scarcely felt the plate crack at her feet or the jagged crockery edge that tore through her panty hose, slicing into her ankle. All she saw was her beautiful billowing dress dripping with spaghetti, the sauce hot and red as blood as it oozed down the lacy netting and into her shoes. All she felt was pure disbelief.

"What the hell is going on here? If you've hurt her . . ."

Roy's voice floated to her as if from another planet. Slowly, dazedly. Ana raised her head to see him ad-vancing upon her father with an expression of fury taut-ening his features to fine-honed steel. Her eyes dulled as she looked away. If she looked into his face, she was certain she'd see either pity or contempt, and she couldn't bear either one. A paralyzing numbness seeped through her.

"Ana." Roy stopped short at the vacant expression in her eyes. She looked as though she were about to topple over in a faint. He reached out, ready to grab her, but like quicksilver she backed away. "Come on, Ana, let's get out of here," he muttered hoarsely.

She shrank from his touch. She stared blindly from Roy's agonized face to her father's shocked one, then down at her dress. Ruined. Everything was ruined. Hatred bubbled up within her, hot, ugly, raw as a reopened wound.

Above the ticking of the kitchen clock she heard a car door slam. Cindi Jo's and Al's laughter pealed through the open screen door as they crossed the porch. "Hey, folks, how long does it take to pin on a corsage?" Al demanded.

Something snapped inside of her. It all came together in a surreal blur: the sounds of her father's raspy breathing, the ticking of the clock, Cindi Jo's low-pitched giggle. She saw the half-horrified, half-defiant look on her daddy's face and closed her eyes, rocked with hatred. The pungent, overpowering smell of spaghetti assailed her nostrils.

Ana bolted for the kitchen door.

"Ana! Wait!"

She heard Roy's cry, but never looked back. She was across the yard before he could run after her. Before the screen door had slammed, she had slipped under the rotting wooden fence, across the alley, and into the dark tangle of the woods, bramble tearing at what was left of her gown. Then all she could hear was the pounding in her ears as her blood pumped furiously and her feet slammed into the soft, springy earth.

She cowered in the darkness with only the gnats and mosquitoes for company until Roy and the others had given up searching for her. At four in the morning, when she knew her father would be passed out colder than a stiff in a coffin, she crept out of the woods, across the yard, and back into the house. This is the last time, she told herself, the last time I ever set foot inside this door.

Everything was exactly as she had left it. The beer and broken crockery still littered the floor, the dried crusty pasta and meat sauce had hardened on the linoleum. Fighting back nausea, she picked her way to her room. With trembling hands she peeled off the now-stiff, sour-smelling dress and hurled it into a corner. She ran a cold washcloth over her skin, fearful of waking her father if she turned on the shower. Dressing hastily in a T-shirt and jeans, she stuffed shorts, tops, and underwear into a gym bag and emptied her Coke-bottle piggy bank into her denim purse. $23.17. Better than nothing, Ana thought grimly.

She stared around her bedroom at the stuffed animals and Cabbage Patch doll on her patchwork quilt, at the scuffed cowboy boots under her Elvis poster, at the shoebox on her dresser containing all of her lipstick, blush, and half-used bottles of Avon nail polish. A sob caught in her throat as she opened the top dresser drawer and took out the framed photo of her mother, faded to pale yellows and reds. She studied the young, hopeful face smiling up at her, the face of Mother before she was married, then abruptly slammed the photo back into the drawer. *Mother left me and this house. Now it's time for me to leave too.*

Her gaze swept to the other framed photo in the room, the one of Grammaw taken at a family picnic the summer before she died. Ana squashed it into her gym bag, then carefully removed the pearl earrings and necklace she still wore. Listening in trepidation to the sounds of her father's snores from down the hall, she stuck them with shaking fingers into the coin section of her wallet. Whirling about, her throat tight with unshed tears, Ana made a final check of the room. Then she grabbed her denim jacket from the rocking chair.

She stooped over the orchid corsage still nestled in its plastic box near the front door. She reached for it, then pulled her hand back.

No, she whispered. Leave it. Leave it in this house. Leave it to wither and die, like everything else in this place.

And then she was gone.

She hitchhiked her way as far as Las Vegas, to the town of tawdry tinsel and neon lights. A town as far removed from the gritty gray gloom of Buck Hollow as she could get.

And in Las Vegas she met Eric Gunn.

The chime of the doorbell snapped Ana back to her airy kitchen with a jolt. She drew in a deep breath. It had all happened so long ago, yet it felt as if it were yesterday.

Ana scrubbed her clammy palms across her sweats and started toward the door as the chime pealed again. Eric Gunn was every bit as much a supporting player in her past as was Buddy Crocker, Roy Cody, and her own father. But his was an even larger, uglier role—the heavy who'd been written out of the script but like Freddy Krueger refused to exit for long.

But Harry Damone is going to fix that, Ana told herself as she opened the pickled-oak door.

Harry stood there, a wad of gum cracking in his mouth, a baggy warm-up suit covering his squat frame. He was a short dumpling of a man with merry elfin features and a salt and pepper toupee. He packed a .45 in his shoulder holster and a package of peanut M&Ms in his back pocket along with pictures of his three grandkids. He might not look like Bogey, Ana thought as she led him into the sunken living room with its turquoise walls and coral leather sofas, but he's every bit as shrewd as Philip Marlowe.

"I haven't had dinner yet, Harry. Can I get you something?"

"A Perrier and a Pepto-Bismol, my ulcer is killing me." Harry sank into the overstuffed peach leather armchair and settled his feet atop the matching ottoman. He crumpled a silver gum wrapper between his fingers and aimed for the ceramic bowl in the center of the coffee table. "Ech. So I don't get two points," he grumbled as the wrapper skidded onto the floor.

Ana regarded him with affection. Harry was going

to help her get rid of Eric. He didn't look much like a knight in shining armor, but that's what he was. By the time Harry and his dauntless companions finished with their little task, the dragon—if not slain—would at least be reduced to a limping lizard bereft of power, danger, and fire.

Chapter Eleven

Sun slanted through the leaves of the palm trees. Ana slathered lotion on her long legs and settled back into the aqua cushions of the chaise longue. She wiggled her toes to the rhythm of Phil Collins's "I Can't Dance," wondering if Eric's overnight delivery had arrived. If so, he wouldn't be doing much dancing today himself, she decided with a grim little smile that didn't quite touch the burning centers of her eyes.

She eased back in the chaise and offered her lotion-moist face to the caressing warmth of the sun. It was only ten o'clock, but the smog had burned off and there was not a rain cloud in sight. For the next hour she refused to do anything but relax. Graciella was gone for the weekend, Louise was camping in the mountains with her latest lover, and the gardener had long ago finished his pruning and primping and had quietly disappeared.

She didn't have to talk to a soul or listen to anyone yell "Rolling—action!" for the seven hundredth time. Once the movie was wrapped—early next week with any luck—she had nothing else scheduled until after her wedding except the *Perfect Bride* shoot in Maui.

The wind sighed through the palms, delicate as a whisper. Ana felt her muscles relax beneath the soothing radiance of the sun. She could spend the rest of the day making decisions on flowers and the menu, but the next hour belonged to her alone, and she would take it selfishly. Such peaceful moments were rare.

She took a sip of her mimosa and set the tumbler back on the glass-topped wrought iron table. For a moment she surveyed the curving pool of shimmering blue water. The gleaming surface captured the reflection of hundreds of roses nestled in the painted aqua tubs bordering the pool's south end. Blossoms of pink, tangerine, yellow, and pristine white seemed to bob in the jeweled depths. The scent of roses, jasmine, and gardenias wafted over to her as she gazed upward at the tranquil cerulean sky. Peace. Harmony. That's what she wanted from her life. That's what she would get once Eric was out of the way.

John would freak out if he knew that she had once shared her bed with the likes of Eric Gunn. His mother would probably drop dead in her Dior suit, perfectly outfitted for her own funeral. And his father . . . she could picture Arthur Farrell's immaculately groomed gray eyebrows lifting haughtily at the first whiff of a lowlife like Eric Gunn, and hear his cultured, Harvard-educated baritone as he'd sniff: "We told you, son, that it wasn't wise to get involved with an actress. When I think of all the delightfully eligible young women who've moved in our circle all these years . . . Well, now you've seen for yourself, John, that all the Pan-Cake makeup and special lighting in the world can't turn an alley cat into a purebred Smoke Persian." And he would pat J. Quincy's silken head, eliciting a grudging meow.

J. Quincy didn't like her any better than she guessed Arthur and Hope Farrell did, but he would— and so would they. Sooner or later she would win them over. For John's sake and the sake of the children who would someday carry on the Farrell name, she needed to carve herself a place in the heart of this exclusive but very tight-knit family. As John's wife she would be entitled to their loyalty and respect. And Ana wouldn't settle for anything less than what was her due.

John's wife. A new role. But one for which she'd been preparing a long time now. And once she and John were married, Ana told herself, she felt certain that she'd begin to truly enjoy their lovemaking—she wouldn't have to act anymore. For now, though she knew rationally that there weren't any cameras when she was with Johnny, emotionally she couldn't seem to believe it. Take a bow, Eric. I owe you for that as well as for everything else.

Luxuriating in the soft perfumed breeze, Ana shifted in the chaise as the CD advanced and Phil Collins's voice husked out the melancholy refrain of "Hold On My Heart."

"We both know we've been here before. . . ." Before, Ana thought. Before Eric . . . there had been Buddy.

She'd lost her virginity to Buddy Crocker out in the garage one Sunday night while Daddy was passed out in front of the living room television. With the set blaring the final game of the World Series over her father's staccato snores, she and Buddy had shared a beer and a blanket in the darkened garage, and in his hungry arms she had discovered the pleasure of pure sex. Their raging hormones had found release in exciting, unbridled experimentation. It had been sweaty, raw, and somehow beautiful. Just the two of them in the darkness, needing, wanting, taking. When she thought now of how careless she had been, she shook her head. Of course they'd taken no precautions. It was a miracle she hadn't gotten pregnant. They'd been so young, so wild, so sure of their own invulnerability that all they'd focused on was the moment.

And what moments they were. For an instant as

she sat in the sun, tears stung behind her closed eyelids. She wondered if she'd ever be so uninhibited and free again.

With Johnny, sex ought to be even better, for she and Johnny truly loved each other. Their relationship had depth and commitment, while hers and Buddy's had been purely physical. Sex with Johnny should be euphoria, Ana reflected bitterly. But ever since that dark period in her life, when she'd hooked up with Eric Gunn, sex had become an ordeal.

It won't always be this way, Ana told herself. She thought of Johnny—so strong and gentle, his muscular body tense with anticipation as he lowered himself over her. Johnny—so patient and giving, always concerned with pleasing her. Even now, remembering, she could feel the urgency in his blue-gray eyes as they searched hers, waiting for the moment she was ready to climax. But even in bed her acting was superb. She never disappointed him. Only herself.

A shadow fell across the sunlight. Ana felt a sudden chill and opened her eyes.

Eric Gunn stood over her. Smiling.

Ana jerked upright, choking back the scream that bubbled up in her throat.

"Goddamn you. Get off my property!" she spat out, her voice hoarse.

Eric flicked a finger beneath her chin. "Who's gonna make me?"

Ana sprang out of the chaise longue and shoved him backward. Fury crackled through her. "Get the fuck out of here before I call the police."

"Yeah, Candy, you always did like to fuck," Eric chuckled. His thick black hair glinted in the sunlight like raw coal, falling over one eye with a studied carelessness Ana suspected he'd spent hours perfecting. Thumbs looped in the pockets of his faded jeans, he was trying very hard to look cool. And he did. He looked like one of those gorgeous Chippendale hunks, all sleek eyes and lean hips, slicked up and ready to swivel.

He ought to look like a bloody pulp, Ana thought angrily. *What the hell happened to Harry Damone?*

Eric's deep dimples sliced into the lean planes of his face. "Well, you know what, baby?" he continued in the mocking tone she remembered too well. "You just go ahead and call the fucking cops, 'cause I've got a real interesting story to tell them. In fact, I've got a couple of stories. Take last night, for instance. I had to hole up on a friend's couch all evening. Seems some bozos wanted to give one of those pricey Hollywood plastic surgeons some new business. Lucky for me, some dudes tipped me off in time. You see, baby, it wouldn't have been so convenient. I haven't paid my Blue Cross lately and I hate doctors." He stepped closer, his gaze menacing as it traveled the length of her bikini-clad body before locking on her eyes. "Just about as much as I hate ungrateful bitches who run out on me without so much as a thank-you, fuck-you, or a postcard home."

"Thank you? *Thank* you?" Ana stared, open-mouthed. Her nails dug into her palms with suppressed fury as she met the icy silver-blue eyes of the man who had put her through hell. *He's enjoying this.* The thought came to her in a flash, and at the same moment she became aware of her near-naked vulnerability. She snatched her white silk robe from the adjoining chaise and punched her arms through the sleeves, tying it hastily and praying Eric couldn't see that her hands were trembling.

"Why do you want to go and do that?" Eric protested with mock dismay. He reached out a ropy arm as if to untie the sash. "Ain't nothing I never saw before, right?"

Ana slapped him hard across the face. "Touch me and I'll kill you. What the hell do you want from me? Haven't you done enough for one lifetime?"

"Still as sweet as candy," he whispered back,

touching the flaming mark her palm had left on his cheek. "I'll bet you still taste sweet too. Come on, baby. Be good to daddy, like you used to."

He advanced toward her, grabbing her wrists and yanking her toward him. "You owe me, baby. You owe me plenty. Ana Cates would be nothin' today if it wasn't for me. Who's the one who gave you your start? I gave you a chance to get some real valuable experience performing for the camera."

Ana sucked in her breath, trying to control the fury exploding through her. For a moment she fought the impulse to shove him sideways into the pool. That would give her a chance to get to the cabana and trip the security alarm. But did she really want the police involved in this? Thinking of the questions they would ask, the triplicate complaint forms she'd have to fill out, the strong probability that someone from the police department hungry for a five-hundred-dollar prize would tip off the tabloids, made her hesitate. A cold, paralyzing knot tightened in the pit of her stomach. She couldn't risk it. It would be suicide for her career, and on top of everything else, she'd lose John.

Never. Eric has taken enough from me. I'll have to handle this on my own. No police. No reporters. I'll have to outsmart this fucker.

"Eric." Ana kept her tone carefully level, her eyes unblinking as they locked on his. "Let me go. Now."

For a moment there was silence except for the gentle warble of a hummingbird. Then Eric's grasp loosened. He nodded, stepped back a pace. "Okay, Candy. I'll say this for you. You've changed since the old days. Used to be I could reduce you to tears with one look. You're a tough little bitch, now, aren't you? I'm impressed."

Sure you are, you bastard. But he was right, she had changed. And he would find out just how much.

The portable phone jangled from the wrought iron

table, startling them both. Ana hesitated only a moment before grabbing it up.

"Angel, sorry I missed you yesterday."

John. Ana rocked back on her heels, her mind racing. She glanced at Eric and saw him grinning from ear to ear.

"That for me?" he stage-whispered, reaching out as if to take the phone.

Ana dodged out of reach, putting the chaise between them. "Darling, I'm sorry too. But it's so good to hear your voice." He didn't know how good.

Eric sidled up to her and began stroking her arm up and down. Ana fought to keep her voice even as she jerked out of his reach. Never taking her eyes off Eric, she drew on all her training to maintain an ordinary tone. "Wait until you see the gorgeous Sèvres candlesticks that came from Senator Kennedy. And I need to ask you something about the menu for the Washington reception, but John . . . can I call you back in half an hour? I'm right in the middle of something."

Eric's grin widened. He was obviously deriving great pleasure from her discomfiture. He returned to the table, took a sip of her mimosa, and made a face. Giving her the thumbs-down sign, he sauntered over to the edge of the pool. As Ana watched in disbelief, he unzipped his fly, fished out his penis, and shot a stream of piss into the glistening blue water.

"Ana . . . Ana, is something wrong?" John's voice was a muffled blur in her ears. He seemed farther than a continent away—more like a galaxy. At that moment she missed him with a pain that sliced through her like an ax. She was in a world apart from the one she inhabited with John—she was back in Eric's world now, and it was a damned ugly place to be.

"I'm sorry, darling," Ana murmured dazedly. "I missed that last sentence. What did you say?"

"You sound strange, Ana. What's wrong?" Suddenly John's voice sharpened. He was listening closely now. Alert. On guard. She could picture his expression —the same one he wore when he suspected a Democratic opponent on the Senate floor was trying to pull a fast one.

"I'm just tired—and I miss you." She prayed that would satisfy him.

Apparently, it did.

"Angel, I'd give anything if I could get away for a few days and fly out there. But it's impossible. At least it's only a few weeks until Thanksgiving. . . ."

John's voice caressed her ear like liquid velvet. She met Eric's insolent stare across the terrazzo. Disgust welled up in her as he shook the last drops of urine into the pool.

Bastard. Fucking son of a bitching bastard.

He was coming toward her, zipping his fly, smirking. Ana wanted to toss the remaining mimosa in his face. But she couldn't let loose with her anger, not yet. She had to suppress all emotion and let her brain take control. Don't let him push your buttons, she warned herself. He's bigger than you, and there's no one else around. Use your brain, Ana. Use your fucking brain.

"Johnny, really, I'll call you back. Let me take care of a little something here, and then I'll be able to give you my undivided attention."

The drone of the dial tone after the line went dead held a dismal finality. She was alone now with Eric, with only her own wits for protection.

"Scared I'd spill the beans to your rich boyfriend?" Eric jeered. "Now, just what do you think he'd say if he knew you were entertaining an old lover? And what do you think he'd say if he knew just what kind of a cheap little slut you really are?"

"Nothing about you scares me, Eric," Ana lied. She forced herself to return to her seat, casually swinging her legs onto the chaise, settling back and looking for all the world as if she were relaxed and at ease. "Now, obviously you've gone to a lot of trouble trying to get my attention. You have it. So why don't you stop playing games and simply tell me what you want."

Staring at her as she reclined with haughty nonchalance, Eric felt the hot flood of color singeing his cheeks. Goddamn bitch. Lying there like fucking Cleopatra. He fought the impulse to overturn the chair and smash her head against the terrazzo. No. Don't be stupid, man, he decided, shifting from one foot to another beneath her snotty gaze. Be cool. Be smart. When the truth came out, she'd tumble good and hard. She'd be the joke of the century. But first he needed the money. Later, he could get his revenge. He'd bleed the bitch for every penny he could and *then* he'd sell her sordid little tale to the tabloids anyway. Eric, you're gonna be one satisfied and wealthy man.

"What do I want? Everything you've got. How's that for starters?" His eyes glinted like sharpened sabers, his words stabbed out at her. He flailed his arms in a wide arc to encompass the pool, the gardens, the estate. "Who'da believed it? Good old Candy Monroe —living the good life. Sleeping on silk sheets. Flying around in private jets. Eating in the finest restaurants. Yes, Miss Cates. No, Miss Cates. Can I get anything else for you, Miss Cates? Need your ass wiped, Miss Cates?" He raked a hand across his chest, pacing back and forth along the edge of the pool with manic energy. Suddenly he kicked a pot of roses, scattering dirt and flowers across the terrazzo.

"Shit, Candy, I'm living in a dump, sharing my breakfast with the cockroaches every day, and you're livin' like this. It ain't fair, you know what I mean? We were partners, remember? I made you, baby, and I didn't get my fucking ten percent. That ain't fair, not one little bit. I figure that with interest, you owe me at least five hundred grand." He watched her carefully. Ana's face remained a rigidly composed mask, cold and lovely as a statue's.

But for one brief instant he caught a nearly imperceptible glint of rage ignite behind those frosty green eyes. "Don't worry, baby, you don't need to pay me all at once. I'm fair. I'll take it in installments." He sauntered closer and swooped down on her suddenly, trapping her in the chair between his sinewy arms. "You won't be getting rid of me quite so easy this time, babe. I'll be in your face for a long time to come."

"Am I interrupting something? No one answered the front door, but I knew we had an appointment, so I came hunting for you."

Eric jumped up and whirled around as the sleek sound of the woman's voice floated from the cabana, punctuated by the soft slap of low-heeled sandals and the tinkling chime of cascading earrings.

Ana was off the chair like a thunderbolt. Who the hell was this? She was still reeling from the shock of Eric's obscene demands and now she found herself further off guard, confronting a stunning brunette who sashayed across the terrazzo right past Eric to dump billowing garment bags on the empty chaise and greet Ana with an outstretched hand and a dazzling smile.

"I'm Monique D'Arcy. Why do I have the feeling I've arrived at a terribly inopportune time?" Her gaze flicked for a moment to the overturned flowerpot and then back to Ana's face with no visible change of expression, but Ana sensed that Monique had witnessed more than she was letting on.

"I'm sorry." Ana shook Monique's hand absently and found her own fingers clasped in a strong, warm grip that seemed to lend her encouragement. "Am I expecting you?" Ana asked blankly, feeling as if her life were slipping completely out of her control.

"Well, Louise faxed me back yesterday, confirming our appointment for this morning. The *Perfect Bride* wardrobe consultation? I brought several items for your approval. *Don't* tell me you don't know anything about this. Dear God, what else can go wrong?"

Fax. Facks? Ana's mind's eye saw the note stuck to

the cupboard glass. Was *that* what Graciella had meant? She hadn't even bothered to check her desk last night for Louise's messages. By the time she'd finished with Harry Damone, she'd decided to let everything else wait until morning.

"Too bad your daddy never taught you manners, Ana," Eric put in with a smile. "You forgot to introduce me to the lady."

Ana bit her lip. She felt as if her head was clamped in an ever-tightening vise. "Monique D'Arcy, this is Eric Gunn. He was just leaving."

"Pleasure," Monique murmured faintly. Her gaze swept over his handsome face and rangy build with cool appraisal. To Ana's relief, Eric didn't leer at her. He was playing Mr. Charm now, a role Ana recalled all too well. "The pleasure's all mine," he responded gallantly.

If he kisses her hand, I'll puke, Ana thought. But all he did was grin. Then he turned to Ana and gave her a peck on the cheek.

"Catch you later, sweet. Why don't I come back and pick up that paperwork on Thursday? That'll give you time to put everything together."

"Fine. You do know the way out, don't you?" Ana turned from him deliberately and with an effort focused all of her attention on Monique. "I'm so sorry for the mixup. It's all my fault. Can I get you something to drink?"

"I'll join you in one of those," Monique said with a glance at the mimosa. She slipped off her sunglasses and her eyes followed Eric through the miniature rose garden and out the latticed portico.

While Ana disappeared inside the cabana to fetch their drinks, Monique sank into a peach-cushioned chair at the patio table and surveyed the curving pool and deck set within the Monet-like backdrop. She reached into her small gold bag and pulled a cigarette from its shiny mesh case, her eyes narrowed against the sun. Monique took a long drag as she studied the lush blending of palm trees, fountains, and brilliant flowers sweeping down the hillside toward the guest bungalow like a colorful Persian rug. Paradise.

But there was trouble in this paradise. Monique had seen the violence with which Eric had lunged at Ana, pinning her in her chair—and it wasn't passion, she was certain, it was violence. The same kind of violence that had decimated that pot of roses, she surmised. What was going on here?

Beneath Ana's composed veneer, Monique recognized the desperation of a caged tigress. And she'd have bet all the gold in Tiffany's that Eric Gunn was her keeper. Was it drugs? she wondered. Sex? Or some kinky variation of both? And where did John Farrell fit into all of this?

None of your business, Monique chided herself. *Just so long as Ana Cates's hanky-panky doesn't interfere with my* Perfect Bride *shoot, she can fuck Manuel Noriega and Long Dong Silver in tandem for all I care.* She gazed at the sun-sparkled pool through the tiny ribbon of smoke twirling up from her cigarette. The warm breeze swaying through the palm trees couldn't dispel the shiver Monique felt when she thought of Drew McArthur and the board twitching for an excuse to throw her out on her ass. She felt more than a little like a caged tigress herself.

But if the June issue did what she projected it would, she'd have ripped away McArthur's whip and chair and set herself free. Free of Shanna's shadow. Free to run *Perfect Bride* the way she wanted. Free to spit in Drew McArthur's eye. She stubbed out the cigarette and fought back the urge to light another.

By tonight she'd be in Maui, prepping for her eight A.M. meeting with the executive vice president of the Maui Haleakala Resort. Together they'd work through all the logistics, security, and accommodation arrangements for the week of the shoot. With an entourage of more than fifty, including the makeup, hair, wardrobe, lighting, and technical crew, not to mention her star-studded ensemble, she wanted to make personally certain of every last detail.

"For you," Ana said, offering Monique a frosty mimosa. She wore a bright smile, and in the sunlight her bouncy red curls framed her face like a fiery halo. "Shall I call you Comtesse, or—"

"Monique." She returned Ana's smile. But all the while she was studying the careful composure with which the actress sipped her drink and then settled opposite her at the wrought iron table.

Good. She's steady as a rock. Whatever the hell she's involved in with that gorgeous devil, she's certainly not going to let it interfere with business, Monique thought. But even as relief settled over her, a sudden gust of wind slammed the portico gate closed and Ana lurched to her feet. She stood wide-eyed, staring at the portico and trembling as if she expected all of Hell's Angels to come roaring up her drive.

"Easy," Monique said softly. "It was only the wind."

Ana sank back into her chair, flushing. She gave a nervous little laugh. "Sorry. Nerves. You caught me on a bad day."

Monique leaned forward and touched Ana's hand. "I saw that guy lunge for you when I came in. I don't mean to pry, but I couldn't help wondering—is your friend Eric Gunn a world-class asshole or just a pest?"

Ana stared. Something in the depths of Monique's gray eyes reached out to her. There was a surprisingly human sympathy under all that polished glamour.

"World-class asshole is an understatement," she blurted out, and tore her fingers through her curls. She gave a rueful laugh. "There are some people born into this world just to make other people's lives miserable. You just met one of them."

"He's not the first I've run across, and probably won't be the last," Monique replied grimly. She took another sip of the drink, letting the cool blend of champagne and orange juice slide over her keyed-up nerves. "Is it serious? Is there anything I can do to help?"

"You already have. Your timing was perfect. If you hadn't come in when you did, I don't know what would've happened." Ana closed her eyes and scrubbed her hands over her temples. "Damn," she muttered. "I need Eric Gunn back in my life like I need leprosy."

Suddenly her eyes flew open. She sat up straight in the chair, reached out, and gripped Monique's hand. "Monique—John doesn't know anything about this creep. I'd like to keep it that way. Eric is someone from my past. I don't know if you've ever had anyone from your past who's like a . . . a demon, or something, but . . . I have to exorcise him by myself. Do you understand?"

"I do understand. But demons can be tough to deal with all by yourself. I'm sure with just a phone call, Senator Farrell could get this creep off your back. . . ." Monique saw the stricken look cross Ana's features and hurried on. "Okay, obviously that's not an option. But Ana, the least you can do is beef up your security around this place. Any Tom, Dick, or Eric can waltz right in and do God-knows-what to you!"

She was right, Ana knew. Now that Eric had found out where she lived, he could pop back anytime he wanted. She'd better make damn sure she wasn't so lax about keeping the security system in the house armed. And as soon as Monique left, she'd get the alarm company out immediately to add some new electronic gizmos to the grounds. That would prevent any more surprise visits. When Eric showed up on Thursday, she'd be ready for him. *If* Eric showed up . . . her mind was already racing ahead of her, clicking off ways to thwart him.

Bingo. She knew what she was going to do.

For the next hour she reviewed the array of swimsuits, beaded gowns, and brightly flowered cruisewear

Monique had brought with her, rejecting only two of the ensembles while all the time her mind was working on her plan. She didn't discuss Eric any further with Monique and almost regretted her impulsive outburst. She could only hope that the entire incident would be forgotten. But at the end of their session, Monique offered a final word of caution.

"Ana, if your demon gets too hot to handle, promise me you'll call me for help. You have my personal number? Use it if you need to."

Touched, Ana squeezed her hand. "I don't think that will be necessary. But I appreciate the offer, Monique. I really do." She smiled slowly, and life sparked once more in her eyes. "I *think* I've got the situation under control. Seriously, you don't need to worry about me."

"It's my job to worry about *everything*," Monique said with a groan, shifting the garment bags on her arm as the two women walked up the drive. "It's a habit I just can't seem to break. Like those damn cigarettes."

"Throw 'em away. Cold turkey. I did when I was eighteen." Her slim eyebrows arched as she shot Monique a challenge. "Something tells me you're every bit as tough as I am. Or am I wrong about that?"

Monique grinned and blew her a kiss as she slid behind the wheel of her rented Viper. "You take care of your demons, Ana, and I'll take care of mine."

Before Monique's car had disappeared beneath the canopy of Russian olive trees bordering the winding drive, Ana was sprinting for the phone. She had to call the security company and she had to call John. But she had to call Arnie first.

Screw Harry Damone and his goons, for all the good they had done her. It was time to try a different approach. "Arnie," she said crisply as his secretary put her right through. She rolled her eyes upward even as she spoke the next hackneyed words. But she was speaking Arnie's language. "I need a meeting, darling. Let's do lunch."

"Great, Ana. Sure. Tuesday, Wednesday—you decide." She could hear him flipping through his appointment book. "How's Monday?"

"How's today? Screw your golf game, Arnie. This is important. How soon can you be here?"

"Ana honey. Gimme a break. . . ."

"One o'clock will be perfect. See you then."

Eric, you poor dumb son of a bitch, Ana thought as she gently set down the phone and gazed unseeingly into her contaminated pool. *I'll bet everything I own you won't be able to resist the bait. I know you too well. Arnie won't have any trouble scooping you into his net.*

Chapter Twelve

"Hilda, you're sure you don't mind my leaving a little early?" Teri's brows knit with concern as she pocketed Mrs. Warnler's tip and pulled on her red boots.

"You've asked me that at least three times, Teri. Stop being such a worrywart. It's no problem. I already told you I'll take care of any walk-ins this afternoon." Hilda waved her dimpled hand carelessly. She was a heavyset woman whose brilliant plum-red hair was styled in an outrageous asymmetrical cut. "If you're going to fly to Maui with all those bigshot celebrities, you need some fancy new clothes. Just don't get trampled by the crowds. You know the day after Thanksgiving is the biggest shopping day of the year."

Mrs. Warnler was bracing her drying nails on the manicure table. Her gaze followed Teri as the manicurist grabbed her purse and denim jacket. "Go to Hudson's," she advised. "Their sales are the best. My daughter-in-law is there today too. She circled so much stuff in that two-page ad that my son will probably need a second job to pay for her 'bargains.'"

Everyone laughed except Teri, who was scowling

out at the gray snow heaping up outside the beauty shop window.

"Hey," Josie yelled, jabbing Teri with a bony finger as she maneuvered her broom across the hair clippings dusting the floor. "Can't you even crack a smile anymore? Next thing we know, you'll be walking around in dark sunglasses, your nose in the air, too snooty to even say hello."

At this, Teri grinned and elbowed her back. "Watch out or I'll start charging you for my autograph."

But as Teri pulled out her carefully delineated list of things she'd need for her trip to Maui, including a new strapless bra, a dinner suit, and a decent cosmetic bag to replace the ratty plastic pouch she kept in her purse, she couldn't shake the uneasiness gnawing at her, that feeling of impending doom she'd been harboring ever since the *Oprah Winfrey Show.* Although she'd had nearly a month to get used to the idea, and she and Brian had been whisked to New York for wardrobe fittings and had actually met Eve Hamel and Nico Caesarone, the whole *Perfect Bride* experience still seemed like a wild dream from which she'd soon awaken.

But, in a little more than a month, she was scheduled to be in Hawaii to have her picture taken for a publication that would be seen by millions of people. *Between that and Oprah Winfrey's show, what are the chances that my cover's blown?* she wondered anxiously.

She left the shop still frowning, and ducked her head against the wind whipping snow into her face. By the time she had pulled her Volvo onto the Southfield Freeway and headed toward Fairlane Mall, she was convinced that it was only a matter of time before she'd have to answer to the past.

Images flashed through her mind. Easter dinner at home. Her brothers and sisters licking chocolate off their fingers and tossing jelly beans and marshmallow chicks at one another, her mother and Grandma Parelli in the kitchen, washing the dishes as she brought them in from the dining room, her father and Grandpa Randazzo setting up a game of bocci in the backyard.

"You better keep your eye on that one," her grandmother had told her mother with an all-knowing nod. "She's too much like my sister, Gertrude. I can see it in her eyes."

"Ma, what are you talking about? Gina's a good girl. She gets straight As. Sister Dorothea tells me she even volunteers to help with the younger children."

"Don't you tell me," Grandma interjected, shaking a wet finger. "She's the spitting image of Gertrude and she's stubborn just like her. She'll bring you trouble yet if you don't lay down the law with her."

"She's only twelve years old! She doesn't even have a boyfriend, Ma. . . ."

"How do you know? Look at her skirts. Two inches above the knee. Whoever heard of such a thing?" Her grandmother turned just then and saw her in the doorway, listening to them.

"Bah, little pitchers have big ears!" Grandma Parelli had exclaimed angrily. "See what I mean? Instead of finishing her job, she's sneaking around here, listening to things that are none of her business. What does that tell you?"

Her mother had sighed, and shooed her from the kitchen with such an exasperated look that Gina had been sure she'd get a lecture later. But instead, when her mother tucked her into bed that night, she spoke in that quiet, concerned way that always made Gina pay attention to her.

"Your Grandma Parelli loves you—you know that. You're her oldest grandchild, and she expects a lot from you."

"I know, Ma," she'd whispered, studying the little holes in the crocheted bedspread. "I try, but she finds fault with everything I do. I wish Grandpa Parelli was still alive so she wouldn't have to live with us."

"You have to understand Grandma a little. She loved Aunt Gertrude very much, and looked up to her because Aunt Gertrude was her big sister. When she got in trouble . . ."

"What kind of trouble, Ma? No one ever says."

Her mother shook her head. "That's not important. She disgraced her family and she was sent to live in the convent. I know you don't ever want to be like Aunt Gertrude, do you, Gina?"

"No, Ma, of course I don't!" she cried vehemently, shocked. "You know I love you and Daddy!"

"That's good." Her mother smiled, and kissed her, and Gina thought she looked relieved. "Grandma just wants to make sure that all her grandchildren stay good and pure, that they don't get into any trouble and disgrace the family. But I know I've brought my children up to be good Catholics, to honor their family, and to do only the right things. I'm not worried about you in the least."

Then why are you discussing all this with me? Gina thought. She felt miserable and confused and she wasn't sure why. When her mother was gone, she crept out of bed and peered at herself in the mirror. Celia, two years younger, was already asleep on the top bunk of the bed she shared with six-year-old Lena, who was snoring softly into her teddy bear's ear. Gina turned on the night-light to see herself better. Do I really look like Aunt Gertrude? she wondered, touching her own long, dark hair, thinking back to the sepia photograph she had seen of a young girl with brown curly hair and doe eyes set within a pretty, wistful face.

No one will come out and say it, but I'll bet she got pregnant and had a baby, Gina decided. She shuddered at the thought. I'd never do anything like that. Why is Ma so worried? Does she believe everything Grandma says?

Gina climbed back into bed, convinced that her grandmother was superstitious and old-fashioned and too eager to criticize. *I hate being the oldest,* she thought. *I always have to set the example for everyone else. Why couldn't Celia, Little Miss Perfect, have been born first?*

Still, she snuggled down into her pillow and said a silent prayer before she went to sleep. "Dear God, please don't let me go astray like Aunt Gertrude. I want my mother and father to always be proud of me."

Teri's eyes filled with tears at the memory. Suddenly, the Mazda in front of her skidded on the snow-glazed pavement and she slammed on her brakes, adrenaline streaking through her. Her car fishtailed into the other lane as Teri pumped furiously at her brakes. After one long, frightening moment, she maneuvered the Volvo out of the skid and crept forward, clutching the wheel with shaking hands.

As if I weren't nervous enough already, Teri thought bleakly. She took a deep breath. *Will I ever feel calm again?*

So far, there had been no word either from her family or from Andrew. And no news was good news, right?

But she couldn't help feeling that all this unwanted publicity—the last thing in the world she would have anticipated the morning of her birthday—would be her undoing.

Anyone else who'd been selected for this kind of adventure would be riding a carousel of happiness, but she felt as if she were on the roller coaster from hell.

She knew Brian was getting pretty fed up with her. She couldn't blame him. But she couldn't ever explain the real reason behind her anxieties. If Brian found out about all the lies, all the deception, she was sure it would destroy his trust in her.

You've got to stop worrying all the time, she told herself as she pulled into the giant slush-filled parking lot and began circling futilely in search of a parking space. But Teri sensed, even as she prayed to St. Anthony, the finder of lost things, to find her a parking spot, that the moment she stopped worrying, something awful would happen.

I've lost enough, she thought, at last wedging her car between a van and a station wagon. *I can't lose Brian too.*

Two hours later she tossed her packages into the trunk and headed home, determined to cook herself and Brian a nice dinner, model the outfit she'd found to wear on the plane, and for Brian's sake drum up some enthusiasm for this *Perfect Bride* fiasco. Even if it was phony enthusiasm.

"Do you have any idea how long you've been fiddling with that clump of broccoli? About twenty minutes." Brian set down his fork and studied her across the chicken-rice casserole.

"You've been timing me?" Teri asked, pushing a strand of hair behind her ears and trying to smile with good humor.

Brian pushed back his chair with a scrape. He carried his plate to the sink and dumped the leftovers into the garbage disposal. "I've heard of prenuptial jitters, but this is getting ridiculous. You're so busy chewing your fingernails all the time, you can't even eat a decent meal. I bet you've lost five pounds since we went to Chicago."

"Stop picking on me, Bri," Teri said in a low tone. "That's not making it any easier."

"Making what any easier, Teri?" Brian exploded, wheeling back to face her. "This should be the happiest time of our lives. We're getting married, and now you've won this contest and we're going to get an unbelievable honeymoon in Hawaii. *Hawaii*, Teri, *Hawaii*. That's been our dream. We never thought it would happen—and it did. What in the world do you have to feel down about?"

Teri stared helplessly at him, unable to offer a word in her own defense. Her heart was bursting with explanations she'd never be able to utter, aching with the secrets she feared would rob her of Brian's love.

"Don't cry, Teri," Brian warned, slamming his fist on the counter. "Dammit, you know I can't stand it when you cry."

But she couldn't stop the sobs that choked her.

"Oh, shit," Brian groaned, and then he was beside her, taking her in his arms. Leaning against him, she wept, and drew comfort from his arms tight around her.

"You know me and my plans, Brian," she gasped at last. "I like to be in control of my life. I like to know everything that's coming up. I never counted on any of this *Perfect Bride* stuff." She wiped the back of her hand across her tear-streaked face. "And you know I hate having my picture taken."

Brian laughed.

She leaned her head against his shoulder. "I just want to get married, get my degree, and settle down. I don't want to be a celebrity, I just want to have a normal life."

"We will, babe, we will." Brian stroked her hair. Teri's hair was always so soft and fragrant, like flower petals. She seemed so delicate in his arms.

He felt like a jerk for badgering her. "I just wish you could try to enjoy your fifteen minutes of fame. Hey, in the click of a shutter this will all be over, and before you know it, we'll be showing those magazine pictures to our grandkids."

"Grandkids—give me a break," Teri giggled. She lifted her face to peer impishly up at him. "Even I haven't planned quite that far down the road."

Brian's lips moved warmly against hers. Teri wrapped her arms around his waist and cuddled closer.

"You just need to relax," Brian said softly. "Let Dr. Michaelson fix you up."

"But the dishes . . . and I didn't even model my sexy new silk outfit for you yet," Teri murmured, curling her fingers around his neck.

"Model your birthday suit," Brian muttered huskily. He scooped her into his arms and carried her into the bedroom. "That's the sexiest suit I ever saw."

A half hour later Teri went still atop him as the doorbell pealed. "Let's just ignore that," she said, leaning forward across him.

"Damned right we'll ignore it," Brian panted. He twined his legs about her, focusing on her breasts bobbing invitingly just out of reach of his mouth. He tried valiantly to concentrate on nibbling them as the doorbell rang again. And again.

"Fuck."

"That's what I'm trying to do," Teri groaned, sighing when Brian's lips ensnared her nipple just as chimes once more sounded throughout the apartment.

"Who the hell is it? If that's Josie, I'll kill her," she vowed.

Brian in exasperation tumbled from the bed and reached for his jeans.

Teri noted wistfully that his erection was gone. Gone but not forgotten, she hoped. She jumped up to throw on her pink chenille robe. Brian tugged on a plaid flannel shirt, buttoning it as he headed for the door.

What a time for company. Not only had she and Brian been in the middle of the best sex they'd had in a month, but the dirty dishes were still strewn all over the table and countertops, the casserole sat hardening next to the half-empty bowl of broccoli and wilted salad remains, and she'd forgotten that the day's newspapers were littering the sofa and coffee table, alongside her pile of Hudson's bags.

Please don't let it be Brian's parents, she prayed as

she rushed into the living room. Brian's mother was a fastidious housekeeper who never left the kitchen without Windexing all the counters. Teri grabbed the newspapers and stuffed them under the sofa cushions just as Brian unlatched the deadbolt.

"Yeah?" Brian said, pulling the door open.

"Yes?" His tone changed as he saw the couple in the dimly lit hall wasn't one of their friends or anyone he recognized.

"We're here to see Gina—I mean, Teri," the woman said hesitantly. Teri stood behind Brian like a deer caught in the oncoming headlights of a semi. The woman in the doorway spotted her and cried out: "Gina . . . Gina, oh, my God, it is you."

Teri's heart seemed to stop as she gazed at the two achingly familiar faces peering at her with a mixture of joy and uncertainty.

The young woman dodged past Brian and hurtled herself straight at Teri. "Gina, Gina," she sobbed repeatedly.

Teri caught her in her arms.

"Celia," she whispered. She closed her eyes and felt her sister's arms tight around her, breathed in the familiar scent of English lavender soap Celia had always favored as a teenager. She touched the rough wool of Celia's car coat, as if to assure herself that her sister was really there.

"I thought I'd never see you again," Teri said.

As Celia buried her face against Teri's shoulder and cried with joy, Teri looked beyond at the handsome blond man in the olive-drab trench coat who was staring at her with burning gray eyes.

Andrew. Oh, God, it *was* Andrew.

Teri started to shake.

"Do you mind if I come in?" The blond man spoke quietly to Brian, who was gazing at Teri and Celia in complete bewilderment.

"Who are you?" Brian demanded. "And who the hell is Gina?"

The blond man's glance swept from Teri to Brian and back. "You know her as Teri Mathews. We knew her as Gina Randazzo."

He extended his hand. "I'm Andrew Leonetti, an old friend of the family." He studied Brian's puzzled face with sympathy. "Got a beer, buddy? I think it's going to be a long night."

Teri lived through the next hour in a haze. She barely spoke, she barely breathed. She sat hand in hand with Celia, the sister she hadn't seen in ten years, murmuring clipped explanations to all Celia's questions. Even to her own ears her voice sounded thin and mechanical. Brian sat across from her in stunned silence. From the corner of her eye she could see Andrew near the window, watching her, carefully keeping his emotions in check.

She couldn't look at him. She didn't have to. The image of his face had been emblazoned in her mind all the years they'd been apart. She could feel the heat of his eyes upon her as she huddled on the sofa wearing nothing but her pink chenille robe.

"So let me get this straight," Brian said, his tone strained and incredulous as he got to his feet and paced around the sofa. "You tripped some old nun outside the confessional, she fell down, and you ran away from home? And changed your name? And haven't bothered to call your family in ten years to tell them you're still alive?"

How could she explain? There was so much more, but she couldn't tell him the rest. Not now. Not ever. The real truth about why Gina Randazzo ran away was something she could discuss only with Andrew. Or could she?

In her mind's eye she saw the elm trees looming overhead, felt the soft fibers of the red and black woven blanket beneath her legs, heard the distant laughter of the parish children playing tag around the picnic tables.

Brian was staring at her as if he'd never seen her before.

"Brian." Teri swallowed. She had to say something to try to help him understand. All this time he'd believed she was an only child, raised by her grandmother in the Upper Peninsula after her parents were killed in a plane crash when she was four. She'd told Brian that after her grandmother had died, there was nothing to keep her in the small town of Houghton. No relatives except distant cousins in Canada. So she'd moved to Detroit to work her way through Wayne State University—leaving small-town life behind.

He must feel as if he's looking at a stranger, she thought. Her hands were clammy within the grip of Celia's soft, tapered fingers. "There's no way I could ever explain it," she started feebly. "I was sixteen. I panicked. I didn't stop and think—I just ran."

"But ten years, Teri. You never thought about it afterward? Never thought to call your parents so they wouldn't worry? Never bothered even to tell me?" Growing more and more angry, Brian came to a halt beside her, and she saw the betrayal and disillusionment clouding his face.

"Brian, listen . . ."

She stood up, but Brian had turned away. He grabbed his coat from the hall closet and spoke without looking at her. "I need some fresh air. I'm sorry, I just can't deal with all of this right now. Don't wait up. Like the man said, it's going to be a long night."

He didn't slam the door. He closed it. But the finality of the latch clicking chilled her heart. She wanted to run after him, but what good would it have done?

She stared into Celia's puffy, tear-streaked face. Ten years had added several pounds to her sister's once-svelte figure, but Celia was still as pretty as she'd been at fourteen. Spiraling chestnut curls framed her face, which was heart-shaped, like Teri's. Her chestnut eyes were still so vividly expressive that looking at her sister now, Teri knew that Celia's heart was in as many pieces as her own.

All these years Teri had imagined how much agony her disappearance had caused her close-knit family. But Celia had lived through it, and every scar was visible in her sagging shoulders and the hollows under her eyes.

"Celia," Teri whispered, "tell me about Ma and Daddy, and Tony, and Dina and everyone. My God, you don't know how I've been dying to know."

"But not dying enough to call us, Gina."

Teri's eyes overflowed with tears. "Don't hate me, Celia. I suffered too."

"Do you know what those Christmases were like? Easter? Ma's birthday? *Ma's funeral?*"

Teri flinched as though she'd been struck. The color drained from her face. "Ma? Oh, God, Celia, Ma's dead? What happened?"

"She was hit by a drunk driver. Three years ago." Celia scowled at the tears streaming down Teri's cheeks. "Sure, cry. She cried enough over you. But you couldn't even take the time to call and let us know you were alive. Why?"

Teri shook with grief. *How could Ma be dead?*

"*Why?*" Celia demanded.

Teri blurted out, "I *did* call. But Grandma Parelli answered the phone. . . . I panicked. I knew she'd ask me a thousand questions. I couldn't deal with it."

"*You* couldn't deal with it?" Celia glared at her. Her voice rose. "Can you even begin to imagine how many hospitals we checked, how many people we called, how many places we looked? Father Andrew can tell you. We searched for *years*."

"Oh, Ma," Teri wept. "Ma, forgive me."

Andrew came forward and stood behind Celia, gently clasping her shoulders, but his eyes never left

Teri's face. "Celia, this is a difficult time for everyone involved. There'll be plenty of opportunities to work through all of the emotions, through all the lost years."

Teri clung to the sound of his low-timbred voice, and willed time to melt away. Father Leonetti, the sensitive young priest she had first encountered at Mass at St. Anne's, had always exuded comfort and wisdom. Right now she needed both. She wondered how he could be so detached from all of this that he could calmly counsel Celia. Had he set aside his own inner turmoil? Or isn't he feeling anything of what I'm feeling?

"You've just given Gina some very hard news," Andrew continued in his quiet way. "I think this is not the time to attack, but to comfort each other."

Sobbing, Celia raised a tormented face to stare at him. "I'm sorry, Father," she gasped. "I can't just yet. I love her, but I could kill her for all she's put us through." With that, she fled into the bathroom and slammed the door.

Teri covered her face with her hands and wept. After a few moments she looked up at Andrew through her tears and read the compassion in his eyes. Wordlessly, he held out his arms to her, and in an instant she flung herself into them.

She sobbed until she was spent. His warm fingers stroked her hair as he held her.

"Andrew . . . I mean, Father," she broke off in confusion.

"It's only Andrew now, Gina. I've left the priesthood."

Teri shook her head slowly, trying to take in this revelation. "When?"

"Two months after you left."

He nodded toward the closed bathroom door and lowered his voice. "We've got to talk alone, Gina. Not tonight. Meet me tomorrow, please." She heard desperation and determination in his words. Gazing into those intense gray eyes, Teri felt herself being sucked into a whirlpool of emotions.

"Tomorrow," she said, trying to keep her voice steady.

Brian, forgive me.

"There's a Burger King a few miles from the beauty shop where I work," she went on. "The lunch crowd is gone by one-thirty. I can meet you then."

God, forgive me.

Teri took a deep breath. "We do need to talk, Andrew. But I'm scared you won't like what I have to say."

His gray eyes bored into her with the same directness she had never forgotten. He must be in his midthirties by now, Teri realized, staring at the slight, fine lines beginning to form around his eyes. Some of the earnest boyishness was gone, but he was still achingly handsome—tall, lean, with a strong face and an air of solid goodness about him. The nearness of him once again was more than she could bear. This was really happening—she wasn't dreaming. She felt as if her legs were about to buckle under her and fought to keep her grip on reality.

How would she tell him? How in heaven's name would she tell him what she'd done?

The bathroom door creaked open. Celia appeared, her face red and swollen from crying. She tried to look at Teri, but couldn't and stared instead at the framed Montreaux Jazz poster on the dining room wall.

"I know Father Andrew is right, and I'll try, Gina, I really will," she said slowly. She picked up her coat from the dining room chair. "But I think we've said all we should for tonight. I'm going back to the motel to phone Daddy and tell them all that we've found you." She hesitated. "Can I call you tomorrow?"

Teri rubbed her eyes and pressed her fingers against her forehead. "Of course. Come for dinner. Both of you."

Suddenly, she ran to Celia and clutched her hand. "Try to forgive me," she begged.

Celia's fingers closed tightly for a moment around hers before they pulled away. "I'm trying, Gina. We're all going to try."

Andrew touched Teri's shoulder. "Tomorrow," he said purposefully.

Teri met his gaze in silent acknowledgment.

The moment they were gone, she began pacing frantically around the apartment. *What a pigsty. What a mess. It will take me hours to clean this up.*

Anything was better than thinking through what had just happened.

She began furiously loading the dishes into the dishwasher. She scooped the remains of the casserole into a plastic container, then changed her mind and dumped the glop down the sink. She scrubbed the casserole dish, dried it, and stuck it in the refrigerator—then stood stock-still, staring at it. *Oh, God, I'm going crazy.*

She glanced at the kitchen clock. Anxiety clawed at her. It was 11:45. Where had Brian gone? Was he coming back?

She ran to the bedroom, opened the drawer in her nightstand, and frantically searched for the crystal rosary beads buried beneath receipts, rubber bands, and canceled checks. Clutching the rosary, she dropped to her knees beside the bed like she had when she was a little girl. The words tumbled brokenly from her lips.

"Forgive me, Father, for I have sinned."

Chapter Thirteen

Teri picked nervously at the garden salad on the tray in front of her and wondered why she'd bothered ordering it. The steaming coffee was all her stomach could handle right now. The prospect of telling Andrew the truth about the past had robbed her of all appetite.

She glanced at her watch. One forty-five. Maybe he wasn't coming. Maybe she wouldn't have to tell him after all. Her stomach roiled with tension. If he didn't show up by two, she'd leave. Hilda had scheduled a 2:30 for her today with Mrs. Campbell, and of all Teri's customers, she was the biggest tipper, especially around holiday time.

Yeah, sure. Teri gulped down the coffee, burning her tongue. She knew there was no way she'd leave without seeing Andrew.

The Burger King was rowdy with kids, all ages, all sizes, racing up and down between the tables, badgering their parents for another order of fries, more ketchup, or pie for dessert. One little boy slipped in a puddle of spilled orange pop and stumbled into Teri, bumping against her arm. Coffee sloshed all over her salad.

"Sorry," he giggled, straightening the Simpsons cap on his head. Teri couldn't help grinning back at his youthful exuberance as he dashed off in pursuit of his brother.

He looks about nine years old, she thought. Someday Brian and I will have a nine-year-old of our own, she told herself. Then her heart sank. Unless Brian never speaks to me again.

At the moment, that seemed like a distinct possibility.

He'd come in the previous night at 1:15 without saying a word and Teri had feigned sleep. He didn't even touch her when he climbed into bed, but turned over and seemed to go straight to sleep, while she stared at the digital clock for hours.

She'd thought they'd talk at breakfast, but he'd slipped out of the apartment while she was still in the shower. *Brian,* she thought, *if you knew the whole story, you'd hate me even more. You and Josie and Marie thought your birthday surprise was so perfect, but you didn't know it was going to turn our lives upside down.*

Even now her hands shook on the cup as she flashed on that moment when she'd seen Celia and Andrew beyond Brian's silhouette in the hallway. How could anything ever be the same again? Was she still Teri, or was she once again Gina Randazzo, or some strange combination of the two?

Her pulse quickened as Andrew hurried through the glass doors. He scanned the crowded booths, spotted her at her window table, and strode over.

"Sorry I'm late—it was tough ducking out on Celia. Let me just get a burger and some coffee and I'll be right back. Want anything?"

She shook her head.

Just like that, she mused, watching him cross to the counter. *He's going to get a burger and coffee.* It was so normal, so mundane that she had to fight back a hysterical laugh. After everything that had happened, all those years apart, he was behaving as if this were an ordinary lunch meeting between two old friends.

But there had never been anything ordinary about Andrew Leonetti—and there still wasn't, Teri reflected. Ten years' time had only enhanced his magnetic good looks, the purposefulness he embodied, the calm, clear-eyed way he naturally took charge.

When he returned to the booth with his tray, she braced herself. No chickening out. She had to tell him. As he slid into the seat opposite Teri's, his knee accidentally brushed against hers. She pulled her legs quickly aside, but not before the brief contact had sent heat through her.

"It's hard to know where to start, isn't it?" Andrew said softly. "I thought you might not come today, Gina."

She met his searching gaze with eyes that held both pain and determination. "Ten years ago I ran away from my problems because I didn't know how to deal with them. I still don't, Andrew, but this time I'm not going to run away."

He sighed. "I'm sorry for upending your life, Gina. I'm sorry for a lot of things. I know that this is a pretty big world, with lots of hiding places. I chose Phoenix for mine when I left Chicago. But when I saw you on the *Oprah Winfrey Show,* after searching for you for so long, I knew that God wanted me to find you again."

"How can you say that?" Teri demanded, leaning forward suddenly. "I don't think God wanted anything that happened between us."

He reached across the table and gripped her hand in both of his. "Gina, listen to me. Who are we to guess at God's will? All I know is that my feelings for you back then were true."

She tried to pull her hand back, but his fingers closed firmly around it, and his eyes locked with hers.

"So true and so strong," Andrew continued deliberately, "that after you left I had to rethink my entire life and what I wanted to do with it. I realized there were other ways to serve God and my fellow man besides the priesthood. And I knew that loving a woman and loving God did not have to be mutually exclusive."

"Andrew." Helplessly, she stared at him. She wasn't seeing the thoughtful, quiet-spoken man in the midnight-blue sweater who sat grimly before her, but the earnest young priest, fresh from the seminary, who had come to assist Father O'Neal in the parish, the movie-star-handsome young priest who was the secret, safe heartthrob of every girl in St. Anne's parish.

She'd come to know him first when she'd turned to him about Jason, a shy toddler she often baby-sat. She'd begun to notice bruises on him, and not knowing what else to do, she'd gone to Father Andrew with her concerns. To her relief, he'd taken her seriously. He had heard her out without interruption, calmed her down, offered her a cup of hot chocolate.

It had been raw and cold that day. Gina had run all the way to the parish, forgetting to put on her gloves and her hat, too upset by the bruises she'd seen on Jason to think of anything else.

Father Andrew had smiled at her while she sipped gratefully at the rich, steaming mug of chocolate. "You did the right thing coming to me, Gina," he'd said. "You're a very level-headed, sensitive girl and your parents must be very proud of you."

She wasn't quite sure about that. Grandma Parelli certainly wasn't proud of her. But at least Father Andrew had taken her worries seriously. That had been a tremendous relief. He'd also called on the family she'd told him about, making frequent visits to check on the child's welfare, all the while establishing a bond of trust with the parents. Andrew had moved slowly but surely. He'd drawn his own conclusions about the troubled young family, had shepherded them into counseling, and in time Gina saw the bruises fade, with no new injuries. And Jason began to blossom into an affectionate and far happier child.

The experience drew her closer to the dedicated young man who had listened to her concerns with such a ready ear, and had acted upon them. Every time he saw her, he thanked her for her astuteness and sensitivity, and assured her that the family was getting much-needed help because she had possessed the wisdom to come forward. He became someone she could really talk to, someone who seemed to understand her as a person. She was convinced he was the most wonderful man in the world.

The boys her age seemed immature by comparison, and besides, they were interested in only one thing. Gina wondered a lot about sex, but she'd heard enough warnings about where making out in the backseat of cars would lead.

She didn't have to worry about anything like that with Father Andrew. Her secret fantasies about him could never be acted upon. He was so committed to God, he would never even suspect the feelings that tingled through her when she was with him. At twenty-five, he was dreamily mature, handsome, kind, and attentive.

But it was more than that. Andrew was more than that.

As months went by, her feelings began to change in ways she hadn't expected. She wasn't sure when her initial schoolgirl crush gave way to deeper feelings, but the more time she spent with Father Andrew, the more she came to understand the man inside the Roman collar. She was afraid of all the new feelings surging through her. Was she going crazy to feel so strongly for a priest? She admired him, yes. She valued his friendship and approval, yes. But sometimes Gina felt that something inside him seemed to reach out to her. She began to stay away.

But one day, so excited she gave in to impulse,

Gina had dashed straight to the rectory from school, waving the first-place ribbon for her Optimist Speech, which Andrew had encouraged her to write.

"I won!" she cried, dropping her books on his desk. "You were right—I didn't think I had a chance!"

"Good girl!"

Andrew had grinned at her exultation, and come around the desk to fling his arms around her in congratulations. But the hug had swiftly changed from one of avuncular affection to something else. Suddenly, his arms tightened around her and she found herself held close and hard against his crisp black shirt, held in arms that were solid and strong. She had tensed at the sudden enveloping closeness and looked up quizzically into his beaming face.

All at once the bright smile vanished from his eyes —replaced by a yearning that only deepened as his lips slowly lowered to meet hers. That kiss, sweeter than honey, stung them both back to reality, and they broke apart. Even with the back of her hand pressed tightly against her mouth, she could still feel the heat of that kiss.

"No . . . it's wrong," she had whispered. "Why did you . . . ?"

"Gina," Andrew's eyes had held such confusion, such torment as she had never seen. "I'm sorry . . . I shouldn't have . . . you'd better go."

Of course she'd gone. She'd run out as if a swarm of wasps pursued her. But in the crowded room she shared with Celia and Lena, she'd leaned her cheek against the wood-framed windowpane and replayed that kiss in her mind over and over.

After that she'd avoided even casual contact with Father Andrew. Every time his fingers brushed her mouth when he placed the host on her tongue during Communion, she trembled. When she tried to pray for forgiveness, she felt only more wicked. *It's not true,* she thought desperately when Grandma Parelli's face loomed accusingly inside her closed eyelids. *I'm not like Aunt Gertrude. I can't be.*

I'm worse.

Because she wasn't truly sorry, not deep down where it counted. She wanted Andrew to hold her, to kiss her again. And again.

To make matters worse, she'd not only lost the chance of ever being in his arms again, she'd also lost the true friend who had come to mean so much to her.

It was in late spring at the parish picnic that they stopped avoiding each other. While everyone else was playing softball or grilling hot dogs, Father Andrew asked her to take a walk with him while he collected twigs the children could use to toast marshmallows.

Gina pulled up the fleece hood of her sweatshirt and glanced around to see if anyone was paying attention. No one was. Even her mother was preoccupied with setting out the coleslaw and potato salad.

Her heart pounding, she followed him silently through the winding trees.

Andrew had obviously meant to clear the air, to return things to normal between them. But somehow—they were never sure afterward exactly how—their talk went askew and turned into a tortured confession of love from each of them.

"I never, ever meant for any of this to happen," Andrew whispered brokenly. "You can't imagine how fervently I've prayed to God to forgive me, to guide me. But Gina, there's something between us that my soul can't deny. I've tried. As God is my witness, I've tried. . . ."

"So have I," she blurted out, covering her face with her hands. "Andrew, I'm so scared. Isn't this wrong?"

"I don't know, Gina, I don't know anything anymore. All I know is what I feel. Gina, my sweet, beautiful Gina, don't cry."

He'd brushed away the tear that streamed down her cheek. Then, somehow, the blanket that he brought to gather twigs in held the two of them instead, hidden away among the oaks and wildflowers of the forest preserve, cocooned beneath a soft, fragrant green canopy. They had made love tentatively at first, then with an innocent, eager passion that left no room for fear or doubt or hesitation.

That brief enchanted half hour was the most vibrant of Gina's life. And when it was over, guilt nearly paralyzed her.

When she and Andrew returned to the picnic site, she was sure everyone could see the guilt on their faces. But Father O'Neal merely tossed Andrew the bag of marshmallows, and her mother called to her to fetch Lena's jacket from the car.

Maybe they don't know, but God does, she thought frantically. She'd go straight to hell, she was sure of it. And she'd drag Andrew down into the fires with her.

Gina didn't sleep a wink that night or the next. Over and over she counted her rosary beads, begging God for forgiveness and finding none. Her chest hurt so much, she could scarcely breathe. Grandma Parelli was right all along, she realized despondently. How many commandments have I broken? How can I ever set foot into St. Anne's again?

But she had to. She had to go to confession and beg God to release her from this sin.

But she couldn't confess to Father O'Neal about the sin she'd committed with his own chosen assistant. She had to confess to Andrew himself.

In the confessional, she managed to keep from crying all the way through, until she heard his voice crack as he absolved her.

"Go in peace, my child, and sin no more."

She wondered, heartsick, if he really meant it. Did he truly wish that they should never repeat what they'd done in the woods, or did the words of passion he'd spoken to her that day reflect the wishes of his heart?

She fled the confessional, convinced that nothing worse in life could ever befall her.

But she was wrong.

When she missed her period, a sickening fear seized her. Maybe it was nerves that was making her late. She'd read in a magazine that stress could alter a woman's cycle. She began praying more desperately than ever, promising God that she would never even *think* about Andrew again if only He would let her period start.

She found herself running to the bathroom every hour to check her underwear.

She felt nauseated. From nerves, Gina told herself while she washed the breakfast dishes and handed them to Celia to dry. All around her in the kitchen the smell of bacon and pancakes lingered, making her want to retch. Her younger brothers and sisters whirled raucously past as they grabbed up lunch boxes and schoolbags and tumbled out the back door. She couldn't be pregnant, Gina insisted to herself as Celia nagged her to hurry. She was only five days late. That was far too soon, she was sure, for morning sickness.

The next few days crawled by. Then three weeks had passed and Gina could bear the anxiety no longer. She rode the bus to a drugstore five miles from home. No one would recognize her there, no one would see her purchasing the home pregnancy test.

It was agony waiting until the following morning to perform the test. And the entire time she was dipping the test stick into the urine sample, Tony was banging on the bathroom door, screaming that he had to pee. She tried to hurry, but her hands shook so badly, she knocked over the urine cup. As urine splashed all over the floor, Gina bit back tears of dismay. Cleaning up the bathroom floor, she realized that now she'd have to wait another day and try the whole thing over again.

She wanted to die.

The next morning the results showed her what she

already knew deep in her heart. She was pregnant with Andrew's baby.

No one would forgive her for this sin. The scandal would destroy her family.

Thoughts of her parents' devastation filled her with dread. They would weep with shame when they knew. Her mother, so deeply religious that she attended daily Mass and cooked for the rectory . . . How would her mother ever be able to face the other parishioners again? And her father . . . Gina couldn't bear to think of her soft-spoken, hardworking father, president of the Knights of Columbus and so proud of his well-mannered brood of children, discovering that his oldest daughter had disgraced the family and the church— and herself—beyond repair.

And Grandma Parelli would never speak to her again.

Scandal. Gossip. Shame.

Her weakness in the face of temptation had brought all of this down on her family. And there was no way out.

Terrified, Gina feigned sickness when everyone left for school that day. Her mother looked in on her before departing with Grandma Parelli to do the weekly marketing.

"You're awfully pale, Gina. Here, I brought you some bay leaf tea. It'll settle your stomach."

"Thank you, Ma," Gina managed to whisper from beneath her huddle of blankets. From the doorway, Grandma Parelli's eyes bore into her.

"I'll be back in an hour. Will you be okay?"

"I'll be fine."

But she would never be fine again. The minute Gina heard the door thud shut and realized she was alone in the house, she gave way at last to the frantic sobs she'd been damming up inside of her. She flung on clothes and made her way to St. Anne's.

Andrew will know what to do, she thought wildly,

running through the hazy June sunshine. She clung to her only thread of hope. *I have to talk to Andrew.*

Why does he have to be a priest? The question seared her heart as she hurried across the empty church parking lot. If only he were any other man, there would be a solution. They could get married. It would be embarrassing, and some people might tick the months off on their fingers and guess the truth when the baby came, but at least it would all blow over. And she and Andrew could be together.

He was the only man she would ever love. Gina wanted to be with him so badly, she could hardly breathe. All this time she'd forced herself to stay away from him had been torture. She'd dreamed about him, thought about him, and fantasized about him, even while watching him say Mass.

She'd even been jealous of God for having first claims on Andrew. It wasn't fair. She loved him, but she couldn't ever have him.

By the time she reached the rectory, Gina's cheeks were flushed and she felt ill. She stumbled up the stairs, but couldn't will her finger to the doorbell. What if Father O'Neal answered? What if Andrew wasn't there?

He wasn't. No one answered the peal of the bell. Desperation washed over her as she ran to the side door of the church and hurried inside toward the bank of candles flickering before the statue of the Virgin Mary.

But instead of Andrew, she found herself face-to-face with Sister Mary Frances, who was placing fresh, fat votive candles into the red glass cups.

"Why aren't you in school?" the wizened nun demanded, gesturing with her black wooden cane.

Sister Mary Frances had recently undergone a hip replacement operation, and was unsteady on her feet, even with the aid of the cane. The kids snickered that it was really a broomstick and warned the youngest ones that Sister Mary Frances was actually a witch who could fly in their window at night to carry them off if they didn't finish all their homework. The strange thing was, the older kids half believed it themselves. With her insistence on a billowing black habit instead of modern street clothes, her straggly gray chin hairs and surly disposition, Sister Mary Frances seemed more a mistress of the devil than an angel of God.

"I . . . I need to see Father Andrew, Sister," Gina stammered.

The nun's sharp, beady eyes narrowed. "He's the last person you need to see. You and those ignorant giggly girls who flock around him so shamelessly should spend more time asking God to give you pure thoughts than chasing after a man of the cloth."

"But Sister . . . there's this problem . . . and I . . . can't discuss it with anyone else."

"Father O'Neal is in the confessional," Sister Mary Frances shot back, wagging an arthritic finger. "Anything you have to say to Father Leonetti can certainly be said to him."

Helplessly, Gina clutched the altar railing. "I really prefer . . ."

"Ha! Shameless little strumpet," the nun muttered almost under her breath. "It's just as I thought. You only want to run after Father Leonetti, like all the others."

Unable to face her a moment longer, Gina turned toward the door. Sister Mary Frances rounded the altar railing with surprising agility and blocked her way. "You go in there and confess your problem to Father O'Neal right now, young lady. If it's something so urgent that you had to miss school, and probably lied to your mother about it too, then you just march yourself in there and speak to the pastor."

"No, you can't make me," Gina cried in panic. She felt that if she said one word to Father O'Neal, he would instantly detect the wickedness in her soul. He

would despise her. And he would send Andrew packing
so fast, the parish would talk about it for months.

She had to get out of there. She couldn't breathe.
The faint sweet smell of stale incense suffocated her,
the candles flickered dizzyingly, and Sister Mary Frances loomed before her, leering at her contemptuously.

She charged forward, attempting to brush past the
nun, but Sister Mary Frances struck out with her cane,
trying to block Gina's way. "Oh, no, you don't, young
lady," the nun began, but the words ended on a choked
sound as the cane swung wide and she lost her balance.
She crashed to the floor with a shriek of agony.

"Oh, my God," Gina cried, starting back to help
the nun to her feet. Father O'Neal rushed out of the
confessional on hearing the commotion, an expression
of alarm on his round, kindly face, but before he could
reach Sister Mary Frances, she brandished her cane in
fury at the girl approaching her.

"Stay away! Don't touch me," she hissed. "You're
nothing but a child of the devil!"

Gina froze. The nun cried out to Father O'Neal,
her voice ringing through the empty church. "Look
what she's done, Father, that wicked child!"

Gina saw shock register on the priest's face and
could bear no more. She broke and ran. All the while
she fled down the shady tree-lined streets, she kept
hearing Sister Mary Frances's scream of pain reverber-
ate in her head, kept hearing those accusatory words
flung at her with such venom. It was true, she thought
as she nearly dashed out in front of a delivery truck.
Sister Mary Frances had merely confirmed what her
grandmother had always suspected. She was evil. She
had entertained wicked thoughts and engaged in
wicked deeds and there was no hope for her.

By the time she reached home, she'd decided that
her family shouldn't have to suffer humiliation because
of her sins. There was only one thing left to do . . .
one thing she must do. She had to leave. The sooner

the better. If no one else knew she was pregnant, no one else would get hurt. Not her parents, not her brothers and sisters, not Andrew.

If she disappeared, there would be no scandal. No venom from Grandma Parelli. There would be pain because she was gone, but it would be nothing compared to what they would suffer if she stayed. *Besides, I'd die if I had to stay here knowing I could never have him.*

And so she'd gone, catching the Greyhound bus to Pittsburgh, the farthest from Chicago her baby-sitting money would take her.

She'd left her parents a note telling them she knew they wouldn't understand why she had to leave, but that she loved them.

She'd asked them to remember her in their prayers.

Now, staring at Andrew in the middle of this Burger King, an older and different Andrew in his casual sweater and slacks, she knew just how misguided her thinking had been all those years earlier. She should have stayed, told the truth, and dealt with the consequences.

Well, she'd have to deal with them now—all of them. Consequences regarding Andrew, and Brian, and her own life. She couldn't go on living this lie.

"Andrew," she said after he'd had a chance to finish his burger, "can we go for a walk? You deserve to know why I ran away all those years ago. It's not just because we made love," she said quickly, flushing.

"We *were* in love," he corrected her.

She glanced around at the crowded restaurant. "Andrew, there's more. I . . . can we go outside?"

He drained the last cold dregs of his coffee. "Let's go."

They walked several blocks without speaking, passing neighborhood strip malls replete with video stores, cleaners, and pharmacies. The temperature had risen, and the previous day's snow was melting into slush. Patiently, Andrew waited for her to begin.

"You know what happened in the church with Sister Mary Frances, don't you?" Teri asked at last.

"I heard about it. Everyone heard about it. Even your family thought you ran off because of the way she treated you. Father O'Neal was appalled."

"And you," Teri asked, "what did you think, Andrew?"

His voice was grim, heavy. "I knew better. I knew it had to do with what was happening between the two of us. I could imagine your guilt, Gina, and your confusion. I hated myself for years for what I'd done to you. I was a grown man, a priest, and I should have been strong enough to keep from acting on my love for you."

"There's something you don't know, Andrew. The reason I went to St. Anne's looking for you that day. I needed to tell you something." Teri stopped walking and faced him as traffic whizzed by on Seven Mile Road.

"I was going to tell you that I was pregnant."

Chapter Fourteen

Andrew's face whitened beneath his tan. "Gina . . ."

"It's Teri now. I started a new life when I ran away, with a new name, a whole new appearance. I dyed my hair blond, cut it short, and then counted the days until the baby came."

"You—we—had a child," Andrew said, raking a hand through his hair. He stared, unseeing, at the piles of dirty slush around them, letting her bombshell sink in. "Thank God you didn't go through an abortion," he whispered.

"I went through an adoption. It was probably just as painful," she replied in a low tone, not looking at him. She dug her fingernails into her palms, trying not to let her emotions swamp her. The last thing she wanted to do was break down now. "The day I signed the adoption papers I thought I'd never know another day's happiness." She swallowed and went doggedly on. "Giving up our son was the hardest thing I've ever done."

Andrew spun away from her, his shoulders tense with silent grief. Teri went on softly.

"I saw him only once, Andrew. But I'll never forget

how tiny and beautiful he was. How much he looked like you."

"Oh, my God, I can't believe what you went through all alone. If only I had known, things might have been so different." He turned back and clasped her by the shoulders, his fingers biting through the wool of her coat. "We could have been married," he groaned, and pulled her close. She could feel his body heat, feel the pounding of his heart. "We could have raised our son together instead of wasting all these years and ending up this way—standing here like two damned strangers!"

It was true, and knowing she had thought the same thing a thousand times herself made her crumble at last. Suddenly she was clinging to him as she had the night before, but this time they were comforting each other. Not with words, just with the closeness of their bodies, her head resting against his shoulder, her heart beating against his—aching for what might have been.

"Where was this?" he asked as a sudden blast of wind ruffled her dark hair. "Where did you go? I want to know everything that happened." He grabbed her arm and pulled her along the street into the fiberglass bus shelter at the corner. They sat on the cold metal bench, away from the gusting wind, and she told him the story she'd kept locked in her heart all these years.

When she was finished, Andrew took her hand. He held it tightly, his fingers strong and encompassing. "So he was adopted through the St. Philomena Home for Unwed Mothers in Pittsburgh?" he asked slowly.

Teri nodded.

"We have to find him."

"No!" She stared at him. "No, Andrew. We can't—Brian doesn't know."

His eyes narrowed. "To hell with Brian. Don't you want to see your son? Don't you want to know where he is, if he's happy?"

"Yes," Teri breathed. "And no." She wrenched her

hands away and stood up, pacing the length of the enclosure as she grappled with her own ambivalence. "Andrew, don't you think I've wondered about him every day for the past nine years? And about you? Do you know what it's like to stir all of this up again after all this time—and then there's Brian . . ."

"Look, if Brian truly loves you, he'll be man enough to stand by you," Andrew said roughly, and there was a hard glint in his eye that Teri had never seen before. "And if he can't—or won't—then, dammit, I will!"

His arms went around her so quickly, Teri gasped, and then he was kissing her and it was as if the years fell away, as if she'd never been kissed by any other man. Teri's lips melted against his and she hungrily clutched his lapels, drawing him closer, ever closer. A wildfire she'd thought long banked leapt to life within her. Her fingers slid upward to touch his face, stroking, reveling in the feel of him, her tongue tasting the warm heat of his mouth. She wasn't cold anymore, and she didn't feel alone.

But reason came spinning back. Abruptly, she pulled away. "Andrew, don't. I'm getting all mixed up —I'm engaged to Brian . . . we can't . . ."

"Sorry." But he didn't look sorry, Teri thought, he looked ready to carry her off to the nearest hotel, order a bottle of champagne, bar the door, and spend the weekend in bed.

Tenderly, he touched her cheek. "I've waited ten years to hold you in my arms again. Do you think I'm going to give up without a fight? It won't be easy, but I can wait a little longer while you sort out your feelings." His gray eyes flashed into hers. "Mine don't need any sorting."

Teri felt as if the ground were sliding away beneath her feet. She tried to fix Brian's face in her mind while she stared at Andrew, but she couldn't even summon up his image. All she saw was Andrew, and that tiny baby she had given away to strangers.

"You've started a new life, a life here in Michigan with Brian. I went on with mine, but I never found anyone I loved as much as you. All I've wanted to do all these years is find you. In my mind's eye I carried the image of a beautiful, sensitive sixteen-year-old, mature far beyond her years. You've changed, Teri. You've grown, if possible, even more beautiful, more desirable. Teri, there's something between us, there always has been. I can't define it, and I can't deny it. I never could. Face it, Teri," he urged, "you know it's still there —I see it in your eyes. I felt it when you kissed me."

Teri took a deep breath. It was hard to be calm with Andrew standing there, looking at her with so much longing in his eyes. She was surprised at the effect he could still have on her despite her commitment to Brian.

"This isn't helping," she forced herself to say. If Andrew touched her again now, she didn't know what would happen. She took two steps back in the bus shelter and felt the coldness of the metal frame against her spine. "I need to get back to work . . . oh, my God, what time is it?"

It was 3:15. She'd missed her 2:30 appointment. "I've got to go," she told him, and hurried out into the street again. Andrew followed, falling into step with her as they half ran back to the Burger King parking lot.

"Look, I know how hard this must be for you. You've spent ten years hiding from the past, and now it's hitting you smack in the face. Let's not rush into anything. Right now I imagine you're still in a state of shock. It'll take time to let the dust settle, to work things through with your family, and I don't want to get in your way with all that. But I've got to get back to Phoenix in a few days. I'm teaching autistic kids there and it's tough on them if I'm gone."

Andrew paused beside the Volvo as Teri fumbled

for her keys. "Listen, I want your permission to institute a search right away for our son. Teri"—he held up a hand as she started to protest—"I can wait for you—I've already waited ten years. But knowing that our son, a nine-year-old boy, is out there somewhere, that's more than I can stand. I didn't know about him before, but now that I do, I can't rest until I'm sure he has a decent life."

The hell of it was, Teri knew exactly what he meant. How many nights had she wondered if her baby had warm clothes, a loving family, brothers or sisters, if he liked sports or music, if he was good at math. Had his parents told him he was adopted, and if so, did he ever wonder who his birth mother was and why she had given him away?

Teri gulped back tears as she unlocked the Volvo. While Andrew held the door open for her, she fidgeted with her purse, wrestling with what to say.

He waited in silence.

"All right." She was shaking, and not from the cold. "But remember, he's just a little boy. It would only hurt him if we were to barge into his life. We've got to think of *him* now, Andrew, and his parents, not ourselves."

"I know that."

"Let's just find out that he's happy and well, and then leave him in peace."

"Thank you, Teri." He kissed her gently on the cheek. "I still have some contacts through the clergy. I'll let you know as soon as I've found out anything."

That evening she sat at the kitchen table, disinterestedly pulling mushrooms off her pizza and nibbling them one by one. Brian hunched sullenly across from her, eyes fixed on the newspaper. The glib chirping of the six o'clock news anchor and the crisp rattle as Brian turned the pages of the *Free Press* were the only sounds in the room.

Teri felt as if she were about to scream. She tossed

her napkin on the table and stood up, speaking with forced calm.

"Brian, this isn't getting us anywhere. Tomorrow we're supposed to pick out our china and silverware at Hudson's and we're not even on speaking terms. You won't even look at me, for God's sake."

Brian lowered the newspaper and peered at her.

"I'm looking at you."

"Well, then talk to me."

"What do you think I'm doing?"

"Brian, I've got a lot to talk to you about, but it's not easy when you're looking at me that way and treating me like I'm some kind of criminal."

"Well, just how do you expect me to act, like everything is just peachy keen?" He slammed the newspaper on the table and slumped back in his chair. "And how should I treat you, like the girl of my dreams, the woman I loved, the woman I thought I knew? Should I act like I haven't had the wool pulled over my eyes for two years? I mean, what else could I possibly discover that would put me in a worse frame of mind than I already am?"

"Brian, please. I never meant to hurt you. Be fair."

"Like you've been with me?"

"Brian, dammit, this isn't easy. There's something I have to tell you, and after I do . . . well, if you still want to keep our appointment at the Hudson's bridal registry, fine—and if not . . ."

"Oh, I can hardly wait for this one." He sat staring at her, arms crossed defiantly against his chest. "What are you going—"

"*A baby, Brian.* A baby. That's what I'm going to talk to you about."

Brian's arms dropped. He leaned forward.

"You mean you're . . . ?"

Teri sank back into her chair. "No. I'm not. This isn't about our baby, Brian. It's about mine. I gave him up nine years ago. No one knew about him—not even his father," she whispered, clutching the table.

Brian looked as though he were about to topple off his chair. He jumped up so abruptly that the newspaper scattered to the floor. "Baby, Teri? A baby? I don't fucking believe this." He paced furiously to the window, where freezing rain was beginning to slash against the pane. After staring out for a moment into the wintry grayness, he whirled back, his face and neck as red as his sweater. "And just who the hell was this baby's father?"

Teri gazed at him in silent misery, then turned to study the cardboard pizza box.

"Well? Don't keep me in suspense. Who was the father?"

"Andrew," she said softly. "His father is Andrew Leonetti."

Brian stared at her in astonishment. "Leonetti?" He took two steps forward. "That guy who was here with your sister last night?"

Teri nodded, then lifted her chin to meet his dumbfounded stare.

"And Brian, there's something else. We've decided to try to find our baby."

Chapter Fifteen

The clangorous din of the jammed department store assaulted Teri's ears as she and Brian rode the escalator to Hudson's upper floor. But the silence between the two of them hadn't been breached all during the long drive out to Fairlane Mall, or when they'd parked the car on the outer fringes of the overflowing parking lot or even when they'd trudged through banks of slush to reach the brightness and warmth inside. Brian hadn't spoken more than five words since breakfast—but at least he was here, Teri reflected, yanking off her paisley scarf as she stepped off the escalator. *Maybe despite all his hurt and anger he still loves me enough to want to work things out.*

Why else would he be here to look at china patterns and bed sheets when he could be playing basketball with his buddies at the Y? Or checking out the new line at the tool and die shop?

"Can I help you?" offered a cheerful, middle-aged saleswoman in an ivory shawl-collared suit seated at the bridal registry computer.

"We're here to register our gift selections," Teri said, trying to smile, trying to summon up some of the joyful anticipation she'd felt only a short time ago, before her carefully planned new life had taken a very crooked turn.

"I'll need you to fill out these forms," the woman said warmly. She smoothed ash-blond hair back from a furrowed brow. "When's the happy day?"

"April thirteenth."

"Here's a pen. Now, now, young man," she chuckled up at Brian. "Don't look so glum. It's not as bad as you think it's going to be. Some of the grooms actually enjoy picking out items for their new home once they get started."

Brian was looking gloomily around. Teri managed a small smile. "He's not into shopping. I wasn't even sure he'd actually come along today. Right, honey?"

That got his attention. He hated when she called him honey.

Brian threw her a glance that would have vaporized a snowball. "I don't think I've ever let you down, *honey*," he said evenly.

Teri flushed, and scribbled more rapidly on the papers before her. The woman peered from one to the other, cleared her throat, and prattled on to fill the silence.

"Um, when you're done filling out all the information below the blue line, we'll type it up on the computer, and then you can take this list through the store and mark down everything you possibly think you'll need."

"An aspirin." Brian muttered under his breath.

"Excuse me, sir?" the woman asked with a blank stare.

"An iron," Teri said quickly. "We need a steam iron."

Without looking at Brian, she scooped up the forms and retreated to a small ivory table to finish filling them out. Brian paced alone through the shimmering aisles of china, sterling flatware, and crystal displayed under carefully angled spotlights.

They couldn't agree on anything that afternoon. Teri liked the Mikasa and Brian wanted Pfaltzgraff. She preferred lace tablecloths with intricate cutwork and he pushed for fifty-fifty polyester solid-color cloths, arguing: "Who do you think we're going to be entertaining —Fergie and Di? I thought you were practical. But then, I guess I thought wrong about a lot of things."

Teri stopped dead in her tracks and whirled around to confront him, nearly knocking over a crystal clock.

"That's enough, Brian. What are we doing here anyway? If this is how you really feel, maybe we should just call the whole thing off."

"Maybe you're right. But, gee, then we won't get our pictures in that magazine. And you'll have to give back all those clothes."

"Fuck the magazine, and fuck the clothes. And fuck you." She tossed down the silver napkin rings she'd been considering and tore the registry list from his hands. Gritting her teeth, she ripped it into bits of confetti, and flung them in his face.

"I thought I knew you too, Brian. I thought you'd stand by me no matter what. Guess I'm not the only one who thought wrong."

She bolted toward the escalator, furious beyond tears. Through a red haze of anger she dodged baby strollers and women balancing bulky coats and bulging shopping bags, while overhead "Winter Wonderland" tinkled through unseen speakers. Just as the tip of her red boot landed on the first step of the escalator, Teri felt herself yanked backward so forcefully, she nearly knocked into a gift display of sterling picture frames and bud vases.

Brian swore. "Where the hell do you think you're going?"

"Anywhere—as long as I don't have to see you!" Teri spat out, wrestling her elbow from his grip.

"Just stop a minute and listen to me, Teri." Brian hauled her out of the fray of staring shoppers and into the semiprivacy of a narrow hallway outside the rest rooms.

"Teri, I'm sorry. I know I'm acting like a real bastard, but all this stuff has really thrown me for a loop."

"Look, Brian, you know perfectly well I never meant to hurt you. . . ."

"But you *did* hurt me." Brian's face was taut with frustration. "You lied to me. You didn't trust me enough to tell me the truth. And maybe you didn't *love* me enough to tell me the truth."

"I do love you, Brian." Teri's knuckles whitened as she gripped her shoulder bag. "And you know it."

"Yeah? You could've fooled me."

Teri felt her anger fading. He looked so miserable that she suddenly wanted to throw her arms around him and comfort him. She stepped toward him, reaching out, but Brian backed away.

"I don't know, Teri. I don't know. Listen, can't we table all this gift-selection business for another day? I don't think either one of us is quite in the mood."

He was right about that. Teri didn't even have the heart to go back and ask that chirpy saleswoman for another form.

"Fine, let's get out of here," she muttered, and pulled her scarf from her pocket. "I just want to go home."

That night Celia joined them for dinner and campaigned throughout the evening for Teri to accompany her home to Chicago for a reconciliation with the rest of the family.

"Look, I talked to everybody last night and all they care about is seeing you. Dad hasn't stopped crying. Tony wanted to jump on the first plane out here, but I convinced him to wait. And Lena is eight months pregnant with her second kid—that first one, little Dino, is such a pisser, he'll win you over in a second. You come too, Brian. Everyone is dying to meet you. Not only do we get our sister back, but a new brother to boot."

Brian poured another splash of Chianti into Celia's glass.

"It sounds great, but don't count on my being able to get away until at least February. It's hard enough right now taking time off for that *Perfect Bride* thing while I'm trying to get this new job running smoothly at the shop."

"I can't believe my big sister is going to be in a magazine with Ana Cates and Eve Hamel." Celia speared a wedge of chicken cacciatore and popped it into her mouth, talking all the while. "But jeez, forget them. What about that gorgeous Senator Farrell and—be still my beating heart—Nico Caesarone." She rolled her expressive eyes, then leaned forward to grin coquettishly at Brian. "Hey, Bri, aren't you jealous?"

Brian set down his fork. He glanced across the table at Teri. "Not of them."

Abruptly, Teri pushed back her chair. "More broccoli, anyone?" she asked with forced gaiety. It was good to be with Celia, and Brian was making a heroic attempt to be pleasant and charming, to behave in front of her sister as if everything were fine, but beneath the glossy surface Teri knew that her relationship with Brian was seriously scarred. And she had a feeling it was going to take a lot of elbow grease to buff out the gouges.

Though Andrew was leaving for Phoenix the next day, he'd declined to join them for dinner, and she could only be relieved. Brian was trying hard, but she knew he would have rather broken bread with Saddam Hussein than sit down to dinner with Andrew Leonetti.

And sitting between Brian and Andrew at this table, attempting polite conversation while trying to digest chicken cacciatore, would have been for Teri only slightly more delightful than running naked through a jungle of cacti.

Studying her sister's animated face and thinking of how quickly soft-hearted Celia was moving toward forgiveness, Teri wondered what Celia would think if she knew the entire truth. It would have to come out soon enough. When she went back to Chicago, they would all want an explanation, and after all this time they deserved one.

Maybe Andrew would never find their son. Adoption records were closed, weren't they? How many people had she seen on television, lamenting their frustration in trying to locate their biological families? She probably had nothing more to worry about. She probably needn't ever have told Brian. But she was glad she had. No more secrets.

So maybe I'm not a "perfect bride," Teri thought. *But I still want to marry Brian and make him happy.*

Yet, when she was at the sink, filling the coffeepot, the memory of the way Andrew had kissed her the day before stole into her mind. Suddenly she felt again the heat of his mouth on hers and remembered how closely and protectively he had held her inside the bus shelter.

"Hey, watch what you're doing," Celia called out. "Haven't you heard about the water shortage in this country?"

Looking down, Teri saw she was letting enough water to fill three pots overflow the rim and slosh across the counter in an ever-widening puddle.

Brian tossed her a checkered kitchen towel and continued to clear the table. But he was watching her in a way that made her wonder if he'd been reading her mind.

She had to get a hold of herself. She had to forget about Andrew and concentrate on rebuilding her life with Brian. And if Andrew did find the child, well then, she'd just have to deal with that and not let it sidetrack her from becoming Mrs. Brian Michaelson.

Gina Randazzo is gone, she told herself, plugging the coffeepot into the wall socket. And so is the past.

She had to focus on the future. And that future was with Brian. But first there was something she had to do. She had to go home with Celia and make peace with her family.

"Celia, what time is your flight tomorrow?" she asked suddenly.

Her sister jumped up, her face lit with hope. "You're coming?"

"How big's your suitcase?"

"You'll fit," Celia laughed, running to Teri and hugging her. "Brian, quick—call the airlines before she changes her mind."

Somehow Teri got through the emotional hurricane of her family reunion. She spent an hour alone with her father before all her brothers and sisters and their spouses and children converged on Chicago's North Side in the small brick ranch-style house cluttered with bric-a-brac.

It was the hardest hour of her life. Her father listened in silence even when she told him about Andrew and about the baby. *"Dio mio"* was all he muttered when she was finished. Teri could have sworn he aged before her eyes, his body seeming to shrink with anguish like a shriveled balloon as he took in the full impact of her words.

"And the baby?" he managed to get out in a thick croak.

"Adopted, Daddy. Andrew is looking for him. We'll see."

Silence fell in the little living room. Teri studied the familiar swag curtains, doily-topped tables, and the White Sox souvenirs cluttering her father's corner desk.

"Basta, Gina. Enough." He grasped her hands in his giant ones. "I'll talk to your brothers and sisters about this later. But for tonight, we celebrate. Thanks be to God, our Gina is home."

And celebrate they did. Teri kept expecting her mother to sail out of the kitchen with a huge platter of homemade sausage, but it was Angela who brought the sausage, Celia who sliced the ham, Rosemary who made the cannoli, and her brother Tony's wife, Connie, who prepared the green beans and potato salad.

Relatives of relatives crowded into the modest home to visit her, and her baby brother, Vince, opened all the dining room windows to let the smoke out and fresh air in.

Teri wiped away countless tears as she watched her nieces and nephews tumble through the house the way she and her siblings once had. She had missed so much during these ten years, and yet she felt as if she'd never been away.

It was only as she lovingly placed a bouquet of pink carnations on her mother's grave that the fullness of what she had lost crushed her. She dusted off the snow accumulating on the headstone and traced her fingers over each letter of her mother's name.

"I'm sorry, Ma," she whispered. "I let you down. And now it's too late to make it up to you. I wanted to call, but I knew the love in your voice would force me to come home. And I just couldn't. I couldn't face Grandma Parelli, or Andrew, or all the questions. It was easier to bury Gina Randazzo than to admit that Grandma Parelli was right about her. And the longer I stayed away, the harder it became to pick up the phone and make that call. I don't know which I feel more guilty about, the pain I caused, or the pain I spared—or tried to spare."

Her father covered his face with rough, knobby hands as tears dripped onto his topcoat.

"She's looking down on you, Gina *mia*. She's smiling now because you're back with us and you're happy. That's all she wanted."

But I'm not happy, Teri thought as she moved haltingly to Grandma and Grandpa Parelli's graves and stared at the crosses carved on either side of the simple twin headstones. Her silent questions were tinged with bitterness.

Well, Grandma Parelli, is this the outcome you expected? Did it make you any happier gloating to everyone that you were right about me? I can only hope that in heaven you've found a way to make peace with Aunt Gertrude. I wonder if you have.

Teri's mind was still in turmoil as she flew back to Detroit. Things were so unsettled with Brian that she knew she'd feel like a total fraud when they went to Maui for the *Perfect Bride* shoot in three weeks. They were supposed to be a deliriously happy couple—so in love, they couldn't wait to get married. But Brian hadn't called during the entire three days she'd been in Chicago, and when she'd tried to reach him late one night, he hadn't been at home.

"I was bowling," he told her that evening while she unpacked her makeup from the overnight case. "If you don't believe me, check with Fred."

"I believe you, Brian. I trust you. And I hope one day you'll be able to trust me."

"I'm working on it," he said, and catching her off guard, leaned down to kiss her. He traced her lips with his finger. "Welcome home, babe."

Her heart leapt. "Does this mean you missed me?" she asked, throwing her arms around his neck. It felt like ambrosia to hold him again, to feel the silkiness of his hair, to savor the clean, earthy scent of him.

"Like crazy." Brian cupped her chin in his hand and stared into her eyes. "Look, I hate what's been going on between us. I want this to work—more than anything." He kissed her again, the fervor of it more telling than any words. Pulling her down on the bed alongside him with one hand, he used the other to toss her suitcase from the bed.

Together they sank into the floral chintz bedspread. Teri kicked off her half boots and wriggled delightedly over him, leaning on her elbows as she began unbuttoning his shirt. Brian's mouth was warm and hungry on hers, the way she remembered, the way she loved. They stopped kissing just long enough for Brian to rip off her sweater and skirt and for her to slide his jeans past his narrow hips and fling them onto the floor.

Teri felt swept along by a tide of relief so great that she was light-headed with desire. Every inch of her tingled with anticipation as Brian rolled her onto her back and eased a finger into the welcoming moisture between her legs. She arched to meet his hand and bit a row of hungry kisses along his shoulder as she rocked against him. Brian's mouth devoured hers ever more urgently, and she pushed aside his hand and reached between his legs to pull him to her. "Now, Brian, please," she panted, unable to bear another second until he was deeply inside her.

"Teri, oh, God, I love you. . . ." Brian's hoarse moan as he entered her shot delicious shivers down her spine, echoing the spasms of pleasure coursing through her. She never wanted this moment to stop. Brian filled her body and soul. Now she was certain. Now she had no doubts. This was where she belonged. In Brian's arms, in Brian's bed—in Brian's heart.

Afterward, when they both remembered they hadn't eaten dinner, Brian rummaged through the kitchen and returned to bed, tossing Teri a bag of potato chips, a can of diet Coke, and a Snickers bar. "Sorry, it's pretty bare in there. If you want, we can order a pizza. . . ."

"This is perfect," she said, tearing open the bag of chips. "Maybe I should leave town more often."

Brian plopped down beside her and grabbed a handful of chips. "Not if I can help it."

Taking a swig of beer while propped up beside her, Brian rehearsed how he would ask the question that had been weighing on his mind ever since she'd told him about that fucking priest. Just do it, he finally told himself.

"Do you still love him, Teri?" There, it was out. He felt her stiffen up beside him and held his breath.

"How could I, Brian?" she returned softly. "It's been ten years."

"So what? Not seeing you for ten years wouldn't change the way I feel. When you met with him the other day and actually told him about the baby—you must have felt something then." Brian set down the beer can and turned to study her face in the half shadows cast by the bedside lamp. "You can level with me, Teri. I won't lose my cool, but I've got to know. I've got to know how things stand."

Teri struggled up to a sitting position. Brian looked so worried, she wanted to reassure away all his fears, but that wouldn't be fair. She had to be honest. First of all with herself, and then with Brian.

"I care about Andrew," she said slowly, feeling her way. "It was tough telling him about the baby. It was awful, so emotional for both of us. But that's history," she went on quickly. "This is my life now—you, school, the new house we're working toward, our wedding. I love you, Brian. And I'm going to marry you. Period. Any more questions?" She cupped his face in her hands and smiled deep into his eyes.

"Yeah, just one." Brian tossed the empty bag of chips into the wastebasket. "Ready for round two?"

"And three and four," Teri tried to say, but his lips crushed hers, muffling out her words and then neither of them spoke again for a long time.

Yet later that night, as she at last drifted off to sleep, her naked body curled against Brian's lanky frame, Teri found Andrew hovering still in the corners of her mind. She couldn't forget the longing in his eyes or the urgency of his kiss. She couldn't help wondering if he'd found out anything about their baby. Knowing Andrew, remembering the driven young priest who'd protected that abused toddler, who'd worked so tirelessly on behalf of all of his parishioners, she knew he'd overturn heaven and earth in his search.

Running her fingers up and down Brian's muscled arm and studying the strong angle of his jaw outlined in moonlight, Teri wondered if her life would ever completely return to normal—the way it had been before she was thrust into the limelight on the *Oprah Winfrey Show*, before her carefully constructed life began to unravel like a slipped stitch, leaving a multitude of raggedly dangling threads.

As the days flew by, she busied herself almost obsessively with work and wedding plans. Every customer at the Hair and Now had a different opinion on what style dress would look best on her, which photographer she should hire, and which celebrity's autograph they wanted her to bring back from Maui—"but only if she could." Between coats of polish and idle chatter, Teri's thoughts vascillated from wondering if she'd ever get to meet her son to how he would look and what she'd ever say to him if she did—and then swung to the opposite extreme, hoping that Andrew's search would screech to a dead end.

Each time the phone rang, her breath caught in her throat and she had to force herself not to run headlong to answer it. Until she knew who the caller was, she didn't even dare look at Brian, but she sensed he was waiting as tensely as she. Despite their passionate homecoming reunion, things were still somewhat rocky between them. Sometimes Teri felt as if she were walking on clouds and sometimes she felt as if she were walking on eggshells.

She was on the phone with Brian's mother, discussing what to bring for Christmas dinner, when she heard the call-waiting signal. When she picked up the new call, Andrew's quiet voice sliced through her like a carving knife. "Teri, I've found him. I think you'd better prepare yourself for this."

Teri forgot all about her future mother-in-law dangling on the other line. She turned to stare blindly out the kitchen window at the jauntily capped snowman standing sentinel on the lawn across the street.

"Adam is living with a foster family outside Pittsburgh in Aliquippa," Andrew continued quickly. "He's lived with a lot of foster families these past nine years, Teri."

Teri's heart stopped. A dizzying nausea seized her. She gripped the phone with both hands. "What are you talking about?" she cried. *"Foster families?"*

"I mean the adoption never went through, Teri. Shortly after Adam's first birthday, the adoptive parents brought him back."

Horror descended upon her like a suffocating fog. This couldn't be true. All those years she'd imagined him nestled in a loving family, asleep at night with a familiar teddy bear, running through a flower-bordered yard alongside a rambunctious floppy-eared dog.

"Brought him back?" she repeated dazedly. "Why?"

"They couldn't deal with a less than perfect baby. They rejected him. Teri . . ." Andrew's voice broke as anguish overtook him.

"Our son—Adam—was born deaf."

Chapter Sixteen

A baby.

She couldn't believe her eyes. Eve stared blankly at the pink test strip in her hands. With a squeak of disbelief she cupped her hands protectively against her toned, flat belly and shook her head.

"Are you really in there?" she whispered. Joy spilled through her. She sank dazedly down on the closed lid of the toilet seat, the folds of her ivory silk robe trailing on the marble floor.

Nico would go wild when she told him. Coming from a family even larger than hers—ten kids—he was always talking about getting started on their own brood as soon as possible.

"But I don't think he intended it quite this soon," she reflected wryly, staring at herself in every angle of the mirrored walls. Nico was probably old-fashioned enough to care about what his relatives would whisper when she waddled down the aisle in August.

And the Estée Lauder people, Eve thought, seeing her contract shrivel into a wisp of smoke. What were they going to do with a pregnant spokeswoman? She quickly dismissed her fears. It's your face they want,

Evie B, not your bod. After all, they'll need only por-
trait shots, and if my boobs fill out a little more, so
much the better.

She danced into the living room and scooped Ragamuffin from his windowside perch, spinning the cat in
the air while she twirled around the room as if the
crystal ballerina sculpture had come to life.

"Listen up, Rags baby, your days as an only child
are numbered. You've got a brother or sister on the
way."

*There's no hope of reaching Nico at the hotel now,
not at four o'clock in the afternoon,* Eve thought. She
set Ragamuffin down on the sofa and hurried back into
the bedroom to dress. How would she be able to wait
until after the shower to tell him? Why did he have to
be in Italy *now*? It was going to be torture sitting
through an entire bridal shower with fifteen of her closest friends, corked up like a bottle of champagne, ready
to burst and overflow with the delicious announcement
that she was pregnant.

She wanted to call her mother. *And Nana,* she
thought with quickening excitement.

What would her father say? she wondered, pulling
a beaded lemon sweater dress from the closet. Finally
she could give him something Margo couldn't—his first
grandchild. When she sent him baby pictures, would he
finally value something of hers enough to put it on the
living room mantel next to Margo's mementos?

But there was no way she could make any calls
until after she told Nico.

Exhilaration bubbled through her.

How was she ever going to keep a straight face?

An hour later Eve could scarcely nibble at her vegetable frittata and the casaba melon wedge served up
on her friend Delia Terebelo's pale blue handcrafted
pottery plates. The coffee mugs steaming with cinna-
mon-laced cappuccino were of myriad shapes and sizes,
collected from galleries and art fairs all over the world.

Delia was a pencil-thin French model Eve had met early in her career, a Sorbonne graduate who spoke seven languages fluently and was convinced she had been Josephine Bonaparte in a previous life. They'd worked together on various jobs over the years, becoming even better friends when Delia had relocated to New York and signed on with the D'Arcy agency.

As Eve gazed around Delia's dining room table at the young women chattering animatedly, all of whom had been invited to the airy penthouse in her honor, she struggled against the temptation to blurt out her secret. After all, it was a rare enough chance to find them all together here in New York. Everyone seemed to have jobs coming up that would take them out of the country until August—that's why Delia had whipped up plans for a shower so far ahead of the wedding.

We're all here together, Eve thought. *It would be the perfect time to tell them.* God, how she wanted to do it.

But Nico would kill her.

Still, she could just picture each of their reactions: Elke Berlin, the vivacious brunette fashion editor of *Image* magazine, would instantly press her to do an exclusive mother-to-be glamour cover for next year's Christmas issue; MTV video director Cookie Palter's giant turtle-shaped silver and amethyst earrings would jingle as she jumped up from the table to wish her an effusive mazel tov and offer to film the birth, and Cynthia LaFond, the bohemian, silver-haired stylist Eve had met on her very first *Sports Illustrated* assignment, would begin spouting out a list of dozens of eccentric names. Then there was Jenna. Jenna Elliot, a lanky free-lance journalist best known for her pungent pieces in *Ebony* magazine, would immediately compute the baby's astrological future and advise Eve on the type of crystal she should wear for optimum health during her pregnancy.

Eve continued her silent game as she looked

around the table, savoring the imaginary reaction of each of her friends until at last she came to Monique.

Monique will probably shit in her pants wondering if I'll be allowed to fly to Maui during my first trimester and worrying that none of the clothes for the shoot will fit me—but all she'll do is smile serenely, blow me kisses, hint to be godmother, and insist on buying the baby's entire layette.

Eve grinned to herself as she watched Monique, dramatic as always, holding court at Delia's elbow. Monique's heart-shaped diamond necklace glinted at the throat of her turquoise fringed-suede jacket, catching the glimmering rays pouring in from the skylight above her. *She's in top form today,* Eve thought. She temporarily forgot her own news as Monique regaled them with details of her run-in with the insolent workman building an enclosure of some sort at her country home.

"And *then* he had the nerve to say that I should stick to sampling the perfume strips in *Perfect Bride* and stay the hell off his turf because I didn't know shit about architecture, landscaping, or carpentry and probably couldn't tell a plumb line from a molly to save my life. Did you ever? Who the hell does he think designed all those gardens around the house?"

She agitatedly stirred the whipped cream into her cappuccino and leaned toward Delia. "By the way, your father was a builder, you ought to know—what the hell *is* a molly?"

Cookie nearly choked on her melon, and Eve whooped along with everyone else.

"I'm serious. *What* is a molly?" Monique demanded.

Elke rolled her eyes.

"I'd have fired the son of a bitch on the spot," Delia declared, waving her spoon in the air. "Sounds too damn full of himself for my taste."

"But who the hell would I get to finish a job that's

three-quarters completed?" Monique demanded. She lit a cigarette and watched smoke curl upward through the hazy beams of light.

"Besides, he's not exactly hard on the eyes," she added casually.

A little too casually, Eve thought.

Delia lifted one sculpted brow. Cookie and Cynthia exchanged glances, then turned back to stare expectantly at Monique. The others all stopped chewing, stirring, swallowing, or chattering to peer at the dark-haired editor of *Perfect Bride*. Monique, oblivious, inhaled another long, slow drag on her cigarette before glancing up to find fifteen pairs of mascaraed eyes boring into her from around the room.

"Why are you all staring at me like that?"

"Details, girl, details," Elke purred.

"Does, ahem, Richard know about this hunky little handyman?" Cynthia drawled with a wink at Eve.

"What the hell is there to know?" Monique shot back. "The guy's nothing but an infuriating asshole." She shrugged. "A cute infuriating asshole, but an asshole just the same. So can the dirty thoughts, ladies. Come on, Eve." She pushed back her chair and rose, dismissing the matter as only Monique could. "Time to inspect your loot."

"That silver box is from Rory," Delia pointed out as Monique led Eve into the living room where presents were piled on a Chinese lacquered table. "She wanted me to tell you how pissed she was that her final run-through for *Driving on Shabbos* coincided with the shower, but she's counting on seeing all of us at the opening-night party tomorrow. God, for her sake I hope it's a success. Until this show came along, she hasn't even had a callback in the past eight months."

"Word is it's a dud," Jenna said bluntly. "Her Mercury is in retrograde—I *told* her to try to postpone the opening, but she couldn't convince the director that next week would be far more auspicious."

"Cookie," Monique interrupted as Eve reached for a pink-and-gold foil-wrapped package. "Grab your video camera. I want a permanent record of her face when she opens my gift."

And so Eve opened the elegantly wrapped boxes from Tiffany's and Bloomingdale's and Gucci, exclaiming over champagne flutes, crystal vases, Sèvres candy dishes, and personalized luggage. The expression on her face when she unwrapped Monique's sleek pink-and-gold box was one of shock. Nestled inside the gold tissue paper was a photo of a fourteenth-century Moorish castle, complete with fountains, mosaic-tiled courtyards, and a massive wooden drawbridge. Beneath the photo lay two open-ended first-class tickets to Seville. "Don't expect anything else for the wedding, darling. This is it for both. My way of making it up to you and Nico for that time in Milan when I interrupted your secluded weekend to bail me out of that mess."

"Monique, this is incredible!" Eve gasped.

"Happy honeymooning, darling. You have the castle and a staff of five for a week. Just give them six months' notice," Monique said. She kissed Eve and hugged her warmly. "Just go, relax, and make lots of Italian babies."

It was all Eve could do to keep from blurting out that bambino numero uno was on the way. Only thoughts of Nico's fury should he ever discover that Monique D'Arcy knew about his baby before he did kept her quiet. So she only kissed Monique's cheek and whispered, "You angel. After this, how could we do less than make you a godmother?"

Delia pushed a green envelope into Eve's hands. "Don't forget this one—last but maybe not least."

Eve was still laughing as she glanced down at the paper in her hands. The smile died from her lips, replaced by a look of terror.

"Catch her, Monique, she's going to faint!" Cookie

exclaimed, lowering the video camera as Eve swayed on her feet and the envelope fluttered to the jade carpet.

Monique eased her into the mahogany Queen Anne chair.

"I'm all right," Eve protested, but her voice was thin and reedy. The buzzing that had erupted in her ears when she saw the envelope began to fade. Suddenly, all she could think about was safeguarding the tiny life cocooned inside her.

Oh, God, my baby. I won't let him hurt my baby.

"No, I don't need any water . . . Elke, I'm *fine*," she said in a clearer, stronger tone. "But . . . no! Don't touch that envelope," she ordered, leaping up to intercept Cynthia's reaching hand.

Everyone gaped at her.

"What is going on with you, darling?" Monique asked slowly.

Eve looked around the room, fighting the impulse to hug her arms protectively across her belly. "Does anyone know how that envelope got here?"

"It was on the table with the rest of the gifts, that's all I know," Delia replied with a puzzled and very Gallic shrug. She handed Eve a glass of ice water and eased her back into the chair.

"You're shaking like aspic. Tell us what this is all about."

Eve silently regarded one worried face after another, weighing her response. Monique's penetrating gray eyes would see through any bullshit she might concoct. And suddenly she didn't want to concoct anything. She wanted to unburden the truth to her friends —and to get Tom Swanson up here as fast as possible.

"There's a bodyguard downstairs—*my* bodyguard," she said wearily. "Someone call the doorman and have him send up the blond guy in the camel-hair coat. His name's Swanson. I didn't see any reason to scare you guys, but some creep has been stalking me. That envelope is from him."

.   .   .   .

Monique poured two fingers of Glenlivet into a tumbler and gulped it down like apple juice. "Sure you don't want some? You look like you could use it."

Stretched out on the sofa, Ragamuffin curled on her stocking feet, Eve remembered the tiny life growing inside her and shook her head. "I'm fine. I'll be damned if Billy Shears is going to drive me to drink."

"How long has this shit been going on, and why didn't you tell me?" Monique asked. She plopped into one of the vanilla chairs, kicked off her scallop-vamped pumps, and leaned back, downing a refill of scotch.

"No one knows except the security firm. Not even Nico."

Monique set the tumbler down with a thud. "Why the hell not?"

"I didn't want him to be distracted when he's racing. I worry about him enough as it is. Besides, Monique, whoever expected this to drag on so long?"

"Exactly how long has it been?"

"A few months, I don't know. The problem is"— Eve sat up, pulling the meowing cat onto her lap— "despite the investigation, the bodyguards, everything I've done to protect myself, he keeps drawing closer. The letters and snips of clothing keep coming, more frequently than at first, and the messages are getting scarier."

The phone rang as Monique sucked in her breath. Eve snatched it up. "Maxine—any prints?" she asked eagerly.

Monique watched her expression deflate.

"No, not after I saw it," Eve continued dejectedly. "Shit. Okay, go ahead. I've got a pencil."

Eve's eyes darkened almost to violet as she listened to Maxine relating the contents of the envelope. She scribbled furiously on a pad. "Sweet," she sighed. "I can hardly wait."

Her fingers stroked Ragamuffin's fur as she replaced the phone and met Monique's questioning gaze. "Maxine Goodman thinks it's a good idea that I join Nico in Bologna for the holidays instead of going home to my family. Interpol will be on alert to see if anyone follows me through customs and out of the country. Doesn't that sound like a fun Christmas?"

"Prints?"

"A partial, blurred. But the letter—now, this one was a real doozy."

Eve stared into the cat's green eyes. "In addition to a few strands of red leather fringe from the jacket I wore yesterday, he sent a love note." She read from her notepad, keeping her voice in a monotone, trying to keep the fear under control as she recited the unnerving words.

"*Christmas is right around the corner. So am I. So wrap yourself in a big red bow. Soon I'll unwrap you, layer by layer. And then we'll ring in the New Year all alone, just the two of us, covered in red. I love the color red, Eve. It's warm and velvety—like blood.*

"And then he signed it the way he always does— *Billy Shears.*"

Monique took a deep breath and regarded Eve through narrowed eyes. "Sounds to me like one fucking psycho. Eve, I can't believe you've been dealing with this all alone. Are you sure you have enough protection?"

Eve bit her lip. "Champion Security is supposed to be the best . . . but when you're dealing with someone like this Billy Shears . . ."

"Do the police have any kind of a handle on this guy?"

"That's the scary part. He's a stalker. The psychological profile—as Maxine puts it—indicates that he's some kind of misfit who's getting off on terrorizing me. Some of these guys zero in on celebrities, some on their ex-wives or girlfriends, and some on a poor soul they happen to spot on the freeway." Eve raked a hand through her hair. "We know he's probably someone nondescript but intelligent. Someone who is obsessed with me, and fantasizes an intimate relationship with me." Her glorious eyes met Monique's, but their usual sparkle was dulled by months of living with intermittent apprehension, weeks of going through each day with one eye or the other constantly cast over her shoulder.

There were brief respites from the relentless uneasiness, times when she nearly forgot, but fear lurked low in the pit of her belly, ready to send tiny reminders of adrenaline pumping through her veins at moments she least expected.

She had lost weight. She could feel the difference in the way her clothes fit, in the hollow of her stomach as she lay in bed, peering into the night-light–illuminated hallway. She had lost sleep. She could see the dark shadows deepening beneath her eyes each morning before she covered them with concealer, and tiny new worry lines feathering around her lips.

She looked through Monique, her eyes hazed over with visions of green envelopes and bodyguards, her ears reverberating with the echoed memory of Maxine Goodman's carefully chosen words that day the security agency director had phoned her with the results of Champion's initial investigation.

"Monique, do you remember Bobbie Sue Griffin?" she asked abruptly.

"The country singer? The one they found a couple of years ago sliced up in the backwoods of Georgia?" Monique sat frozen, eyes wide, heart pounding. "No, Eve, don't tell me this," she groaned.

"Billy Shears." Eve tossed her pencil onto the coffee table and leaned back into the sofa cushions. "Bobbie Sue Griffin received letters like this too. So did Lianna Caruthers—the tennis star from the eighties."

"But the papers said she died of a blow to the head during a scuffle with an intruder," Monique protested.

"The police always keep certain information close to the vest, holding back crime details from the public, the kinds of things only the killer would know. Monique, you're sworn to silence about all this. Promise me. They know that these two women were killed by a man calling himself Billy Shears. The weird thing is, several years elapsed between Lianna Caruthers's death and Bobbie Sue Griffin's murder. Maxine Goodman theorizes that he might have been incarcerated during that time for some unrelated offense . . . but now he's out again and . . . well, lucky me. I guess it's my turn."

"God, Eve, you've got to tell Nico. He has no damn business running around Europe, leaving you alone, bodyguards or no bodyguards! I can't believe you stay here all by yourself every night with a cat, no less, for protection. Do you have a gun?"

"No, but Swanson and Tamburelli do and one of them is always around."

"Around! How around can they be? This lunatic is cutting off pieces of your clothes and Batman and Robin can't even catch him in the act?"

"Monique, Champion is the best security agency on both coasts. Everybody uses them. You know that." Eve set the cat on a pillow and stood up. She paced across the living room, twisting the engagement ring on her finger.

"What more can I do? I don't want this garbage stinking up the newspapers, and I refuse to be held hostage by a fantasizing psychopath. He's not going to force me to give up my life, or send me into hiding like they did to Salman Rushdie."

"Tell Nico."

"I'm going to." Eve thought again of the baby. For the baby's sake, for all of their sakes, she had to bring Nico into this. It would be a relief not to have to shoulder it alone any longer, to have Nico nearby—for she knew he would be nearby. As soon as he knew what was going on, he wouldn't leave her side.

Great, Eve sighed. *We'll be a twosome like Fred and Ginger, yin and yang, Minneapolis and St. Paul—and pickles and ice cream.*

"Cara mia," Nico murmured as he rained kisses down her throat and across the lush mounds of her breasts. "Oh, *sì, carissima, sì.*"

Taut with excitement, he pulled her close, drowning in her woman scent mingled with the rosewater fragrance of her hair. Her breath was silky warm against his ear as her tongue traced the sensitive lobe. Nico grinned, kissing her even more fiercely. Ah, she was talented—beautiful, brilliant, and skillful as a courtesan.

The brocaded topaz bedspread slid unnoticed to the floor as they writhed, sweaty and single-minded in the tangle of cinnamon sheets. The phone jangling on the marble bedside table intruded like the whine of buzzsaws in a primeval forest.

"Fuck," Nico said.

"I'm trying to, love."

"Could be Biaggio," Nico muttered apologetically as he reached across her to yank the receiver to his ear.

"Nico darling."

Double fuck. Nico rolled away from her and bolted upright to a sitting position.

"Bambina," he exclaimed. "I was just this moment thinking about you."

Eve's voice sounded quavery as it crackled across the Atlantic. He had the instant feeling that something was wrong.

"Nico." She was hesitating between slices of intermittent static. "I've been thinking about you too. I have to tell you something. I'd planned to tell you in person, but it can't wait another minute. Can you talk now?"

"For you, always, bambina. What is wrong?"

He grimaced as Margo slanted a mischievous smile up at him and reached out one slender hand. Her fingers twirled through the matted black curls on his chest in a sensuous motion, then trailed down his abdomen toward the more thickly matted hair below, deliberately trying to distract him. But Nico was no longer in the mood.

He grasped her wrist and his eyes blazed fire. *Not now,* the message telegraphed clearly. She slumped back against the pillows, glaring at him, watchful of every expression that crossed his lean, unshaven face.

Steam from the radiator fogged up the stained glass windows of the stately Via Terranova Hotel, one of the best-kept secrets in Rome. But Nico noticed neither the hissing mist that filled the antique-laden room, nor the sun-splayed prisms dancing off the half-empty green wine bottle resting on the carpet of the sunken parlor, nor the speculative expression Margo wore as she waited naked and sweaty beside him in the canopied Louis XV bed.

He was aware only of Eve's low-pitched voice, distant, yet unnervingly close, speaking to him so rapidly he could barely follow the tumbling words.

"Nico, there's so much to tell you, I don't even know where to start. Promise me you won't be angry that I didn't confide in you sooner."

"Angry? When was the last time I was angry with you, Eve?"

"The night we went to dinner with Margo and I kept changing my clothes," she offered with a shaky laugh.

"Ah, yes, Margo," he murmured, and flicked his gaze to the *dottoressa,* regarding her with mingled amusement and desire.

Margo shot him the glance she usually reserved for

upstart residents posing ignorant questions, and rose naked from the bed. She sauntered across the sun-dappled Aubusson carpet to pour herself another glass of wine, smoothing back her tousled cap of silver-blond hair. It took all of her considerable self-control to refrain from snatching the phone out of his hands and disconnecting the call.

Let Eve think it was a transatlantic snafu, she thought spitefully. But Nico would be furious, and Margo wasn't quite sure she could control him in a fury. Still, she was tempted to try.

Instead, she dipped a chunk of fontina cheese into a dish of caviar, never taking her opal eyes from his face. He was watching her too, she observed with satisfaction. Seductively, she nibbled at the cheese, lolling the caviar luxuriously on her tongue, allowing the tiny eggs to burst one by one. She savored the salty flavor that enhanced the lingering taste of Nico's semen.

"What?"

Nico's voice rasped out so abruptly, Margo nearly dropped her wine goblet. His skin had gone pale, and his eyes blazed with a sudden dangerous intensity that was totally centered on Eve.

"What the hell letters are you talking about? Billy Shears? Eve, bambina—slow down. I must hear every word of this. Now, start again from the beginning."

As Eve told him, he paced, stark naked, magnificent—185 pounds of explosively contained male energy ready to blow. When she told him about the baby, Nico sank down on the edge of the ornately carved bed. He closed his eyes. But the tears trickled out, and his voice was raw with emotion.

"A bambino? Or maybe it's a bambina? Then I'll have two bambinas. Oh, Eve. Oh, *Dio mio.*" Suddenly he laughed out loud, pure joy beaming from the swarthily handsome face. "Are you sure? Have you seen a doctor?" He suddenly surged to his feet. "Listen to me, Eve. You stay right there. I'm coming to New

York to get you. Don't you set one foot out of that apartment until I get there. Promise me. I don't want you going *anywhere, capish?* I'm going to call my family and tell them to expect us both in Bologna for Christmas, and then I'm catching the next plane for the States."

He paused, listening, then continued harshly. "I'll protect you if I have to kill this Billy Shears with my own bare hands. But Eve, promise me again you'll stay put until I get there."

Listening to him, Margo felt her insides grow cold. So Eve was going to have Nico's baby. For a moment she couldn't breathe for the jealousy that raged through her. *You're going to be an aunt,* she told herself contemptuously. *Big fucking deal.*

And who the hell was this Billy Shears? She'd never seen Nico this worked up about anything except sex and race cars.

Margo lifted her silver charmeuse robe from the back of the chair and slipped it on, trying to warm herself against the chill that was growing in her heart like frost feathering a windowpane. Quietly, she studied Nico's rapt face. Eve had him now. She'd captured his attention—his heart, soul, and body—all while she was several thousand miles away. *Damn her.*

And damn her baby.

I hope you get stretch marks from here to Beijing. And gain fifty pounds.

Margo thought of how long it had been since she'd felt men's gazes following her across a room instead of nailing in on her sister. Not since Eve's senior year in high school, when the gangly tomboy had suddenly blossomed and totally eclipsed Margo's own position as the family beauty had any man looked twice at her when Eve was in the room. Always before, Margo and everyone else had taken for granted that she was the smart, pretty one and Eve merely the sweaty, long-limbed jock who crossed the finish line at high school meets smudged and sans makeup, looking as nondescript as a sturdy station wagon in a used car lot. But then, suddenly, just as Mom had always predicted, Eve had become some snazzy top-of-the-line convertible, red hot, polished, and sexy, zooming off at dizzying speed and leaving Margo gasping in the dust.

The worst part of it was that even Daddy thought Eve was prettier. Daddy, who had always called her his little princess, who had bragged that his Margo was the smartest, prettiest girl in the world—even Daddy had turned on her.

Standing there in the Via Terranova, watching Nico's glowing face, Margo's eyes stung with unshed tears as she remembered her father's betrayal. She'd come home from college for Easter vacation and had started downstairs late one night for a glass of juice, when she'd heard her father bragging to his poker buddies.

"I always thought Margo was my prettiest daughter, but Eve sure proved me wrong. Good thing Margo's so smart, or this'd really be hard for her to swallow. Oh, make no mistake, she'll do all right for herself with her medical career, no doubt about that— Margo's a real smart girl. But unless she wins a Nobel Prize or something, she'll never be famous."

On the stairs she'd frozen in shock, his words more painful than a slap in the face. Gripping the railing and thankful to be hidden by the near darkness, she'd heard with agony the unmistakable pride in her father's voice, and the murmured agreement of the other men.

"I mean, look at all these magazine covers," he'd said almost in awe. "Who'd have ever thought my Eve would turn into such a gorgeous girl?"

A gorgeous girl. Well, now his gorgeous girl was going to get fat and hormonal, bloated, and puckered with varicose veins. Her stomach would stretch and her boobs would sag. Evie B was on her way down and out as far as her modeling career was concerned, and as far as Nico was concerned . . .

I'm not giving up yet, she thought, swallowing the last warm drops of the wine. She studied the magnificently handsome man with the blazing eyes and midnight hair, the man in whose arms she had known such ecstasy only an hour earlier.

No, Margo decided, setting down the goblet. I'm not finished with Nico Caesarone. Not by a long shot.

Chapter Seventeen

"The longest two hours of my life," Richard muttered.

Monique dug her elbow into his ribs. "Shh, here comes Rory. Tell her she was wonderful."

"No question about that," Delia concurred in an undervoice. "But even that stellar performance won't be enough to save this dog."

Eve watched in sympathy as a grinning Rory Fitzgerald sashayed through the crowd. She was dazzling, her white leather fringes heightening her impish brunette beauty. "She looks upset. She knows."

Nico's voice rang above the susuration of the glittering throng clustered in the dining room at Tavern-on-the-Green.

"*Bravissima*, Rory. You were magnificent. I never had two hours pass so quickly in my life."

Rory hoisted her champagne glass above her head as she maneuvered through the maze of well-wishers gathered to celebrate the opening of *Driving on Shabbos*. The place was packed. Waiters passed silver trays overflowing with salmon-mousse-stuffed peapods and escargot nestled on garlic rounds. A tuxedoed violinist strolled among the elegantly garbed men and women who had turned out for the opening-night party.

"Don't bullshit me now, guys," Rory said, a grin still plastered on her face. "It was a bomb. I stunk. You all hated it. Waiter, another glass of champagne, please. Make that a whole bottle."

Monique kissed her flushed cheek.

"You were terrific. If only the writing was half as good as your performance, you'd have it made. The audience absolutely loved you."

"Rory, you had them in the palm of your hand," Richard added, adroitly lifting a second glass of champagne from a passing waiter's tray. "So what if the play sucks? You, my dear, were mesmerizing."

"Shit," Rory said. "Well, I'll be damned if I'm going to wait up for the reviews on this one. Jenna, grab me one of those salmon things from the waiter behind you. I'm starving."

Nico turned and scooped four hors d'oeurves from the doily-lined tray, passing one to Rory and pressing the rest into the napkin in Eve's hand. "*Mangia,* bambina. *Mangia,*" he urged.

Eat? Eve disinterestedly regarded the three appetizers in her hand. *I've heard of eating for two, but if he thinks he's going to get me to eat for three, he's sadly mistaken.*

Monique's hand was quicker than her tongue. "Oh, no, you don't," she scolded, grabbing the salmon-stuffed peapods and passing them to Rory. "Eve has to maintain her girlish figure. Or did you forget we have a big shoot just weeks away? As a matter of fact, Nico, I'd suggest you'd better go easy on the goodies yourself."

Nico grimaced and raised his empty champagne flute. "Excuse us, everyone. Time for a refill." Fuming, he steered Eve by the elbow toward the bar. "I'm going to kill that woman myself, Eve. Just watch me."

"Not a nice thing to do to your own baby's god-mother," she laughed.

"Godmother?" he exploded, coming to a halt. He waved his hand like Toscanini for emphasis. "Never. That woman will never be a *padrina* to a child of mine. I don't care *how many* we have."

"I love when you get angry and that little dimple deepens in your cheek," she murmured, raising up on tiptoe to kiss his mouth. "And I love the fact that you're here with me. I haven't had so much fun in ages."

It was true. Since Nico had arrived that afternoon she'd felt more relaxed, more like her old self, than she had since this whole business with Billy Shears started. They'd left a trail of clothes across her apartment as they made their way to the bedroom to celebrate not only their reunion, but the baby, with an afternoon of luxurious sex. She had giggled hysterically when Nico had crooned lullabies to her belly. And she'd felt so secure that she'd managed to choose her outfit for the evening in an instant, instead of deliberating for half an hour. Things would be better now. Billy Shears couldn't touch her, not with Nico around. Even so, Eve scanned the crowd, watching faces, automatically noting Tamburelli over by the bar, drinking his customary mineral water.

Habit, she told herself as Nico led her toward the curtained alcove where Jenna and her art-director husband, Luis, were deep in conversation. *You're looking over your shoulder only out of habit.*

People surged and drifted about Rory and the rest of the cast, gossiping, nibbling, and rinsing away the sour taste of bad comedy with rivers of Dom Pérignon. Gradually, Monique became aware that Richard was leading her steadily toward the door.

"Going somewhere?" she inquired dryly, her diamond earrings catching the light as she looked up at him.

He looked especially handsome tonight in his evening clothes, the electric colors of his bow tie and cummerbund adding flair to the formal black and white of his attire. But Richard didn't seem to be in the mood for the festivities. Monique had noticed the restlessness of his eyes, the repeated glances at his watch throughout the play.

"I've got a nightstand full of reports to go over. And let's face it, this party's a dud. Just like the play," he added with a wicked grin. "Do you really mind cutting out?"

"Yes, I mind. I haven't had a chance to talk to Eve yet, and she's leaving in the morning for Rome." Monique tucked her arm firmly in his and led him in a direct path toward the alcove where Eve and Nico were ensconced with Jenna and Luis. Thank God Nico was back, she thought. He hadn't left Eve's side for a moment all evening, even escorting her to the door of the ladies' room. Though there was no love lost between her and Eve's fiancé, Monique had to give credit where it was due. Nico looked to be guarding Eve with the cool-eyed vigilance of an attack Doberman. At least for tonight, Monique prayed, that maniac wouldn't get anywhere near Eve. And maybe when Eve left for Rome in the morning, Billy Shears would try to follow, make a mistake, and be snared by Interpol.

All night long Monique's gaze had trailed Eve, trying to decipher which tuxedo-clad man was Eve's bodyguard for the evening and which was that lunatic who was sending her the notes. She was amazed at Eve's outward composure, her radiance in her amber velvet tuxedo jacket and palazzo pants.

But Monique knew that beneath the serene veneer, Eve was about to come apart at the seams. She had observed her clasping and unclasping her evening bag all during the play. *That bastard had better be caught and caught soon. The last thing I need is a psycho loose on Maui.* She made a mental note to contact Maxine Goodman herself so that Champion could interface with the Hawaiian police department and the resort staff. She needed all her bases covered.

Before they reached Eve and Nico, a foghorn of a voice stopped them in their tracks.

"Richster, there you are!"

James Evans shifted a chewed cigar stub from his pudgy, ring-laden right hand into his left and grabbed Richard by the arm. Shit. Evans would bore them with his obnoxious drivel until at least next Tuesday.

"James. A pleasure as always," she bit out as the portly butterball pumped Richard's arm nearly out of its socket. Four people she had never met hovered at Evans's elbow, regarding her with curiosity through the haze of smoke pluming from the fat cigar.

"Big wedding coming up soon, eh, Richster?" James Evans laughed. "Not getting cold feet on the little princess, now, are you?"

"Comtesse, James, comtesse," Richard replied. "And my feet are warm as jalapeños toasting on a barbecue grill."

James Evans was the biggest advertiser in all three of Richard's top business publications. He owned a national chain of hotels catering to business travelers, but his social savvy had never equaled his financial success. In his dress, conversation, humor, and taste in women, he remained the grubby busboy who'd gotten his start in the Poconos.

"Some people I'd like you and the comtesse to meet, Richard. I don't think they believed I'm on a first-name basis with Prince Rainier's second cousin and her soon-to-be husband—who's not too shabby in his own right, eh, Richster? This is Simon Paulson and his ladyfriend, Ginger—what's your last name, honey?" he asked the tall redhead with the five-inch eyelashes.

"Velour, like the material. I'm the original material girl," she giggled.

Spare me. Monique rolled her eyes. And where the hell did he get this "Prince Rainier" business? Why does everyone keep embellishing *my* story? Silently she tugged on Richard's tuxedo sleeve. But Richard remained attentively tuned to James Evans and his introductions, and she quickly realized why. The dapper man with the silver hair and glinting eyes turned out to be Henry Theogustus, owner of the fifty-thousand-watt radio station in Los Angeles that Richard had his eye on. Richard immediately cranked up the volume on his charm and with instinctive cunning piled it on thick about her noble roots.

"You didn't have the pleasure of meeting my fiancée, the comtesse, when we met in San Francisco, did you, Henry?" Richard drew Monique forward and squeezed her hand to let her know it was time to ladle out the charm.

"A comtesse!" Henry exclaimed, kissing her fingers and bowing playfully in salute. "I am truly honored." His black eyes sparkled with good humor, yet there was a tinge of awe beneath his lighthearted gallantry.

Richard, you see them coming every time, Monique acknowledged silently as she flashed Henry her most dazzling smile. Henry Theogustus, like so many others in this democratic country, appeared to be enthralled by any hint of feudal nobility. And Richard knew just how to play it to his own advantage.

Well, why not, she thought to herself even though the charade always made her itchily uncomfortable. You did it yourself when it suited your needs. You invented this story, and Richard believed it. He's merely exploiting it for all it's worth. She kept the glowing smile frozen in place as she made small talk with Henry and his companions, but tugged again on Richard's sleeve until he began politely edging away.

"Please don't scoot off just yet, Richard," Henry urged. "My date for the evening stepped away momentarily, and I'm sure she'd love to meet you both."

Damn. From the corner of her eye Monique saw Eve and Nico moving away toward other friends. "I hate to be rude," she said quickly, "but we really must . . ."

"Right." James Evans unexpectedly jumped in to support her. "You've got people to see, we've got people to see. Richard, lunch. Next week."

Monique stared curiously into James Evans's agitated face. The man was nearly popping a blood vessel in his sudden eagerness to be rid of them. Strange. He began bundling off his little entourage, but not before Henry had peered past Monique's shoulder and spotted an approaching figure.

"Here she comes now. Richard Ives, Comtesse D'Arcy, please say hello to my lovely friend, Shanna Mulgrew."

Monique went cold as Grecian marble. She turned her head in shock to see a sleek blonde in a hot pink leather sheath skid to a stop beside them.

"Mulgrew?" Richard asked with a bemused smile.

"Clean slate, darling," Shanna retorted.

Shanna Mulgrew Ives. To think of how many times I've dreamed of this moment, Monique thought, staring icily at the woman she'd hated for so long. *Twenty years, but I'd have recognized her anywhere. A few crow's-feet on the old witch,* she thought, *a few miles on her, but she still has that same Bonwit chicness—despite that dreadfully unbecoming steam pouring out of her ears.*

Monique plastered on a smug, impervious smile and deliberately snuggled her arm possessively through Richard's.

Shanna flicked a long, sharp look at her, eyes narrowing contemptuously. As the other woman's glance swept from Monique's face all the way down to the beaded fringe skimming her knees, Monique lifted her chin and stared her down. Beside her, Richard cleared his throat.

"Still getting all choked up when you see me, darling?" Shanna cooed.

You little bitch, Monique thought venomously. Still as smarmy as ever.

"So you two know each other?" Henry faltered, glancing from Shanna's icy demeanor to Richard's grim one with uncertainty.

"Oh, yes, they've met," James mumbled, rolling his eyes.

"But *we* never have," Monique lied coolly, extending her hand in her most regal style. She flashed Shanna a smile smooth as satin. "How do you do?"

Shanna ignored her extended hand and turned to Henry. "Darling, it's rather cloying in here, don't you think?" She placed one slim, red-manicured finger against his black bow tie. "I could really use some fresh air. Nothing personal, of course," she added over her shoulder to Monique, her mouth twisting with the faintest of smiles.

She has no idea just how personal this is, Monique thought, her expression hardening. *Shanna Mulgrew hasn't the faintest clue who I am.* Satisfaction rippled through her. *The bitch probably dismissed all thoughts about Mireille D'Arcy and her daughter three seconds after I fled Bonwits in tears,* she thought. Shanna would never guess that the "stupid little jerk" she ejected from her precious store twenty years ago grew up to become a woman clever enough to steal both her man and her job.

"Don't let us keep you," Richard interjected dryly.

"No, we'd hate to spoil your evening, dear." Monique smiled sweetly. "You're not getting any younger. Run along now and try to have fun."

"You fucking bitch," Shanna snapped under her breath, stepping forward, but at that moment Eve whisked out of nowhere to grasp Monique's arm.

"There you are! Rory is doing the tarantella with Nico and Jenna. *This* you've got to see."

She dragged both Monique and Richard away, leaving Shanna seething.

Eat my dust, Monique gloated, flushing with victory. *And you still wear too much perfume*, she added in silent scorn before being swallowed up by the clapping crowd encircling the dancers.

Later, cloaked in the sleek darkness of Richard's limo as they threaded their way through late-night Manhattan traffic, Monique studied his face. He was lost in thought over a sheaf of papers, his pipe smoke curling through the backseat.

"Are you ever sorry?" she suddenly asked. "Do you ever wish we hadn't met?"

"Mmmm?" he murmured, sucking on the pipe, eyes still locked on the report before him.

"Shanna," she persisted. "Do you ever wish you were still with her?"

"Monique." Richard sighed, glancing up from the papers, his gaze bleary. "I don't have time to assuage feminine insecurities right now. If I wanted to be with Shanna, I'd be with her. Period. In the meantime, pray she doesn't screw up my deal with Henry Theogustus. I can only imagine the talk going on in that bedroom tonight." He grimaced. "And while you're praying, throw in one for the success of your June issue. Word is McArthur has sweet Shanna just waiting in the wings, hoping you'll fall flat on your ass. And I'm warning you right now, Mo, I won't be able to fend them off without some damn good numbers behind us."

A pinching anxiety assailed her. Monique shivered inside her sable coat. For just a little while tonight, basking over her successful joust with Shanna, she'd forgotten how quickly she could lose ground. *Perfect Bride* was still very much up for grabs, and only solid numbers skyrocketing from a dynamite June issue could block any political maneuvering against her. She had a long way to go before this fight was really over.

She slumped back against the upholstery, suddenly exhausted, and more than a little disheartened. "I know," she said tensely, "believe me, Richard, I'm working on it."

What she really wanted was for Richard to set aside that blasted report and enfold her reassuringly in his arms. She thought of how protective Nico had been of Eve tonight. He'd stayed close to her, held her hand, and smiled attentively into her eyes as if no other woman in the room existed. Even though Monique couldn't stand all Nico's blazing machismo, she wished that Richard would just once set aside his belief in her self-sufficiency and smother her with caring attentiveness, the way he had at the inception of their relationship.

I am strong, she thought, *and Richard knows it as well as I do, but dammit, sometimes I wish he knew that even Wonder Woman needs a little tender loving care after a day of battle.*

She cracked the back window to allow the haze of pipe smoke to dissipate and stared out at the lights of New York, glimmering on the slick pavement. She felt cold inside, empty, and lonely. It's nerves, she told herself, prewedding jitters, work stress, and that mess with Eve—not to mention coming face-to-face with Shanna. God, I could use a two-hour massage and a couple of margaritas right about now, she reflected, her eyes closing as tension built in her head.

Things will all come together after Maui, she told herself. The pressure will be off. Richard will see that I can ace this job. And by then we'll be in the homestretch of all the wedding plans.

As the limo delivered them to the curb of the Dakota, a light snow began pirouetting through the darkness.

"I'll build a fire," Richard said as they stepped off the elevator and hurried into the marble foyer. "Put up a pot of coffee, will you? It's going to be a long night."

As Monique flung her sable across the red settee and headed into the kitchen, she noticed the message light flashing on her answering machine. She pressed the button and reached for the coffee grinder.

Ms. D'Arcy. Dorothy's crisp voice echoed through the room. *Don't worry, but we're leaving right now for the emergency room. It's—let's see—ten-fifteen and your* maman *is quite uncomfortable. Mr. Lambert is getting her into the car right now, but I wanted to let you know in case you want to meet up with us there. If we don't see you at the hospital, I'll call you as soon as we get back. Don't you worry now, I'm sure everything will be fine.*

The line clicked off with a double beep just as Richard appeared in the doorway. There were no other messages.

Fear clawed at Monique as she ran past him to grab her coat.

"Richard, will you come with me?" she asked, trying to keep her voice steady as she plunged her arms into the sleeves.

He blanched. "Mo, you know how I hate hospitals. Besides, I've got all this reading. . . ."

"I need you to be there with me," she implored him. "Richard, I'm scared."

"Who—you?" he said, smiling and coming forward to brush a kiss across her cheek. "Impossible. Nothing scares my indomitable Mo. Besides, Dorothy said there's no reason to worry. It sounds like she's got everything under control. Who's Lambert?"

"That carpenter who's working on the terrace," Monique replied distractedly, slinging her purse over her shoulder. She hurried toward the door, her heels sinking into the Oriental rug.

"Sure you won't come?" she tried once more.

"Tell you what." Richard picked up the phone. "Let me catch the driver before he garages the limo. I'll plow through your report when I've finished mine so that I can brief you in the morning. That way you'll be all caught up. And if I hear from Dorothy, I'll buzz you in the car."

That's the best you can do? Monique thought, glaring at him in silent fury.

Richard pretended not to see her anger. He spoke rapidly into the phone, giving orders to the driver.

"If it's a real crisis," he said when he'd replaced the receiver, "I'll zoom right up there. Promise."

Monique set her lips together and slammed the door behind her. *Asshole,* she thought. She paced across the lobby, shivering as she waited for the car to return.

God, please don't let it be anything serious, she prayed, clasping the brass bar of the door. Why hadn't Dorothy given her some clue about what was wrong?

She ran wordlessly past the staring doorman before the limo had even nosed up to the curb. As the car plunged through the twirling snowfall, Monique hunched forward in her seat. Her hands shook as she tried to light a cigarette.

Shit. At this time of night it would take close to fifty minutes to get to the hospital.

Fifty minutes of wondering; fifty minutes of hell.

Chapter Eighteen

The phone call came too late. By the time Richard dialed the car, Monique was already inside the hospital, scouring the emergency room, questioning everyone wearing a hospital ID tag, demanding the whereabouts of Mireille D'Arcy.

When she returned to the car with no more information than that her mother had been sent home, the driver gave her the message from Richard.

"Mr. Ives called five seconds after you went in. He said to tell you he'd heard from Dorothy. Your mother's back home and Dorothy's making all the necessary arrangements. He wants you to phone him as soon as possible. He said it's imperative."

Right, Monique thought, reaching for the cellular phone and punching in the number at the country house, *I'll get right on it. Just as soon as I've filed my nails and shoveled the circular drive.*

Richard was the last person she wanted to speak with right now. She was still steaming over his refusal to accompany her to the hospital. She was sick of his excuses. Maybe he hated hospitals, maybe he hated sickness, but if he loved her, he could at least try to be there for her when she needed him.

And she did need him. She was coming apart. If anything happened to *Maman*, she didn't know what she'd do.

A busy signal. How in the hell could there be a busy signal? She tapped the redial button. The same.

Monique let out a strangled hiss of frustration. She couldn't get through once during the entire twenty-minute ride to the estate, and by the time she ran into the foyer and dashed up the stairs, Monique was in a state of frantic anxiety. She burst into her mother's room to find Dorothy seated in the cushioned oak rocker beside the bed and Mireille asleep, swallowed up in the huge four-poster.

Monique's heart lurched. *Maman* looked so tiny and frail and ashen—and old. *She looks ten years older,* Monique thought in dismay.

"What happened?" she cried as Dorothy set down her knitting and came swiftly to her feet.

"Pneumonia," the nurse replied in her steady tone. "She started having trouble breathing late this afternoon. Up until then, we thought it was just a cold."

"Shouldn't they have kept her in the hospital?" Monique hurried to the bedside and smoothed the down comforter, searching her mother's wan face.

"They kick you out fifteen minutes after surgery these days," Dorothy snorted. She patted Monique's shoulder. "But don't you worry, Ms. D'Arcy. They've already started her on antibiotics and I've gone ahead and ordered her ventilator. And with your permission, a private duty nurse can be here in an hour to alternate shifts with me so that someone can stay with her round the clock."

"Of course, Dorothy, absolutely. Why don't you arrange for that, and then get to bed? It's already after two. I'll stay with her until the nurse gets here."

Monique pulled the rocker closer so she could hold

Mireille's hand. Exhaustion dragged at her, twinned with fear. *Maman* had been weakened enough by her stroke. How would she be able to fight off pneumonia?

"I've got strength enough for both of us, *Maman*," she whispered in the dimness. "I'll help you."

Maman's hand felt so small and weak. Her breaths came in shallow labored rasps that seemed to cut right through Monique. She thought of her desk piled high with work, of the trip to Maui later this week that was supposed to run through Thanksgiving, of everything involved in setting up the shoot.

How could she do it? How could she leave with *Maman* so ill?

With a sigh Monique eased out of her beaded heels and plucked off the large square tourmaline earrings that suddenly felt too heavy for her ears. She stared at the gems twinkling in her palm. Richard had given them to her as an engagement gift.

A lot of good they do me now.

She needed *him*, not earrings, not furs, not all these stupid trappings. Just someone to be there when she was scared. And she was scared right now.

It was nearly three by the time the private duty nurse arrived. After getting her settled in Mireille's room, and kissing her mother's clammy forehead, Monique stumbled off to the eerie silence of her own room.

Wearily, Monique stripped, sank into a steaming tub, and tried to soak strength and comfort from the warm, lilac-scented water. Tired as she was, she knew she couldn't sleep with this knot of tension grinding inside her.

It wasn't until she was downstairs in the kitchen, bundled in a thick pink terry-cloth robe and compulsively munching Oreo cookies slathered with peanut butter that she remembered Richard's message.

Imperative, he'd said. Whoop-de-do. She poured a

tall glass of milk, downed it in one gulp, and reached for the desk phone.

Off the hook. Damn. Monique stared at it angrily. *That's why I couldn't reach Dorothy from the limo.*

She listened to the phone ringing at the Dakota, all the while pacing barefoot around the center island of hand-painted Italian ceramic tiles.

On the fourth ring Richard picked it up.

"It's about time," he snapped. He sounded wide awake and on edge.

"My mother is doing just fine, thank you."

"I know. Dorothy explained the situation to me. I told you everything would work out. And now I need you back here ASAP so that I can brief you on these reports. You, my dear, have got big problems."

"At three-thirty in the morning? Richard, are you insane?"

"No. But you will be when you see this mess."

"What mess?" Monique slumped into a bamboo chair and raked a hand through her still-damp hair. She couldn't handle much more tonight, not without some sleep, but she had to know what was wrong. She stretched her legs across one of the plushly cushioned eighteenth-century bamboo chairs that ringed the pine table inlaid with tiles to match the island's.

"Didn't you even glance at any of the reports Linda left you? Or were you so busy getting ready for your friend Rory's opening that you took the whole afternoon off?"

"Get to the point, Richard," she said tersely.

"The point is that your June issue is going to hell in a handbasket. Oh, your shoot will come off okay. Maybe. But the editorial end is falling apart."

"What the hell are you talking about? There are four articles on my desk awaiting final approval, and the other three are due next week. What could possibly be falling apart?"

"Item number one: your article 'How to Survive

the First Six Weeks of Marriage.' Belly-up. The author got a book contract with a heavy duty advance and a deadline to match and she's backing out. Said you could sue her if you like.

"Item number two: your spread on bridal fashions designed to hide figure flaws. Canceled. Linda discovered that *Bride and Groom* has the same article *with* the same designer slated for May. Seems the eager young artiste thought he could get mucho mileage peddling the same idea to everybody. And—if that's not enough to brighten your day—Deanna, the art director you insisted on promoting, has quit without notice and gone to the competition. There's more. Shall I go on?"

Shit. Monique wanted to lay her head on the table and cry. Instead, she heard herself shouting into the phone. "Richard, my mother has *pneumonia*. She just got home from the *hospital*. Don't you think you could try to deal with some of this for me? I can't even think straight right now. I don't even know what time I'll be in tomorrow. Or *if* I'll be in tomorrow."

His voice slicked down her back like an ice cube. "Monique, I'm sorry about your mother. I really am. But you know damn well she's in good hands. You're just being neurotic."

"Neurotic? Since when is concern and compassion *neurotic*?"

"Look, Monique, it's not going to do your mother any good to have you hovering over her while *Perfect Bride* goes down the tubes. One thing I'll tell you about Shanna—she never let *anything* interfere with getting the job done. Hell, she once broke her leg skiing, but did she let that stop her? She set up an entire office in her hospital room, conducted interviews, *and* directed a shoot by video remote, for God's sake!" Richard bellowed. "She might have been a bitch on wheels, but she got things done."

"You bastard! How dare you throw Shanna in my face at a time like this?" Shaking, Monique fought to gain control of herself. She'd been screaming at him like an escapee from Bellevue.

"I'll call Linda in the morning and straighten everything out with her," she bit out, reaching desperately for the box of Oreos. "Then you won't have to worry your precious head about your precious magazine. Right now I'm going to try to get some sleep. And don't you dare tell me that your precious Shanna could get by on only three hours a night."

"Four."

"Asshole!" Monique shrieked into the phone, and slammed it down.

From the darkness beyond the kitchen she heard a low, amused voice.

"Guess that's telling him."

Monique screamed. She whirled around, grabbing up the butter knife coated with peanut butter.

"I surrender," said Pete Lambert, squinting as he stepped from the darkened terrace into the light. With a start Monique realized that the doors opening onto the nearly completed addition had been ajar, but who would have expected anyone to be lurking there in the dark—least of all this tall, muscled carpenter with the attitude from hell.

"And you're another asshole," she flashed, brandishing the knife without realizing it. "What in the hell are you doing here at this time of night? How did you get in? And how long have you been eavesdropping on my private conversation?"

"Long enough to know that you're hooked up with a real jerk. I thought you were smarter than that," he said, reaching for an Oreo and dipping it into the peanut butter jar.

"Please. Just help yourself," Monique invited him sarcastically.

Pete's eyes swept from the damp tendrils of jet-black hair dangling on her forehead down to the V-necked opening of her robe. Her skin still glistened a pale, pearly pink from the steaming effects of the bath. Nice. His gaze took in the lush fullness of her breasts, the long curve of hips and legs sweeping down to her delicate bare feet with their pink-polished toenails. Stunning. Once again his gaze slid up and down the sensuous length of her lilac-perfumed body in one slow, appreciative glance.

"Don't mind if I do."

Monique drew in her breath. Her heart had only barely recovered from the start he'd given her, and now it leapt again at the thinly disguised innuendo. Silhouetted against the darkness of the terrace, Pete Lambert looked even taller and more rugged than ever. And right at home.

In gray sweats, with his fair hair tumbling carelessly, he looked ready to stretch out in front of the fireplace with the evening newspaper, a glass of brandy, and a labrador retriever. Not *my* fireplace, she thought, but she couldn't help admiring the ripple of muscles beneath his easy-fitting casual clothes, the firm slant of his jaw, and the undeniable power of those cobalt-blue eyes.

And she couldn't help but feel the spark flying between them, a spark that made her acutely aware of his potent masculinity and of her own vulnerability as she stood there barefoot, and naked beneath the terry robe.

Deliberately, sensuously, Pete licked the smidges of peanut butter from his fingers. Monique fought the urge to wrap herself deeper into the folds of pink terrycloth.

"Not bad," Pete commented with a wry grin, his gaze lingering on her mouth. "Nope. Not bad at all."

"An old family recipe," she retorted. She tightened her sash. "Now, would you mind telling me exactly what you're doing lurking on my terrace at four a.m.?"

"Is Mireille all right? The nurse is with her?"

"Must you always answer a question with a question?"

"Does it annoy you?"

"Does Baryshnikov dance?" She glared at him. "Oh, *excuse me,* you probably don't have the faintest idea who that is."

"No." Pete leaned forward suddenly. "*You* excuse *me.*" His thumb dabbed lightly at the corner of her mouth. "Peanut butter," he explained, grinning as she flushed. "Comtesse, I didn't take you for a snob." He shook his head. "An adorable, high-handed, determined, and formidable woman. But not a snob. Even I, peon that I am, know who the exalted Baryshnikov is—he's that Italian tenor who's a little on the hefty side, right?"

He did it perfectly, dead-on, straight-faced.

In spite of herself, Monique couldn't contain a gasp of laughter. "You're impossible!"

She planted her hands on her hips and fought to squelch her smile. "Mr. Lambert, I can't figure you out. Not that I want to bother!" she added hastily.

She was still trembling—from her conversation with Richard, she assured herself, *not* from this intimate one-on-one with Pete Lambert. But for good measure she grabbed the jar of peanut butter and scooted around the granite kitchen island, putting its solid bulk between them under the pretense of stashing the jar in the cupboard.

"You still haven't explained what you're doing here," she reminded him.

To her chagrin, Pete Lambert followed her around the island to the cupboard. "Come here, I'll show you."

He tugged her out onto the darkened terrace. "Sit down right here," he instructed her, patting the overstuffed pillow in the center of the ceramic tile floor and then crossing over to flip on a wall switch.

Soft, silvery light danced across the lacquered walls and onto the crystal-clear glass panels that overlooked the snow-laced gardens and the forest beyond. The smell of varnished wood and fresh paint mingled with

the scent of cherrywood logs in the fieldstone fireplace
that had not been completed the last time Monique
was at the house. Now it was, magnificently so, and the
terrace was no longer a roughed-in work-in-progress
but a cozy, glassed-in parlor overlooking the natural
beauty of the estate. It was a haven adorned with nature's ever-changing artwork—the feathering of trees,
the expanse of diamond sky, with snowflakes tumbling
like wayward stars right at arm's reach. Yet it was shel-
tered from the elements, a panoramic sanctuary filled
with comfort, warmth, and light.

And music. For as the lights came on, so did the
sound system, flooding the room with the hypnotic
voice of Jose Carreras.

"I finished the wiring right before we left for the
hospital. When we got back, I stopped in here to check
it out. Guess I fell asleep." Pete watched her face
soften as wonder and delight erased the tension. "It's
the concert of the three tenors—Pavarotti, Carreras,
and Domingo. It's one of my favorites. In a minute
you'll hear Baryshnikov," he added, eyes twinkling as
Luciano Pavarotti burst into "Torna a Surriento."

"You *are* impossible." But this time Monique's
tone was appreciative. "I *hate* to admit it, but you've
done a pretty fair job with this."

She was being stingy, she knew, but somehow
couldn't help it. In truth, he'd done a breathtaking job
—the terrace was a dream. And when she brought in
the floral chintz sofa with the huge pillows and the
wicker side chairs and table, and filled the room with
baskets of plants and flowers, it would be a year-round
garden, a haven from work, from pressure, from . . .

My God, she'd almost thought: *from Richard.*

Appalled, Monique gave herself a mental shake.

"Not bad, Mr. Lambert," she continued briskly to
cover her own confusion.

Pete took three steps toward her and yanked her to
her feet. "Look up."

She marveled at the snowflakes glittering above the curved glass ceiling, then realized that the twinkling diamonds overhead were actually stars. Close enough to touch. Bright enough to blind.

"I'd like to stay here forever," she sighed.

"Is life that bad?"

"No, of course not." Monique tried to assume her usual hard-boiled pose. "It's just that I'm worried about my mother, and I'm supposed to go out of town in a few days for business, and my magazine is going to hell, and my fiancé is acting like a son of a bi—never mind." She bit her lip. Why on earth was she telling Pete Lambert any of this?

"I know what you need."

She stiffened. Sure he did. A lay. Men always thought a good lay cured everything.

Before she could step back, he slipped an arm around her waist and grasped her right hand in his. The rich Russian strains of "Ochi Tchorniye" filled the terrace as he began waltzing her around the starlit room. "You need to dance, Monique D'Arcy. Don't think, just move. Dancing is like letting your soul fly free. It lightens the heart. It softens the pain."

"I don't need pain-softeners, Mr. Lambert. I'm tough as nails and perfectly capable of dealing with all of my problems."

"Yeah, you're tough all right," he muttered, shaking his head at her. Monique felt the raw strength in his callused hands as they guided her across the smooth, tiled floor. "Tough as Cool Whip."

Monique winced. No man had ever detected her vulnerability before; everyone thought of her as a mountain of iron. Cool Whip? Oh, yes—tonight Mr. Lambert was right on target. Down in her soul she felt as weak and airy as a mountain of fluff.

Unnerved, she tried to pull free, but he held her close. "What's wrong, Comtesse? What's really wrong?"

"It's late . . . I should check on things upstairs."

"After the song."

When the music ceased, he released her. Monique felt strangely bereft as his hands slid away, as the warmth of his body receded. She couldn't read the expression in his eyes.

"You've been . . . very kind." She sounded stiff as a British headmistress. Why was she having such difficulty thinking what to say? "Thank you for taking my mother to the hospital."

"Don't mention it. I adore Mireille. She's a special lady." His eyes flickered with concern. "Do yourself a favor . . . get some shuteye, okay? I'll be seeing you tomorrow. Unless you're going back to the city?"

"Not a chance."

He nodded, and glanced around the nearly finished room. "Well, one more coat of paint and I'll be out of your hair."

He lifted his leather bomber jacket from the corner and let himself out the terrace door, making off through the wind and the snowy darkness without a backward glance.

Monique watched him until he disappeared through the trees. Despite everything that had happened, she felt oddly relaxed. And she made a decision. She wouldn't think about Richard tonight, or the problems with the magazine. Time to take a hint from Scarlett O'Hara—she'd think about it all tomorrow.

Mireille was sleeping like a tiny doll when she poked her head in the door and the private duty nurse, a plump young creature with wiry red hair and a perpetual smile, assured Monique that her mother was doing fine. It was all Monique could do to stumble down the hall to her own high-ceilinged room. She collapsed into the featherbed too weary even to brush her teeth, but not before she had slipped Pete Lambert's compact disc into her bedside player. She fell asleep to the crooning of the three tenors and the sensation of waltzing in snow.

She didn't make it into the city the next day, or the one after that. Richard called, Linda called, and everyone at the magazine except for the maintenance man called. Monique was on the phone for eighteen hours out of the day.

But there were some things she couldn't handle long distance. The day before Thanksgiving she drove reluctantly with Richard to LaGuardia and boarded a plane for Hawaii, with a three-hour layover in L.A.

She'd tried everything she could think of to postpone these meetings, but had been unable to coordinate the calendars of Antonio, Mimi Cohn, and everyone else involved, all of whom had been looking forward to a sunny working vacation over the holiday. So Thanksgiving night found her eating lukewarm sliced turkey and runny cranberry sauce in the hotel suite with ten of her closest business associates, forging plans and counterplans.

For Friday, she'd set up a private meeting with the police chief and the security staff of the Maui Haleakala Resort. Only Richard knew about it. No need to alarm everyone else about a problem that might never even come up, she thought.

"Anyone for dessert?" Richard lifted several ornately knobbed silver covers on the linen-draped serving cart. He pursed his lips. "Looks like a choice of pumpkin or pecan pie smothered with Cool Whip."

Cool Whip. Monique's gaze darted to the snowy mounds dolloped on the pie, but her thoughts drifted beyond tropical beaches and mountainsides dripping with bougainvillea and orchids to the snowdrifts hugging a cozy glassed-in terrace, where a fire blazed in a fieldstone hearth. She could picture *Maman* lying across the new sofa, a blanket tucked around her as she basked in the glow of the cherrywood logs, with Dorothy beside her, knitting and sipping steaming tea.

And Pete Lambert, he was there too, stoking the logs and drinking elderberry wine, as comfortable and natural as the Navajo throw rug Monique had selected to warm the tile floor.

She jolted herself out of her absurd reverie, embarrassed to find that Richard had asked her the same question three times.

"No thanks, no pie for me. I don't have the stomach for Cool Whip tonight."

Richard placed a hand on her shoulder and leaned down to whisper in her ear. "After we get rid of this crowd, let's take a moonlight walk on the beach."

Monique regarded him coolly, betraying neither pleasure nor objection. Let him sweat, she thought. Let him coax me.

Just leaving New York had seemed to soothe Richard's relentless pace. Though they planned to work straight through the weekend, the beauty of the island and the mesmerizing lapping of the ocean waves outside their lanai seemed to put him in a better mood than he'd been in for quite a while. Monique smiled tightly up at him, wishing she could feel truly enthusiastic.

Richard was trying hard to appease her. He'd even ventured to the country this past week to visit Mireille and had stayed through dinner. She supposed the least she could do was forgive him. She would soon enough —but let him grovel a little first, she decided, reaching for the portfolio of location sites.

It was after eleven when Monique and Richard set out barefoot across the cool wet sand. Richard had rolled up the cuffs of his white cotton twill trousers, and knotted a loose-woven cotton sweater around his waist. He held out his hand to Monique and they left the shadow of the resort behind, roaming down the empty beach with only scattered torchiers and the moonlight to guide them. Monique's oyster-white jump suit reflected the creamy light onto her face, and the evening's humidity wisped the dark strands that escaped from the ponytail high atop her head.

"Tomorrow we'll check out the yacht," Richard said as they rounded a shoal where a stand of palm trees fluttered in the breeze. "If you change your ticket and stay a few days longer, we could sail around the islands and really have a chance to relax."

"But Richard, you know I have to get back."

"Not necessarily. The office is under control. The X-rays showed your mother's lungs have improved fifty percent. Dorothy's taking good care of her, so what are you so worried about?"

"She's still weak. I hated leaving her for Thanksgiving. You know I'm all she has."

"Fine. Change of subject. Have you decided on the flowers for St. Patrick's? I want that cathedral filled top to bottom with exotic blossoms—birds of paradise, orchids, protea—and the like. Nothing ordinary, Mo, remember that."

She nodded. Richard above all else hated the commonplace. "They're already ordered, even for the reception," she assured him, splashing through the foaming tide. "Even you won't be disappointed, Richard."

How many men would take such great interest in every detail of a wedding? Monique wondered. Yet it was so characteristic of Richard. He needed to control everything around him, and appearances were crucial. He worried that if the minutest detail wasn't unusual and extravagant, people would think he'd fallen on hard times. When the economy soured, Richard splurged. Image was everything.

Monique knew how to play that game. As a matter of fact, she could teach him a thing or two, she thought as she stooped to pick up a seashell glinting beneath the wash of water.

"I'm not going to tell you about the orchestra, but let me just say three words: Harry—Connick—Junior."

"You didn't?" He grinned.

"That's only the start. By the way, the people at the

Plaza have been fabulous. But we really have to nail down the menu. Linda showed me pages and pages of delectable choices. For appetizers, how about asparagus and prosciutto strudels, crabmeat in coconut milk served on the half shell, ouzo-marinated Greek cheese and wild mushroom pie?"

"Perfect."

"I know you love the escarole soup with roasted garlic, tofu, and red peppers. And I've already decided on the spinach, Brie, and walnut salad, but for the main course do you want lobster in saffron butter with artichoke rosettes or rack of lamb with eggplant pancakes?

"Both. Next choice."

"My favorite," she laughed, warming to her subject and to Richard. "Dessert. I can't decide between the peach mousse in pine nut cookie baskets, the margarita sherbet with candied lime peel, or a summer fruit compote with bourbon and mint. Which one do you want?"

Richard stopped and grasped her by the waist, pulling her close. "Right now I want only you." His dark eyes glistened in the moonlight. They roamed over her body with flagrant desire. "It's been weeks, Monique, and I'm *very* hungry. Starved, actually. Let's not wait another minute."

This was more like it. There was fervent desire in his face, and that ardent, tender look she had first seen on Ivana's balcony. Saucily, Monique tossed back her head and challenged him with her eyes. "Who's stopping you, sailor?" she murmured.

The thought of making love to him on the beach, under the moonlight, with rhythmic accompaniment of lapping waves and the perfume of the islands enveloping them brought an eager smile to her lips. Deliberately, she tossed the seashell aside and unfastened her jump suit with slow, seductive movements, keeping her eyes locked on his.

The jump suit glided down her body like a dewdrop down the stem of a flower. Richard unhooked her wispy bra and slid her lace bikini panties to her ankles, trailing kisses down her calves. Laughing, Monique stepped out of her panties and with a mischievous chuckle darted toward the ocean.

"Last one in writes all our thank-you notes," she sang out, and made a great noisy splash as the water showered her with salty droplets.

"Cheater," Richard bellowed, tossing his sweater to the sand and tearing out of his clothes with such haste that he jammed his pants zipper and had to hop on one leg, trying to pull off his slacks and underwear in one motion. He dove after Monique, catching her with ease and kissing her as they sank beneath the warm, shimmering indigo water.

Only the moon watched as they explored each other's bodies, serenaded by slapping waves that undulated around and through them in counterpoint to their urgent movements. Breathlessly, he hoisted her against him and carried her to the sand. She shivered in the cool breeze, but only for a moment before Richard covered her with his own body and pressed her into the grit of the sand. He plunged inside her again and again while stars swam dizzily above her in a velvet sky that stretched into eternity.

Richard's hands teased and tantalized her. Monique gasped and inhaled the scent of the ocean mingled with the spiciness of his cologne. Her tongue flicked against the hollow of his shoulder, tasting ocean salt. She clutched at him, driving him deeper inside with quickening movements. The stars flared in her eyes as he encircled her waist, yanking her to him—and suddenly she was dancing, twirling through time and space.

Pete Lambert's blond hair and rugged face blazed in her mind even as Richard called her name.

My God, what was she thinking? Monique blinked and forced herself to focus on Richard's darkly compelling features. But in her distraction, the dizzying sensations of sexual ecstasy drained from her even as she tried to cling to them, swept away like a handful of wave-washed sand.

Afterward, as they strolled hand in hand back to the hotel, Monique tried to quell her restlessness.

"Richard," she said impulsively, "let's go someplace and dance."

"You've got to be kidding. Mo, I'm too beat to hang the room service order on the doorknob, much less boogie the night away. Tomorrow, okay? I promise."

Monique wondered as she slipped into bed beside him if it had snowed back home, if the last coat of paint was dry on the terrace, and if Pete Lambert was out of her life now for good.

Check immigration records. Check French passport office. Call Salt Lake City—Latter-Day Saints' Family History Library.

Shanna Ives paused, pencil in hand. Amber light dribbled from her ivory bedside lamp, making the twisted satin sheets around her shimmer like mother-of-pearl. CNN droned from the TV. The fish in her forty-gallon aquarium built into the cantilevered wall darted silently among their ferns and colored stones. She stared down at the lined legal pad propped on her lap and nibbled the eraser end of the pencil.

"One call to that Mormon Library and their researchers will get the goods on little Ms. Comtessa in no time. I'd bet my life her title is as phony as that dime-store smile. There has to be some dirt that McArthur and I can use against her."

Shanna reached for the bottle of sleeping pills on the nightstand. Four A.M. and she hadn't yet slept five minutes. She gulped down a Halcion tablet with a mouthful of mineral water, and clicked off the TV.

"Screw you, Monique D'Arcy," she said aloud. She

paused, her eyes narrowing in concentration. "D'Arcy.
D'Arcy." Frustrated, she rolled the name around on
her tongue. It burned like bitter acid.

Why was that slut's name so damned familiar?
Shanna'd never been able to shake the feeling that
she'd heard it before. Not just from the D'Arcy agency.
Not just from industry gossip. It was driving her crazy.

It'll come to me.

She threw herself back on the pillows and tugged
the satin blanket across her chest.

Sooner or later . . . she flung herself over, punching the pillow into shape . . . *if it kills me, I'll remember.*

Chapter Nineteen

Four days later Monique was back in her office. She reviewed cover poses for the May issue, conferred with Linda and managing editor Phoebe Martinez about the new page format, okayed the wedding banquet article, and kept jet lag at bay with nicotine and mug after mug of espresso. She interviewed the four final candidates for art director and wearily told Linda to keep looking. She ran out at lunchtime for a preliminary fitting of the wedding gown she'd designed herself, and bought her mother a pair of earrings that caught her eye in Tiffany's window.

The afternoon was full of meetings and endless decisions, including scheduling an interview segment with *Entertainment Tonight.* Leeza Gibbons was all set to do a feature on Ana and Teri that would be filmed right before Christmas. The segment would preview Ana and Teri in their *Perfect Bride* wedding gowns and would build on the hype for the June issue.

Put that in your stogie and smoke it, Drew McArthur, Monique crowed, elated, as she finished all the arrangements with the ET producer.

By the time she reached the country house that

night, she was exhausted, bleary-eyed, and badly in need of a hot meal, a crackling fire, and tea laced with cognac.

"They're beautiful," Mireille exclaimed as Monique lifted the tarzanite and diamond teardrops from the blue velvet pad. Monique fastened them for Mireille and held up the ivory hand mirror so her mother could see the crystal-blue glow of the tarzanite capture the light.

"I notice the terrace hasn't been painted yet. Where has Mr. Lambert been all this time?" she inquired casually. "Did he desert you?"

"Of course not. He spent Thanksgiving here, but he decided I shouldn't be breathing in paint fumes just yet. He's been working on the Parker place."

"What a dear," Dorothy remarked, bringing in Mireille's eight o'clock pills along with the overpowering scent of Jungle Gardenia. "He never comes by without bringing some little gift for your *maman*. For example, yesterday he brought that," the nurse said, pointing to a slim volume of French poetry. "They certainly broke the mold with that man."

Thank God, Monique muttered to herself, remembering the insolent way he had looked her up and down in her very own kitchen. Well, she was thankful he wouldn't be coming by anytime soon. This weekend while Richard was on the West Coast trying to nail down his deal with Theogustus she could hole up here with *maman* and wade through the pile of work that had accumulated while she was on Maui, and she wouldn't have to worry about running into that insufferable egotist.

But the next day, while taking a break from her work, she found herself meandering down toward the bridge and crossing the path that led toward the Parker place. Bundled against the cold in her sheared-mink parka, Monique kicked snow as she strolled along, luxuriating in the biting cold and the dazzle of sunlight on icicles that dangled like diamonds from spindly branches.

She came to the crest of the road from where she could catch a glimpse of the Parker house and hesitated only a moment before plunging on up the path. He'd done wonders with the old place. Gone were the crumbling brick, the drooping shutters, and the weed-strewn, neglected grounds that had made the place resemble a ramshackle leftover from a Stephen King movie set.

In its stead stood a masterpiece of striking simplicity, a redwood and granite showplace with expansive glass windows overlooking a two-story deck perched above a fish pond, stone-bordered gardens, and grounds dotted with bird feeders and salt licks to attract the forest deer.

Beyond snow-dusted hedges she saw the carriage house, freshly remodeled in the same rich redwood, smoke curling from the chimney.

Impressed in spite of herself, Monique started forward. "Lambert! Hey, Lambert."

She didn't really expect him to answer. She didn't even know if she wanted him to, but suddenly a snowball cuffed her in the back. She whirled around.

A second snowball splattered against her shoulder. "Shit—missed." Pete stooped to gather another handful of snow.

Before he could toss it, a hard-packed cruncher hit him in the forehead. "I didn't," Monique shouted across the expanse of sloping ground as she turned and ran.

The fight was on. Like a pair of ten-year-olds, they shrieked and dodged and hid behind trees until at last Pete tackled her and washed her face with a leather ski glove full of snow.

"Had enough?"

"You'll pay for this, Lambert!" she gasped.

He grinned and hauled her to her feet. "Truce?"

"Beats another snowball down my back."

He pulled her toward the carriage house. "I know just how to warm you up."

He poured steaming coffee into mugs and topped them off with a splash of amaretto. "Delicious," Monique sighed as she took stock of her surroundings.

The carriage house was stunning. A high-beamed rough-hewn hideaway. There was an open redwood loft complete with built-in bed extending halfway over the expansive living room below, where a glazed redbrick hearth blazed. The floor was patterned in the same red brick, warmed by thick Dhurrie rugs.

Monique rubbed her fingers across the pebbled-suede throw cushions on the cordovan sofa. "Nice digs. No wonder you're stretching out this job."

"The owner isn't in any particular hurry. Which suits me just fine. Want to see what I've done so far?"

It was even more beautiful inside than out. Pete Lambert obviously took great pride in his work. The craftsmanship of the curved bay windows, buffed oak floors, and twelve-foot corniced ceiling, was flawless. She ran her hands lightly over the creamy wainscotted walls, luminous enough to reflect light back toward the mullioned windows.

"What color is this? I love it!" she exclaimed.

"It's a blend. White eggshell finish paint dolloped with a trace of rose to warm it up. Come on, I'll show you what I'm working on right now in the master bedroom."

Drop cloths rimmed the parquet floor, and buckets, rollers, brushes, paint cans, and a stepladder littered the room, but even so, the space was enormous—huge and open, with skylights, vaulted ceilings, a pale marble fireplace floating between two wall-to-ceiling windows, and an adjoining dressing area the size of a small boutique. The bathroom was a self-contained spa, where additional skylights illuminated the sauna, sunken whirlpool, two-person shower stall, and his-and-her sinks that wrapped around two walls.

"I think I like my new neighbors already. Who are they?"

Pete bent closer to examine the finish work around the gold-fauceted sink. "One guy. Kind of eccentric. Probably not your type," he threw at her.

"What do you know about my type?"

"If Richard Ives is any indication, you like high-powered moguls who live and breathe big business and don't like to get their manicured hands dirty." Pete's dark blue eyes gazed challengingly into hers. "What about you, Comtesse? Feel like getting your hands dirty?"

"What do you have in mind?" Monique asked suspiciously.

"I could use an assistant today—unless you've got something better to do."

"Well, there's a whole stack of perfume strips that need stuffing into the next issue of *Perfect Bride*," she drawled.

For answer, he tossed her a car-wash sponge. "I'm going to show you what real work is like." Kneeling down, he poured paint into the metal tray along the baseboard, then dipped a second sponge into the wheat-colored paint. Baffled, Monique stared at the pristine white walls. "More blending?" she guessed.

"Uh-uh. Kindergarten stuff. Watch." He scraped excess paint from the sponge and climbed the stepladder. Pete stamped the sponge against the wall, leaving an imprint resembling Swiss cheese. Then he pressed it again and again in a row across the upper wall, and Monique watched a lovely pattern emerge.

"I get it."

"Great. I'll take the top half of the room, you work the bottom."

"Terrific. Another guy who insists on being on top."

His chuckle was deep and resounding through that enormous room. "Richard Ives must be even more of a tightass than I thought."

Your ass looks pretty firm from where I'm standing, Monique thought, gazing up at him, but merely said, "Drip paint on my head and you're a dead man."

Two hours later, with one wall completed and the daylight nearly gone, they quit for the day.

Pete served pizza and cold beer in the carriage house while Monique phoned home to tell Dorothy not to wait dinner.

"I didn't realize I was so hungry." Monique chomped blissfully on her third slice of pizza. "This is scrumptious."

"An old family recipe."

"Liar. I saw the Bertino's box in your garbage pail."

Pete helped himself to another slice from the ironstone serving plate. "Think you're pretty smart, don't you, Comtesse? Then answer this—why are you marrying that jerk?"

Monique stiffened. She swallowed and patted the corners of her mouth with a paper napkin. "You don't know anything about Richard Ives or about me," she said quietly.

"You're wrong. I've seen you with your mother—seen the soft side of you. I wonder if Richard Ives really knows how to make you happy."

"You overheard one phone call, and *that* makes you an expert on my relationship with Richard Ives? Well, I've got news for you, Dr. Ruth—every couple fights. I don't know what kind of rose-colored glasses you look through, but it isn't always champagne and daffodils in the real world. I know that, Richard knows that, and if you don't, then maybe I've taught *you* something today."

She pushed back her chair. "Thanks for the painting lesson and the pizza. I think I should leave now."

Pete stopped her as she reached for the mink parka

she'd tossed over the sofa. His paint-freckled hands were warm on her shoulders. His lips sought, and briefly tasted hers. "I wonder if Richard Ives would go to bat for you as enthusiastically as you did for him," he said softly. "He's a lucky man."

"You bet your ass he is. Guaranteed."

The door slammed behind her.

Pete watched from the window as she stomped up the path through the deepening twilight. When she'd disappeared, he carried the plates to the sink. He'd met a lot of women, but never anyone as dynamic, complicated, or infuriating as Monique D'Arcy. Beneath her bravado, her tough exterior, she was real, she was intense, not a shallow mannequin with plastic for a heart, but more like a dreamy-eyed kid with her nose pressed against a toy store window, yearning for everything. And the hell of it was, Pete thought, rinsing the last soapy plate in hot water, he wished he could be the one to give it all to her.

Chapter Twenty

Ana's glinting curls emerged through a diaphanous webbing of silver-shot tulle and airy lace as Angelina gently tugged the wedding gown into place.

"Gorgeous, my pet. Absolutely gorgeous!" Angelina stepped back to admire her creation. She was a reed-thin stick of a woman with a slew of movie credits going back to the forties, and two Oscars on her mantel for best costume design. Angelina Vargas had dressed more Hollywood stars than anyone but Edith Head.

"One little tuck here and you're all set. Don't move, child! I'll stick you with this pin if you don't stand still. Want dried blood all over your wedding gown? Shit, you're as fidgety as Katharine Hepburn was when we made *The Philadelphia Story*."

Ana made a face at Louise in the mirror.

"I'm just trying to see the back, Angelina."

"You see the back when I tell you to see the back. There. Now. Go ahead and look."

Ana stared at the magnificent gown of silver-white tulle. Angelina had outdone herself. The dropped poufed shoulders studded with satin rosettes and seed-pearl stars accentuated Ana's tiny waist, enveloped in tightly ruched fabric.

Since the wedding was to take place on the Fourth of July, Ana and John had decided on a red, white, and blue motif, complete with fireworks. The maid of honor and bridesmaids would wear blue, and would carry bouquets of red roses, violets, and beautiful white star stephanotis.

Ana herself would be all in silver-spun white, and her bouquet a confection of tea and baby white roses entwined with red and blue satin ribbons.

It's all going to work, she thought excitedly. *It's going to be spectacular.*

And this gown would be the show-stopper.

"I look so skinny," Ana breathed, unable to tear her eyes from her reflection. "Angelina, you're a genius."

"No. You're a toothpick," Louise interposed, moving off her velvet stool and fluffing the sweeping Cinderella skirt. "A toothpick with boobs," she added enviously, eyeing the neckline that was as low as Angelina dared push it without breaching the decorum befitting a potential First Lady. "John Farrell's going to drool like a baby when he sees you in this."

Delighted, Ana dipped and pirouetted before the blur of mirrors. She studied the scalloped hemline and chapel train in the rim of lights across the softly lit studio. It was perfect. It was more than perfect. It was a dream dress.

"Angelina, thank you, thank you. I adore it."

"Naturally. Now. What are we going to do about a headpiece?"

As Angelina experimented with veils, lace, headbands, and combs, and Louise slipped into her blue douppioni silk bridesmaid's sheath, Ana found herself looking ahead with unfettered enthusiasm to the coming months. There was nothing now to mar her happiness. Between now and the wedding, her only work commitment was the *Perfect Bride* shoot on Maui after New Year's, and cohosting an AIDS fund-raiser in late spring—unless she had to go back to the studio to loop some lines. Arnie had a script he was hot for her to accept; he swore that Sidney Pollack was all but signed to direct, but it wouldn't be shot until late summer, so she was pretty much free and clear.

Free and clear.

That's how she felt in general now that Eric was out of her hair. Out of the country, too, and hopefully for a long time. She smiled to herself, thinking of how clever she'd been arranging with Arnie for Eric to get that part. So long, sucker. She hadn't heard one word from him since Arnie had put the call in to the producer filming in Oslo.

Thank God Arnie was a man who collected favors like some men collected *Playboy.* The producer owed him, and had agreed, though cursing all the while, to offer a minor role in his political drama to an unknown wannabe named Eric Gunn.

Eric must have thought his fairy godfather had come through in spades, Ana reflected as she tried on a pearl-encrusted tiara. His greedy little ego meant more to him than revenge, just as she'd surmised. She only prayed the filming, scheduled to last four months, would go longer, and that he'd surprise even himself with a credible performance. If it led to more film work and a real break, maybe he'd leave her alone. Or maybe he'd stay in Europe and get caught up in the drug scene there, frying his brains so badly, he wouldn't even remember her name.

Please, Ana thought, gazing unseeingly into the mirror, her face framed by a coronet of tulle and lace. *Please let him fall off the Matterhorn or drown in the English Channel or overdose on Ecstasy in Pigalle.*

"You're going to be late for your meeting with Arnie," Louise said, breaking into Ana's thoughts. She was tapping at her watch. "Should I call the Polo Lounge and leave word?"

"Shit. Angelina, my head is spinning with all these choices. You pick and let me know. Louise, let Arnie know I'm on my way. Tell him to order my usual."

A short time later she was dashing through the lobby of the Beverly Hills Hotel toward the Polo Lounge. Her hair trailed behind her as she breezed through the maze of pink tablecloths and green chairs to the booth where Arnie was yakking away on his cellular phone.

The moment she sat down, Carlos whisked a pink napkin onto her lap, and the McCarthy salad onto the table before her.

"Mineral water, Miss Cates?" Carlos inquired.

"A glass of Soave, Carlos—thanks." Ana picked up the script Arnie pushed toward her while he continued to hammer out some deal on the phone. She flipped through it until he was finished.

"Looks intriguing. You're sure Sidney is in?"

"The ink's not dry, but it's a done deal, baby, you can take that to the bank." Arnie gulped at his grilled chicken breast. He swallowed noisily, then wiped his mouth on his napkin as daintily as a debutante. "This part's you, Ana. You want another Oscar—you got it with this one."

Ana promised she'd read it on the plane. "I've got an ET segment in New York tomorrow afternoon, and then I'm flying straight out to Rhode Island to spend the holidays with John's family. How soon do they need to know? And who's the male lead?"

Arnie leaned forward, his tanned, smooth-shaven face very close to the fresh flowers adorning the center of the table. "The male lead? The male lead, you want to know? Okay, sweetheart, here's your dessert." The words rolled off his tongue like a splendid present.

"Kevvv-innn Cossst-nerrr," he enunciated with exquisite slowness.

Ana grinned. "Okay, okay, I said I'd read the script. So maybe I'll plow through it tonight instead of on the plane."

Satisfied, Arnie waited until she had finished her salad before broaching the next topic. "So, you want to hear the bad news?"

"I never want to hear bad news." Ana suddenly noted his nervous fingering of the salt and pepper shakers, and her stomach constricted. "Arnie, what?"

"You know that friend of yours, the one I finagled that part for on Bettendorf's picture? He fucked up."

"What do you mean?"

"He's history. Bettendorf wants my ass for this one. Seems your friend Eric Gunn was either stoned, drunk, or a no-show from day one of the shoot. Bettendorf axed him from the picture a few weeks ago. Word gets around, your friend won't even be able to get work in a dog food commercial—as the dog."

"Do you know where Eric is now?" Ana reached shakily for her wine and tried to mask the frustration raging inside her. *Fucking idiot.* Couldn't even keep himself straight enough to take advantage of the one break he's had in his whole miserable life. She prayed Eric was still in Europe, too strung out to find his way home.

Arnie's next words offered her little comfort. "Who the hell knows? Or cares? Honey, scratch this guy off your list. He's a loser." He tossed his crumpled napkin onto his plate. "Come on, speak of the devil, I just saw Kevin come in. Let's go say hello and see if he can twist your arm."

That night Ana kept waiting for the phone or the doorbell to ring, expecting to hear from Eric in some insidious way she couldn't even imagine. *Don't be paranoid,* she told herself, the words of the script blurring before her eyes. *It's been weeks since he was canned and you haven't heard a word. Maybe he's completely self-destructed by now.*

But maybe Eric had nine lives. She'd thought she'd taken one of them years before, but she'd been wrong. Funny how scum, like cream, also rose to the top.

Ana tossed the script aside and unfolded herself from the living room sofa with a stretch. She wandered through the kitchen and out onto the veranda, sinking into the overstuffed wicker chair. Staring out at the moonlit palms reflected across the pool's glassy surface, her eyes darkened with old, unpleasant memories.

What an idiot I was to get hooked up with sleazebags like Eric and his crowd. Sixteen years old, naive as they come, and lonely as a minnow in a school of sharks. Eric had no trouble convincing me that he would take care of me. He took care of me all right. She covered her face in her hands and sighed as the ugly memories welled up.

When she'd stepped off that bus in Las Vegas, she hadn't known where her next meal was coming from. Eric approached her in the lobby of the Lucky Dice Hotel after she'd been turned down for a job waitressing tables. He bought her a steak dinner and introduced her to champagne—and to a side of nightlife she spent years trying to forget.

With a face like yours and that body, Ana, you got no business waiting tables. You're a star, baby, in every sense of the word. She wanted to believe him, she needed to. She was in a fairyland of flashing neon lights, where laughter and music played backup to the tinkle of slot machines, where no one slept and everyone dreamed, and she believed Eric all the way to the tips of her dusty cowboy boots.

He got her a job dancing in the second row at the Pot o' Gold Casino downtown, where the girls wore more makeup than clothes and the customers were too drunk to notice. Ana didn't care. She was making more money than she'd ever dreamed possible, and she was Eric's woman. She danced by night, slept by day, and partied with Eric in between. She had her choice of drugs from Eric's candy store of pills and powders, but was too chicken to dabble in more than a few joints and an occasional upper. And as for sex, the boys in Tennessee were fumbling choirboys compared to Eric. He taught her to make love like a woman.

The only thing that scared her was the gun, his father's black .45 which Eric kept under his pillow. It gave her the creeps. But for the most part, she was so high, so dazzled, she thought she was on top of the world. It took her months to realize she'd been mired in the gutter.

I've got a job for you, baby. A real acting job. You want to be a movie star, or not?

Something inside her had shrunk from the idea of taking off her clothes and making love with him in front of a camera, but she went ahead anyway to make Eric happy. The drugs helped her blot out what she was doing, helped her pretend it was only her and Eric making love. He was her costar in the first three porno films, and it wasn't until he brought in his friend Curt for a sadomasochistic menage à trois scene that she'd started to rebel. Before then she'd figured it wasn't hurting anyone—lonely guys in the downtown hotels rented these films for a little titillating company, that's all. And Eric told her this was how all the big movie stars got their start.

But Eric had tied her down, gotten rough, hurt her when she balked at scenes with Curt and his girlfriend, Gayleen. Before Ana realized it, she'd lost control over her life and her body. Eric was holding her prisoner, taunting her with that gun—the only thing of his father's that had returned in one piece from Vietnam. He was obsessed with it. He'd even taken his stage name from it. Ana never knew what his real last name was.

Don't even think about leaving me, baby. I'll see you dead first. You owe me. I took you in, fed you, and got you started in the business. I made you a star, baby. You ain't goin' nowhere.

Then one night Ana had enough. There had to be more to life than sex, booze, and grass—and Eric Gunn's fists. She'd actually started out the door with only his car keys and the clothes on her back, but Eric caught her and knocked her halfway across the room.

When she'd come to, he'd been asleep, sprawled across the sofa, his gun beside him. He must have kicked her. Her ribs were on fire, and her jaw throbbed beneath her black and blue eye. It took every ounce of her determination to stagger up and out the door. Somehow she was in the car, turning the key in the ignition, hope rising in her so agonizingly that she started to cry. She threw a glance in the rearview mirror and suddenly saw Eric plunging across the parking lot. He pointed the gun at her.

Bitch. You ain't goin' nowhere.

She threw the car into gear as a shot rang out, shattering the rear passenger window. With a scream she stomped on the accelerator. The engine died. Tears rolling down her face, Ana fumbled desperately with the starter. She glanced in the rearview mirror again. Nothing. Where had he gone?

As the engine fluttered to life once more, she floored the accelerator and the car lurched forward. Suddenly Eric sprang into the street directly before her, his face contorted with rage. Ana screamed and tried frantically to swerve.

The car hit him with a sickening thud.

She was halfway out of the car when she saw him lying twenty feet back. She moved closer a step, then another, her chest heaving with pain and nausea. His left leg was twisted in a sickening contortion of denim and mangled flesh that made her want to retch. His glazed eyes stared at the night sky.

He's dead. I killed him. Oh, God, what should I do now?

She glanced around. The street was empty.

Get out! a voice screamed inside of her. *Get away.*

And she did.

How stupid I was to run, she thought now as she crossed the patio steps leading down to the pool. The scent of the tub roses and bougainvillea drifted about her on the gentle gusts of the evening breeze.

Ana slipped off her moccasins and dangled her feet in the heated water. All those years I thought he was dead. I should have known Eric wouldn't let me off that easy.

I should have known a lot of things.

There should be a special place in hell for fucking lowlife bastards like him, she thought, splaying droplets of water off her polished toenails.

And the sooner he checks in, the better.

Maybe he already has.

Chapter Twenty-one

Teri stared with disbelief into the spotlight-framed mirror at Vidal Sassoon on Fifth Avenue.

Josie'd never recognize me if she tripped over my feet right now, she thought, watching Heidi, the six-foot-tall stylist with purple nails, massage coconut-scented gel through her hair.

When I get home, Josie will memorize every strand of this ninety-dollar haircut. I just hope she can figure out what makes it work so well.

Teri's jet-black hair had been trimmed to chin length and parted on the side. A sweep of bangs, a sleek curve slightly longer in front, and auburn highlights now framed her heart-shaped face.

But it wasn't only the haircut's upbeat new style that had transformed her. Dramatic makeup made her look as chic as Monique D'Arcy herself. The makeup artist had rimmed Teri's eyes in smoky charcoal with cinnamon shadow in the crease, and accentuated her slim eyebrows with deft pencil strokes. Teri rarely fussed with much more than a gloss of powder, blush, and lipstick, but Jeannine had dipped into a dozen pots, tubes, and jars to create drop-dead glamour.

It had been all but impossible to observe, much less study, the painstaking procedure: a blending of foundation, a sweep of highlighter, then blush, mascara, concealer, and lip liner—and a dizzying assortment of brushes. Jeannine's final touch had been coloring in Teri's precisely lined lips with deep ruby lipstick. And then a spritz of finishing spray "set" her exotic new look in place.

Grinning wickedly, Teri wondered what Grandma Parelli would think of the dark-eyed sophisticate smoldering back from the mirror.

She'd make a run for her rosary beads, Teri thought. *And pray for my soul.* Then she forgot about Grandma Parelli as Heidi lifted her bangs and accidentally shot hair spray into Teri's eyes.

"Oops, sorry about that, sweetheart. You okay? Don't worry, if the mascara runs, Jeannine will fix it."

How could she not be okay? Surrounded by all these stylists in high-tech hairdos and funky clothes, getting VIP treatment in this famous salon, being the focus of such frenetic activity—it all seemed unreal.

Livonia, Brian, school, and her problems seemed light-years away.

Behind her, she overheard Monique consulting with the cameraman and producer from *Entertainment Tonight.*

"Almost done," Heidi murmured, fluffing the sides of her hair.

Teri tried to calm the nervousness tightening inside her. She'd been so fascinated by Heidi's wizardry that she'd hardly paid attention to the camera dollying around her as Heidi had snipped and scrunched and brushed and blown.

But from here she was headed straight to the studio for an interview segment with Leeza Gibbons and Ana Cates. She only hoped that when they stuck the microphone in her face she would remember her name.

"Hold that right there, Teri. Now tilt your head to the left and smile. No, no, don't look in the camera. Look in the mirror. That's it, sweetheart, great."

The director ordered several more close-ups to intersplice with the interview segment, but just as Teri felt she was getting the hang of it, Monique said, "Time to scoot. The producer left five minutes ago." She stabbed out her cigarette and whisked Teri from her chair.

All around them, the crew began packing up.

"I *knew* you were a natural," Monique told her as she grabbed their coats. "Stay this relaxed with Leeza Gibbons and it'll be a cinch."

Monique swept her out of the salon, through the courtyard, and up the stairs before Teri even said thank-you to Jeannine and Heidi.

As they passed F.A.O. Schwarz, Teri exclaimed: "Oh, could we run in for one minute . . . ?"

But Monique shook her head and shooed her into the waiting limo.

"Sorry, we're barely going to make it. You'll have to do your Christmas shopping later."

Teri bit back her disappointment. There'd be no time later.

"I have a five-thirty flight out of LaGuardia," she reminded Monique. She watched as the enchanting window display receded from view.

"Right, right. You and Ana will share the car. She's headed to Rhode Island for the holidays."

Teri lapsed into silence, her hands folded in her lap. Monique was telling her something about changing into the tangerine suit once they arrived at the studio, and about lighting and sound checks, but Teri couldn't concentrate. She was fine when she was busy, but while the limo darted in and out of traffic her thoughts kept returning to the ordeal she faced.

Tomorrow she would meet her son for the first time. Tomorrow she would have to come to grips with the real person she had left behind so many years before.

As she'd glimpsed that wonderland of toys displayed in the F.A.O. Schwarz window, she'd suddenly yearned to bring Adam something wonderful.

But what do you give a child whom you've abandoned? The whole store wouldn't be enough to make up for what she'd done.

Andrew had been in Pittsburgh since Friday, meeting with attorneys on her behalf. Tomorrow she would have her own meetings—with the attorneys, the social worker, the pediatrician, the administrator of St. Philomena's—and with Adam.

Teri knew she had to get custody—at any cost— even if it cost her Brian. When she'd left yesterday, Brian had said he wasn't sure he could raise another man's child.

"I don't even know how to be a husband yet, Teri, much less a father. A father to a nine-year-old, for Christ's sake. I'm afraid that every time I look at him, all I'm going to think about is you and Andrew Leonetti. Not exactly a great way to start a marriage."

"Brian, I know you. You'll learn to love him."

"Sign language—*that* I know I can learn. Learning to accept another man's son is a different story."

"Is that a no?"

"It's a maybe. That's all I can give you right now, Teri—a maybe."

She had no choice but to be content with that. She wondered abruptly what Monique would think if she knew that one of her dream couples was enmeshed in a nightmare.

Oh, God, maybe I should tell her.

The thought had never occurred to her before. But suddenly it seemed important.

Could *Perfect Bride* sue her and Brian for breach of contract if they broke up?

She took a deep breath and glanced sideways at

Monique, who was engrossed in reading a sheaf of memos.

"You may want to kill me," Teri began, "but I think it's only fair that I tell you something. Only . . . I'm not sure where to start."

Monique said nothing, but a film of perspiration misted her face.

"Just start," she said tersely, rapidly lighting up another cigarette.

Her expression remained fixedly impassive as Teri haltingly told her the reason behind her trip to Pittsburgh.

"I guess it's kind of late for you to pick somebody else," Teri finished miserably.

Damned straight it is, Monique thought. Her hands shook ever so slightly as she shoved the sheaf of papers back into her portfolio.

What more could possibly go wrong? Eve's being stalked by a madman. Ana's hiding something regarding that weirdo I met at her pool. And now my Cinderella is about to lose her prince in a tabloid tale to rival anything out of Buckingham Palace.

The whole damned June issue was cursed, Monique decided. It could fall apart at any point for all sorts of idiotic reasons—none of them within her control.

I'm going to have apoplexy. Next thing I know, Richard will tell me that his annulment from Shanna never went through.

"Teri, I'm simply going to trust that everything between you and Brian will somehow work out," she said with far more calmness than she felt. "Let's proceed according to plan. I'm no marriage counselor, but I've seen the way he looks at you, and the guy is clearly bonkers. I'm going to gamble on this."

I've got to, she thought. *I have no other choice.*

Beside her, Teri stared out at Manhattan streets choked with traffic. She wished she had as much faith as Monique. But Monique didn't know the full story, she didn't know that Andrew had come back into Teri's life—or of the feelings for him still tugging at her.

She wished she had a crystal ball that would let her see into the future, show her which path she would take, and reveal who'd be waiting for her this April when she walked down the aisle.

But she didn't. She had only her instincts and her resolve to be a mother to Adam at last. The rest she'd have to make up as she went along.

Teri watched the monitor in the Green Room as Leeza Gibbons interviewed Ana Cates about preparations for her July fourth wedding to Senator Farrell.

Ana Cates was shorter than she appeared on-screen, but she was every bit as beautiful. *I've got to remember to get her autograph for everyone at the shop,* she reminded herself, plucking at the skirt of her tangerine suit. It wouldn't be as difficult to ask as she'd anticipated. Ana Cates had greeted her warmly when Monique had introduced them, given her several tips to help her relax on camera, and insisted that Teri join her in the VIP room at the airport until their flights were called.

Who'd have thought such a famous movie star would be so down to earth? Teri wondered as she glanced over at the olive leather satchel Ana had left on the settee. A hardcover book peeked from the outside pocket. Teri couldn't resist.

What did a movie star read in her spare time? She reached over and pulled the book up so that she could see the title.

Reaching Sexual Satisfaction: How to Relax and Reach the Ecstasy You and Your Partner Deserve by Ellis B. Severance, Ph.D.

Flabbergasted, Teri guiltily began stuffing the book

back into the tote, but not before the door flew open. Monique called in, "Your turn, sweetie. Break a leg."

Must be research for a role, Teri decided moments later as the sound man fastened her microphone to the lapel of her suit. There's no way that someone as sexy as Ana Cates could be having trouble in bed. Was there?

Wait'll I tell Josie.

Then Leeza Gibbons was smiling at her, the red light flashed on, and she didn't have time to think about anything except trying not to make a total fool of herself in front of millions of viewers.

Ana snapped the book closed and flipped it facedown onto her lap as Monique breezed into the Green Room.

"It went well, don't you think?" Ana asked quickly.

Monique nodded, and tossed down her portfolio. She'd meant to watch Teri's interview on the monitor, but unnerved by Teri's comments in the limo, she couldn't help grasping for some straw of reassurance from Ana.

"So, have you heard any more from your friend Eric?" she asked casually as she poured coffee from the silver thermal pot.

Color rushed into Ana's face. "As a matter of fact, no, Monique." Her voice took on a wary note. "I trust you've kept this to yourself. You promised me you wouldn't mention anything to anyone. . . ."

"I haven't, don't worry, I can keep a secret. Guaranteed. I'm keeping tabs on all my perfect brides only to make sure everything's cool. Think of me as the mother hen, and you're all my little chickadees—at least until the shoot is in the can."

Ana laughed and visibly relaxed. She accepted the cup of coffee Monique handed her, taking care not to spill any on the book in her lap or on her rust-colored leather skirt. "I guess I'm just not used to being mothered," she said. "But if it makes you feel better, Mother Hen, you can relax. You must have scared Eric off, because I haven't heard a word from him since that day."

"Good." *Thank you, God.* Monique sent up a silent prayer. "And how's John?"

"Like a kid waiting for Christmas." Ana's face lit with animation for the first time since the cameras stopped. "He adores this time of year. His family has a lot of traditions, I guess, and he's pretty sentimental about it all. His parents are planning a monumental New Year's Eve celebration." She sighed and took a sip of her coffee. "Half of Rhode Island society will be there. Personally, I'd rather hole up at a secluded ski lodge where the cider is warm, the nights are cold, and the phones are disconnected."

Monique laughed. "I know what you mean. But you'd better get used to kissing up to babies and society matrons if you plan on moving to Pennsylvania Avenue." Monique eyed the overturned book on Ana's lap. "What's that? *How to Survive a Weekend Among the Rich and Stuffy*"?

"Not exactly," Ana began as the door opened and Teri bounced in.

"It was fun," she bubbled. "I could get used to this."

Monique started gathering up coats. "Traffic's horrendous at this time of day. I hate to shove you ladies out the door, but if you don't want to miss your flights . . ."

As Teri reached for her overnight bag, her gaze fell on the book Ana still held. "Isn't that mine?" she asked slowly.

"Caught in the act." Wincing, Ana handed over the slim green volume: *Sign Language Made Easy.* "Sorry, I'm a hopeless busybody. I couldn't resist checking out what you're reading."

"That's okay, Miss Cates." Teri met her gaze squarely, a slight smile playing about her lips. "We're even. I checked out yours too."

"National Enquirer. How may I direct your call?"

"Gimme your best reporter."

"One moment, please."

Eric shifted the telephone into the crook of his shoulder, freeing up his hands to light the joint he'd rolled. Why did every female under the age of twenty suddenly drone with that same nasal accent? Was this some Valley version of *The Stepford Wives,* for chrissake?

"Enquirer." The voice was female and chipper.

"Uh, yeah, I was curious about what you'd pay for a juicy bit of cover material."

"Depends. Is it substantiated?"

"No, I made it fucking up. Of course it's substantiated."

"Is it about a prominent celebrity?"

"About as prominent as they come, lady. How much?"

"Photos?" She sounded matter-of-fact, as if she were simultaneously filing her nails.

"And videotapes. *If* the price is right."

"Who's calling, and what's this about?"

"I need to know what you pay—ball park—"

"And I need a little more than you're giving me, pal. I've got better things to do than play knock-knock games all day."

Bitch. Screw you.

"I'll get back to you." Eric slammed down the phone.

You ain't goin' nowhere, lady. We'll do this later. On my terms. But first, back to Plan A. Ana owes me a whopping late charge, and it's time to collect.

He picked up the .45 and spun it, gunslinger fashion, then fired off two shots into the wall beside the phone. Immediately, he felt better.

From downstairs came the familiar thud of arthritic old Kodiac pounding the ceiling with his broom.

"Fuck you!" Eric shouted into the cold-air return, and stomped his boot repeatedly in reply.

For good measure, he fired off another shot.

Half an hour and two joints later, Eric tilted back in his chair and reread his little masterpiece:

> Something old, something new:
> I've still got the goods on you.
> Pay the money, I've upped the price.
> Or I'll throw shit instead of rice.
> Enquiring minds would love to know
> That Ana Cates was Candy Monroe.
> The hit-and-run should get you jail.
> Trailing chains instead of a veil.

Eric chuckled to himself as he reread the lines he had written and then squashed the letter into a beer-stained red envelope. Sitting at the wobbly table littered with fast-food containers and sogged cigarette ashes stuck in place by long-dried booze, he wrote Ana's name and that fancy address of hers and imagined her shock when she realized that he was back on her case.

Man, she probably thinks she's off the hook, figures I've forgotten about the money. Babe, if you think I'm kissing off one red cent of that half million, you're out of your beautiful little mind.

He licked the stamp and then sucked down a long swig of warm Bud to wash away the taste.

As he headed toward the door of the one-room walkup, he tripped over two weeks worth of dirty laundry he couldn't afford to wash at the Suds and Spin. It had been molding there since he'd returned from that lousy job in Sweden.

Shit, he had to get out of this slime hole. He was

cut out for better things than this. He could have been rich, he should have been on top of the world. Too bad there'd been so many assholes stinking up that movie set in Oslo—that job had sounded real sweet at first. It was his first break in years, a chance to show what he could do. He had more talent in his left testicle than Ana Cates had in her whole damn body. But that A.D. on the set had been after him from day one. Shit, everyone did coke, but who did she report? Only me. And the call sheet had been all screwed up. He hadn't been late—not one goddamn time. Who the fuck cares, Eric told himself, sneering at the bottle of beer. The picture sucked anyway. The director was a no-talent moron. The only thing he regretted was the money. That's okay, he'd get it from Ana.

He'd better get it soon. He could barely scrape up enough cash to keep his supply flowing, especially since that bastard Vinnie stopped dealing on credit.

He kicked at the mound of rancid clothes. Stinking laundry. Stinking place. Stinking bitch. He'd given her a start when she was nothing but a runaway hick. What had she ever done for him? Paid him back with the front end of his own goddamned car. He wanted to kill her just thinking about it.

Well, it was her turn to pay. And later, when the truth came out, she'd get hers in spades.

What will stuffed-shirt Farrell think of his Hollywood slut when the tabloids explode with the pictures? Or when he gets a load of the tapes showing his little honey in action?

Oh, yeah, he'd call that reporter back—when he was ready.

Ten minutes later Eric dumped the letter in the mailbox on Western Avenue. The lid banged shut.

Read it and weep, slut. That private jet you're flying is about to crash.

. . . .

"Hey, Rudy, can you make out this address? Some genius used a red marker on a red envelope, and naturally didn't bother with a return address." Otis Rorchin flipped the envelope to his fellow postal clerk with a snort.

"I think they were dipping into some early holiday cheer too," Rudy remarked. "Look at all the crap slopped over this—washed off half the writing."

"Betcha somebody's gonna get scratched off somebody else's Christmas list. Too bad."

"Nah, less work for us." Rudy grinned, nodding toward the lobby congested with customers, all balancing bundles of envelopes or brown packages laced with strapping tape.

He tossed the red envelope into the dead letter pile, plopped the Closed sign in front of his station, and whistled on his way to the john.

Chapter Twenty-two

Nothing Teri had read in her psychology classes, no crash course in sign language communication, no soul searching, and no prayers prepared her for the experience of meeting her son.

With Andrew beside her, she walked up the shoveled walk leading to the small brick home in Aliquippa, where Adam's foster parents lived. A painted swing set in the hilly backyard creaked in the wind as she scanned the modest neighborhood plunked between the steel mills on the river and downtown Pittsburgh.

What would he be like, this little boy of hers?

Andrew had told her he loved comic strips, the Lakers, and Nintendo. He had a ready grin, freckles, and a surprisingly mature sense of humor. And he was athletic. She'd clung to these precious, meager tidbits all during the endless meetings with the lawyers and social workers. When she'd met with the pediatrician, he'd assured her that Adam's deafness hadn't hampered his development. In fact, he was an exceptionally bright and well-adjusted child.

Teri'd wanted to know what had caused the deafness, and if there was any hope Adam might someday be able to hear. Had she inadvertently done something during her pregnancy to cause it? The pediatrician had shaken his head.

"Your son's deafness is irreversible," he told her gently. "And it's no one's fault. I've reviewed Adam's medical records as well as the ones you and Mr. Leonetti have supplied. Ms. Mathews, one in every thousand babies is born with a hearing impairment. Sometimes it's genetic—when both parents carry a recessive gene. But sometimes, as in this case, it's a sporadic occurrence with no known cause."

He'd gone on to reassure her that the chances of deafness in any other children she might have were remote.

But at the moment Teri wasn't concerned about any other children.

Now that she was finally here with the letter she'd written to Adam in her hand, she only hoped she had found the right words to tell him what was in her heart.

"I wasn't this nervous meeting Ana Cates," Teri whispered as they started up the front steps, where fresh broom strokes were etched in the dusting of remaining snow.

"Relax. He's a great kid, he takes after his mother." Andrew grinned. He squeezed her arm. "Go on. Ring the bell."

"Please, come in," said the attractive thirtyish-looking woman who answered the door. "I'm Natalie Morowski, you must be Teri Mathews."

Strands of tinsel clung to her slim-fitting jeans and oversize cable-knit sweater. "Adam's been waiting so you could help him hang the last ornaments on our tree. We spent the morning baking gingerbread men, and he must have combed his hair twenty-five times in the past hour," she said, taking their coats and ushering them into the wood-paneled family room. "He couldn't be more excited if Bart Simpson were coming."

Teri scarcely heard. She moved trancelike toward

the boy, who stood motionless beside the gaily decorated tree.

Long-lashed gray eyes swept over her appraisingly. He looked very serious. No smile lit that scrubbed little face with the pointed chin and rosy cheeks splattered with freckles. The dark straight hair falling over his forehead belied whatever care he had given it, it was as shiny as the tinsel clutched in his fist, as casual as the red and black geometric sweater draping his skinny form. His jeans looked new, his sneakers did not.

Teri's heart pounded in her ears as she knelt before him.

"Hello, Adam, I'm so happy to meet you," she signed in the way that she had practiced half the night in the motel mirror.

Adam signed back something Teri struggled to follow. Sweating, she glanced at Natalie for help, then turned wildly back to Adam. *What was he saying? And still no smile.*

"He said, 'Me too,'" Natalie put in, her voice cracking a little.

Andrew sauntered forward and slapped high-fives with Adam. "Teri and I want to take you downtown for lunch. Okay?" he signed.

It was obvious Andrew and Adam had already established a good rapport in the short time Andrew had been visiting him. Wide-eyed, Adam nodded eagerly, and signed something back so quickly, Teri again couldn't follow. In frustration, she turned quizzically to Andrew.

"He wants to know if we'll come back and help him finish the tree, and eat some gingerbread cookies," he told her with an encouraging smile.

She hoped she didn't look as nervous as she felt. She envied their rapid, silent fluency. Andrew's work with autistic children required proficiency in signing. His experience was obvious, and in sharp contrast to her own faltering efforts.

"I'd love to," she signed slowly, crossing her wrists on her chest, palms in.

She waited, holding her breath. Had she done it right? Had he understood?

And then at last, Adam smiled. Smiled and nodded and walked right up to her.

He took her hand and began leading her to the front door. Her fingers tingled at his touch. It had been more than nine years since she'd enfolded that little hand in her own, marveling at its tiny perfection. Nine years since she'd said hello and good-bye in a single sentence, sending Adam off to what she'd thought was a far better life than she could ever give him.

And now he was back, tugging at her hand, tugging at her heart—tugging Teri out the door and toward a future they could share.

It's almost as if he's waited for me, Teri thought later, watching Adam wolf down his ketchup-sodden burger, double order of fries, and tall root beer beneath the twinkling holiday lights in the TGIF dining room. *Waited for me to grow up and be ready to take care of him.*

But she'd missed so much. His first smile, first tooth. First day of school. Christmases and birthday parties and everyday kisses and hugs.

I'll make up for it now, Adam—we both will, she added silently with a quick, warm glance at Andrew, who was comfortably munching a mushroom cheeseburger beside her. Andrew was marvelous with his son, calm and steady, at ease in a way that was purely instinctual. And they were so alike, Teri noted, watching them together in the noisy restaurant. The gray eyes, so clear and intense, the same quicksilver smiles, the same enthusiasm for life, for people.

I wonder if Andrew sees anything of me in Adam, she mused, sipping her Coke. *He has my dark hair, but what else? My eyebrows. And Daddy's chin, I think. Thank God he didn't get Grandma Parelli's nose.*

The afternoon passed in a whirl of ice cream cones, bowling, and arcades. Andrew already told her that Adam was mature for his age, funny, bright, and athletic. She found he was right on all counts. She didn't give Adam the gift she'd brought him until they'd returned to the house and put the finishing touches on the tree. The Morowski kids helped, but Natalie shooed them into the kitchen when she saw Andrew lift the packages from the rental car's trunk.

Andrew gave his gift first, a pair of high-tech high-top athletic shoes in size three. The salesman had promised him they were the hottest shoe of the moment, and from the expression on Adam's face when he pulled them out of the tissue paper, he hadn't lied.

Teri quietly handed over the box wrapped in Santa Claus paper. "I hope you like it," she signed slowly, guided by Andrew.

Adam's gray eyes, so beautifully sensitive and alive, just like Andrew's, lit with joy as he held up the Turbo Express Portable, the hand-held video game system Marie's kid brother swore was the most awesome Christmas gift in the world.

Teri had spent a chunk of money she'd socked away toward a down payment on the new house, but it was worth every nickel, she decided when Adam threw his arms around her and squeezed tight.

She didn't need an interpreter to tell her she'd made him happy. *It's only the beginning,* she promised him silently, hugging Adam to her as tears filled her eyes. *I might not be able to give you rooms full of fancy toys or closets full of designer gym shoes all the time. I can't give you hearing. But I'll give you love, Adam, I promise you that. You'll be able to count on me from now on—no matter what. I'll always be there for you, starting now.*

On the drive back to the motel, Andrew reached over and clasped her hand. "He's pretty terrific, isn't he?"

"Very terrific. Did you see the way he brought us the biggest of the gingerbread cookies? I thought I would cry right there."

"I got a kick out of the way he opened the packages. Ripped that wrapping paper to shreds," Andrew chuckled, "and then got so engrossed in that video game, he almost forgot to wave good-bye."

"He'll win Brian over, I know he will," Teri almost whispered.

Andrew said nothing. She glanced over at him. His eyes were locked on the road ahead.

"I'm going to skip next semester at school," Teri went on brightly to fill the awkwardness. "And I'm going to work out a different schedule at the shop. I want to spend as much time with Adam as possible once he comes home with me."

"The social worker thinks the final custody hearing will be scheduled for mid-January," Andrew said, pulling into the motel parking lot. "We can go over the paperwork at dinner."

As they headed through the small courtyard bordering their rooms, Teri stopped abruptly and faced him. "Andrew, I told her I want to share custody with you. You can come see Adam anytime, and he can spend holidays with you. . . ."

Her voice trailed off at the expression blazing in his eyes as he turned to her and grasped her arms. His fingers unintentionally bit right through her sleeves as he held her hard and his breath steamed in the chill air.

"That's not what I have in mind. I'll accept it if I have to, Teri, but only as a last resort. What I want is something completely different—I want *full* custody, *joint* custody, along with you. A real home for our son, not two homes, not shipping him alone back and forth between Arizona and Michigan."

He yanked her close, urgency heating his voice.

"Come on, Teri, reach for the brass ring," he urged. His eyes burned into hers, compelling and yearning all at once. "We can be a family. You, me, our son." He smiled, a smile full of such eagerness, he could have been nine like Adam. "You can't tell me you don't want that as much as I do."

"I don't know what I want," Teri gasped, frightened by her own insane urge to throw her arms around his neck in agreement, to succumb to both the logic and emotion of his appeal.

"Don't run from me this time, Teri. I want to be a part of your life. Dammit, I *am* a part of your life—from now on. Don't relegate me to watching from the sidelines."

Teri wanted to tear herself from his arms before she surrendered to them. Her head and her heart were at odds with her soul—and with each other, and she was torn in two. "This isn't fair, Andrew," she rasped, trying to think clearly, trying to stay focused despite the emotions swirling through her. "Brian . . ."

"Brian be damned." Andrew's usually gentle face grew hard, rigid as stone. "Don't you see, Teri? He can't make up his mind. What kind of love is that? I don't have a doubt in the world. Doesn't that matter to you?" Suddenly, he leaned down roughly and kissed her, his lips warm and demanding against her mouth.

"Teri. I've missed you so much."

His hands slid up to cradle her neck and the kiss softened, deepened, became tender and hungry and needful. "Teri," he said quietly. "This could be the happiest Christmas of our lives."

And the worst of Brian's, she thought dismally. Yet she found herself lifting a hand to caress Andrew's lean cheek, red and rough from the cold.

She said softly, "Give me time, Andrew. I just met my son today after nine years apart. I can't possibly make any decisions that may last for a lifetime, not now. I can't look beyond this afternoon, or tomorrow."

"I won't ask you to. I just want you to know how I

feel. Last time around I never had the chance to tell you."

There was no note of recrimination in his voice. Teri felt a warm surge of gratitude. Not once had Andrew ever condemned her for the choice she had made, a choice that had cost him nine years of knowing his son—and had cost Adam nine years in foster homes. Yet there was only understanding and tenderness in his face as he gazed down at her now. Could it work? Could they be a real family after such a belated start?

Slowly, Teri stepped back, disengaging from his arms, from the emotions flowing between them.

"Let's take Adam sledding tomorrow," she suggested, turning back toward the motel door. "Is there a good hill nearby?"

"I'll find one," Andrew told her. He was right behind her. "I'll find whatever you want."

That was the problem, she reflected as she fit her key into the lock. She didn't *know* what she wanted. But she did know one thing.

Someone she cared about would be deeply hurt once she finally figured it out.

Mister D's Sports Bar erupted in a chorus of raucous jeers as the Detroit Lions fumbled the ball on the goal line with no time remaining in the fourth quarter.

"Assholes. Fucking assholes. How could they screw up a play like that?" Linc Armstrong shouted into Brian's ear.

"Because they stink," Brian said in disgust, and signaled the waitress to bring another pitcher to the table.

Garlands of green and gold roping framed the wide-screen TVs scattered strategically around the packed bar. Monday night was standing room only at Mister D's, but this group was a regular fixture in the front corner under the moose head. Tonight, in honor of the season, a blinking red light was affixed to the beast's nose.

Brian's mood, however, was anything but festive. Teri had been gone four days and he missed her like hell. All he could think about was that tonight she was probably with Andrew Leonetti. She'd phoned yesterday, elated after her first meeting with Adam. Yet when he'd asked her if she'd be home by Christmas Eve, she'd hesitated. "It depends," she'd said evasively, and changed the subject. He'd wanted to ask her about Andrew Leonetti, if she was spending much time with him, but he'd already guessed the answer to that.

Brian's eyes narrowed. "I'd like to punch that jerk's lights out."

"Who? Fontes?" Linc asked. "It's not his fault the team sucks."

"Not him," Brian muttered. "Someone else."

He couldn't figure out why it felt so strange to be there watching *Monday Night Football* with the guys. He was a regular—he usually enjoyed the rowdy atmosphere, the endless pitchers of beer, the pretty waitresses in their tight red shorts and black jerseys. There'd been a time when he'd come here as much to eye the tight-jeaned single women who decorated the barstools as to hang out and watch the games with his friends.

Until he'd met Teri.

There is nothing wrong with being here, he told himself. Teri had even encouraged him to keep busy while she was gone. But for some reason, it wasn't much fun. He couldn't even concentrate on the game.

Through the smoke haze he saw Josie and his sister, Tina, sail through the front door, stomping snow off their boots. He waved them over.

"Heard from Teri?" Josie demanded as she pulled up a chair.

"Sure did."

"Well . . . what did she have to say?" Tina

prompted him, nudging him and helping herself to a sip of Linc's beer.

"Not much."

"Well, did she say when she's coming home?" Josie pressed.

"Nope."

Josie and Tina exchanged glances.

"You're not exactly Dan Rather tonight," Tina remarked with exasperation.

"Hey, Teen, give the guy a break," Linc's brother, Steve, interjected from across the table. "What's with the third degree?"

But before Tina could argue, Brian stood up and tossed a ten-dollar bill on the table. "Forget it. I'm going home."

He didn't feel the biting cold as the door swung shut on the clamor and their pleas that he stay for one more round. Restless, Brian left his car in the parking lot and began walking home, needing to discharge some of the bitter energy churning inside him. He followed his steaming breath across deserted intersections and dim side streets, crunching ice and snow beneath his hunting boots.

What was it he had told Teri? He couldn't raise another man's child? What a load of crap. It wasn't the kid that bothered him, it was the other man. Andrew fucking Leonetti. That's what it all boiled down to.

In frustration, he suddenly scooped up a handful of icy snow and packed the meanest, hardest snowball he could mold. He threw it hard against the rear brick wall of the 7-Eleven.

"Right over the plate," he muttered. "Leonetti, you're *out!*"

He wished it were that easy.

When Brian was eight, he wanted desperately to pitch for his Little League team. He wanted that more than anything in the world. But the coach put him at third base and told him to work on his curveball—and maybe he'd get the chance to pitch relief.

He practiced till his arm ached, he begged the coach before every game. "Better," the coach had told him. "Keep working on it, and we'll see." But when the regular pitcher got the chicken pox, it was Henry Saganski the coach put in.

Disgusted, discouraged, and mad as hell, Brian quit the team that night. Nothing his father said or did could dissuade him. "Quitters never win," Glenn Michaelson told him, but Brian refused to listen. Pride wouldn't let him stay after he'd been so blatantly passed over.

Two days later Henry Saganski broke his leg.

"I could've used you," the coach told him regretfully when he bumped into the Michaelsons at Baskin-Robbins. "I had to put in Paulie Corrigan, and he doesn't have half the arm you do, son."

His father said nothing, but Brian knew exactly what he was thinking. *Quitters never win.*

He had quit before he'd given himself—or the coach—a chance. He'd had the rest of the season to think about that lesson, to regret letting his pride ruin his opportunity.

Maybe I'm doing it again, Brian thought. *Letting my pride get in the way of what I want. Do I really want to call it quits with Teri?*

Quitters never win. And Leonetti knows that. He's not quitting. He's in there pitching his guts out.

And what the hell am I doing?

Suddenly Brian began hurling snowball after snowball against the brick wall like a coin-fed pitching machine gone wild. In a burst of newfound zeal, he let out a whoop and started running toward home. His mind reeled with plans.

Tomorrow, on the way to the shop, he would swing by the library to check out some books on sign language. And after dinner he'd rummage through his parents' attic for his old Lionel train set. And somewhere, if his mother hadn't thrown it away, he still had his old comic book collection. Yes! Adam would love that.

This ball game's going into extra innings, Leonetti, he thought with fresh determination. *And this time I'm going to be on the field when the last ball is thrown.*

Chapter Twenty-three

"You're going to love panettone," Nico said to Eve across the small café table as traffic whizzed through the streets of Bologna. He watched her bite into the raisin-studded loaf that was a cross between a cake and a sweet yeast bread as he studied her face expectantly.

"Heaven," Eve breathed.

Nico sipped his marsala with satisfaction. "You see? We Italians know what's good."

Eve felt as if she were floating, as light and airy as this orange-flavored panettone farcito layered with chocolate cream filling. This time in Italy had been a blessed reprieve from the pressures she'd faced alone in New York.

She actually felt safe. Billy Shears couldn't touch her here. Not in the roomy ochre house on the out-skirts of the city, its two stories overflowing with Nico's warm and lively family. Not in this charming café on the Via Rizzoli, with Nico right beside her and Tom Swanson dutifully stationed near the front door six small tables away.

Interpol hadn't detected anyone suspicious trying to follow her to Italy. And Maxine Goodman had left a message on her machine right before she left, assuring her that there would be an extra bodyguard assigned for the shoot in Maui.

Maui.

Suddenly Eve shivered. There must be a draft. Or was it something else? A premonition?

Ridiculous, she told herself, and sipped her espresso. *I'm just tired. Mama Caesarone warned me I'd be pooped during the first trimester. It's perfectly natural.*

She forced herself to look ahead, past the *Perfect Bride* shoot, past her Estēe Lauder commitments in February, to the wedding in May and then the baby's birth at the end of summer.

Think about those things—the good things—not Billy Shears, she scolded herself.

She fingered the miniature gold *cornu,* the horn charm secured on the gold chain around her neck. "It will ward off the evil eye and protect you, bambina. Wear it every day," Nico had told her on the plane from Rome to Bologna.

So far, so good.

But why did she suddenly have such a weird feeling—a feeling that something terrible was about to happen?

"Bambina." Nico broke into her thoughts, covering her hand with his. "I think we walked too much tonight. You look like a woman who needs her bed."

He settled the bill and wrapped Eve's mohair cape around her shoulders as they stepped out into the cool, starry night. Eve looked so beautiful these days, low-key and comfortable in her ponytail and sweats, her face scrubbed and glowing without all those layers of makeup. Au natural she was magnificent, as beautiful and timeless as the terra-cotta Madonna they'd admired while strolling in the Piazza Nettuno before dinner.

I was an imbecile to fool around with that sister of

hers, he reflected as Eve nestled against him in the taxicab. Tom Swanson stared out the window from the front seat as the driver caroomed through the medieval streets.

Nico was furious with Margo for persisting in calling him. He'd thought she was sophisticated enough to understand it had been a fling, nothing more. He should have remembered that American women were not like Europeans; they simply didn't understand.

Her phone calls were increasingly annoying. He had nothing more to say to her. He had told her from the first what she could expect, and now that it was over, she seemed to have forgotten that he had never promised her anything more than the most casual of affairs.

A pleasant pastime, these dalliances, but he had made a mistake choosing Eve's own sister, intriguing as she was.

His father had told him at the age of seventeen: "When a mistress and a wife know each other's names, you'll find yourself in court trying to defend yours."

Stupido. That idiotic affair with Margo Hämeläinen could ruin everything. Granted, she'd been exciting and had possessed a surprisingly adventurous appetite, but she hadn't been worth the risk.

How could he have been such a fool?

Well, it was over now. *Finito.* Nico brushed a loose strand of hair back from Eve's face and kissed her cheek.

"There's nothing to worry about," he murmured half to himself. "I'll take care of you, my precious bambina. Rest easy."

Easy, Billy Shears gloated as his fingers danced over the security alarm keypad in Eve's New York penthouse. *That was mindlessly easy.*

The black cat watched him unblinkingly as he

flipped on the recessed lighting and stared expectantly into the room. The housekeeper, Clara, had left hours earlier and wouldn't be back until the next day. He knew her schedule by heart.

He knew plenty.

Containing his euphoria with great effort, he prowled through the apartment. The ballerina sculpture drew him immediately.

"Pretty girl," he purred, stroking the sparkling crystal. Suddenly his fingers recoiled. "But cold and hard. Not soft and warm like my Eve." His obsidian eyes narrowed as he struck the ballerina from her perch and a thousand shards of crystal shattered across the marble floor.

"Not . . . like . . . my . . . Eve . . ."

He was oblivious of the scrunch of glass against marble as his feet grated through the foyer. His own ragged breathing echoed in his ears as he stole down the hallway to her bedroom.

He touched all of her clothes.

Smelled them.

Buried his face in her pillow.

And lost all track of time as he writhed beneath the rose and cream comforter in the huge satin-sheeted feather bed. Soft. So soft. Like her.

His hand sticky with his love for her, he traced his fingers along the mirror where he pictured her standing.

Soon, Eve. Very, very soon.

He inspected her dressing table, touching every bottle and jar. Then he saw the silver-framed picture— of that man, the one who had given him the car keys.

Nico, she called him. Eve, how could you? he wailed. Bringing another man into our bedroom? You must be punished.

He slashed the bed sheets to thin, shimmering ribbons. He hurled the framed photograph of Nico against the mirror. The cat shrieked its protest. He chased it, but it disappeared into one of the darkened rooms down the hall and he grew bored with searching for it.

Next time.

He played the answering machine before he left.

Silly drivel. Business mumbo-jumbo. Christmas calls.

Week-old messages, boring and meaningless.

Halfway out of the dimly lit room, a woman's crisp voice stopped him in his tracks.

Bingo.

"Eve. Maxine Goodman. Nothing new on this end regarding Billy Shears. If there's no break by Christmas, I'll be sending an additional bodyguard to meet you in Maui. Just a precaution. Dean Everett is with our L.A. office—he's top-notch, a former Secret Service agent. You'll be in very good hands. I'll be in touch."

The answering machine clicked off with two beeps.

Dean Everett. Dean Everett.

Billy Shears let himself out of the penthouse as easily as he'd let himself in. They thought they were so smart. But he was smarter than all of them.

He'd gotten close to Eve time and time again, outwitting them without breaking a sweat. He knew every circled date in her appointment book, every phone number, every address. He knew what she wore to lunch, what she ate for dinner, what she kept in her glove compartment.

Easy. It had been so easy.

Take the keys. Park the car. Fondle all the goodies she left behind.

And always snip, snip, snip.

An hour later he was home, poring over his bankbook. Three thousand, two hundred and forty-seven dollars, Billy read gleefully.

Aloha.

Chapter Twenty-four

"I can't, *Johnny.* Not in this house. Not with your parents sleeping down the hall."

The logs in the guest bedroom fireplace were ablaze and so was John, but Ana felt as cold as the icicles fingering down from the eaves outside her window.

Senator John Farrell, his tanned, fit body clad only in a paisley brocade robe, stared at her in bewilderment. "You've got to be kidding."

"I'm not." Ana hunched up defensively in the high four-poster feather bed. She pulled the straps of her pink teddy onto her shoulders with a sigh. John was staring at her as if she'd just doused him with ice water. Really, she couldn't help how she felt. His parents sent off vibes that could make Madonna frigid.

But John was evidently oblivious of them. "Ana, don't be ridiculous. They're five rooms down the hall."

It *was* ridiculous, she thought. She tried to remember the sensible advice in her book. *You have permission to relax. Focus on the pleasure. Center on the sensation. Let yourself go.*

None of it was working. *Dr. Severance, you're a crock.*

She felt tight as a drum and devoid of any passion. Maybe it was this house.

Fine old Chippendale furnishings, antique mahoganies, and rich leather worn to a high gloss. Costly Oriental rugs, priceless gilt-framed paintings, and the elegant comfort of brocade tapestry and fresh flowers spiking out of vermeil pots that had been in the family for generations.

Everything seemed dark and heavy and New England. She felt more like a visitor to the Smithsonian than part of a warm and cozy home. Maybe it was because John's mother had said: "We're delighted to have you, dear. Please make yourself comfortable," but her eyes had conveyed, "You don't belong here. You'll never belong here."

John jumped from the bed, his robe falling open. Ana noted his erection hadn't completely given up on her. Guilt ate at her. A little voice inside kept screaming that it was all in her mind—sex was supposed to be fun.

It was easy and natural. That's what all the books said. That's what all the movies said. That's what Dr. Severance said. Loving John should be enough to make it work.

But she felt dry and cold and miserable. And the accusing look on his face didn't help. A sheen of tears blurred her vision.

She whispered, "I feel like they're going to know."

"Ana, they think I'm in my own room, resting up so I can play tennis with my father at the club at seven and still be home and showered for breakfast by nine. And they've probably been snoring in each other's faces for hours already." He sat down beside her and took her hand, his fingers rubbing back and forth across her palm.

"You've been so tense these past few days. What's really bothering you? And I want the truth."

Ana answered immediately. "Your parents don't like me."

"They don't like anybody born west of the Hudson," he laughed. "It's nothing personal, Ana. Believe me."

His lightly tracing fingers made her palm tingle. "I'm dreading the party," she confessed. She bit her lip and met his gaze with soulful directness. "All those bluebloods looking down on me, waiting for me to pour ketchup on my shrimp cocktail or slurp my soup."

John shook his head as he gathered her close. "You're a movie star, darling. They'll be at your feet. You could spoon caviar on your ice cream and they'd simply assume it was the latest rage in California cuisine." He pressed a kiss against her ear and whispered into it: "Where is all this insecurity coming from? I've never known you to worry so much about what other people think."

"It's just that these are the people you're depending on to back your campaign. I don't want to do anything to jeopardize their support, or to make you look bad."

"You couldn't if you tried. Come on." He snuggled up beside her. "Enough worrying about my parents, about the party, about the campaign. Don't even think about the wedding. Think about you and me. There's snow at the window, a fire in the hearth, and a horny guy who thinks you're the sexiest, most desirable, most lovable Mrs. Farrell to ever hit this family."

John kissed her with lips that were warm and insistent. His fingers slid the delicate teddy straps down her shoulders. His mouth followed.

Ana fell back against the satin pillows, willing her mind to relax, her body to let go. John caressed her, stroked her, and nibbled at her. He moved slowly at first, then urgently upped the tempo, trying to draw her into the excitement he was feeling, but instead of ascending to the heights he promised, Ana found herself falling further and further behind.

You're an actress. So act, Ana commanded herself at last in frustration.

So she faked it. All of it. The passion. The arousal. The orgasm.

John came with a long, shuddering sigh and a groan of satisfaction. He playfully kissed her breasts. "Do I hear footsteps?" he stage-whispered, propping himself up to stare into her sweat-filmed face. "Is that Mommy coming down the hall?"

She swung a pillow at him, suddenly giggling. "Creep. And she's going to stick *you* in the corner."

"That's okay—so long as you're in that corner with me."

"I'll always be in your corner, Johnny," Ana murmured, her gaze suddenly serious, her arms sliding around his neck. She drew him to her and kissed him earnestly. "I love you so much. Don't ever leave me."

"Never."

Ana fell asleep snuggled beneath the goosedown comforter, John's arms around her, solid, strong, secure as the very foundations of this ancestral home. As she drifted off, lulled by his rhythmic breathing, she told herself that things would go better in Maui.

Ocean breezes, swaying palm trees, and tropical sunsets were conducive to good sex—all the experts said so. Didn't they?

Then it must be true, Ana reflected as she stared into the dying logs of the fire and listened to the nocturnal creakings of the house.

All she had to do was learn to let go. It would get easier, she promised herself. Kind of like bungee-jumping—once you threw yourself over the edge, it was all downhill.

. . . . .

Liz Smith's column taunted him from the kitchen table.

Eric taunted back.

Ho-ho-ho. He paced frenetically around the room, always circling back to the column. *So the bitch was spending the holidays in Rhode Island with her future fucking in-laws and the boy senator. La-de-fucking-da.*

He ripped up the entire newspaper and tossed the confettied pieces out into the night. Swearing, he slammed the window shut on the stench of garbage and dog shit in the alley.

Then he paced some more.

Stupid move, Candy. You had your chance and you blew it, babe. Santa's going to have one big, belated surprise for you.

He grabbed up his .45 and stared at it longingly, the anger building inside of him. Christmas Eve had come and gone—and so had the deadline he'd given Ana.

She doesn't think I've got the guts to do it.

He tossed the revolver from hand to hand.

Well, you just made the worst mistake of your life, sweetheart. Kinda like plunking coal in my Christmas stocking. Can't play with coal, baby, and not get yourself dirty.

Time to get dirty, Ana. Real dirty.

He turned and lunged into a graceful crouch, pointing the gun at his own reflection in the grimy window.

Merry Christmas, slut.

New Year's Eve. She had to get through only one more night. Tomorrow, Ana reminded herself as she sipped her champagne, she'd be out of this stuffy mausoleum. She'd be soaring like an uncaged bird, flying with John to Maui.

The party was huge, pretentious, and sedate as a Sunday-school tea. Ana wandered from room to room, feeling lost and adrift despite the multitude of guests. The air was close and warm. With all the chandeliers and fireplaces aglow, she felt overheated and sweaty in her tight-sleeved wine velvet gown.

The gown was terrible. All wrong. It was too low-cut, too sexy. She'd had a feeling it would be, but John had assured her she looked stunning. Once downstairs, though, mingling with the one hundred and twenty guests dribbling through the mansion, she felt overdone, overdressed, and flashy with her smoky eye makeup and brilliant burgundy lips.

And her earrings were inappropriate as well. John had insisted that the dangling ruby-encrusted diamonds she'd bought for herself after she'd won her Oscar set off the gown's burning jewel color to perfection. He'd urged her to wear them.

But Hope Farrell and her society friends all wore simple pearl studs, tailored dresses, stiff smiles, and polite makeup.

They must think I look like a hooker, she thought miserably.

The hours till midnight stretched agonizingly before her.

John and his father had withdrawn to the library for cognac with the governor, several state congressmen, and his two biggest campaign contributors, Jeffrey Tobes III and William Gordon.

Ana felt like a cheerleader at a funeral home. For God's sake, this was New Year's Eve. It was supposed to be festive, wild, and celebratory with rock music and funny hats and noisemakers. The only noise here was the tinkle of silver demitasse spoons against dainty floral teacups.

She'd scream if she didn't get some air. Five more minutes in this stifling parlor with all the ladies sipping from heirloom bone china and droning endlessly about their spring debutante balls, and she'd go bonkers.

She threw on her black velvet hooded cape and

slipped out into the frosty New England darkness. She inhaled deeply of the fresh tangy air and set off down the front walk, the path flanked by twinkling luminaria winding toward Ocean Drive.

John had taken her this way along the Cliff Walk that afternoon, pointing out the various "cottages" built by the Astors, the Vanderbilts, the Belmonts, and other wealthy industrialists during the late-nineteenth century. Ana had shaken her head in disbelief. Even after the excesses of Hollywood, she was amazed. The ocean-fronted "cottages" looked like palaces plucked from European estates. John had told her that they'd been originally fashioned after the great castles and chateaus of Europe. She tried to imagine him growing up here, amid such unbelievable wealth. She'd grown up in Buck Hollow, where the greatest show of affluence was a pillared porch in the center of Main Street, where the only thing reminiscent of Newport was the invigorating scent of the pines.

Buck Hollow. She hadn't been back in all these years. After her Oscar nomination, she'd received a fan letter from Buddy Crocker. He was married to Shirleen, and they had four kids. All boys.

Her father had written, too, looking for a handout.

That was when Ana had instructed her lawyers to set up an account at Buck Hollow First National. Working with Reverend Bowles, the local minister, the lawyers had arranged for all of Warren Cates's grocery and medical bills to be paid from the account. But nothing else. Ana had made it clear that she would not contribute one penny to her father's alcohol abuse. And she didn't want to be involved in any way with either her father or the disbursement of the account's funds.

She walked along, pushing her father and Buck Hollow from her thoughts, giving herself up to the heady fragrance of pine trees, smoky chimneys, and sea air. The Atlantic rolled beyond the horizon, shimmering beneath the starry midnight-blue sky.

Someday my children will sail out there in Narragansett Bay, Ana mused. *They'll play tennis at the country club, swim in the ocean, and mingle with the grandchildren of all those stuffy Yankees inside.*

Poor kids.

But I'll be damned if I let them fall into the mold. Their father may have come into this world with a gold money clip tucked in his diaper, but their mother was a poor country girl who still remembers what it was like when she didn't have squat. They'll be bicoastal kids, she reassured herself, *California dreamers and Washington pragmatists.*

John and I will have to make sure they keep their sense of humor, their sense of balance, and their feet planted on the ground. I won't have them turning out spoiled or full of themselves.

The church bells chimed from somewhere beyond the moon-washed cliffs. Eleven o'clock. John would be looking for her.

She let herself in and was about to hang up her cape, when Wendall, the butler, an imposing scarecrow with blue-veined hands and a bald pate, stopped short in the middle of the hall.

"Oh! Miss Cates . . . forgive me, please. I'm so terribly sorry."

"What's wrong, Wendall?" Ana inquired with a smile. The poor man looked so flustered, she thought he'd pop his cummerbund.

"The package that came for you and Senator John before the party. With all the last-minute preparations, I completely forgot. It's in the library. Shall I get it for you?"

"Don't bother. I'm sure I'll find it, Wendall."

J. Quincy meowed at her from the mantelpiece as she entered the library. But when Ana reached out to stroke the Smoke Persian's silky fur, the cat leapt gracefully away.

"Be that way," she grumbled.

The men had obviously rejoined the women in the south parlor, but the rich aroma of cigar smoke remained. Ana found herself pleasantly alone in the massive mahogany-paneled room filled with comfortable leather Chesterfield sofas, matching gooseneck chairs, and glass-fronted mahogany bookcases teeming with well-worn leather-bound volumes.

She saw the UPS package at once, resting beside the bronze candlestick lamp on the Louis XV desk. Maybe Louise had forwarded a late Christmas gift. Funny, there was no return address.

Ana slit the wrapping with an antique gold letter opener she found in the desk drawer. She tore off the brown butcher paper and lifted out a videocassette—accidentally scattering the enclosed black and white photos to the floor.

Oh, God.

From the pale Aubusson carpet, glossy images leapt up to stop her heart. Images of herself—*no, of sixteen-year-old Candy Monroe*—romping naked with nameless men she'd long since banished from her mind.

She stifled a scream and fell to her knees, haplessly swooping at the scattered photos. Her heart seemed to convulse in her chest as horror gripped her.

The video. She knew exactly what it was—one of Eric's smutty little masterpieces. That bastard!

Trembling, she stared at the yellow legal page stapled to one of the photos. Beneath it, a picture of herself sandwiched between Eric and a man she couldn't recall mocked up at her with sickening clarity.

That *bastard*.

She read the note while choking back the urge to vomit.

Something old . . . something blue.
A New Year's Party treat for you.
The star, I'm sure, you'll recognize.

Oh, yes . . . you can believe your eyes.
Your White House bid will be no more.
When voters see she's such a whore.
You'll view this first, by just a week.
Then the tabloids get their peek.
She's not the girl you thought you knew.
She's screwed half the world, plus me . . . and you.

Below the printed block letters, Eric had scribbled a crude postscript:

> *Ana babe, you just blew your last chance. I waited two hours at the drop point, but you stood me up. Now it's time for truth or consequences. The tabloids will pay me big-time for these goodies. Kiss your cushy life and your Prince Charming good-bye.*

Still on her knees, Ana stared blankly at the almost indecipherable scrawl. Drop point? What drop point? What was he talking about? Feverishly, she collected the photos, video, and note and crammed them back inside the plain tan box, her thoughts racing.

Eric must have tried to contact her after the movie role fell through. It was the only explanation.

But she'd never received his demands. No phone calls. No letters. No messages in bottles or surprise visits. Something had gone wrong—and now it was too late.

She clutched the box in numb terror. What if Wendall had delivered this to John instead of me? Cold, clammy despair drained the strength from her body. Somehow she pulled herself to her feet and leaned on the desk for support.

Next week John would know anyway—along with everyone else. Her life was disintegrating and she was helpless to stop it.

Or was she?

John's voice startled her from the doorway.

"Hey, gorgeous, where've you been hiding?"

She nearly dropped the box.

He strode into the room, looking as comfortable in his black tux as he had walking along the cliffs that afternoon in his jeans and hooded sweatshirt. "Guess who wants to have their picture taken with you?"

"Wh-ho?" Ana's voice emerged a hoarse croak. She cleared her throat and tried again. "Who?"

"The governor and his wife. They're waiting by the Christmas tree with their press photographer. And William Tobes the third requested your autograph for his mother. Ana, what've you got there? What's wrong? You look like you're going to faint."

"This? Nothing, it came today from Arnie. Business. Can you imagine, I can't get a minute's peace, even on New Year's Eve." Oh, God. She was babbling. She sounded like a total idiot.

Deep breaths, Ana. Slow down. Focus and act your ass off.

Ana forced herself to grimace with pain and pressed her fingers to her temples. "I think I had too much champagne before dinner," she said with a small, rueful laugh. "I stepped outside to try to clear my head but . . . if I don't get an aspirin, I'm going to die. Darling, I'll be right back."

He slipped an arm around her shoulder, his blue-gray eyes darkening with concern. "Let me get it for you."

"Don't bother. I know you have to mingle, mingle." She slanted him an overbright smile and started toward the door.

"Hang on, I think you dropped this." John stooped to reach for the glossy paper lying partially under her heel.

Ana's heart lurched into her throat. She'd missed one of them. . . .

She couldn't breathe as he turned the glossy square of paper over in his hands.

"Just a Christmas card." John tossed it onto the desk. "Must've fallen from the mantel."

"John," Ana said weakly, breath barely flowing from her lungs. "If I don't get that aspirin, you'll be picking *me* up off the floor."

"Make it quick, sweetheart, it's nearly midnight. . . ."

"Two seconds. Promise."

Alone upstairs in the guest room bath, she vomited into the toilet. Afterward, she gargled with Scope and sprawled in despair on the ice-cold tile floor.

Her throat burned raw. Perspiration filmed her cheeks. Yet inside she was freezing cold.

Her mind blank, Ana commanded herself: *Think. Think.*

John would be looking for her.

Think. Hurry.

She willed herself off the floor and scooped up the tan box from the bed, knowing only one thing.

"I won't let you get away with this, Eric Gunn. Not on your life."

The photos and note she flung into the fireplace, watching them curl into blackened ash. She stuffed the video into her overnight bag.

She wasn't sure exactly when she made the decision.

From downstairs, as she packed, she could hear the faint strains of "Auld Lang Syne." "Should old acquaintance be forgot and never brought to mind . . . ?"

"Yes," Ana whispered fiercely, her eyes full of tears.

"They should."

No one except J. Quincy saw her leave.

Chapter Twenty-five

The *Comtesse* was alive with lights, music, and the perfume of tropical flowers as she glided through Maalaea Bay, streaming white water in her wake. Even in the daylight, no one could detect a trace of her former name, *Shanna*.

But for Monique, the festive moonlight cruise she'd planned to kick off the week-long shoot was turning into a voyage on the *Titanic*.

Where in hell were Ana Cates and John Farrell?

The driver meeting their flight had reported that they never got off the plane and were not on the passenger list. She'd instructed him to wait for the next flight. He had, and the one after that. He hadn't left the airport all day.

Ana Cates and John Farrell had never arrived.

Monique had frantically called the mainland to no avail. In L.A. she reached Ana's answering machine. At Senator Farrell's family residence in Rhode Island, a clipped voice informed her that the senator was not taking any calls.

"Miss Cates," she'd demanded.

Miss Cates, he'd sniffed, was "unavailable."

"I'll sue their asses," Monique fumed as the *Comtesse* sliced through the marigold-tinged bay. She threw the phone across the king-size bed in the master stateroom and downed a shot glass of Maalox.

What if they didn't come at all? What the fuck was she going to do?

She tried to calm herself. *It'll all work out. They'll be here in the morning with a perfectly good explanation. And if not . . .*

Forget the "not." They'll be here. Guaranteed.

"Who's ready for more champagne?" she called with forced gaiety as she breezed onto the twilit open deck where Eve and Nico, Teri and Brian, Mimi and the rest of the shoot crew were toasting the New Year and the June issue.

"Did you reach them?" Eve asked.

"Not yet," she responded airily, and ducked inside and up the spiral staircase in search of Richard and the other guests.

Richard was in the saloon with Antonio and his long-time friend, Phil, who, along with Eve's bodyguards, was admiring Richard's fishing trophies mounted above the brass bar.

"I hear there's some great blue marlin fishing toward Kailua-Kona," Tamburelli commented, reaching for a handful of macadamia nuts.

"I'd rather land a girl than a marlin," Swanson quipped.

Everett choked on his pu pu. "You got that right."

"Well, if you're serious fishermen, you guys ought to see about booking yourselves on a fishing cruise after the shoot wraps," Richard suggested.

"Maybe next trip." Tamburelli looked out onto the open deck, where he could observe Eve feeding broiled pineapple chunks to Nico. "This one is strictly business."

Richard shot an inquiring glance at Monique. "Any luck?"

"I make my own luck," she answered brightly.

He took her arm and led her past the appetizer tray, out of earshot of the others. "You know damn well what I mean, Monique. Did you reach them?"

"We'll talk about it later," she snapped back, flashing her most generous smile as Teri wobbled into the cabin.

"Anyone remember to bring Dramamine?" Teri asked hopefully.

The girl looked green as a dollar bill. In the light glowing from the crystal lamps, lit when the sun finally slipped below the shimmering topaz water, she appeared ready to upchuck.

Monique hurried toward her sympathetically.

She knew just how Teri Mathews felt.

The Dramamine didn't work.

Hours later, huddled in the Maui Haleakala Resort's king-size water bed with Brian's arms around her, Teri still felt like a cork in a storm-tossed sea.

"Brian, don't move. I'm going to barf," she groaned, "and you keep jiggling this damned bed."

Brian sighed, giving up his last hopes for the romantic night he'd envisioned. Things were not exactly going according to plan. *You'd have thought that with champagne, leis, and a moonlit dinner cruise on a luxurious megayacht beyond anything I've ever seen on* Life-styles of the Rich and Famous, *the night would have ended in scorching passion.*

Not.

Instead, Teri'd locked herself in the head and spent the entire evening throwing up. That idiot bodyguard Everett had spilled red wine on Brian's white dinner jacket—the one he was supposed to wear in the shoot tomorrow. And Richard Ives and Monique D'Arcy had quietly feuded all through the five-course Polynesian dinner served in the yacht's teak-walled dining room.

So much for idyllic beginnings.

He needed a beer.

He needed a reality check.

He needed to make love to Teri.

Ever since Christmas Eve, when she'd come back from Pittsburgh, she'd seemed somehow distant. Now that *he* knew what he wanted, it seemed *she* was up in the air.

What had happened in Pittsburgh to make her draw away from him? Brian would have bet the new Chrysler account he'd landed for the tool and die shop that Andrew Leonetti was the reason.

If I can't make her forget about him in this place, I'm a complete asshole.

Their private villa was fantastic. Luxury beyond description. Outside, a waterfall thundered into their own free-form swimming pool flanked by lava-rock gardens overflowing with orchids. A personal bonfire pit and sunken Jacuzzi nestled beside swaying palms in the walled courtyard, hidden from view. They could make love beneath the stars, and no one in a neighboring villa would know.

Inside, there were five incredible rooms, each one spacious and furnished in Japanese textured pastel fabrics, with thick carpets, native art, and baskets spilling over with fresh flowers and fruit. The floor-to-ceiling picture windows framed the ocean like a living postcard.

Brian couldn't believe people lived like this.

Lights turned on automatically whenever he or Teri entered a room. The phones featured built-in answering machines. In the living room and bedroom, wide-screen televisions disappeared into state-of-the-art entertainment centers.

But Brian hadn't planned on watching TV.

"Teri, can I get you something?" he whispered into the darkness, and gently rubbed her shoulder.

"A new stomach, a new head, and ten hours sleep,"

she groaned back. "Oh, God, I'll never survive a back-roads' jeep ride to the shoot location in the morning."

The very thought of it made Teri shudder beneath the satin coverlet. She had never felt more nauseated or miserable. Even morning sickness hadn't been this bad.

She thought about Andrew and Adam. They were in Disneyland right now. The trip had been Andrew's surprise Christmas gift to the little boy. *I could've been shaking hands with Mickey Mouse on terra firma instead of throwing up all night on a yacht,* she thought, squeezing her eyes closed.

She felt so sorry for Brian. He was really trying hard. But every time she began to imagine the two of them raising Adam together, she kept seeing Andrew's face. She saw him bear-hugging Adam on his lap as their sled whipped down Buttertop Hill that last day in Aliquippa. She'd never forget the sound of their laughter, or the delight on their faces, or the growing closeness between the three of them.

Teri buried her face in the pillow. She had to make a decision. It wasn't fair to Brian. It wasn't fair to Andrew.

And it's killing me, she thought.

"Shoot me, Brian. Put me out of my misery."

He kissed her brow. "Shh, you'll feel better in the morning."

That's what he thought.

She wanted to die.

"You're not going to die," Nico protested. "Come to bed."

Eve paced with a leonine stride across the Cuenca carpet and paused to stare out the French doors. She gazed unseeing beyond the palm-lined walkway descending to the pool. "He was in my bedroom, Nico. He destroyed my statue and smashed your picture. You heard Maxine—she called this an escalation. The guy's a madman. If I'd been there, he'd have killed me."

"But you weren't there. Bambina, you're here with me in paradise and there are three bodyguards protecting you like guardian angels day and night. That lunatic is thousands of miles away in New York. He can't touch you here. And what about the good news? Eh?" He punched up the pillow behind him and leaned back.

"This time they got some good fingerprints. He's slipping up, Eve. And somebody—I don't know, Eddie, a neighbor—*somebody* had to have seen something unusual. They'll nab this criminal before we get back. Half the NYPD is on the case now."

"I hope Maxine was able to convince the press to keep this quiet," Eve fretted. She crossed to the refrigerator and poured herself a glass of fresh mango juice. "The last thing we need is a media circus right now." She set the glass on the countertop with a sharp clank. Her aquamarine eyes blinked back tears.

"Nico, I'm scared—scared out of my mind."

He threw back the covers and went to her. "Bambina, I won't ever let anything hurt you, not ever."

Eve buried her face in the cologne-scented silk folds of his jaguar-print robe. "Promise me," she whispered, but even as he said the words she knew it was useless.

Only Billy Shears's capture would heal the terror.

"I hope he doesn't know about the baby," she murmured into Nico's shoulder. She shuddered. "That scares me the most."

"What scares me is what all this worrying is doing to the baby. And to you. Try, Eve, try for the next few days here in Maui just to forget this nightmare. We can stay on as long as you like. We don't need to go back to New York until he's caught."

"The wedding plans . . ." she began.

"The wedding is five months away," Nico said

firmly. He took her by the hand and led her back to the circular king-size bed. "Come, let's rehearse for our wedding night. That's the important part anyhow. And we have only five months left to practice."

In spite of herself, Eve smiled. How could she resist Nico when he looked at her that way, smiling his dazzling bedroom smile, his hair falling adorably over his eyes?

He was right, after all, wasn't he? This was paradise. A beautiful, heady, sensuous paradise. No harm could come to her here.

She made up her mind. She wasn't going to allow Billy Shears to invade this Eden. She stared into Nico's eyes and with a wriggle let her backless ruffled nightgown slip to the floor in a cloud of ivory. She stood naked and nymphlike, the Italian gold *cornu* Nico had given her glinting in the pulse point at her throat. Nico's grin widened.

"You know what they say." Eve drew him down with her onto the bed. "Practice makes perfect, doesn't it?"

She snared a finger into the knot of his sash and loosened it, glancing down mischievously as the robe drifted open to reveal his engorged penis.

It was her turn to grin. She slanted a wicked look up at him and reached out a caressing hand.

Her whisper was the only sound in the villa.

"Perfect."

"The Perfect Bride *month-end reports—how do they look? Circulation's up that much? I see. Interesting.*

"Now, remember to change the figures on Ms. D'Arcy's copy of the report and bury the actual file the way I told you. There's a lot riding on this. As always, I appreciate your loyalty.

"Remember, no one, especially Ms. D'Arcy, can know. . . ."

•   •   •   •

"They'd better be here in the morning."

Richard glanced up from his wicker chair on the torchlit lanai as Monique stepped out into the starry night, carrying two crystal glasses of cognac.

Richard, you sure know how to build a mood, she thought, watching his pipe smoke curl upward and his mouth curl down.

"They'll be here," she repeated for the twentieth time. And pushed aside the nagging fear that Ana and John had stood her up.

If they didn't arrive by eight A.M. for the bridal shoot, her whole schedule would be blown from the outset. She'd need to decide whether to proceed without John and Ana and cut them from the issue, or work around them, and squeeze in their shots later, which would translate into overtime and over-budget.

She'd never have taken Ana Cates for a Hollywood prima donna. Ana had a reputation for being completely professional. What the hell could have happened? Why hadn't one of them called her?

If they didn't show up within the next thirty-six hours, they'd miss the sunrise formal-wear shoot at the Haleakala Crater, the one location that couldn't be rescheduled.

"I hope to hell you have Plan B figured out, Mo. Looks like you're going to need it. You've really painted yourself into a corner this time."

Richard stood up, frowned out into the balmy night, and accepted with a scowl the glass of cognac she handed him. He brushed past her into the sunken living room without another word.

"Thanks for all the support," Monique muttered into the darkness, her words drowned out by the roar of the surf.

She gazed up at the stars, his words echoing in her head.

Painted yourself into a corner.

The smell of paint seemed to rise up from the palm trees swaying over the moon-washed cove. She remembered a fresh white room, its paint tinged with rose. She remembered a ladder, a sponge, and sunlight filtering through expansive windows that overlooked rolling hills dusted with snow. She remembered Pete's grin as he served pizza in the carriage house. She remembered his kiss and how she had pushed him away.

Better remember that your ass is in a sling, she told herself furiously. *Quit this ridiculous daydreaming and work on Plan B.*

And C, and D, and E.

She went inside to hunt up her cigarettes. It was going to be a long night.

Chapter Twenty-six

Monique was living on black coffee and Maalox.

The weather had cooperated for the sunrise shoot at the Haleakala Crater, but she was racing to stay ahead of the rainstorms predicted for the rest of the week.

John and Ana had fallen off the face of the earth, and the press had descended upon the resort like a colony of anemic vampires.

"Ms. D'Arcy, is it true that Ana Cates and Senator Farrell have eloped?"

"Rumor has it that Ms. Cates has checked herself into the Betty Ford Clinic. Do you know anything about that?"

"Has Ana Cates or Senator Farrell contacted you at all to explain their absence?"

"Isn't it true that Ana Cates despises Evie B and is refusing to work with her?"

"We've heard a report that John Farrell had a heart attack and is undergoing bypass surgery—any confirmation of this?"

"They've been abducted by three-eyed aliens,"

Monique wanted to scream at them, but instead she offered only a crisp "No comment."

Head throbbing, Monique slammed the Polaroids of the morning's bridal shoot onto the poolside table. She couldn't even look at them.

"Alfie," she said to Mimi's assistant as he dropped an armload of pool props near her feet. "Run to the giftshop and buy me another bottle of Maalox and some Extra-Strength Tylenol. *Now*. And check the weather report."

"Stop worrying—it won't rain," he told her cheerily. "This is paradise, remember?"

More like hell, she thought disgustedly. Thank God Richard was gone. One less thing to worry about.

They had finished the cruisewear session aboard the *Comtesse* the previous day. The only time Richard had set down the phone was to pose with Monique, or to change from his crisp navy blazer and white twill slacks to outrageous black and fuchsia swim trunks. Even the gold lurex bikini Monique wore in the sundeck shoot failed to capture his attention. Then, in the morning, he had grimaced his way through the wedding extravaganza before abruptly heading to California, following a phone call from Theogustus.

Not a moment too soon either. He'd been a grouch the entire morning. Come to think of it, Brian Michaelson hadn't been much better. Not grumpy, exactly, but down in the mouth, Antonio having to coax out that cute smile of his. He and Teri must still be having problems, Monique concluded with a sigh.

Thank God all that was left were a few more swimsuit poses around the pool and the women's final boudoir shots. The men were wrapped.

They'd strutted in their bikinis and bathrobes and silk pajamas, and dazzled the cameras in their tuxedos and boutonnieres. Antonio had done a superb job with them. If only Ana and John had been here, everything would have been fine.

But they weren't and the whole issue was screwed up. Even if they showed now, it would be too late. The group shots were done. Even the best photo retouchers couldn't cut and paste them into the pictures.

But Monique had more to worry about now than the nonappearance of Ana and John. *Just let me get these fucking pool shots done before five o'clock and then I don't care if Typhoon Tillie blasts through here,* she prayed.

Although the sun still blazed down, a frenzied wind was beginning to whip through the palm trees as Heather freshened Teri and Eve's makeup.

Richard ought to be halfway to L.A. by now, Monique thought. Probably on his own steam.

But she couldn't complain about the way the rest of the shoot had gone. For the most part, Teri and Brian had been adorable—wholesome, fresh, and photogenic beyond her hopes. They were exactly what she had envisioned in her rosiest scenario of her Cinderella couple. And the prints of them on the white sands of Papalua Wayside's beach, in particular, with the kiawe trees as backdrop, were her hands-down favorites. The camera had perfectly captured the mischievous boyishness of Brian in his leopard-print bathing trunks, trying to capsize a straw-hatted Teri from her raft as she lolled unsuspectingly, maitai in hand.

Fabulous.

Eve and Nico had been pure dynamite together. They'd snuggled their way through the honeymoon suite photos, and couldn't have looked more in love. They made a stunning couple, she fair and lithe, he with those swarthy, dangerous good looks and penetrating sea-green eyes that seemed to strip Eve every time he looked at her.

Yes, for all of his arrogance and initial reluctance, Monique reflected, Nico had been the picture of professionalism all during this production. But the minute he'd stripped off his tuxedo and bow tie that morning, he'd jumped behind the wheel of the resort jeep and headed off down Hawaii 31 toward Kipahulu, eager to pit himself against the challenge of the narrow winding road.

He didn't care about the views of rain forests, black lava shores, or rugged coastal cliffs. He wasn't interested, Eve had explained, in the pineapple fields or waterfalls. He was itching to drive, and to drive fast.

Brian had deserted them too.

He'd struck up an easy friendship with Eve's bodyguard, Tamburelli, and the two of them had split for the day. With the guard shift rotating three ways, Tamburelli had the day off, and he'd coaxed Brian into joining him for a quick hop to the Big Island while Teri finished her layout.

The only male Monique had to deal with for the next few hours was Antonio.

"It's raining!" the little tyrant suddenly shrieked.

"But the sun is still shining. Keep shooting!"

"And ruin my cameras? Are you insane? Cut. Cut. *Cut!*"

Monique stormed across the pool deck as icy bullets of rain pelted her gold maillot.

"Everybody inside," she shouted resignedly. A cavalcade of people thronged toward the clubhouse doors, technicians dragging cameras and lighting equipment, Mimi and Heather scooping up plastic garment bags crammed with swimsuits, sunglasses, hats, and thongs.

Eve and Teri didn't have to be told twice. Shivering, they threw themselves into thick terry robes and dashed out of the whipping wind.

"You may have to make do with the earlier water shots, Monique. Aren't one hundred enough to choose from?" Antonio grumbled. "In the meantime, I'll set up the final boudoir shots—give me at least an hour—then we finish this monster."

Monique studied the blackening clouds scudding

in from the west. She could see rain sheeting out of them as they tumbled toward the island.

"Everyone else has pissed on me," she muttered as she rammed her schedule book into her tote. "Why not Mother Nature?"

A long soak in the tub or a quick nap? Eve mused, unlocking the door to her villa. *Which do I crave the most?*

The combination of tropical sun and the pregnancy had drained her of all energy. She welcomed the hour hiatus. But looking back at the clouds billowing ominously in the distance, she fought off a sudden uneasiness. Those clouds were right about where Nico should be at the moment.

"Thanks, Tom," she called to the bodyguard as he lowered the umbrella and swept through the villa ahead of her.

"Looks clean to me, Miss Hamel. I'll park myself outside in the gate house. Unless you want me to wait here until Mr. Caesarone comes back."

"I'll be okay. I'll hit the beeper if I need you."

Eve latched the front door. At the moment, she was more concerned about Nico than about Billy Shears. *You'd think he'd have enough sense to come in out of the rain.* Her heart skipped a beat whenever she imagined him maneuvering those wet, unfamiliar roads in this god-awful weather. The native guide who'd taken them across the island had respect for the highway, but she knew even this torrential downpour wouldn't slow Nico down.

Think of our baby, she implored him silently. *You don't always have to be a daredevil.*

Eve tossed her straw satchel onto the coffee table and peeled off her wet bathing suit. Giving in to a luxurious yawn, she crossed with longing toward the made-up bed. But as she picked up Nico's robe which the maid had laid out neatly across the pastel flowered spread, something tumbled from the pocket and landed at her feet.

She stared at it. A marcasite earring set with onyx and rubies.

Suddenly taut, she stooped to retrieve it.

Margo's. She'd recognize it anywhere. She herself had given the set to Margo as a medical school graduation gift. Margo had worn them the night Eve and Nico met her for dinner in New York.

Eve turned the earring over and over in her palm.

How did this get in Nico's robe?

She sank onto the bed, clutching the earring in a trembling hand.

No.

She stared at it.

No.

The earring burned her palm. She dropped it to the floor as if it were a searing hot coal and stared numbly down at it, dazed by its twinkling mockery.

Eve covered her face with her hands. He wouldn't, she whispered. He couldn't.

But then how . . . ?

There has to be an explanation, she thought, trying to stay calm.

There was one, of course. And only one.

Bambina, I won't ever let anything hurt you, not ever.

Her eyes filled with diamond-hard tears. Tears of bitterness, devastation, and rage.

Right, Nico. Right.

"Bambina, what is it? You look like . . . what's wrong?"

Nico's dark hair and bronzed face dripped rain as he stared at Eve, who opened the door of the villa in frigid silence and stepped aside.

Thunder rumbled beyond the French doors. A slash of blue-white lightning crackled across the sky.

"Eve . . . you're scaring me!" He paled. "Is it Billy Shears?"

She shrank as he grasped her by the shoulders. She pushed his hands away.

"Don't touch me."

Nico dropped his hands to his sides. "Eve, what is all this about?"

"Lies. It's about lies, Nico. And betrayal."

"I don't know what you're—"

"Yes, you do. I have only two things to say to you, and then I never want to see your face again. Not ever."

Nico froze. "Bambina . . ."

"Don't call me that! Did you call *her* that, Nico?"

"Who?" It came out as a croak.

Eve, ice cold, furious as the avenger goddess Nemesis, tossed him the small object embedded in her hand.

"Catch."

He stared blankly down at the earring in his broad palm.

"Don't want to lose part of your trophy collection," Eve bit out. It was all she could do not to spit in his face.

"Eve, this has gone far enough. You're scaring me. Has this Billy Shears made you crazy too? None of this is making any sense. I want you to calm down, sit down —think of the baby—"

"Don't mention my baby!" Eve reached him in two steps. She drew back her arm and let the full force of her rage explode across his face.

But as she reached up to hit him again, Nico, in shock, grasped her wrist.

"Let go of me!" Eve cried. "Didn't you say practice makes perfect?" She struggled to free her hand. "Well, let me practice."

"You're crazy!"

"Did you practice with her, Nico? Did you practice for our wedding night—with *Margo*?"

Nico sucked in his breath. He let go her arm and stepped back, his face first flushing and then draining of all color. He stared down in dazed shock at the earring still in his palm.

"Eve, listen to me . . ." he began slowly.

"Two things, Nico. *Ciao*. Forever."

White-faced, Eve ripped the engagement ring off her finger and flipped it toward his feet. The *cornu* pendant followed.

She turned on her heel and headed toward the bedroom. "Your suitcase is in the lobby with the bellboy. You can tip him yourself."

Through the roaring in her ears she heard the quiver in his voice as he cried after her. "Eve, I can't let you do this. Not without giving me a chance to explain. She meant nothing to me—you mean everything! I'll make it up to you, I swear. I broke off with her because of you and the baby . . . I knew it was a mistake, I told her—"

"Get the hell out!" She whirled around, screaming now with fury and betrayal.

"Don't you understand, Nico? I can never trust you again! You've ruined everything." Tears streamed down her face, the bitter, resigned tears of loss and desolation. "We can't go back ever, not ever."

"You don't know what you're saying. Let me stay to protect you. I know you're upset. You have every right to hate me. But please . . . oh, God, Eve, please don't do this now. I don't want to leave you, I love you!"

She only looked at him, a cold hatred creeping into her eyes. She didn't trust herself to say another word. And he didn't deserve it.

Eve snapped her heart closed with chilling finality. She went into the bedroom and slammed and locked the door.

Nico paced and raged and cursed and begged for the next hour, but Eve wouldn't respond. At last Tom Swanson knocked at the villa door.

"Miss Hamel asked me to escort you to the lobby. This way, Mr. Caesarone."

If the bodyguard felt any sympathy toward Nico, he didn't show it. His easy grin had been replaced by a stoically set jaw. He no longer looked like an easygoing tennis player. He looked like he meant business.

Nico glared at him. In frustration and blind rage he spun about and shouted at the bedroom door: "Fine. I'm out of here. I'm going to New York. When you come to your senses, call me."

Moments later Eve emerged from the bedroom to funereal silence. She ached all over, as if she'd been beaten. It hurt too much even to cry. She could only stare in mute agony around the empty villa, so outwardly lovely yet so devoid of comfort.

There was no comfort here or anywhere. And her head was pounding with the force of a thousand waves.

She refused to take a Tylenol. She didn't want to risk *any* medication. It might not be good for the baby, no matter what the doctors said.

The baby.

She fought back more tears. It'll be just the two of us now, she whispered, her hands sliding along her faintly rounded belly. *But that's all right. I'll take care of us both.*

Suddenly Eve remembered that she hadn't yet taken her daily multivitamin.

Moving like an automaton, she reached for her straw satchel on the coffee table and fumbled for the dark plastic bottle containing the pills.

Her fingers stiffened as they brushed against a square of fabric. She drew it out slowly. Time shrank, expanded. Seconds or maybe hours passed as Eve gazed at the blood-soaked scrap of beaded satin cut from the wedding gown she'd modeled that morning.

Her scream was shrill and tortured. When its last echoes faded, she saw the green paper still tucked in the center pocket of the satchel. One word was scrawled across it in blood.

SOON.

Chapter Twenty-seven

She studied herself in the streaked mirror of the Starlite Motel in West Hollywood.

Not bad.

Ana nodded approvingly at her zebra spandex leggings, purple sequined bustier, and the droopy gold lurex cardigan draping her shoulders. Assorted chains dangled down her cleavage, and bangle bracelets chimed on her wrists as she slipped on the short blond spike-haired wig. With calm deliberation she threaded purple elephant earrings through her pierced ears and then donned John Lennon–style glasses with blue-tinted lenses. Finally, she yanked on a dusty pair of black motorcycle boots.

Thank God for the Salvation Army thrift shop, she thought, where shopping for sleaze was a breeze.

Smiling grimly at her own nearly unrecognizable reflection, she added gobs of bright orange lipstick and dotted on a fake black mole above her left eyebrow.

Hooker Hanna.

This performance should win her a second Oscar—though unless she screwed up, no one would ever know.

Ana's heart thudded painfully in her chest as she stuffed two hundred dollars down her bustier and planned out the next few hours.

When she was ready to leave, she slipped on the black rhinestone-studded leather gloves and tossed back a shot of courage from the bottle of scotch she'd bought out of loneliness yesterday at the drugstore. From the next room she heard a woman's shrieking laughter, a man's mumbled curse, and then the furious creaking of bedsprings accompanied by moans, gasps, and ardent squeals.

She glanced at her watch. It was time.

Grabbing up her canvas slouch bag, she carefully double-locked the metal door on her way out.

The apartment was empty. Of course. She knew his pattern by now. She'd been watching his comings and goings for three days, biding time, building courage.

He was at the Royal Bar, shooting pool, bullshitting the big-boobed bartender, trying to win a few bucks to score some crack.

He wouldn't be back until after three. Then he'd crank up the radio and do God-knew-what until after dark, when he would slither back onto the streets with the rest of the vermin.

But not tonight.

She stole up the creaking steps of the walkup and jimmied the lock the way Buddy Crocker had taught her when her father was passed out drunk on the couch and she couldn't get into her house.

What a pigsty. Ana covered her nose with a gloved hand as the stench of rancid clothes, stale smoke, and food rotting in an open garbage pail assaulted her. Dirty laundry carpeted the floor and overflowed from the threadbare sofa, which dipped in the center to perfectly mimic the shape of Eric's backside.

Ana tiptoed around the littered desk and hoisted

the window open to gulp some fresh air. She was almost afraid to go into the bedroom without a fumigator in hand.

Ugh. Even in the semidarkness she could smell the slimy sheets, feel the grit of hopelessness and evil. With one gloved finger she lifted the pillow. She knew exactly what she would find.

And it was loaded.

She checked the .45's safety before secreting the gun in the pocket of her cardigan. Then she started her search.

The videotapes were easy to find. She remembered all too well Eric's favorite hiding places. She yanked the unmade twin bed away from the wall and reached behind the dust-caked headboard for the leather pouch. Bingo.

Five tapes were inside. "Eating Candy"—lovely. "Candy Kisses"—she grimaced.

Candy pukes, she thought.

How many copies had he made? she wondered, feeling sick. And how many had he already sold?

She remembered that he sometimes stashed valuables in the toilet's water tank and headed for the tiny bathroom. With a chalky scrape she slid aside the ceramic cover, but all she found sealed in the two-by-two Ziploc bag was a small empty vial dusted with cocaine crystals, two reefers, some pills she didn't recognize—maybe pink ladies—and a dirty syringe.

Where were the photos?

She shoved the toilet top on with a clank and headed back to the bedroom. But though she searched furiously through the bureau drawers, under the bed, behind the door, inside an old pair of sneakers, she found nothing.

She tried the living room with equally frustrating results. Again, nothing.

Then her gaze fell on a copy of *Comes a Stranger* peeking out of the loading drawer of Eric's VCR. *Is that what's feeding your anger, Eric?* she thought, heading toward the kitchen. *My success?*

Growing more desperate, she opened the refrigerator and checked under the empty vegetable crisper.

And there it was.

A manila envelope addressed to *The Enquirer.* It was paper-clipped to a plastic sleeve that bulged with negatives.

The crudely written letter inside promised more to come—for a price.

Well, we'll just see about that, sucker.

Ana stuffed the envelope and the videotapes into the bottom of her canvas bag, zipped it shut, then scraped a wobbly wooden chair across the floor until it faced the front door.

The digital alarm clock on the end table flashed its rhythmic red message. Two forty-five.

Soon this would all be behind her. Forever. This time she would make sure of it.

Ana stationed herself squarely in the chair, legs braced apart, feet planted firmly in the spot she'd kicked free of squalor.

She cocked Eric's gun and with steady arms trained it on the doorway dead ahead.

She mentally rehearsed what she had to do.

And waited.

Chapter Twenty-eight

"Do you read me, Everett?" Static sputtered from Tom Swanson's walkie-talkie.

"Everett here," came back the choppy reply.

"Security's been breached," Swanson barked into the black handset. "The stalker is in the compound."

Lightning streaked across the sky, and the lights in Eve's villa flickered. She gasped and hugged herself, trying to stop shivering.

"He's been in Miss Hamel's purse. Alert compound security and double-back here pronto."

"Will do."

A clap of thunder startled Eve. She eyed the table lamps, willing them to stay lit.

"Tom, we have to warn Monique and the others," she urged as he turned back to her, his jaw tight. "I'll call them . . . but please don't leave me alone."

Swanson nodded, his eyes light and cool. "I'm staying right here, Miss Hamel. You'll be perfectly safe. From this moment on, I don't leave your side."

Eve's fingers trembled so much, she could hardly dial Monique's room.

"Monique," she began with a strange, flat calm. "I

can't believe what's happening. Nico—Nico's gone. And Billy Shears is here—he's in the resort." Near-hysterical laughter almost overcame her then.

"He's going to kill me, Monique. As if what Nico did wasn't enough." The panic started to take hold. "He's going to finish me off, I feel it. . . ." Gently, Tom Swanson took the phone from her and spoke to Monique in a controlled, rapid manner, his ice-chip eyes scanning Eve's lanai and the surrounding landscape all the while.

"I'm bringing you to Ms. D'Arcy's villa," he told Eve when he had finished with Monique. "He won't expect that—he'll come here first, and when he does, we'll be ready for him."

She nodded, but she felt with dread certainty that Billy Shears would find her no matter where she tried to hide.

Five minutes later Eve tumbled into Monique's arms, whispering, "I don't understand, how could he have gotten in here?"

"It doesn't matter. They'll get him, Evie B. Or I will. Nothing is going to interfere with this shoot." Monique tried to joke, but it fell flat. She saw Swanson roll his eyes as he headed into the master bedroom to begin his sweep through her quarters. *So I'm no Jay Leno—but if I don't keep my sense of humor, I'll never get through this.*

She led Eve to the sofa and gently settled her amid the pillows. "I'm fixing you a drink."

But Eve shook her head as Monique began to slosh ice and scotch into a tumbler.

"No booze for me."

"Come on, sweetie, it'll help calm you down—"

"I'm pregnant."

Monique stared at her, dumbfounded. "Oh, Eve— that's wonderful . . ." Her voice trailed off at the stricken look in Eve's glazed eyes. "Isn't it?" she finished uncertainly, setting down the bottle of scotch and hurrying back to the sofa.

Eve was staring straight ahead, her arms limp at her sides.

"I won't let Billy Shears hurt my baby," she vowed, so low Monique had to strain to hear.

Monique exchanged grim glances with Tom Swanson as he returned to the living room.

"Of course not," she continued soothingly, "no one is going to hurt you or the baby. Eve, for God's sake, where is Nico?"

"Who the hell cares?"

"Sweetie," Monique said carefully, "you're not making any sense."

"I don't know how to make sense out of my fiancé sleeping with my sister. Do you?"

Monique's eyes widened. "No," she breathed. An image of Nico kissing Eve under the waterfall while Antonio snapped away flared bright in her mind. Then she saw him helping her across the flower-strewn bridge, carrying her over the mock honeymoon threshold. . . . They were so obviously in love. He *couldn't* have been acting. "Eve, come on, are you sure?"

"I found her earring. It was in his robe. He admitted the whole thing not more than an hour ago." Eve's face was drawn and ashen, the color of oatmeal. She forced a feeble smile and a shrug. "I guess this just isn't my day, Monique."

Then she crumpled into sobs.

While Swanson surveyed the rain-swept grounds from the window, Monique held Eve, stroking her hair, murmuring gently, her mind racing.

Teri's all alone—Brian's off with Tamburelli. My God, I've got to get her over here and make certain the Hawaiian authorities are taking this seriously. Where the hell is everybody? I want this place sealed tighter than a drum—all my people curfewed in their villas under guard until this nut is caught.

She put Alfie in charge of alerting her staff. Swanson made the other calls—to Teri, to security, to the local police. And to Maxine Goodman in New York. But Maxine was out of the office and he was forced to leave an urgent message.

"Eve, you're staying put for the night," Monique announced when Swanson had finished his series of calls. She knew she'd get no argument. While Swanson checked in with Everett on the walkie-talkie, she tucked a light cotton coverlet over Eve and put up a pot of tea. Then she flung a rain slicker over her red terry-cloth romper.

"When I get back with Teri we'll have a pajama party."

"Well, don't bother renting a horror movie," Eve muttered, "we've got one in progress."

That makes two of us trying to keep our sense of humor, Monique reflected. *Never mind that I'm losing my June issue.*

What the hell am I going to do without Eve Hamel and Nico Caeserone?

"Listen, Evie B," Monique said bracingly as she carried steaming cinnamon tea to the sofa. "Swanson and I have everything worked out. I'm going with a security guard to get Teri and then we'll swing by your room for your stuff. We'll be back before you can say Kaanapali."

Eve hated for her to leave at all, but she said only, "Don't be long, Monique. Please."

After Monique had gone, Eve stared into her steaming teacup. *Stop acting like a baby. You've got plenty of protection.*

Still she couldn't help shivering as Tom Swanson checked his revolver and spoke alternately with Dean Everett and the compound security chief on his walkie-talkie.

It occurred to her that she had blurted out all the sordid details of her breakup with Nico in front of Tom

Swanson. Oh, God, he'd even been just outside the doorway during their fight—he had to have heard that too.

Great. She knew practically nothing about the man except that he had a wife and three little kids waiting for him in New Jersey. And he knew everything about her—the most hurtful secrets of her life. Yet he'd given no sign of having overheard any personal conversations. He went on about the business of protecting her with cool professional detachment, which was comforting and face-saving for them both.

"Everett's found no evidence so far of an intruder in the compound," Tom informed her, shoving the walkie-talkie into his belt clip. "Neither has security. The local authorities are on top of the situation, Miss Hamel. Everything is under control."

Eve gulped her tea.

Everything except my life.

The security guard used his master key to unlock Eve's villa and preceded Teri and Monique inside. While they waited uneasily in the entrance foyer, he made a quick check of the rooms.

Teri paced nervously in the small space. She had just ended a phone call with Andrew in L.A. when the call had come through about this "emergency." One minute she was hearing about Adam's delight at the Pirates of the Caribbean ride, and the next she was listening to Tom Swanson curtly instruct her to pack an overnight bag and prepare to spend the night in Monique D'Arcy's villa. Monique had explained briefly what was going on, but Teri couldn't absorb it all. The idea of a deranged stalker on the loose was too bizarre, and the storm added Hitchcockian special effects that seemed larger than life. She wished Brian were back from the Big Island. She wished she were back in Livonia, polishing Mrs. Warnler's nails.

She wished Monique had warned them.

"Why didn't you tell us what was going on?" she demanded, spinning toward Monique. "I think we had a right to know."

"No one expected the worst-case scenario, Teri— or that *any* of us would be in danger. Every possible security precaution was taken, and the odds of this happening were so remote that there seemed no point in worrying everyone and violating Eve's privacy. . . ."

It took Monique three attempts before her cigarette lighter caught. She exhaled a long stream of smoke and peered down the hallway where the security guard had disappeared. "Besides, we couldn't be safer if we were in FBI headquarters—there's enough policemen around here to start our own precinct."

Teri bit her lip as the security guard lumbered back. Her rain-spattered silk shirt and walking shorts clung to her skin, chilling her in the air-conditioned room. She wished she'd changed into jeans and a sweatshirt.

"Doesn't look like anyone's been here," he reported. "You ladies grab what you need and I'll get you back to the other villa ASAP."

"Start in the bathroom," Monique directed Teri. "Just throw her stuff into this tote, and I'll find her nightclothes and a sweatsuit. The sooner we get out of here, the better."

"Hey, sweetie," she added, noting Teri's pinched white face, "don't worry so much. We'll all live happily ever after. Guaranteed."

"I know." Teri swallowed. She squared her shoulders and headed toward the bathroom. "But this is giving me the creeps."

"Tell me about it," Monique muttered, and yanked open the walk-in closet door.

Dean Everett crouched inside, the muscles of his face drawn in a taut grimace, his gun pointed in a very businesslike way at her head.

Monique shrieked at the top of her lungs until she recognized him.

The security guard bounded into the bedroom, gun drawn. Wide-eyed, heart thudding, Teri peeped around him from the bathroom door.

Monique gave a nervous laugh, half frustration, half annoyance, her heart banging like a drum in her chest.

"You scared the shit out of me, Mr. Everett. Don't point that thing at me. *I'm* not the stalker."

Everett stood up and lowered his gun. "Sorry, Miss D'Arcy." He was silent as Teri hurried forward, clutching toiletries and makeup. "Didn't mean to scare you. Or you either, Miss Mathews. I heard a muffled noise and thought I might have surprised our suspect."

"Well, did you find anything?" Teri asked.

Monique frowned. Didn't you hear our voices, you idiot? she wanted to demand, but at that moment the phone rang.

"Don't touch that," Everett ordered as Teri reached for the phone. "If that's Billy Shears, let him think the place is empty."

Suddenly the whirr of the answering machine clicked on and Maxine Goodman's crisp voice blared into the bedroom. Dean Everett whirled in the direction of the sound.

"Eve. Swanson. It's Maxine. This is a dire emergency. Your lives are in danger. Dean Everett has been found dead in L.A. All his ID was missing. Do you understand? Your Dean Everett is an impostor—we have to operate on the assumption he's Billy Shears. My next call is to hotel security and the Maui police. *Use extreme caution.* I'm taking the next flight out."

Then everything happened simultaneously.

Teri dropped the toiletries with a gasp and stared in stunned horror at the face of Eve's bodyguard.

Monique froze, aghast, her eyes locked with those of "Dean Everett."

Dean Everett, who had been a guest on Richard's yacht. Who had danced with Mimi. Who had helped clear the pool deck in preparation for the shoot.

Who had been tormenting Eve with such calculated cruelty for months.

The security guard whipped out his gun, but not quickly enough.

Everett fired two rapid shots.

The first cut short the security guard's terse "freeze" warning and hit him squarely between the eyes.

Monique heard a gargled moan as the guard fell in slow motion to the floor, the red stain widening silently around him like spilled wine.

The second sharp blast ricocheted off the mirrored teakwood bureau and ended in an agonizing scream.

Monique gagged on the smell of death and gunpowder and gaped in helpless terror at the blood spurting through Teri's fingers. *Oh, God.* Teri was clutching her shoulder, shrinking against the blood-splattered wall, her eyes fixed incredulously on her attacker.

This can't be happening, Teri thought. A blue wall of pain blinded her. She was cold. So cold. Adam. There was Adam on Andrew's lap, sledding down the hill. Laughing.

"Poor little boy," she gasped aloud.

Dean Everett glared at her. "Shut up."

My poor little baby. You lost your mother once. And now you're losing her for good. But your father will love you. You belong with him. You belong with Andrew . . . Andrew. . . .

Cold blue darkness swallowed her. *Like the Detroit-to-Windsor tunnel. She was going through the tunnel with Brian. They were going to spend the day picnicking along the waterfront in Windsor.*

Brian.

Brian held out his hand to her. *It's cold in here, and so dark. Brian, we're lost.*

Monique gasped as Teri crumpled to the floor. *Stay in control*, she willed herself. *Don't lose it now. Don't panic*, she repeated to herself in a silent mantra. Her breaths came in icy, rapid gulps. Slowly, her eyes riveted on the man she knew as Dean Everett, she made her way to the corner where Teri huddled.

"Lie down on the floor next to her," Everett said in a mechanical voice.

"Can't you see she needs a doctor . . ." Monique began.

"*Now*, Miss D'Arcy. On the floor. Don't make me hurt you too."

"Teri, I'll help you." Monique touched the girl's lily-white cheek with shaking fingers. "Hang in there. Don't leave me," she urged, staring over at the frighteningly still form beside her, as if willing lifeblood back into the girl. Blood gushed from Teri's wound in a ribbon of liquid crimson.

Monique flung a desperate glance at Everett.

"Let me get a towel and stop the bleeding," she begged. "It will take only a minute. Then I'll do whatever you say."

"I can't wait another minute." He smiled dreamily at her. "I've waited long enough. I have to go to Eve."

Monique recoiled from the madness in his eyes. She couldn't believe this was the same stolid-looking young man who'd been with them all during the shoot. Before, he had appeared so normal, so ordinary. So average he was almost invisible in a crowd, with his medium height, side-parted brown hair, brown eyes, and clean-cut boy scout features.

The kind of person you'd pass on the street and never notice. The kind of guy who'd order a hamburger medium-rare every day for lunch, who spotlessly shined his shoes each Sunday before going to church, who shoveled his neighbor's walk and tossed a football on the lawn with the kids down the block. An ordinary, nice-looking, nondescript guy whose only quirk was that he killed people.

With pounding heart she avoided looking toward the dead security guard sprawled a few feet away on the once-pristine carpet, and instead focused on Teri. She was unconscious. *Only unconscious*, Monique told herself. *Not dead.*

Where the hell are Maui's finest? Didn't Maxine get through?

She groped frantically for Teri's pulse, even as she saw Everett unbuckle his belt.

What now? Rape? she wondered, gritting her teeth. *Over my dead body.*

But she should have known it was only Eve he coveted.

Methodically, he tied their arms behind their backs with his belt and the sash of Eve's bathrobe. Monique was grateful that Teri couldn't feel the biting agony.

When they were securely trussed, Monique felt him tugging at her jump suit. "What the hell are you doing?"

He didn't answer, but moved away to stoop over the guard with a slashing movement. Monique saw the glint of metal in his hands.

Then he straightened and stared at Monique, his head cocked to one side.

"You worked her so hard. So hard. 'Eve, do this.' 'Eve, do that.' You shouldn't have done that. You'll have to pay for being mean to her, Miss D'Arcy. I'll come back for you. But first I have to take care of my Eve. She's been waiting so long. And I promised, you know. I promised."

He walked out without a backward glance, leaving the door flapping in the wind. Gale-driven rain splayed into the room, bringing with it the damp, rich smell of eucalyptus, moist earth, and the Pacific.

Monique felt Teri's blood dampening the carpet beneath her chest. She fought back a wave of faintness.

Tough as Cool Whip. Pete's teasing words came starkly back to her. *You're wrong, Mr. Lambert. I'm tougher than you think. And I'm going to live long enough to prove it to you.*

Eve startled at the crackle of the walkie-talkie on Swanson's belt. Where were Monique and Teri? she wondered uneasily. It shouldn't be taking this long. But Tom Swanson appeared unconcerned even as he told her that Everett had radioed him for assistance outside.

"Everett says Miss Mathews twisted her leg running back here, and they need me to help carry her." He started toward the door. "They're right outside. I'll be gone only a second."

Chapter Twenty-nine

The door latch clicked. Her body twittered, as tense as a bird staring down an alley cat. He was back.

About time.

The door swung open on creaking hinges.

He didn't notice her until he'd kicked it shut and staggered partway into the room, bringing with him the odor of barroom smoke and unwashed flesh.

"Hello, Eric."

Dumbfounded amazement spread across his unshaven face. He blinked and almost dropped his beer can.

Who the hell was this broad with the gun? He rubbed his eyes and squinted across at her, trying to recognize the boldly painted face. Not bad-looking. Had he brought her home last night? He must be losing it. Usually he remembered the dishy ones.

"Whoa, baby." His words slurred as he eyed her with a crooked grin. He shoved his coal-black hair out of his eyes. "Didn't anyone . . . ever tell you it's rude to point?" He chortled at his own joke.

Ana noticed the zipper on his molded jeans was half undone. There were chalky stains of deodorant mixed with sweat ringing the underarms of his faded green T-shirt. Pig. She kept the gun trained on him, her eyes as hard and cold as sequins.

"Look," Eric said, swigging from the can. "If it wasn't good for you baby, we'll go at it again. But, hey . . . put the gun down. Broads with guns make me nervous, ya know?"

He edged forward tentatively, keeping an eye on the spike-haired bimbo with the no-shit attitude.

"Don't move. Stay right where you are, you slimy son of a bitch." Ana's voice shot out electric and controlled, despite the hammering of her heart.

Eric blinked at her again. Familiar. That voice . . .

"Shit! It's you." He gaped at her—a dark red flush crept from his neck upward. "Candy, what the fuck are you doing here all dressed up like it's Halloween? What, you think you're going to pay me off? Oh, no, baby," he scoffed, "it's too late for that. You had your chance and you blew it. I can get more money from the tabloids than you could ever fork over. So put that fucking gun down and stop playing games."

"This isn't a game, Eric. This is my life. And you're not going to ruin it. You tried before, but I got away. I thought I was rid of you—but this time I intend to make sure of it. I've given you more of myself than you ever deserved. You're not getting one ounce—or one penny—more."

"Big talk." He laughed, his eyes blinking drunkenly. But he stayed where he was. "Candy baby, what's that bigshot fiancé of yours gonna say when the tabloids get a load of your *real* film debut?" He belched, loud as a fart in church. "Did he like my Christmas present?"

"He never saw it and he never will." Ana struggled to stay calm despite the anger threatening to explode like a hand grenade inside her. Staring at Eric—drunk, strung-out, and swaggering like a basketball star who's just sunk a three-pointer, she felt a crawling disgust.

Long ago she had endured the drunken taunts of her father. She'd helplessly let Warren Cates ruin her dreams of love with Roy Cody, let him make her feel worthless and hopeless. But she was a different person now from that miserable runaway who'd left her Cabbage Patch doll and her innocence behind when she fled Buck Hollow. She was strong, powerful, and pissed.

And not helpless anymore.

She let the icy anger harden through her, steeling her for what she had to do. Her father had destroyed her first chance for happiness, had driven her away from a caring and gentle boy—and she wasn't about to let Eric destroy her chance for happiness with the finest, most decent man she'd ever met. A man who loved her, believed in her, and could himself be destroyed by the secrets she'd kept hidden.

No. She couldn't let that happen.

"Eric, you went too far."

He took another swig of beer, belched in her face again, and laughed.

"You're bluffing. You don't have the guts."

"Don't bet on it." Ana stood up, leveling the gun at his chest. She was breathing hard now, fury whistling through her. "I was sixteen when you sank your filthy hooks into me and turned me into your slut mistress. I was a stupid kid, but you were an amoral monster. You used me like you use everybody, you hurt me, you made me into something I hated, and now you think you can control me again? And again, and again? Well, you thought wrong, mister. You thought fucking wrong."

"Don't be crazy, babe. You loved it. You know you loved it. If only you'd kept on being good to your daddy, things wouldn't have gotten to this point. Candy, you shoulda never run out on me. Never left me for dead. If we'd stuck together, we both would have made it big. . . ."

Now it was Ana's turn to laugh, a high, hysterical laugh that made the gun tremble dangerously in her hands. "If I'd stayed with you, I never would have made it out of the gutter! Look at you. You're disgusting, you're a piece of worthless vermin." Her voice rose. Red rage swirled before her eyes. "You've always fed off other people. You never could stand on your own two feet. Want to know something, Eric? That job you got in Oslo? I got you that job. I thought it would get you out of my hair and give you a chance. But you blew it, like you blow every good thing that comes along. You haven't changed one damn bit. The world will be a better place without you!"

The red flush had faded from his cheeks. He was pasty now, and backing up against the closed door. "Ana baby . . . come on . . . you're talkin' cold-blooded murder here. This ain't no movie set, you know. There's no retakes. Ice me, and you'll spend the rest of your life in the big house instead of the White House. . . ."

He steadied himself against the door, one hand clenching the beer can, the other fumbling behind him for the knob. "We can talk about this. Hey, I didn't send the pictures out yet. . . ."

"Shut up!" But his pleas were distracting her. The palpable fear in Eric's voice leapt across the room and grabbed her by the throat. She'd suffocate from her pent-up fury unless she released it in a torrent of gunfire, but yet . . .

Just go ahead and shoot the son of a bitch. What are you waiting for? You know how to use the gun. You watched him shoot up the walls plenty of times.

Pull the trigger.

It was the only thing she *could* do—except lay down and play dead for Eric Gunn. She thought of John, of how destroyed he would be if he learned the truth.

No matter what happened, John mustn't be hurt. He didn't deserve it.

She clicked off the safety, her gloved finger looped across the trigger.

"Adios, Eric. I wish I could say it's been fun."

"C'mon, please . . . oh, God, Candy . . . no . . ." He began to whimper and a wet stain slowly spread across the front of his unzipped jeans.

Pathetic son of a bitch. Pees in my pool. Pees in his pants. Just shoot him.

"Don't!" he pleaded.

Her finger quivered on the trigger. *Do it*, she willed herself. *Get it over with and get out of here.*

She stared at him, stared hard, letting the loathing and disgust rise up her throat until she thought it would choke her. But it wasn't Eric whom she loathed. It was herself.

He'd done it again.

She felt dirty all over.

How low would he make her go?

"You aren't worth it," she whispered at last, lowering the gun with a bitter sigh. Suddenly the blond wig felt horribly hot and itchy. The bustier dug into her rib cage.

"You aren't worth killing, Eric. You're already dead —in every way that counts. When I thought I'd killed you before, I spent years looking over my shoulder for the cops." She shook her head, suddenly drained, exhausted. "You made me do a lot of things I regret. No more. No one, not even you, will ever make me stoop that low again. You won't make me kill you. Go to the tabloids, do your dirtiest. I don't care. Now get out of my way."

But as she started wearily toward the door, he blocked her path. Relief gave him a wild bravado.

"You ain't goin' nowhere, slut. Not with my father's gun."

"So call the cops." Ana gestured impatiently with the .45. "Move!"

But Eric, still drunk, and suddenly infuriated that he'd been afraid of her for even a minute, lunged at her and wrenched the gun away with one fluid movement.

"Now who's going to crawl?" he chortled, and pointed the barrel between her eyes. "You won't look so pretty with a bullet in your face, will you, Candy? Oh, excuse me, it's Ana now."

She felt a faintness wash over her. Yet everything was vivid, clear as a country night.

This couldn't be happening.

"Eric, don't be crazy. You'd never get away with it. John knows exactly where I am," she bluffed, trying to sound offhand. "They'll crucify you if you kill me."

"Nah, I'll be famous. It'll be worth it. I think I'm gonna do it. Yep, I am."

She saw the crazed purpose gleaming in his eyes, saw his finger shift to the trigger. Oh, God, he *was* going to do it.

Fear, instinct, rage, all converged within her—she jumped forward without thinking.

"Bitch!" he screamed.

She grabbed his wrist, held it fast, and kneed him in his urine-soaked groin. Eric grunted in pain. For a split second his grasp on the gun loosened. She clutched at the .45 with both hands and they fell, tussling, against the rickety table before crashing together to the floor.

The room spun in slow motion as Ana fought for her life. John's face loomed more vividly in her mind with each blow as Eric backhanded her, and through the haze of pain she could taste the copper tang of blood on her tongue. But she held fast to his gun arm, struggling with the ferocity of a pit bull. If she didn't get it away from him, he would kill her. . . .

Then Eric was on top of her, his weight pinning

her to the floor, his elbows stabbing into her rib cage.
He pointed the gun at her face. And laughed.

"So long, Candy."

Somehow, she flung up an arm. Somehow, the gun
discharged.

The bullet pierced his forehead like a shiny red
star.

Blood and brains vomited out the back of his skull,
splattering down on her, hot and slippery.

Like limp red spaghetti, Ana thought right before
she passed out.

She crawled to the bathroom, sick and dizzy, and managed to pull herself up with the help of the knob.
Fighting back nausea, she scrubbed manically at her
face and wig.

Out, out, damned spot. Ana fought back the hysterical tears that bubbled in her throat as she yanked the
leather gloves back in place. *All the perfumes of Arabia
will not sweeten this little hand.*

She'd always wanted to play Lady Macbeth. . . .
Oh, God.

Flinging hangers aside in the bedroom closet, she
found a frayed khaki trench coat. Every pore quivering,
she stuffed her arms into the ripped sleeves and yanked
the belt tight over her death-soaked clothes. She
moved carefully to her satchel near the TV without
looking over toward Eric.

She saw no one as she slipped out of the apartment. Head down, she crept along the stairs and
through the open doorway before blending into the human jungle on the street.

Chapter Thirty

The thunder and lightning transported Eve back to her little bedroom in Duluth, where buffeting rain-storms had provided a perfect backdrop for Margo's nighttime terror stories. She could still hear the voice from the top bunk, an ominous voice that pierced the dark like jagged glass, punctuated by wind, rain, and thunder. And Margo wouldn't stop. She'd keep adding gruesome detail after gruesome detail until Eve would flee down the dim hallway to her mother's arms for reassurance.

Where was Swanson? He'd said he'd be right back. Eve rose from the sofa and ventured cautiously to the glass panel framing the front door.

Not a soul in sight.

Rain slashed diagonally across the sloping gardens fronting the villa, sending bougainvillea and slender palms swaying to the ground as if in supplication.

She cupped her hands around her cup of tea and sipped the fragrant, comforting liquid. Her mother had always given her tea when she was sick—delicious tea laced with honey and stirred with a cinnamon stick.

She reached for the phone. Big girls did cry sometimes, and at those moments they needed their mothers. But just as she heard the first ring begin on the line to Duluth, a deafening clap of thunder boomed directly outside, making her jump.

Or *was* that thunder? Oh, God, was it a gunshot?

Eve dropped the phone into its cradle. Her heart began a staccato rhythm of its own. *It had to be thunder, you idiot.*

But she set down the tea and snatched up a letter opener, just in case, before she made her way back to the entryway.

She gasped as a heavy knock reverberated against the door.

"Miss Hamel. It's Dean Everett. Let me in."

It was about time. She peered through the peephole. Reassured that it was indeed the brown-haired bodyguard, Eve slipped the letter opener into her jump-suit pocket in relief. "I was so worried." She glanced past him into the sheeting darkness. "Where's Swanson—and Monique and Teri?"

Everett guided her inside and carefully locked the door.

"Don't worry about them."

"But I thought . . ."

He shook his head, and droplets of rain flew down his flushed cheeks. "They won't be back for quite some time. But I brought you something from them."

Baffled, Eve stared at him as he reached into the pocket of his rain-soaked navy blazer.

"This one is from Monique."

He handed her a scrap of red terry-cloth. Eve stared at it in numb confusion.

"This one is from Teri."

He produced a snippet of white silk, and pressed it into her hand.

"And this one," he added dreamily, holding out a blood-soaked square of cotton khaki, "is from Tom."

Stark madness stared at her from the face of Dean

Everett. Terror immobilized her. She couldn't scream. She couldn't move. All she could do was stare in horror. First at the ragged scraps of fabric in her hand, then at the ordinary young man with the insane glow in his eyes.

"What did you do to them?" she whispered.

"I killed Tom—with this." He brandished a five-inch hunting knife pulled from the leather sheath attached to his belt. "I had to. I forgot my gun in your villa when I was tying up Monique."

Eve swallowed, fighting to keep her balance as the room swayed around her. "Is Monique . . . all right?"

"Oh, she's fine. But Teri's lost a lot of blood. You mustn't worry about them though. The security guard is right there with them." Suddenly maniacal laughter gurgled out of him. "Only problem is, he's dead too. See?" And he produced yet another scrap of bloody fabric.

Oh, my God. Eve involuntarily took two steps backward. *You're insane,* she wanted to scream. But she forced herself to keep silent and to think. Her breath was coming in shallow, winded gasps, her mind rattling in every direction.

What was it Maxine had drummed into her head time and again as they rehearsed unthinkable scenarios? Stay calm, feed his ego, keep him talking—*do whatever you have to do to stay alive.*

My God, he's killed Swanson and the guard—probably Teri and Monique too, Eve realized on a surge of panic. An image of Monique's trussed and bloodied body imprinted itself in her brain. Grief vied with terror.

I'm next, she thought, her muscles turning to water. *Me and my baby. Please, God, no.*

Keep him talking.

"Billy." Her lips were so dry, she had to moisten them with her tongue to speak. "Why don't you come in and sit down. I'll fix us some tea." She moved one tentative step toward the kitchen.

"*No.*" He leapt forward and seized her shoulder with one hand. "You're always walking away from me. No more. I'm here now, and it's time."

"Billy, I wouldn't walk away from you." She tried to smile. Tried not to wince though his fingers bit into her. "I've just been working so hard . . ."

"Too hard." He nodded his head vehemently. "You've got to take better care of yourself. And our baby."

He knew. Even that, he knew. Her lungs constricted. His hand was roaming across her belly, and she wanted to shrink back, but she forced herself to remain motionless.

"So you know about the baby," she said slowly.

He pulled her along with him down onto the sofa, keeping one hand on her, one hand on the knife. He held it loosely, almost as an afterthought.

"You really should have told me about the baby. I was so angry at you when I found out. You know you have to be punished for that."

She could smell his breath, sweet and mediciney, as though he'd gargled with mouthwash.

"And for *him.* Why are you still seeing him when you're having my baby, Eve? Did you think I didn't know?" He sighed. "You're like the others. You're too pretty. They were pretty too. Everybody loved them— they took them away from me—always away from me."

"I'm right here, Billy. I'm not going anywhere. I promise. I'll stay right here."

His pebble-brown eyes grew sad, dreamy. "You love me, Eve, don't you?"

She nodded, unable to force out the words.

Billy's face darkened. He set the knife down on the farthest edge of the coffee table, miles out of her reach, it seemed, his mournful eyes trained on her face. Before she realized what was happening, he cuffed her across the jaw. "Say it, Eve. Stop being so stubborn. I'm sick of it. Say it!"

"I love you." She choked out the words.

"Again." Another blow stunned her.

"I love you!"

A beatific smile spread across his features. "I knew it. I knew if we could only spend some time together, you'd straighten out. Look, I want to show you something." The shiny manicure scissors glistened in his palm.

What else does he have in those bottomless pockets, a grenade, a machete? Eve waited while he held the scissors up to the light. She didn't dare say anything, terrified of inadvertently setting him off.

Billy took her pinky between his blood-stained fingers. "This little piggy went to market . . ." He giggled and snipped off her half-inch French-manicured nail. "This little piggy stayed home.

"You should stay home, Eve." And the ring-finger nail was gone.

One by one he snipped off all ten of her fingernails. Eve's heart thudded wildly as she listened to his half-lucid chatter. She had no idea how long she sat there, her gaze fixed on that scissors. Surely help would be coming soon—if she could just keep him going a little longer. Security would find Monique and the others, would discover whatever mayhem he had wrought in the other villa.

"Bobbie Sue was always on her tour bus, going from town to town, singing her little heart out. But no one loved her like I did. And Lianna—pretty Lianna. She had such soft red hair. It bounced in the sunshine when she swung her racket. Bam! Fifteen–love. Pow. Thirty–love. She was so graceful. I loved her, Eve. It hurt me to punish her. But I had to. You understand, don't you?"

Eve nodded.

Billy stared at her woefully. "You don't really, do

you? You're just saying that. None of you understand."
Suddenly his brown eyes took on a sly look. The corners of his mouth twitched, lifted. "Did you figure out how I did it yet?"

Kill those women? Get away with it? Snip my clothes? What, you asshole? Give me a clue.

"I can't figure it out, Billy. Won't you tell me? I've been wondering how you could be so clever."

Her voice was low, soothing, she hoped, but her muscles clenched taut with fear. She was caught between conflicting urges: the impulse to fight, to flee, or to follow the practical advice Maxine had given her: Keep him talking. Keep him calm.

So far it was working. Her questions were defusing him. He looked pleased. "I am clever," he informed her. "Very, very clever. I could be anything I want to be —I don't have to be a valet, you know. I did that only to get close to you. And it worked." He beamed and dangled the manicure scissors like a set of car keys. "I got to see you all the time—you always looked so pretty. So many pretty dresses. And I loved when you left your appointment book in the car for me. It made me feel so close to you. It was like reading your diary— or your love letters."

A valet. It hit her like a Mack truck. Of course, the nameless, faceless runners who parked and brought the car at restaurants, theaters, parties, hotels. How many times had she turned over her keys, her car, and whatever personal papers were left lying on the seat, never thinking twice about the person entrusted with them.

All Nico ever worried about was that the valet would speed off with her Viper and get a scratch on it. He inspected the car each time he got into it.

"That was so ingenious of you," she said slowly, reminding herself to smile. "You must really care about me to go to so much trouble. I have an idea. Why don't we go on a date together—you and me. I'll get all dressed up in one of my pretty dresses and we could go out and have dinner together."

He grabbed a handful of her honey-blond hair and yanked her head backward with vicious strength, his face contorted with rage. "You don't understand, do you, Eve? You're always going somewhere. I've had to wait *forever*. We're finally alone here together and all you want to do is eat? Or do you just want to go out and show off, have everyone look at you? That's your problem, you know. You're too pretty, too vain. We have to fix that."

The scissors caught the light as he raised them toward her face. Eve gasped and wrenched desperately away, but quick as a snake Billy was on her, pinning her lengthwise beneath him on the sofa.

"Don't!" she pleaded as the scissors flashed over her again. "Please, don't!"

"It's for your own good," he admonished her. "Now, lie still like a good girl, or I'll get angry."

Terrified, she bucked and struggled beneath him, expecting at any moment to feel the slash ripping into her skin, but he merely began methodically snipping strands of her hair, cutting it above her ears, yanking her head, concentrating all of his attention on the ragged strands that drifted onto the couch in a pale halo. He hummed as he did it.

"That wasn't so bad, was it?" Billy said at last, admiring his handiwork. "You don't look quite as pretty now."

He grinned and leaned closer. He was lying full upon her. "Gimme a kiss; now, there's a good girl," he chortled.

Eve fought revulsion as his moist lips covered hers.

"Open your mouth," he whispered.

She wanted to vomit, to scream, to fight, to kick. But she wanted to stay alive more.

She opened her mouth.

•   •   •   •   •

Monique's hands were numb but for the painful tingling in her wrists. Her throat ached from shouting.

No one had responded to her screams for help. Had he killed everyone in the whole place—Antonio, Mimi, all of them?

Teri's blood soaked the carpet. She hadn't moved.

Hard rain blew in, tossing the curtains, flooding the entrance floor. Where in the hell was security?

At least the lights haven't gone out, Monique thought, keeping panic at bay with fierce resolve. *At least I can still see what's coming—my imagination would be freaking out in the dark.*

Okay, she thought. *Enough of feeling helpless. You read fifty million Nancy Drew books when you were a kid. Nancy always came through. What the hell would she do now?*

Wriggle free.

Easier read than done. The belt cut into her flesh as she writhed, twisted, and contorted in a vain effort to loosen the snare.

I've got to get Teri to a hospital. I've got to help Eve. Oh, God, maybe he's already killed her. Maybe Teri's already dead, too. She's lost so much blood.

Monique would have gladly traded her Porsche at that moment for one tiny razor blade. Damn . . . this . . . fucking . . . belt.

She collapsed, out of breath. It was no use. Turning her head with an effort, she saw the ever-widening pool around Teri.

Tears of frustration scalded her eyes. She gulped back despair and began wriggling furiously again, her arms wrenching in their sockets, her legs kicking out.

The phone jangled suddenly atop the sofa table. Monique focused on the sound with alacrity.

It might be her only chance. She jackknifed across the damp carpet, ignoring the pain bursting in her joints. Three rings . . . four . . . furiously, she hurled herself against the leg of the table as the belt strained agonizingly around her wrists.

The phone stayed put and ceased ringing before the answering machine had a chance to pick up. But the jolt knocked the lamp to the floor. It cracked and splintered, the bulb showering her with fragments of glass.

Monique screamed a curse as she was plummeted into inky darkness.

"I have to go to the bathroom."

Billy stopped kissing her long enough to eye her warily. "I don't believe you."

"Billy, I'm pregnant. With our baby. Pregnant women have to go to the bathroom all the time."

He hesitated, then nodded. "This better not be a trick, Eve."

"I'll come right back—I promise."

He eased off her and allowed her to stand up. Eve tried not to wobble as she crossed toward the bathroom. For the baby's sake, she prayed this would work.

"Wait."

Billy brushed past her into the john. Her heart lurched as he ripped the phone from the wall with both hands and tossed it into the sunken marble tub.

Eve's muscles were taut, her senses heightened. *He doesn't have the knife. It's still on the table. So is the manicure scissors. You might not get another chance.*

He edged out of the bathroom and stopped before her. Her breathing quickened, but all he did was joyously fluff his fingers through her mangled hair. "Lovely. Even shorter than Lianna's." Abruptly he scowled and leaned in close to her face. "Don't close the door."

"I won't."

She tried not to stare at the locked front door as

she turned. Billy was walking backward toward the
sofa, humming, watching her, a tiny smile playing about
the corners of his mouth.

Now or never. Make a run for it.

Her heart banged against her rib cage as she
forced her gaze to fly to the French doors behind him.
"Don't shoot, Tamburelli!" she shouted, and in the split
second that Billy jerked his head to look, she flung herself toward the locked front door.

Terror exploded through her as she wrestled with
the bolt. Her hand was on the knob, pulling, when Billy
slammed into her.

"Liar! Slut! You're just like all the others!" he
screeched, the veins in his neck bulging with rage. Spittle flew from his lips and his eyes had gone completely
mad.

"You have to pay, Eve. Pay dearly. It's your own
fault!" His hands closed around her throat.

Through the ringing in her ears and the white
lights blinking before her eyes, Eve groped in her
pocket. She prayed she had enough strength. . . .

The lights flashed like a strobe lamp. She couldn't
see.

With a hiss she lashed out maniacally, stabbing
toward his groin.

Billy Shears's scream drowned out the thunder. He
let go of her throat and sagged backward, clutching at
the letter opener jammed into his bloody crotch.

Eve spun toward the door, but as she reached for
the knob it flew wide.

"Freeze!"

Six Hawaiian cops and Monique burst toward her.
Silent red and white flashers punctuated the darkness
outside.

The cops charged past. Monique caught Eve in her
arms as an ambulance siren howled through the night.

"It's okay, Evie B. It's okay," Monique murmured,
caught between hysterical laughter and tears. "I told

you everything would be okay. And when I say it, darling, it's guaranteed." Tears streamed down her cheeks as she looked at Eve's butchered hair, her pinched white face, the terror convulsing her slim body.

Behind them, Billy Shears was bellowing obscenities as the officers restrained him, walkie-talkies squawking.

"Suspect wounded. Losing blood. We have two dead, one wounded."

Staggering, Eve dragged Monique out with her into the storm-tossed night and lifted her face to the sweet pelting rain. Together they collapsed against the bamboo gate.

"My baby, Monique!" Eve whispered, and turned to hug Monique wildly. "Thank God, you'll be a godmother after all. I did it. I saved my baby."

Chapter Thirty-one

Adam was curled up on the sofa of the Disneyland Hotel, lost in the dizzying adventures of his treasured hand-held video game. He didn't notice the news bulletin flash across the TV screen. He couldn't hear the announcer's interruption:

". . . a tale of death and terror on the island of Maui. Two people are dead, both of them male security guards, and two others have been hospitalized, including the suspected serial killer who held supermodel Eve Hamel hostage for several hours before he was apprehended. Injured in this bizarre chain of events was a young woman named Teri Mathews, of Livonia, Michigan. Miss Mathews was in Maui to participate in a special promotion for *Perfect Bride* magazine. We have no word on her condition yet, or on the condition of Miss Hamel, who is reportedly pregnant by her fiancé, race car driver Nico Caesarone. They were participants in the magazine promotion, which was also to have featured actress Ana Cates and her fiancé, Senator John Farrell, as well as *Perfect Bride's* billionaire publisher Richard Ives and his fiancée, the Comtesse Monique D'Arcy, its editor in chief. Neither Cates nor

Farrell showed up in Maui, however, and there has been no official word on their whereabouts. The pieces of this story are still filtering in to us. More details as we receive them."

His heart tight with fear, Andrew lunged for the remote control. He clicked through all the other channels in desperation. CNN? ABC? Where else could he get more information about Teri? Why didn't they say which hospital she was in?

Despite the air-conditioning, sweat dripped down his forehead as he placed three phone calls. One to the number Teri had left him, one to the Maui Police Department, and one to LAX.

Adam was so mesmerized by his game that he didn't look up once as Andrew swiftly packed their belongings and set the bags down by the door.

"Time to go, sport," he signed as he knelt beside the child, then ruffled the boy's dark hair.

"Where?" Adam signed back, his dancing gray eyes expectant of wonders yet to come.

"On an airplane." Andrew tried to keep his expression cheerful despite the fear gripping him.

He was grateful he didn't have to speak, because he knew his voice would have broken. "We're going to see your mother—Teri," he signed as Adam stared at him questioningly. "She needs us."

Teri was ensnared by a tangle of tubing and wires, and precisely tucked sheets that were as white as she was. Her heartbeats blipped across the monitor at the head of the bed, rhythmically reassuring Brian that she was still breathing. But he didn't feel reassured. He was terrified.

She looked so fragile, so utterly still. How could someone lose so much blood and still live? The nurses were cordial but noncommittal.

"We can't give you any information until the doctor is out of surgery, Mr. Michaelson."

Brian and Tamburelli had arrived on the last flight out of Hilo shortly after the surgeon had joined the team operating on Billy Shears.

Brian glanced at his watch—three A.M. Eve Hamel and Monique D'Arcy had left with Tamburelli less than fifteen minutes before, after the resident had threatened to strap them into a hospital bed if they didn't go back to the resort for some rest. But it seemed that he'd been alone here for hours.

That Monique was something else. She'd probably saved Teri's life. Destroyed her wrists on broken glass —but sawed herself free in time to summon help before Teri bled to death. With steely optimism and unflappable determination, her wrists bound up in layers of gauze, she had circled the hospital corridors for hours, constantly checking on Eve in the emergency ward and then returning to the foot of Teri's bed to inform Brian in no uncertain terms that Teri was going to be *fine*.

He wished desperately he could believe it.

Wearily, he hoisted himself from the molded orange bucket seat supported on chrome legs. In the faint fluorescent light from the panel above the headboard, Teri looked like a wilted lily. Her lips were cracked and dry. Blood dripped through yards of plastic IV tubes into her. Her shoulder and upper arm were engulfed by the cast that extended to her collarbone. Only that morning she'd been gloriously vibrant, laughing in the sunshine, her black hair whipping in the breeze as they'd cavorted for Antonio's camera.

Now she was barely there—diminished—like the hazy image on photographic paper as it floats in the chemical bath that will bring it to life.

He stroked her cheek with a tentative caress. He'd been such a shit to her the day they went to Hudson's.

He'd been so angry, so full of hurt pride. All Teri'd ever asked was that he love her.

And he did. But did she know it now, when she needed his love, needed every drop of love and strength to survive?

"I love you, Teri," he whispered. "God, how I love you. I know you can hear me. Maybe it's not too late. I told you that I found my old Lionel train set for Adam. Picture how much fun the three of us are going to have with it. We can set it up on the Ping-Pong table in the basement for now, and when we get our house, Adam can keep it in his room if he wants. Hang in there, babe. I'm with you every step of the way. I love you," Brian finished on a gulp.

A shadow fell across the bed.

"I love her too," Andrew spoke beside him.

Brian's hands involuntarily balled into fists. He willed them open again and turned to face Andrew Leonetti.

"Then I guess one of us is going to have a problem." Brian took a deep breath and then unwittingly echoed the words Andrew had spoken to him that first night in Livonia. "Have a seat, buddy, it's going to be a long night."

They sat, they paced, they watched.

Teri's eyes never even flickered until eight A.M., when the nurses came to replace the IV. When the nurse adjusted the drip, Teri suddenly opened her eyes and began to moan.

"Lie still, Teri," the nurse directed cheerfully. "Everything's fine. It's all over, you're in the hospital and you're okay."

"Brian . . . I want Brian. . . ."

Andrew was on his feet, bolting to the side of the bed at the nurse's first words.

Teri peered into his face. "Andrew," she breathed,

and clutched his hand. Her face was puffy, pale as candle wax. "Where's Brian? I want Brian," she pleaded, wincing with pain. "Where is he?"

Andrew's face crumpled. He reeled two steps backward. Brian edged past him.

"I'm here, babe. I'm right here." His eyes locked with hers. He reached out and tenderly smoothed away a wisp of her hair. She looked so weak, so drained, his heart tightened with fear, but at least she was awake and coherent, clinging to his hand as if it were a lifeline. "I've been here all night, and I'm not going anywhere," Brian told her. "You really know how to give a guy a scare. Hey, if you want to leave me at the altar, there are easier ways to do it."

"I don't want to leave you at the altar. I don't want to leave you at all."

Andrew's shoulders slumped. He stared at the couple before him, feeling as invisible and empty as lost dreams. Teri had forgotten him already. She was completely intent on Brian.

"I was so scared," she was murmuring. "Brian, I thought I'd never see you again."

The words were thick on her tongue. But they were the most beautiful words Brian had ever heard.

Neither of them noticed Andrew Leonetti turn and walk out the door.

Chapter Thirty-two

John Farrell slammed the car door and leaned against it, composing himself for the scene ahead of him. Ana was already at the cabin, her rental car parked under the giant redwood tree. She'd said so damned little on the phone when she'd begged him to meet her that all of his questions still hammered inside him. It had been nearly a week since she'd walked out of his parents' house without explanation, seemingly dropping off the face of the earth.

He could never forgive her, not for this. A whole week without a word. There could be no excuse.

Still, he'd come. He'd hear her out and then he'd show her the statement his press secretary would release in the morning.

He'd been dumbstruck when he found her cryptic note—*Johnny, something urgent has come up. Sorry to leave so suddenly. I'll explain later*—then frantic with worry when he'd heard nothing more. Somewhere in the next two days, anxiety had succumbed to fury. The reporters had swarmed mercilessly, Monique D'Arcy had burned up the phone lines between Maui, Rhode Island, and D.C., and worst of all, his parents had shot their usual reproving looks and taken great pains not to mention Ana's name.

No one knew where she was—not Arnie, not Graciella, not Louise. Until the phone call.

"Well, Ana, I'm here," he said when she opened the door of the cedar A-frame and stood aside for him to enter.

"Johnny, I never meant to hurt you or worry you," she began in a low voice, but he cut her off as ruthlessly as an opponent on the Senate floor.

"You did a pretty good job of it nevertheless."

She flinched from the rage in his eyes.

Well, she hadn't expected this would be easy. "I know you're furious. But can you sit down and listen, please? I do have an explanation."

He sat. Belligerently, in the center of the plaid sofa, forcing her to perch opposite him in the cushioned mission chair. He didn't want to be close to her, not yet. He had to keep a clear head for whatever shit she was about to unload.

The only sound in the room was the hiss of the wood fire flickering in the rustic hearth. The leaping orange flames gave color to Ana's wan face. The baggy fisherman sweater she wore over skin-tight black jeans seemed to swallow her. There were sunken hollows under her eyes. John had never seen her look so pale, so dejected. She almost looked sick.

"Are you all right?" he asked reluctantly, wondering with a sudden knife thrust of the heart if she was ill. Seriously ill. He half rose from the sofa. "Ana"—*my God, how selfish can I be*—"what's wrong with you?"

She shook her head, reading the unspoken fear behind his words. "I don't have cancer, I don't have AIDS, it's nothing like that. It would be easier for me to tell you something that awful. This is so much harder. Please listen. If you hate me afterward, I'll understand. I'll have Arnie release a statement that by mutual agreement we've decided to go our separate ways." She stared down at her hands a moment, then lifted her head to meet his eyes. "Only remember that I love you. I always have, I always will."

What the hell was she going to say? John tried to keep his expression impassive as Ana began to talk, but what he heard quickly wiped away any hopes of maintaining an air of detachment.

And so she told him. All of it—every ugly detail. His usually noncommittal expression vanished at the first mention of Eric Gunn. The porno films made him blanch. The hit and run sent him pacing to the window, his fingers tearing through his hair. And when she told him about the blackmail so recently started, he spun about and glared at her.

"Why didn't you tell me? Dammit, Ana, why didn't you trust me with this?"

She dropped her head into her hands, suddenly exhausted. "You don't know the worst, Johnny. Eric is dead. I shot him."

"You *what*?"

That was when she began to cry. John swore a stream of words he usually saved for the Democrats. He struggled within himself, pacing, kicking the logs in the brass cradle alongside the hearth. But seeing her utter desolation, hearing her heart-wrung sobs, tore at his self-control and vanquished all of his shock.

He went to her and gathered her close. His mind raced to take in all the repercussions of the bombshells she kept dropping. Any one piece of this could destroy him. All of it together would decimate him.

Part of him said cut your losses and run.

The other part said screw the consequences.

He tentatively touched that bright halo of hair, burnished the color of new pennies in the firelight. "It's all right, Ana. Tell me how it happened."

Three hours later John set down the phone. "It's all taken care of. Anything in his apartment that could link you to that slimebag has been obliterated. My people said the police haven't even found him yet."

Ana shuddered.

"Anything you missed has disappeared. Anyone who remembers anything has already forgotten."

Ana curled her knees beneath her on the sofa and reached for her cocoa. "I hate involving you in this. You had nothing to do with it. If it ever came out, John, it would ruin you."

He stared at her a long time. "I haven't gotten this far steeping my hands in baby lotion," he said ruefully. He crossed to the window and gazed out at the claret dusk spilling like a glass of wine across the mountains. "You should have come to me on day one."

"I wanted to handle it myself. I didn't want to risk losing you. Johnny, you're the best thing that ever happened to me."

"You almost got yourself killed." Suddenly, a new kind of anger rushed through him. He went to her and grabbed her so abruptly, the cocoa sloshed out of the cup she held. John set the cup aside and pulled Ana into his arms. "Going up against Eric Gunn one on one like that was the stupidest thing of all. If he'd killed you—"

His voice broke. His hands tangled suddenly in her hair, then slid down to crush her against him. "I couldn't bear losing you," he breathed violently.

With wonder Ana saw the sheen of tears filming his eyes. Relief and impossible hope lurched through her. But she was afraid to hope.

"I'm so scared that every time you look at me now you'll think of those films," she whispered miserably.

"Oh, shut up, silly." John ruffled her hair. "Every time I look at you I think of that vibrant, caring woman who wowed me at the AIDS benefit, the woman I couldn't stop thinking about for days afterward. The woman I want to spend the rest of my life loving. Making up to you for all this shit in your past. It's over, Ana, dead and gone. Along with Eric Gunn."

He took off her sweater, then unzipped her jeans. "Let's make a pact."

"What sort of pact?" Standing there clad only in her cream lace bra and panties, Ana felt a strange pleasant pull inside her. She actually giggled as John yanked her down with great firmness onto the alpaca rug.

"Never to talk about Eric Gunn again."

"I'll drink to that."

"Later," John said, silencing her with a kiss. "We'll toast it with champagne or root beer or whatever you say, but right now . . ."

Hurriedly he unbuttoned his white chamois shirt and tugged off his shoes, his erection straining against the fly of his charcoal twill pants. Ana felt oddly excited, oddly . . . free. She didn't know if it was John's eagerness affecting her or what . . . but . . . merely looking at him she felt a warm wetness blossoming between her legs.

As he unhooked the front of her bra and welcomed each rosy nipple with a kiss, Ana let out a quivering sigh. She could hardly believe that John hadn't walked out on her. He knew the worst, and yet he was standing by her, loving her, wanting her. . . .

His mouth trailed kisses along the center of her body to the curve above her bikini panties. Ana strained against him, lifting her buttocks so that he could remove the last article of clothing, then cried out as his tongue slid lower, bathing her in warmth more welcome than the flickers from the fireplace.

Slowly his tongue teased her, then his fingers joined in the heady tantalization. Incredibly, she felt the warmth low in her groin intensifying from a delicious tingle to an insistent throbbing ache. Just when she thought she'd go mad from anticipation, he spread her legs apart with his own strong thighs and slid inside her.

She forgot to grow tense, forgot to freeze up. She was lost in sensation, lost in happiness. John truly loved her . . . he was standing by her . . . he didn't want to dump her because of her past. . . .

His muscular body pulsated with energy and strength as he covered her, claimed her—and Ana found herself wrapping her legs around him with abandon, molding her body with his, thrusting her hips along with him. . . .

John captured her, carried her off. She was lost in a land of wild, fragile sensations and she didn't want to ever come back. . . .

It was wonderful, magical, perfect. Ana couldn't believe how relaxed she felt afterward. A film of sweat glistened on her body, she felt warm, drained, and sated, and she gazed happily back into John's eyes as he grinned down at her.

"I love you, Johnny," Ana murmured.

"For a few days there, I wondered," he replied, rolling off her to prop himself up on one elbow. He wound a lock of her hair around his finger and rolled it up and down.

"Don't ever do that again, okay? Don't shut me out, or walk out like that without a word. It's not fair, Ana."

"I promise."

He kissed her breasts and trailed a gentle hand across her belly. "I love you too much to lose you. I'll do whatever it takes to keep you safe, to keep us together."

Ana didn't know how long she slept. It was the first long, untroubled sleep she'd had in over a week, and she awoke refreshed and cozy in the huge feather bed facing the master bedroom's picture window. Inky darkness obscured the mountains outside, allowing only a few glittering stars to penetrate the clear, still night.

Ana threw off the goosedown comforter and padded toward the bathroom.

"Sleep," John called out from the leather lounge chair, lowering his book as she entered the living room a minute later.

"Uh-uh. I feel like being with you." Ana encircled his shoulders from behind the chair, burying her face in the warmth of his neck. She kissed his cheek and snuggled, content. "I wish we could stay here forever. This place is perfect. Perfect! Oh, my God, did you ever get ahold of Monique D'Arcy?"

"Yep. You'll never believe it. Thank God we weren't on Maui."

She straightened up at his tone and came around to plop down in his lap. "Why?"

"Haven't you been listening to the news?"

Ana closed her eyes and shuddered. "No. I was afraid I'd hear something about you-know-who. I just wanted to block it all out."

"Well, they've had quite a party over there in Hawaii. A few shootings of their own. Eve Hamel was held hostage. And that manicurist was shot by some deranged serial killer. The tabloids are going nuts. So is D'Arcy."

"Oh, my God. Is Teri all right?"

"She lost a lot of blood, but she's going to make it. And Eve Hamel actually stabbed this guy and held him off until the police got there."

Dazed, Ana closed her eyes, then opened them wide. "How horrible. I suppose they had to scrap the shoot?"

He grinned. "Are you kidding? Monique nearly tore my head off. She wants us there ASAP. Are you up to it?"

"I guess if we do it," Ana said slowly, watching his face, "it means we're still on for the Fourth of July. Right?"

"Only if you promise me the same kind of fireworks we had a little while ago."

"Senator, I think it can be arranged. Want a sneak
preview?" She slanted him a sideways siren's glance.

"No, a full-length double feature."

Ana uncurled herself from his lap and raced him to
the feather bed.

Chapter Thirty-three

Maxine Goodman's cab pushed through the throng of reporters camped at the Maui Haleakala Resort entrance gate, and after a flash of credentials was waved inside the lush grounds of the compound. The reporters went crazy.

Maxine found Eve Hamel sunning beside the main pool, looking iceberg cool despite the blazing sun. The air was tinged with an almost electric heat bearing the fragrance of pineapple fields. Palm trees stood around Eve like tall, silent sentries, replacements for the fallen guards.

Maxine envied Eve her bathing suit. She was perspiring and uncomfortable in her magenta linen traveling suit, but she hadn't wanted to take the time to change. She'd come to the resort straight from the police station, and she had news.

"We expect Billy Shears will never have the chance to waive extradition. He's being arraigned this afternoon on two counts of open murder, three counts of assault with attempt to commit murder, breaking and entering, attempted rape, and felony firearm. He'll be locked up so long in Hawaii, he won't remember his name by the time he has to face those other murder charges back on the mainland, let alone the B and E of your apartment."

Maxine tossed down the legal papers from which she'd been reading and leveled her gaze at Eve. "Too bad stalking isn't a crime here as it is in California, or they'd throw that at him too. I'd say even if he's let off on an insanity plea, he'll never see a day of sunshine like this one again in his life."

All the while she listened, Eve had been watching the tall, sandy-haired man in the black boxer trunks playing water Frisbee in the pool with the young boy. Someone had told her the child was Teri's. She had no idea who the man was.

"So it looks like Billy Shears's scissors will be sheathed for good," Eve sighed. "Did he tell you his real name? Not that it matters, I suppose . . ."

"William Kendricks. Age twenty-three—first run-in with the law at fifteen. Once we got his real name and ran a check on him, we discovered why he was so quiet between the Caruthers murder and the Griffin one. He was in jail."

"Just as you thought," Eve murmured. She picked up her glass of pineapple-guava juice but didn't drink it.

"He served three years of a five-year sentence for B and E with malicious destruction of property, got out early for good behavior, then broke parole and vanished. That must have been when he began stalking Bobbie Sue Griffin."

Silence fell between the two of them, broken only by the frivolous splashing in the pool. "It's awful about Swanson," Eve said in a low tone. "His poor wife and three little children—they were all he ever talked about. He couldn't wait to bring his wife here someday. Life's weird, isn't it? My baby is safe, and someone else's husband and father is dead." Eve looked away into the distance as tears threatened to spill over.

Maxine placed a hand on her shoulder. "He was a good man. As good as they come. But he knew the risks —in this business we live with them every day." Her tone became crisp and professional once again. "Swanson's body is being flown back tonight. I hope to finish up the paperwork here and return to New York in time for his funeral. Dean Everett—Tom Swanson . . ." Maxine rubbed her temples wearily.

"I can't believe they're both gone," she admitted. "It's these kinds of cases that can make you crazy. Fill you with all those nagging 'if onlys.' " She lifted her head, sighed, and gave Eve a measuring stare. "So, how are you?"

"Hanging in there. Like my new look?" Eve touched the ends of her bobbed hair and managed a wan laugh. "Thank God Monique's stylist was able to salvage Billy's chop job. Don't know if the Estée Lauder people will agree." She shrugged. "I can always wear a wig if it hasn't grown out by then."

"Eve." Maxine's piercing amber eyes held hers relentlessly. "How are you really?"

"Shell-shocked. Glad to be alive." She set the drink down on the small poolside table. "Maxine, those briefings you gave me saved my life. I'll be eternally grateful."

"Take credit where it's due. You were smart, Eve. You kept your head."

"Every time I started freaking out, I kept reminding myself what you told me about playing along, feeding his ego, stalling for time."

"Time is what you need now to put this all in perspective."

Maxine scribbled hastily on the back of her business card. "Here's the phone number for a victim's assistance program in New York. You might want to get in touch with them when you get back. It helps to talk things out with others who've gone through a similar ordeal."

At that moment the Frisbee skittered through the air and crashed into the frosty juice glass, sending it spinning and the contents splashing across Eve's lap.

She yelped in surprise as the icy liquid hit her sun-baked legs.

"Sorry," the man signed from the pool, then suddenly gave a self-conscious laugh and called out, "Sorry!" He hoisted himself over the edge of the pool, and with water dripping behind him padded to Eve's chair.

"I guess we got a little carried away."

Eve was already blotting up the juice with her towel. "No problem." She glanced ruefully at Maxine, stuffing the papers back into her briefcase. "This isn't exactly the stickiest situation I've been in this week."

"So I heard," the man said grimly. There was quiet sympathy in his engaging gray eyes. And something else, a fleeting flicker of sadness. It disappeared as soon as he stuck out his hand. "I'm Andrew Leonetti—an old friend of Teri Mathews's."

Eve introduced Maxine, who excused herself a moment later, saying, "I have an appointment with Monique D'Arcy and then the D.A., but I wanted to fill you in first, Eve. I'll be in touch."

Eve plunked her sunglasses in her tote and folded the damp towel into a neat rectangle. All the while Andrew Leonetti kept his gaze trained on the boy jack-knifing off the diving board. "You've had a tough time of it, Miss Hamel," he remarked at last with a quick, steady look as she swung her legs off the chair. "Not many people could have kept their heads in a situation like yours and come out of it intact."

Oddly, Eve didn't mind the stranger's comments. They were offered so quietly, with such genuine sensitivity, she felt no annoyance. She watched the boy do a choppy somersault off the board and said slowly, "I guess I'm a survivor. I come from hardy Scandinavian stock. And," she added unexpectedly, "I'm pregnant—I kept thinking about my baby the whole time and how I couldn't let anything happen to him—or her."

Why was she telling this stranger something so personal? But there was something reassuring, innately decent, and quietly compassionate about this tall, light-haired man who'd spent the past hour entertaining Teri's little boy. The words were out before she realized it.

He looked at her then, a warm, level gaze that thankfully bore no pity. Yet Eve had the strange impression that he could see straight through to her soul, that he saw all the trouble, all the hopes and anguish there. "It's amazing how children can bring out the best in people," he said, and smiled. "Adam and I are going to have lunch in the Jungle Room. Care to join us?"

Eve hesitated. For a moment she wanted to be in the company of this comfortable man and the skinny boy in the Ninja Turtle bathing suit, to forget about Billy Shears, Nico, Margo—everything—just for half an hour.

But she shook her head. "Thanks, but I don't have much of an appetite these days, and I'm afraid I'm not very good company."

"Party-pooper." Andrew Leonetti chuckled. "Can't say I blame you. Chicken fingers, video games, and Maui Zowie Sundaes are not exactly gourmet fare. But if you change your mind, you know where to find us."

He summoned Adam from the pool with a flash of silent gestures, wrapped a towel around the boy's shoulders, and set off through the winding path to the main concourse.

Eve started toward her suite in the main building, then turned. "Andrew," she called after him, and he paused at the trellised archway below the banyan tree, "if you go to the hospital later, I'd love to hitch a ride. I want to see Teri myself."

"Three o'clock," he called back, shading his eyes

from the beating sun. "Kids' visiting hours. Meet you at the taxi stand."

Maui Zowie Sundae, Eve mused, walking back to her brand-new blood-free, Nico-free suite. "Wonder if they put macadamia nuts on it," she said aloud.

"Yes," room service replied when she called and asked them. "And whipped cream and fresh crushed pineapple."

"Perfect. Give me one scoop of guava and one scoop of coconut ice cream, and go heavy on the macadamia nuts."

"I spent several hours early this morning bicycling with Adam," Brian said, looking for a spot to place the box of chocolate-covered macadamia nuts he'd brought Teri.

"And?" She paused to look at him, a chocolate poised midway to her mouth.

"And all the sign studying I've been doing seems to have paid off. We stopped for a Coke and had a rather interesting conversation about arcade video games and fifth-grade math." He sat down next to her and smiled. "Teri, I think he likes me. I think everything is going to work out."

Teri popped the chocolate into her mouth and settled back into the fresh pillowcases on the hospital bed. "The kid obviously has good taste. He takes after his mother, you know."

A nurse scurried in, checked Teri's temperature and pulse. She scribbled on the chart hooked to the metal post at the foot of the bed before scurrying out again.

Teri turned her head toward the window and a vista of turquoise sky, thinking, *It's funny how you know when you've made the right decision. And I have. Andrew is part of my past. But Brian is my future.*

She felt Brian's gaze on her, but when she looked

at him he began brushing imaginary lint specks off his jeans. He cleared his throat.

"I also spoke with Andrew this morning," he began. "He's going back to Arizona at the end of the week. By then Adam will be officially ours." Brian took a breath. "I told him I wanted to adopt Adam. Teri, I don't want Adam to feel any different from the other children we might have together." Teri nodded, her eyes warm. Her heart was suddenly too full to chance words.

"Andrew had some misgivings. He wants to think it over." Brian went on, smoothing the sheets between his fingers. "But as long as Adam knows the truth. That Andrew is his birth father. And as long as Andrew is able to be part of his life—spend some time with him during summers, vacations, things like that, it could work out best for all of us. What do you think?"

"I think I know why I love you so much, Brian Michaelson," Teri whispered, reaching for his hand. She squeezed it and cradled it against her cheek. "And I think I can't wait to get better and go home, and *really* start planning our life together. Beginning with our wedding."

"Oh." Brian grinned suddenly. "That reminds me."

Brian had that devilish twinkle in his eye. Teri studied him suspiciously, "What now?"

"Talked to Tina today. It seems Josie met Hilda's grandson, Frank, at the Hair and Now Christmas party. He was home on leave from the navy. The poor guy's being shipped out to Germany in two weeks and guess who's going with him? He and Josie eloped New Year's Day."

Brian laughed at the flabbergasted expression on Teri's face. "Guess you'll need to find yourself a new maid of honor, babe. *Auf Wiedersehen*, Josie."

.   .   .   .

"Yes, yes, yes, yes, yes." Even with the receiver held at arm's length, Richard's tirade still reverberated in Monique's ear.

Outside her window, Ana and John Farrell posed arm in arm on the narrow garden bridge suspended over the brook. As Monique watched, Mimi fluffed out the wedding gown's train, drifting it behind Ana in a froth of satin and lace. Blue ribbons had been tied along the bridge posts. They curled among the garlands of white and red roses spilling from pots lining the bridge, and the miniature waterfall that fed the brook provided a graceful backdrop.

"Cheat your glance to the left a little, Senator," she heard Antonio order, and then Richard's bark blasted again, reclaiming her attention.

"I'm going to think of something to save this damn issue," she screeched finally, yanking the receiver back against her ear. "Cates and Farrell are doing their thing even as we speak. I don't *know* what I'm going to do about Eve and Nico yet—let me think about it, for God's sake. Until I get the proofs back, I won't know how many group shots we have to discard. Richard, tell McArthur to go fuck himself. If you're not man enough to tell him, I will. Now go play mind games with someone else and tell the circulation department to start busting their buns, because this is going to be the most sensational, sought-after issue of *Perfect Bride ever.*"

She slammed down the phone and stabbed out her cigarette. She glanced ruefully across the littered desktop in her temporary office, then picked up once more the L.A. paper Maxine Goodman had left behind. WEST HOLLYWOOD MAN SHOT DEAD.

The three-paragraph story was buried on page eleven, but it had caught her eye. So had the name of the victim—Eric Gunn.

I wonder if Ana knows about this, she mused, and then immediately her eyes narrowed with a realization that was pure instinct.

Of course she does.

She dropped the newspaper into her wastebasket and sank down at her desk. She forced away a fleeting image of Eric Gunn crouched over Ana alongside her backyard pool, but not before it sent goose bumps prickling down Monique's spine.

Well, Miss Disappearing Cates, I'll ask you no questions, you'll tell me no lies. But I'll bet your New Year started off with a bang.

Monique glanced outside again at Ana and John. They were flirting for Antonio's camera beneath a rainbow that arced off the waterfall. They looked as carefree as the blue ribbons fluttering in the breeze.

She wouldn't allow herself to speculate whether John Farrell knew anything about this Gunn person. She wouldn't allow herself to speculate at all.

It was none of her business.

But getting this issue back on track was. Monique opened the desk drawer and extracted a pad of legal paper along with three sharpened pencils. Across the top of the first blue-lined yellow sheet she wrote: New Articles for June Issue.

On the next line she began a list.

1. What to do when your life is falling apart and your fiancé is making you crazy?

Call your mother.

"*Mon Dieu,* Monique. I can't stop thinking about that terrible man and what he could have done to all of you. If I hadn't immediately spoken to you myself, I would never have believed you were all right after such an experience. And now? Tell me, *petite,* when are you coming home?"

"Tomorrow. *Maman . . .*"

Mireille heard the hesitation in her tone and said instantly, "What's wrong, *chérie?*"

"Nothing. Everything's fine. I just wanted to hear your voice."

"Is it Richard?"

"Of course not." *Don't cry, Monique.* "I talked to him right before I called you. He sends his love."

Was it a sin to lie to your mother even if it gave her peace of mind? she wondered.

"Hmmm."

"I'll see you before you know it. Now, no more worrying. *Maman*?"

"Yes, *petite*?"

"Has Pete Lambert finished painting the terrace yet?"

"Yes, he finished before he left. We haven't seen him since."

Finished before he *left*?

"Well, I can't wait to see how the terrace turned out," Monique went on slowly. "Do you know where Pete's gone?" She tried to sound casual.

"Since when are you so interested in Mr. Lambert's comings and goings?" Mireille asked with a tinge of mischief in her voice.

Monique felt herself flushing as her mother continued. "He said he's done all he can do with the Parker property down the road. But before he left he brought me a homemade ginger fruitcake and a beautiful fringed silk shawl. Oh, Monique, wait until you see it. The man has such excellent taste. And he gave Dorothy a lovely little brooch. Oh," she added, and Monique could almost picture the laughter in her eyes, "did I mention that he left a small package under the tree for you?"

Monique suppressed a wave of pleasure. What could Pete Lambert have possibly given her? A box of carpenter's nails or a monogrammed paintbrush?

She swallowed a grin and said matter-of-factly, "How nice of him. *Maman*, I have to go now and somehow try to salvage this issue . . . see you soon . . ."

Somehow. Without Eve and Nico. With minimal photos of Ana and John. With my Cinderella bride shot down by a lunatic. It'll take a miracle. . . .

She doodled. She scribbled. She fidgeted with the diamond bracelet Richard had given her for Christmas. She chewed the eraser off her pencil.

And finally she wrote: Costner, Taylor, Houston, Beatty, Brinkley, Estevez, Willis, Shriver, Swayze.

The list went on and on, until there were fifty.

Chapter Thirty-four

By the time Eve returned to her Manhattan apartment, Clara had scrubbed out every trace of Billy Shears—and of Nico Caesarone.

But his letters flooded her mailbox. She returned each one unopened and refused to take his calls.

He might have broken my heart, but he'll never break my will, Eve resolved.

In spite of what he had done, she knew she could never deprive him of his child. She left arrangement of the details to her lawyers and busied herself with designing the nursery and reading Drs. Brazelton and Spock.

In January her mother came to visit, and begged to know what had caused the breakup. Eve never told.

February brought a dismal Valentine's Day dinner with Jenna, whose husband, Luis, had requested a trial separation only the week before. "Midlife crisis strikes again," Jenna cracked, tossing salad with a vengeance. They heated up Bertino's frozen pizza, cursed the selfish egotistical arrogance of men, and rented *Thelma and Louise*. That night Eve felt the baby kick for the first time.

"It's got to be a girl," Jenna cheered, and raised her glass of Chianti. "A feminist in training."

Eve clinked her root beer bottle against the wineglass. "Amen."

March brought Eve the relief of work with a *Good Housekeeping* cover and a week of head shots for Estée Lauder. Her cropped hair started a raging trend. At the end of the month she trudged off to Lamaze classes with a fluffy feather pillow and her coach, Delia, in tow.

She hadn't heard a word from Margo.

Or spoken one to Nico.

And she allowed herself no sympathy for the bereft Ragamuffin who slept on Nico's pillow and prowled the closet with piteous meows in search of Nico's belongings.

She decided against going to Michigan to attend Teri and Brian's wedding. It was their day, and she didn't want to spoil it by heightening the media circus that had been raucously converging on every follow-up story to the soap-opera turn of events on Maui. She sent them her best wishes and a crystal punch bowl set from Neiman-Marcus, along with a glog recipe Nana had given her years earlier.

For Adam she enclosed box-seat tickets to the upcoming Pistons-Lakers series at the Palace. As she handed the package to the postal clerk, she decided she must have basketball on the brain. Every time she looked in the mirror, she was convinced she'd swallowed one.

On the day of Teri's wedding, Margo called from Paris. Eve was too stunned to think of hanging up.

"I'll be in New York for a meeting next month. We have to talk. Save the twentieth for lunch."

They were all there—the Randazzos, the Michaelsons, Hilda and the gang from the Hair and Now, Teri's regular customers, the guys from the tool and die shop, local reporters and their camera crews attracted by the local-girl-involved-in-celebrity-hostage-taking angle. Everyone was at St. Bartholomew's Church to witness Teri and Brian exchanging their vows.

Everyone except Andrew Leonetti.

Teri's father beamed through tears as his family crowded into the tiny bridal room. "If only your mother were here today . . ."

His son, Tony, handed him a starched linen handkerchief. "She is, Dad. Just like you always say, she's smiling down at us—at Gina—from heaven," he told his father as Celia and Lena passed out the bouquets. "Right, Gina?"

Teri nodded wordlessly. *If only Ma were here, everything would be truly perfect.* Her absence was the only empty corner in a heart full of happiness.

Moments later, Teri's nieces, Nickie and Lauren, danced down the aisle, sprinkling their flower petals between the jewel-toned sunbeams bouncing down from the stained glass windows. Adam, his hair slicked in place with mousse and his face shining as brightly as the rings he carried on the lace-trimmed brocade pillow, bounded down the aisle and stood alongside the groomsmen in front of the first pew.

Teri was radiant, her dark hair pinned in a mass of abundant curls spilling from beneath her simple pearl headpiece. Tiny diamond stud earrings winked in the sunlight, almost as brilliant as her smile. She wore the Vera Wang gown she'd chosen courtesy of *Perfect Bride.* Brian wore the biggest grin of any man in the church and a white morning tux with a kelly green cummerbund and bow tie. There were shamrocks tucked into his boutonniere for luck.

When Mass ended and the priest introduced the new Michaelson family to the assembled guests, Brian and Teri shared a Hollywood-style kiss that went on and on, to the delight of the crowd, and then knelt to throw their arms around Adam.

Monique dabbed at her eyes and threw the first handful of rice as the Michaelsons sailed out the door, past the sea of photographers and into the waiting limo.

Pete Lambert. What do you know.

As Monique accelerated along the road snaking toward the country house, her breath caught in her throat at the sight of the familiar pickup truck visible through her rain-spattered windshield.

She didn't bother to pop open her umbrella but dashed up the front steps balancing the huge white box wrapped in plastic.

Laughing voices led her to the terrace, where she found *Maman* and Pete munching on chicken salad sandwiches.

"Don't let me interrupt," Monique announced airily, "but when you're finished, *Maman*, I brought something to show you."

"And hello to you too, Comtesse." Pete slanted a wink at Mireille. "Or must your subjects bow down before you recognize them?"

Monique was chagrined at the flush of crimson suddenly heating her face. "I thought you'd taken your two-by-fours and set off for greener pastures," she breezed. Without looking at him, she set down the box and bent to give Mireille a kiss.

"Hurry, *petite*," Mireille urged, her face aglow with eagerness. "Go try it on. I can't wait another minute."

Monique let herself glance for the first time at Pete Lambert. Why did he have to look so good in jeans and a hooded sweatshirt? "What about him?" she asked, jerking her thumb.

Mireille's laugh tinkled like tiny crystal bells in the sun-washed terrace. "Silly, it's bad luck only if the *groom* sees you in your dress before the wedding. Go."

Twenty minutes later Monique reappeared, feeling shy for the first time since she'd tried on her first bra.

The dress was so personal, so much her own, that entering the terrace, she felt almost as if she were naked.

Mireille exclaimed in delight, but it was Pete's reaction Monique couldn't help but take in. He was staring at her, at the dress, with unchecked appreciation.

The gown was captivating, a regal vision of voluminous satin generously spangled with gold sequins and appliqués. The low-cut, tight ruched bodice outlined in gold ribbon was cinched at her waist, dramatically emphasizing her breasts. The gown was daring, sophisticated, and elegant—pure Monique panache. Instead of buttons, tightly coiled gold satin rosettes shimmered from the nape of her neck to the skirt's hem threaded with matching thin gold ribbon. Gold rosettes also studded the yards and yards of skirt that billowed like a satin sail full with the wind on a dazzling June day.

"That's some dress," Pete managed to say in a choked tone as Monique performed a flawless runway turn and finished with a flowing curtsey.

"Magnifique," Mireille breathed, her face alight, as Dorothy joined them, clapping her hands with approval.

"It took the patience of a saint to button, but I've *never* seen anything as beautiful as this dress," the nurse exclaimed. "Miss D'Arcy, you're in the wrong business."

"Are the gold sequins too much? Are the sleeves full enough? *Maman*, tell me the truth."

"Don't change one stitch, or I'll disown you. It's perfect. Isn't it, Pete? Is my daughter beautiful, or is she not?"

"She's beautiful."

Monique felt a giddy pleasure warm her and had to fight to maintain her nonchalance. Pete looked serious. More serious than she'd ever seen him. Her color deepened to a lovely rose blush.

Idiot, are you sixteen or what?

To cover her discomposure, she turned to Mireille

and babbled, "Most of the arrangements are in place for the ceremony. With the videotape, *Maman,* you'll have a better view than if you were sitting in the front row of St. Patrick's. Did I tell you the florist made up a sample bouquet for me and it was heavenly? Oh, and the cake, *Maman,* the cake will look like café-au-lait dotted Swiss, the most elegant cake imaginable, piped with white accents and topped with champagne-colored roses. And the minute we leave the cathedral, the Plaza is sending a driver here with the video and a complete wedding supper for you and Dorothy."

"Sounds like all that's missing is a diamond-studded ball and chain." Pete walked over to the expanse of windows and stared out at the budding rosebushes, flowering fruit trees, and beds of crocuses, daffodils, pussy willow, and forsythia that lilted in the light spring rain.

Monique shot a narrow-eyed look at his broad back. "Sounds like you're not the marrying kind, Mr. Lambert."

"*Au contraire,* Comtesse," he retorted, turning to face her. "Only problem is, I've never been able to escape the feeling that the ladies are after me only for my money."

She laughed. "Couldn't be your charm, looks, or personality," she pointed out affably. She started toward the door. "Dorothy, can you help me out of this thing?" Then she caught the wistful look in her mother's eyes.

"What is it, *Maman?*" she asked, dropping down on one knee in a billow of glowing satin.

"Oh . . . nothing important . . . it's just that I, well . . . I wish I could be there to see you dance in this dress."

"How about a sneak preview?" Pete didn't wait for an answer, but strode to the entertainment center in search of a tape.

"Looks like you did get my Christmas present," he

commented, lifting up the cassette of the three tenors' concert and slipping it into the tape deck.

"I would have thanked you if I'd had a forwarding address," Monique started acidly before she was scooped into his arms and spun across the terrace to the strains of "Memory."

"See, Mireille, how she'll dance in the arms of her true love?" Pete's cobalt eyes glinted into Monique's smoky ones. "How he'll sweep her across the floor, and off her feet?"

Monique's heart fluttered like the wings of a captured bird. The terrace flew by in a whir as he spun her, holding her ever more tightly, more possessively, filling her with dizzying euphoria.

The flowers outside whirled by in a pastel blur, her mother's and Dorothy's rapt faces blinked in and out, the voices from the stereo floated through the air, but only Monique heard Pete whisper insistently into her ear.

"I love you, Comtesse. Don't throw yourself away on someone who can't appreciate you."

Had she heard correctly, or was she imagining it? His rugged face was an unreadable mask, but his arms nearly crushed her.

The dance was over. Monique stepped back, breathless and unsure. She managed an airy little laugh.

"Thank you, monsieur. My last waltz as a single woman. I'll remember it always."

And after a curtsy performed on shaking legs, she swept from the room and out of sight.

"Bambina, please don't hang up."

"Nico," Eve said through a blur of tears, "you're drunk."

"Only a little . . . what the hell does it matter? . . . I have to talk to you!"

Eve hugged her arms around herself in her lonely bed. The baby shifted low in her belly, making her wince as a tiny foot or hand pressed on a nerve. Okay, kid, I'll listen to him, she promised blearily, though it hurt even to hear Nico's voice after all this time. For two minutes, no more. Then—*finito.*

"Tomorrow would have been our wedding day . . . bambina, please, don't do this. Don't throw away everything we had because of one idiotic mistake."

"You're the one who threw everything away, Nico. I have to go."

"No . . . wait! Please . . . Eve . . . my beautiful bambina. Listen to me. There is a fine gold thread between Bologna and New York that's been damaged, but it can never be broken. The heat of our passion can solder it whole again. If you'll only give me one more chance . . . I swear to you, I haven't so much as seen your sister since you told me about the baby. She meant nothing to me . . . nothing, Eve. You have to believe me."

"I could never believe you again." Eve battled the tears congesting her throat. "This conversation is pointless, Nico. From now on, say whatever you have to say through the lawyers."

She hung up the phone, terminating the torrent of words still pouring over the line. Eve slumped down onto her side, melting into the rose and cream comforter to weep.

I'll get over him someday, I swear it, she vowed as the tears streamed onto the pillowcase. *It'll take time, but the pain will go away. It has to.* Resolutely, she stared Ragamuffin down.

"He's gone for good and you'd better get used to it," she informed the cat coldly, rubbing the tears from her face.

She went into the kitchen, drank a glass of milk, and poured some for the cat. "Small consolation," she told him, "but better than nothing." She tried not to think about what might have been . . . about the shower gifts she'd returned, the Finnish lace tablecloth she'd sadly packed into a hope chest, about the excitement she should have felt the night before her wedding. . . .

She didn't know when she fell asleep, a copy of *Parents* magazine across her chest, but she awoke to the drone of the morning news blathering from the clock-radio. She groaned. Monique was arriving at nine to take her to breakfast.

As Eve wearily swung her legs off the bed and set her swollen feet on the floor, the eight o'clock news continued, and the words began to penetrate her sleep-fogged brain.

". . . ironically, has been killed in an auto crash. Witnesses say the car skidded wildly across the narrow mountain path before plunging off the shoulder into a ravine eighty feet below. One of the great race car drivers of the century, Nico Caesarone had set more records than anyone else in racing history. In recent months he has been dogged by rumors of heavy drinking following his breakup with international supermodel Eve Hamel, but there is as yet no evidence to indicate if alcohol was involved in the fatal crash. . . ."

No. Eve's arm swept the radio off the nightstand. Her eyes were mirrors of horror. "No!" she screamed.

Nico couldn't be dead. She had talked to him last night. . . .

No!

She sank to the floor, her legs too numb to hold her. A freezing, feverish sweat drenched her. She closed her eyes, shuddering and nauseated, and through the filmy blackness saw a dreamily handsome face . . . silky jet hair . . . mesmerizing bedroom eyes . . . she saw the man who had rescued her from

the crowds in Lisbon, fed her panettone in Bologna—
and broke her heart in Maui.

Nico, *please, no,* she wept, caught between paralyzing grief and a fury that went deeper than the gates
of hell. *My poor, stupid, lost Nico.*

Chapter Thirty-five

I never should have agreed to this, Eve told herself as she listened to Margo order the shrimp with carrot and Thai spices. Eve glanced around Jo Jo at the other diners, engaged in animated chatter and oblivious of the melodrama being played out at her table in the Upper East Side bistro. Maybe they're playing out their own melodramas. Maybe that's all life is.

She put a hand to her swollen belly. The baby was due in a month and had chosen this moment to launch into another attack of uncontrollable hiccups.

But you, my little one, don't you worry. I intend to see to it that we have our share of comedy. I'll give you laughter along with love—no matter how much life tries to make us cry.

She stared across the table at the silver-blond stranger opposite her and felt only sadness and loathing and hatred. What was the point of meeting with Margo? Nico was dead, and as far as she was concerned, her relationship with Margo had strangled long ago—long before she'd discovered her sister's ultimate betrayal.

This was merely the funeral. The corpse has been cold a long time.

"Well, at least you're not wearing widow's weeds. I'll give you credit for that," Margo said, turning her attention again to Eve as the waiter bobbed away. "But for God's sake, grow up, Eve. You can't even bring yourself to look at me, can you?"

"I wonder how you can bear to look at yourself in the mirror."

Margo lifted her chin. "There's no point in blaming this all on me. It takes two . . . and all that. Personally, I think I did you a favor. Let you see the real man Nico was instead of the fantasy lover you had created for yourself."

Eve grabbed the napkin from her lap and started to rise from the table, twin spots of color staining her cheeks. "I refuse to listen to this. Don't try to justify what you did. There's no excuse for it, no rationale, and no logic. You were never much of a sister to me, Margo, but this whole thing is incomprehensible, even for you." She shook her head, fighting back sobs of pain, sobs so bitter they stung her throat. "The same blood runs through both our veins, and at least for me, that meant something."

Margo jumped up to block Eve's path. "Sit down and face me for once in your life. You're such a baby. Always have been. Running down the hall to Mom's bedroom, crying over a few ghost stories. Running to Mom now? Going to tell on big sister?"

"Get out of my way, Margo," Eve spat out.

"Not until we're finished here. Sit down, and let's get this over with."

Eve took a deep breath. There was so much she wanted to get off her chest. So much that had been pent up these past months. *Do it before the baby is born. Say what you have to say and get rid of the anger,* she told herself. *Once and for all, let it go before it does you more harm than* they *ever could.* She dropped heavily back into her seat as the waiter reappeared with their meals. The nearby diners had stopped eating to stare at them, and Eve toyed with her roasted chicken, waiting until their attention and her own emotions cooled down.

Margo tore with relish into the fried carrot basket cradling her shrimp as the waiter refilled their water goblets. Eve ignored the icy opal eyes studying her. At last she took a bite of the cilantro-flecked ginger chicken and forced herself to chew.

"Well, are you planning to tell Mother?"

"What would be the point? It would only hurt her, and I doubt it would matter to you." She added coolly, "But Dad might be a little disillusioned with his golden girl—I think that's what's really on your agenda, isn't it?"

The shot hit home. Margo actually flushed. She reached into her silver cigarette case, extracted a long cigarette, and lit it in one fluid motion.

"You'd like that, wouldn't you? To upset Dad. To cause trouble between him and me." She blew a thin stream of smoke into the air and narrowed her eyes. "You always have been jealous of my relationship with him. It was laughable, watching you running yourself silly, rolling around in the backyard mud with the boys, climbing the tallest trees—anything—just to get his attention away from me. As if he really cared about all those track trophies . . ."

"Shut up, damn you." Eve leaned forward, her hands clenching the tablecloth so tightly that her knuckles shone whiter than the linen. "This isn't about Dad. We're not kids anymore. What you did was a very grown-up, thought-out act of treachery. The only reason I agreed to meet you is to find out why."

Margo gave her head a tiny toss, sending her pale hair flipping over her shoulders. "Sorry to disappoint you yet again, baby sister. I don't have any deep Freudian reasons. The man was available. I was available.

Nothing more. As a matter of fact, until you dangled a baby in front of his macho nose, he seemed quite unattached—official engagement to the contrary. You didn't know Nico very well, did you? He was a passionate man, a thinker, a lover of life . . ."

"He was a liar and a cheat."

"Maybe he just got bored with your small-town girl-next-door puritanism. European men are different, baby sister. They don't stick with the apple pie. They need to sample everything on the dessert cart."

Eve stared at the arrogant, cold-eyed woman opposite her, disgust rising like bile in her throat. It was hard to believe that fifteen years earlier they had slept in the same bedroom, sat at the same dinner table, opened Christmas presents around the same tree. Blood was supposed to be thicker than water. But in this case, she doubted Margo had anything but vinegar running through her veins.

"The night he first met you," Eve said slowly, "Nico called you an ice princess with nicotine breath." Her lips twisted in a tight, bitter smile. "Guess you found some mouthwash. But you know what?" she asked, setting her fork down with a tiny clink. "If this was your idea of a contest, we both lost. We lost Nico. And we lost any chance to ever be friends." Eve folded her napkin with an air of finality and placed it on the table. She felt sad inside, infinitely sad and old and drained.

"But Margo, I want you to remember one thing."

The waiter hadn't brought the check yet, but Eve was finished. She threw down a $100 bill and pushed back her chair.

"You may have had a brief, meaningless fling with him," she said with quiet contempt, "because no matter what you think, that's all it was." She took a deep breath. "You may have destroyed my life with him, and destroyed Nico in the bargain, but I'm the one carrying Nico's child. I want you to remember that. I will *always* have a part of him with me." A cold, triumphant smile quivered about her lips as she started to walk away. Suddenly, she paused. "And something else—I'll always have my dignity. No matter what you do, how much you lower yourself, big sister, those are two things you can't *ever* take away."

Eve strode out of Jo Jo into the noise of the city. Bright May sunshine spilled between the buildings along East 64th Street. She didn't bother hailing a taxi. Amid the noise of the city, she slung her purse over her shoulder, popped her sunglasses on her nose, and walked away through the mass of pedestrians without once looking back.

"I've got her, the bitch," Shanna gloated as she watched the numbers on the elevator panel flicker by one by one. "The only royal treatment she'll get from this point on is a red carpet out the door to the unemployment line."

She clutched her briefcase containing the documents with delicious excitement. Richard would see them later today and she could only imagine his rage. Richard hated being made a fool of. Almost as much as he hated losing money.

Her call to the Family History Library in Salt Lake City had paid off in a major way. The Mormons had the largest collection of genealogical documents in the world, and the researcher she'd hired there had hit pay dirt. When Monique D'Arcy saw what was locked inside this briefcase, the bitch would have to eat crow instead of pheasant under glass.

Comtesse. Shanna threw back her head and gave a contemptuous laugh as the elevator doors whooshed open at the twenty-second floor.

Finally, after months of vague, nagging memories, it had come back to her—where she'd first met that pushy, dark-haired manipulator. Of course.

D'Arcy . . . Mireille D'Arcy and her brazen little daughter, the girl who'd come begging for her mother's job in a stolen dress.

What colossal gall, to pass herself off as nobility. What a joke. *Well,* Shanna thought with satisfaction as she marched toward the marble and brass reception area, *we'll see who has the last laugh.*

Shanna's perfume arrived three seconds before she stormed into Monique's office, barely able to contain her glee.

Her perfume intensified the sinus headache throbbing to excruciating proportions across Monique's forehead.

"Did we have an appointment?" Monique asked coldly, glancing up from her desk and from the just-published June issue she'd been pretending to peruse.

"Your only appointment should be with Impostors Anonymous," Shanna replied evenly, closing the door and advancing with quick strides. She sank gracefully into a chair and leaned back with a smug half-smile. "We've come a long way from Bonwit's, you and I, my darling. But maybe not quite so far as we'd have others believe?" She raised one eyebrow, waiting for a reaction. Monique's face remained impassive.

"I was wondering how long it would take you to remember." *Don't let her smell blood,* Monique warned herself, trying to ignore her throbbing temples. The rain beat at the windows like tapping fingernails. "You made a dangerous enemy that day, but you were too impressed with yourself to realize it."

"Dangerous enemy? Oh, you think you've won, don't you?" Shanna came out of the chair in one smooth movement and hefted the briefcase onto the clutter of Monique's desk. "Your infantile revenge games are over, you stupid bitch. And so is your charade. You played with my life and with Richard's. He'll be very interested to find out that you deliberately broke up our marriage and conned your way into this job over the dismissal of a lying, inept seamstress who pilfered from her employers. It stands to reason you'd turn out to be just as sneaky and incompetent as she was."

Monique's calm façade burst like a punctured balloon. Rage suffused her and she rounded the desk in a flash. "Get the hell out of here," she spat out, seizing Shanna's arm and yanking her toward the door. An image of *Maman* on that awful birthday so many years earlier flashed through her mind—*Maman*, beaten, worried, her pride as ruined as the uneaten ice cream melted on the plates, her precious dignity wounded by this self-centered bitch.

"My mother was the most honest, upstanding, hardworking employee that store ever had, and you threw her away like torn stockings. Say anything about me that you like, but if you say one more word about her, I'll knock you on your ass."

Shanna jerked her arm from Monique's grasp and hurried back to the desk. She opened the briefcase with shaking fingers and pulled out a manila envelope. "If your mother's so damned honest, why are you such a conniving liar? *Comtesse?* Has a nice ring to it, but it's hollow as a bell. Take a look at these, 'Comtesse,' and tell me what Richard will say when he learns that your illustrious pedigree is more mongrel than show dog."

Monique went pale as candle wax when she saw the official French seal on the immigration documents. She already knew the names that would appear on the line that listed parentage.

Mireille D'Arcy née Lovette, seamstress, and Jacques D'Arcy, head groomsman.

"Read it and weep, my dear. This ought to knock that phony crown off your head. When I show this to Richard and the press, everyone will know you're nothing but a cheap fraud. You're not the daughter of the Comte de Chevalier—you're not a D'Arcy at all—you're an illegitimate nobody."

Monique was about to thrust the papers back into Shanna's smarmy face but at this she snatched them back. And stared.

Giraud?

She peered at the document more closely. Jacques D'Arcy's name was nowhere to be found.

There had to be some mistake. Her father's name was listed as Pierre Giraud, landowner.

It hit her like the cork popping off a bottle of champagne.

Landowner . . . the comte. Pierre Giraud had been the Comte de Chevalier. How . . . ? What . . . ?

Maman, why didn't you ever tell me? All these years, you let me go on with this masquerade, and it was the truth all along . . . the Comte de Chevalier was my father.

If that doesn't make me a comtesse, it's pretty damn close.

A million unanswered questions swirled through her head, but all she could do was whoop.

"*Merci*, Ms. Mulgrew." Monique grinned, hugging the papers to her chest. "If you weren't so inept, you would have done a more thorough job of snooping and discovered that Pierre Giraud was in fact the name of the Comte de Chevalier—my father. Being illegitimate is no disgrace these days, darling, but being an asshole is. You qualify hands down. Guaranteed. Now, will you get the hell out of here, or do I have to call security?"

Shanna gaped at her as though she'd gone mad.

Linda stuck her head in the door. "Staff meeting starts in five, Ms. D'Arcy. Can I get you more coffee?"

"Screw the coffee. Pop the Taittinger—a magnum —we're celebrating today." She locked the papers in her desk and pocketed the key, ignoring Shanna, frozen in dumbfounded silence in the center of the room. Monique grabbed the June issue, suddenly overcome by a feeling of soul-touching satisfaction.

She'd done it. She'd pulled it off. And she'd bested Shanna yet again.

She gazed with pride at the magazine, with the princesslike Teri Michaelson beaming from the cover—and a feature article inside detailing her dream wedding, made perfect courtesy of *Perfect Bride*.

Below the masthead, the issue's revised lead feature jumped out in big blue letters: *Fifty Wedding Tips from the Stars!*

And therein was Monique's coup. Bolstering the original concept, and filling in for the loss of Eve and Nico, she had recruited a galaxy of Hollywood's brightest to offer their suggestions for the perfect wedding, complete with never-before-published photos of their own nuptials and honeymoons.

Also inside was a knockout Hawaiian spread featuring Ana and John, Teri and Brian, and her and Richard—all traces of Eve and Nico had been airbrushed out. And with the fifty celebrity tips and unique photos, and all the advance publicity the fiasco in Maui had garnered, Monique had delivered a walloping good issue with advance sales catapulting past all expectations.

Miraculously, her headache was gone. But Shanna lingered, looking as if she were searching for ammunition for a gun that was clean out of bullets, even as Monique sailed toward the door.

"You know, darling"—Monique paused, one hand on the brass-handled knob—"there's something I've been meaning to tell you for years. Makeup and lighting have done wonders for your looks, but all the perfume in Paris can't camouflage a piece of shit."

She left before Shanna could frame a coherent reply. Linda waited at the doorway of the office and regarded Shanna warily. "If there's nothing else, Ms. Mulgrew . . ."

Shanna snapped her briefcase shut. She swung out the door like a Doberman, bristling through the reception lobby without a glance at any of her former staff.

Afterward, several members of the typing pool swore they'd heard the sound of grinding teeth.

Chapter Thirty-six

The heat was palpable. The fluttering canvas canopies dotting Arnie's sprawling canyon ranch did little more than spare the guests the relentless rays of July sun. Champagne bottles prematurely popped their corks in a burst of protest, for as rapidly as the tuxedoed waiters replenished the red, white, and blue tubs of ice in which they floated, the chunks melted to the temperature of a lukewarm bath.

Everyone was there. It could have been a post-telecast Academy Awards gala or a White House formal dinner. Julia Roberts wore a slinky column of lipstick-red moiré. Paul Newman and Joanne Woodward huddled deep in conversation with Sylvester Stallone near the free-form swimming pool bobbing with a rose-petal configuration of the American flag, and Dustin Hoffman, Robert De Niro and Francis Ford Coppola nibbled shashlik and Beluga caviar rounds with Hillary Clinton and Jeane Fitzpatrick.

Valets scurried up and down the mountain roads, parking Ferraris, Jeeps, Mercedes-Benz, Vipers, and Rolls-Royces. The cars snaked through the canyon in a coil of pricey, glittering metal.

Waiters wove through the crowd, offering delicacies as muted strains of vintage Elton John floated from the loudspeakers that were scattered across the patriotic landscape.

Ana was in the guest suite, breathtaking as a fairy princess in Angelina's masterpiece gown. As Louise wound white gardenias through her hair, Ana trembled with excitement. She was terrified that for the first time in memory she might be so nervous she'd forget her line.

I do.

I do love you, John Farrell. More than anything or anyone in the whole world.

Last night John had made love to her in Arnie's swimming pool with the moonlit reflection of the tents shimmering around them. While the water lapped at their shoulders, he buried his face in the damp tendrils clinging to her neck and murmured: "Guess what? Arnie convinced me to do a cameo in the picture you're shooting with Costner."

Ana pulled back to peer quizzically into his face, half-shadowed in moonlight.

"I play the judge who sentences you to prison at the beginning of the movie."

Ana laughed. "So *you're* the louse who buys into the crooked D.A.'s setup. Think a screwball comedy will catapult you into a new career? Or are you just there to keep an eye on me during my love scenes with Kevin?" she teased.

"Well, the thought did cross my mind. . . ."

"Johnny."

"Hmmm?" he asked, reaching out to draw her close again.

"Don't give up your day job."

She'd splashed water in his face and he dunked her, their laughter echoing through the trees and twining around the wedding bowers the designer had placed at the crest of the hill.

Like water nymphs, they played until the wee hours of the morning, grateful to be together, content in each other's arms, and carefree as the white satin ribbons streaming from the bowers in the faint evening breeze.

"Finished," Louise pronounced, stepping back to admire the blossoms entwined in Ana's hair. Ana regarded herself from every direction in the full-length triple mirror. Perfect.

Louise handed her a small lace garter threaded through with pale blue satin. "This was my mother's—and she and my dad have been married forty-seven years. I'd say that's a lucky token, wouldn't you?"

"As lucky as they come." Ana scooped up the voluminous skirt so that Louise could slide the garter into place.

"Better hurry," Louise urged, "cameras roll in ten minutes."

"I'll be right down," Ana promised, reaching for the small velvet box nestled on the bed as Louise disappeared down the hall. She drew the faded photograph from the box, smiling down with love at the visage in her hands. "You said if I held on to my dreams and worked hard to make them come true, anything I wanted was possible, Grammaw," she whispered. "You were so right."

Ana cradled the photo against her chest, then propped it against the dressing table mirror. Her grandmother's crinkled old eyes watched her as she slipped on the small pearl stud earrings and matching teardrop necklace she'd taken from Tennessee, her only mementos of Grammaw.

"There. That's it. Something old, something new, something borrowed, something blue. I've got it all."

She looked at herself in the mirror a final time before slipping down the stairs and into the spotlight once again.

. . . .

With Richard's hand clasped in hers, Monique wedged through a crevice in the crowd toward the dance floor. As usual, he'd been working that crowd as if *he* were running for office instead of John Farrell.

"You're mine for the next ten minutes, pal," Monique informed him with a saucy toss of her head. The orchestra was playing a hustle, and despite the oppressive midday heat, the wedding guests were oblivious of anything but the music.

As they reached the dance floor, the bouncing beat gave way to the slow strains of a ballad, and Monique melted into Richard's arms. They moved together in small concentric circles until Richard spotted Ted Turner sauntering across the lawn.

"There's Ted—Mo, hang on a second. I've been thinking over his proposition and I have a few questions . . ." And she was stranded on the dance floor, dumbfoundedly watching the back of his head disappear into the throng, until she was suddenly encircled by the arms of the groom.

"*Your* big day is coming up in a few weeks, isn't it?"

"St. Patrick's will pale compared to this, I'm afraid. What a lovely party, Senator." Monique spoke the words automatically, a bright smile pasted on her face, hiding the anger she felt at Richard. *John Farrell is a true gentleman,* she thought wryly. He was carrying on a meaningless conversation with her, giving her time to recover from her embarrassment at being deserted in mid-dance. He'd stepped in as adroitly as if he'd been waiting in the wings for an opening on her dance card.

"We should be back from Cap Ferrat in time to toast your marriage, Comtesse," he said as smoothly as he guided her across the floor. "Ana and I wouldn't miss being there for the world." His blue-gray eyes twinkled down at her. "After all, these *are* the perfect weddings of the summer, are they not?"

His lighthearted words lingered long after the dance. Perfect weddings. *My* perfect wedding. It should be. . . .

Yet something bordering on wedding jitters kept eating at Monique, though every last detail was in place. She had taken the next few weeks as vacation time, leaving Linda to see to the seating arrangements and to notify the caterer of the final head count. The Plaza had everything else under control. Monique had nothing to do except savor a few days at home with *Maman*—her last visit to the country as a single woman.

So why couldn't she shake this nagging feeling that something had been left undone?

Mentally, she ticked everything off again—each detail, each plan. On the surface all was in order. Still, she was bedeviled by a feeling she couldn't quite put her finger on.

Half an hour later she bumped into Richard at the poolside bar. "Fancy meeting you here," she said coldly, and started to brush past him.

"A manhattan for the lady," he demanded of the bartender, grabbing her arm and keeping her by his side. "Mo, of all people, you should be used to how I do business by now. This is benefiting your future too." He handed her the drink, but his eyes were already skimming the crowd. "It's not like you to pout, Comtesse." Before she could respond, he tugged her forward. "Put on your million-dollar smile, there's someone I'd like you to meet."

There's someone you'd like to impress with my title, more likely, she thought wearily—and was instantly angry with herself. She loved Richard's drive, his steely determination, and aggressive powerplays. She loved being part of his team. The man was poetry in motion, he was matchless at the top of his form. Since when had she forgotten the rules of the game? She counted to ten, pushing away her annoyance and reminding herself how much she loved him.

"Point the way, boss, but you do owe me one more turn around the dance floor."

Richard winked at her and brushed a tiny kiss across the tip of her nose. "Consider it a done deal, gorgeous. But first come meet Sheikh Abu ibn Hassan."

Chapter Thirty-seven

Monique assembled the tea and scones on the tray, tucked some extra lemon into the china dish, then carried the whole thing up to her mother's sunny bedroom. She paused in the doorway, struck by the intensity with which Mireille was studying the latest issue of *Vogue*. Even after all these years, with her infirmity and failing eyesight, *Maman* still loved fashion and studied every nuance of tailoring and design with a keen passion. Watching her face, Monique recalled how many times she'd come home from high school to find her mother absorbed in this same way—only then she could whip her visions into reality with needle and fabric. Now she could barely summon the coordination to sip her tea and bring the scones to her lips without assistance.

Monique gazed with aching affection at the dainty woman in the bed who had lived such a hard and lonely life. She tried to imagine her mother as a young woman, in love with the Comte de Chevalier, knowing she could never have him. A few days after Shanna had stormed into her office, Monique had broached the subject, and Mireille had at last told her the full story of her birth.

Mireille's eyes misted over as she peered down at the documents Monique showed her that evening as they sat on the terrace, watching the fireflies. "Yes, *petite*, Pierre Giraud was your father. I have longed many times to tell you—you truly are the comtesse you invented. But I was ashamed, and afraid you wouldn't understand. Let me explain to you now."

They talked long into the night, Mireille's haggard face lighting with the memories of her long-ago love. It seemed that her mother's marriage to Jacques D'Arcy had been nothing but a bleak escape from the convent. He was older than she, a drunkard with a roving eye who'd beaten her whenever he had overindulged his thirst for liquor and loose women. One night the comte had found her weeping at her worktable and saw the bruises on her young face. In a fury he had gone himself to the village in search of Jacques, had thrashed him with his own two fists, and ordered him from the town. Mireille had never seen or heard from him again, but the comte became a frequent visitor.

His own marriage, it turned out, was loveless and childless, the result of an arrangement concocted by his family and a duke in a neighboring province. The comtesse was a bitter and overbearing young woman whose tongue was as sharp as the needles Mireille employed in her work. Pierre found the beautiful, fragile young seamstress enchanting, and in him Mireille found a kind and handsome protector. Divorce was unthinkable for the Catholic comte, but they shared their lives as best they could, behaving with discretion.

Yet sometimes Mireille feared the comtesse could see right through her, and she dreaded the times when she had to meet with the woman and do her bidding.

"He doted on you, *petite*. When you were born . . . ah, such joy was in his eyes. He meant to provide for you, for both of us, but the automobile accident took him from us before the arrangements could be made. He was a fine man," Mireille whispered, clasping her daughter's hand. "You would have been proud to call him *Père.*

Years had fallen from Mireille's face that night as she recounted details about the comte and their love affair. But this morning, dwarfed by the feather pillows supporting her frail frame, she looked to Monique much older than her fifty-six years.

"Thank you, *petite,*" Mireille murmured as Monique offered the fragrant tea. "You can't know how I treasure having these last few days with you before your wedding. It brings back so many memories."

Monique kissed the top of her head, as *Maman* had done to her so many times when she was small. "I'll think of you—and my handsome Père—when I walk down the aisle Saturday."

"Oh, *petite,* I almost forgot. Pete Lambert is moving this week. He mentioned yesterday that he'd like you to stop by."

Mireille regarded her daughter inquisitively. "You two seem to have become friends, no? I'm glad. Is he coming to the wedding?"

"No. And we're not friends, *Maman,* not really." Monique changed the subject quickly. "I hope Eve makes it to the wedding. My little godchild better not preempt my trip down the aisle. Can you imagine being upstaged by a newborn at your own wedding?"

And then Dorothy came in and announced it was time for Mireille's nap. Monique wandered down to the terrace and gazed outside at the blazing blue sky. She'd better remind Dorothy to run the sprinkler system again after the sun lowered a little—the poor roses were wilting in the scorching July heat and the lawn was crisping up like dried hay.

Despite her light words to *Maman,* she regretted that Eve couldn't be her maid of honor. But Eve's obstetrician had warned her to stay off her feet as much as possible, and she wasn't taking any chances.

Not that Monique wanted her to. It still shook her to think of how close she'd come to losing her friend. Eve had come through the whole experience with remarkable stamina, but Monique, who knew her so well, sensed that Nico's betrayal had hit her harder than anything else, much harder even than the nightmare with Billy Shears.

And then the poor bastard had gone and driven himself off a cliff. It was a wonder Eve hadn't miscarried. But she was strong. No Cool Whip about that kid, Monique reflected as she let herself out the terrace door and started toward the little bridge leading down to the carriage house.

Suddenly she could picture that winter's night in her kitchen when Pete had scoffed at her own bravado. She could never look at a carton of Cool Whip in the supermarket nowadays without thinking of him, or at a frozen Bertino's pizza. In fact, she'd been thinking about Pete Lambert a great deal recently.

She reached the little crest overlooking the carriage house and wondered why she was obeying this summons. She hadn't seen Pete Lambert in months.

Yet the sight of a moving van parked in front of the big house made something twist inside her. Perhaps it was best that Pete's work was finished and he was leaving. The timing was perfect. She was getting married on Saturday, and he was moving on at the same time. Whatever crazy relationship they'd forged last winter was over. It was summer now. The snow was gone, the ice was melted, and the carriage-house chimney was capped until winter. No fires burned. Not even a flame flickered. She thought back to the last time she'd been in the carriage house—to the awkward kiss she'd shared with Pete. She thought of his whispered remark the day she'd shown *Maman* her dress. And she knew he wanted something from her that she could never give him.

Richard was the man she wanted to spend her life with. Did Pete Lambert really think she would throw away that relationship because he crooked his little finger? Granted, the guy was sexy, but he was certainly not her type. He didn't have Richard's style, drive, or, face it, Monique, his bank account. Not that she wanted Richard's money. God knew she had plenty of her own. But they moved in the same circles, knew the same kind of people, shared the same goals.

My God, I'm turning into a real snob, she thought with a sudden pang of conscience. Her steps lagged as she crossed the meandering gardens laced with rose-bushes, daisies, oleander, and ferns. She lifted a hand to knock at Pete's door, but he opened it before her knuckles could make contact.

"Comtesse," he grinned, and pulled her inside. "Just in time to help me pack."

"This is why you wanted to see me?"

"That's right—you owe me."

"I beg your pardon?"

"You're breaking my heart, lady." His eyes penetrated hers with a quiet blue intensity that made her heart skip a beat. "The least you can do is send me packing in proper fashion—if you mean it."

She searched his face, trying to see if he was joking. She couldn't.

Suddenly the July heat seemed overwhelming. Had he already shut off the air-conditioning?

"You're *still* impossible," she grated between clenched teeth, then deliberately turned away to glance around the carriage house stacked with cartons and littered with newspapers, packing tape, and twine.

"Hey, still time to chuck the diamond-studded ball and chain," Pete tossed over his shoulder as he hoisted a pile of books from the dining room table and plopped them into a carton.

"What is it you want me to do, Lambert?" Monique asked, fanning herself with a folded sheet of newspaper.

At that, he turned around and came toward her. "Do you really want to know?" he asked softly. Without warning, he slipped his arms around her waist.

"How can I *help* you?" she demanded, stiffening, then added hastily, "with your *packing*."

Pete's hands lingered at her waist. Monique felt certain it must be one hundred degrees in the room, but she forced her expression to remain cool. Reading that coolness in her eyes, Pete released her with a sigh.

"Fine. Here's some newspaper. Grab a box and fill it with some of those knickknacks on the mantelpiece. That shouldn't endanger your manicure. Wouldn't want any broken nails before the big day."

Monique wasn't sure why she stayed. Silently, she wrapped the brass candlesticks and several porcelain figurines, admiring in particular the delicate blue and white Lladro maiden.

"That one was my mother's favorite," he said. "She had a collection of them, but my brother's wife has the rest."

"It's lovely." Monique nestled it in the box and folded the cardboard flaps end over end. She grabbed a Magic Marker and printed Fragile in block letters across the top.

Like you, Pete thought, watching her from the corner of his eye. She was dressed in white cutoffs, a lemon-yellow tank top, and sexy gold sandals. A simple pendant shone at her throat. Her dusky hair was caught back by a yellow ribbon, and she looked young and fresh and luscious. Not like the killer magazine editor who'd have beaten him with his own two-by-four the first time they'd met. But like a wild daisy, shining in the sun.

He pushed the baseball cap back on his head, wiped the sweat from his brow, and studied her as she worked. His hand slipped into the pocket of his sweat shorts and fingered the small square box inside.

Now or never, Lambert, he told himself. *Speak now or forever hold your peace.*

He couldn't do it. Not this way. It had to come from her.

But all he got from Monique that day was a carefully packed box of porcelain, a whiff of her perfume, and a bittersweet handshake as a good-bye.

"When are you moving?" she asked at the door.

"Saturday."

A wry smile. "I guess that's a red-letter day for both of us. Where will you go next?"

"Why? Planning to send me a postcard from your honeymoon?"

"I'm planning to be too busy to write."

"I'll bet you are."

Suddenly he pulled her close and his corded arms were like iron around her, his breath warm on her face. "Monique . . ."

"Pete, I have to go." But she made no move.

"Do you?" He traced her lips with his fingertips and gazed hungrily into those smoky, mesmerizing eyes. "You're sure?"

"Yes." But her voice was breathless.

Oh, God, why was she still standing there, letting him touch her? She was getting lost in those eyes. His hand slid to cradle her neck, the fingers electric on her hot skin.

She jerked back and gave a nervous little laugh. "I have a thousand things to do."

But her voice sounded hollow to her own ears. "Phone calls, last minute changes . . . and I'm meeting Richard in the city for dinner."

He didn't say anything. He let her go and watched as she turned and started walking quickly up the path. Sunlight glittered around her, catching the pendant at her throat.

He knew then it was over. He'd lost.

"Hey, Comtesse."

She paused on the path.

"Don't forget to be happy," Pete called after her. "That's an order."

"I intend to be," Monique called back with a final wave. And then she was hurrying beneath the trees, disappearing into the cool canopy of green. "You too, Pete Lambert," she whispered to herself, her feet rustling along the fallen twigs and dirt of the path. "You too."

Their waiter at '21' knew Richard well, and had their usual drinks whisked to the table the moment Richard and Monique arrived. Richard ordered dinner for them both and leaned back in his chair, watching Monique with an appreciative gleam in his eye.

"You look pretty together for a woman who's getting married in two days. Everything under control?"

"Oh, sure." Monique rolled her eyes and took a sip of her Glenlivet. "Aside from the fact that the banquet manager had an emergency appendectomy a few hours ago and the assistant who's filling in has the cold from hell, and the florist misplaced our order and needs Linda to fax over a copy, and the Alexanders and the Donovans are suddenly coming in from London after all and now the seating arrangements need to be redone . . . shall I go on, or do you get the picture?"

Richard mopped his brow in mock sympathy. "I get the picture. Poor Mo. But don't worry, in a few days we'll be sunning ourselves in the Greek islands. And that reminds me, I have to make a phone call."

"About the honeymoon?" she asked hopefully, visions of their idyllic escape playing cinematically before her eyes.

"Exactly."

She looked around for a waiter, intending to ask for

a phone, but Richard pushed back his chair. "Uh-uh. This is my little surprise. Be right back."

Monique watched him make his way through the restaurant with the suave grace that characterized him.

A tiny sigh escaped her. But she wasn't even conscious of the sound.

His secretary answered the private line on the first ring. Sandra hated being the only person left in the building, but he paid her well enough to overcome her qualms.

"The figures," Richard said tersely.

She read them aloud.

He whistled under his breath. "Excellent. Better than I expected." Richard sketched quick notations on a pad. "Now, make the usual changes on Ms. D'Arcy's copy of the report. And bury the true figures in the coded file on my computer."

"Yes, Mr. Ives, it's already taken care of."

"Good. I'll be in at seven to look it over. Oh, and Sandra, I want ten copies of everything ready for my meeting with Theogustus in the morning."

"They'll be in the locked drawer of your desk."

Richard smiled to himself as he replaced the receiver. The June figures for *Perfect Bride* were astronomical. At this rate, Theogustus would have to pay top dollar for the magazine—and for Monique. As much as the masthead, she was part and parcel of the deal.

He had to give her credit. Monique had done a hell of a job. Too bad he couldn't tell her how successful she'd been. But that would be detrimental to his overall plan. No, he had to keep the pressure on Monique. She worked remarkably well under pressure, and he couldn't afford to jeopardize that momentum.

Richard tucked the pad into the breast pocket of his navy Armani suit, his lips pursed thoughtfully. Monique couldn't ever know that the circulation figures had never been as disappointing as he'd made them, or that they were now damn close to spectacular. Success made people rest on their laurels. He couldn't afford that. He had to keep Monique thinking that sales were still not up to par, he had to keep the pressure on her, keep her working her tail off until the figures for October and November clinched the deal.

When Theogustus signed on the dotted line to purchase *Perfect Bride*, it would be a tremendous coup. And he'd get top dollar from Henry, thanks to Monique's frantic drive and tenacity.

We'll stay a good month in the islands after the sale is final. She'll love it there, she can relax—and a little ouzo and bouzouki music under the Mediterranean moonlight will soften her up when I break the news that she's part and parcel of this deal.

She'd be angry at first, Richard guessed, when she learned that he'd committed her to one year under a new boss, but he knew he could make her see reason—and a twenty-five percent salary bonus would help sharpen her eyesight. Theogustus was no fool. He'd demanded Richard's written guarantee that Monique would stay on as editor-in-chief for one full year after the purchase date—just to see him through the transition.

After that, Richard thought, *I've got other plans for her.*

Richard fixed a tight smile on his face as he returned to the table. "All set. You're going to love what I've got in store for you. But . . . this part isn't so good. I phoned Sandra for the final June figures and—"

She set down her scotch, a knot tightening in her stomach. "What are you telling me? They're good, aren't they? All the indicators have been positive. . . ."

Richard shook his head as he settled back in his chair.

Monique gripped the table's edge.

"Good, yes, but not quite good enough," he said quietly. "Not what we'd hoped for. You're getting there, Mo, you're doing a hell of a job, but the numbers don't quite reflect the growth we want. After the honeymoon, it's back to the drawing board with a vengeance. I think we can hold McArthur off for a few months with these figures—but October and November have to really shine."

"What are they? Tell me," Monique demanded, moistening her lips. "They must be up at least twenty percent."

"Not now." Richard shook his head. "This is our evening; we're not going to worry about business tonight. The only *Perfect Bride* I care about right now is you."

"But—"

"Put it out of your mind until after the wedding, after we get back from Greece," Richard stated firmly. He patted her hand, noted the anxiety in her eyes with a twinge of guilt, and waited until after the waiter had set down their meals before saying with a genial smile, "Mo, relax. This is our night." He brought her hand to his lips with a smooth, loving gesture and kissed it fervently, his gaze locked on hers.

"Have I told you lately how much I love you, my adorable comtesse?"

Chapter Thirty-eight

Monique opened her eyes fifteen minutes before the alarm was set to go off and stretched deliciously across the huge bed in Eve's guest bedroom.

This is it. No turning back now. I have exactly six hours to get to that church, looking slightly more presentable than I do at this moment.

She and Eve had stayed up until three in the morning, talking and laughing like fifteen-year-olds at a sleepover. Neither of them had been able to get much sleep the past few weeks. The baby was pressing on Eve's bladder, and she found herself constantly running to the bathroom, and Monique had so much pressing on her mind that insomnia had taken hold of her as surely as her frenzied need for cigarettes and coffee. Groaning as she stepped into the shower, Monique spun the jets full blast and prayed the bags under her eyes would mist away in the steam.

Still damp, she padded off to the kitchen, following the lure of Irish Creme coffee. She lit a cigarette as she went.

"You really should get rid of those things," Eve

scolded in greeting. "Don't you want to live to celebrate your golden anniversary with Richard?"

Monique made a face and poured herself a mug of coffee.

"Besides, you promised not to smoke here. Remember, the baby?" Eve reminded her pointedly.

"Whoops. Forgot." Monique stubbed out the cigarette and smiled apologetically. She reached into the refrigerator for a grapefruit. "By the way, you never did tell me who your escort is for the wedding."

"No, I didn't."

"Well?"

To Monique's amazement, Eve looked shy as a schoolgirl. "You know him . . . sort of. Remember Andrew Leonetti?"

Monique dropped the grapefruit onto the counter, startling Ragamuffin, who had been about to curl up on a chair. "I didn't realize . . . I never knew . . . are you seeing him?"

Eve laughed, and tucked a loose strand of hair behind her ear. She'd gained forty pounds and her belly was the size of a porcelain Buddha's, but she looked fresh and glowing in her fuzzy yellow chenille bathrobe that barely made it around her middle.

"Well, we talked a little in Hawaii. And when he heard the news of Nico's car crash, he telephoned from Arizona. He's nice."

"And good-looking," Monique remarked encouragingly.

"*And* good-looking," Eve agreed calmly, stroking Ragamuffin's perked ears as he jumped onto her lap. "Monique, don't make a big deal of this. Andrew was in town last month for a conference on autistic children, and we met for dinner, and that's all."

"That's *all*. That's *all?* We were up until three in the morning, spilling our guts and timing Braxton-Hicks contractions, and you save this little news flash for today?"

Eve actually blushed. "Everyone's entitled to a few secrets," she said smugly, and set down her coffee mug. "Scrambled eggs, or sunny-side up?"

Monique protested that she couldn't eat a thing. She watched Eve wolf down four scrambled eggs, whole wheat toast, a doughnut, and a bowl of strawberries, and wondered if she'd eat like a horse when she was pregnant. Right now she couldn't fathom ever wanting to eat again. She tried to imagine being pregnant with Richard's baby, but all she could summon up was the absurd image of a nurse presenting her a bawling infant with a pipe clenched tightly in its tiny fist and a silver money clip dangling from its umbilical cord.

Caught between a shudder and a giggle, she told Eve, "At the rate you're going, my godchild's going to look like a sumo wrestler. Just promise me you won't deliver the little butterball while I'm walking down the aisle."

By two o'clock Eve's apartment was a hurricane of activity. Jenna, Delia, and Eve dashed around in a blur of blue silk, while Monique's hairdresser removed the hot rollers and fashioned her hair in an explosion of glossy curls.

Clara kept coffee flowing for the makeup artist, photographer, and his two assistants, while Linda, smashing in a tube of amethyst silk, gathered up the veil and bobby pins and with great ceremony slipped a good-luck sixpence into Monique's pearled and beaded shoe.

At last, resplendent in her gold and white gown, Monique was whisked off with her entourage in a cavalcade of limos.

"No turning back now," Eve chuckled gaily.

Monique's stomach lurched. Maybe she should have eaten breakfast after all. When they passed Saks and she saw the spires of St. Patrick's loom up into the searing blue July sky, a wave of faintness washed over her.

Get a grip, Monique. "Anyone have some crackers?" she heard herself ask in a tiny voice. Jenna rummaged through her peau de soie bag and came up with a Velamint. "We can always try to sneak you some unconsecrated communion wafers," she kidded.

It was ninety-seven degrees outside, but Monique felt freezing cold as she stepped dreamlike from the limo and up the white carpet that rippled over the cement staircase and into the darkened vestibule.

They were the last to arrive. The cathedral was packed. "Richard looks fantastic," somebody whispered. She thought it was Delia.

Eve embraced Monique. "I'm going in to find Andrew. They'll be starting any minute." She brushed a light kiss across Monique's cheek, taking care not to smear either of their carefully madeup faces. "Be happy," she whispered. "You deserve it."

Monique's knees knocked together beneath the voluminous folds of the gown. *Maybe this idea of walking myself down the aisle wasn't such a good one—I could use an arm to lean on right now. Guess I'm not as tough as I thought.*

A horrifying thought occurred to her. Maybe Pete was right. Maybe he knew her better than she knew herself.

The organ strains floated through the closed doors. "That's our cue," whispered Linda, before she, Jenna, and Delia disappeared into the cavernous cathedral frosted with exotic blossoms and flickering candlelight, leaving Monique alone in the vestibule.

Monique thought of her mother at that moment and knew Mireille and Dorothy would be sitting in the parlor, watching the crystal clock on the mantelpiece, imagining her every emotion. *But they can't possibly imagine the panic I'm feeling right now.*

The videographer's assistant poked his head through the door. "Two more seconds and you're on, Comtesse."

Two seconds. The door closed with a whisper of finality. Monique took a deep breath and pulled the door open a tiny crack. The cathedral was a fairyland of candles, flowers, and white carpet, the packed pews aglitter with elegantly attired guests.

You love this stuff, she reminded herself. *You love making an entrance and being the center of attention. This is who you are.*

She stepped out as a dramatic chord announced her entrance. All eyes turned to Monique, and a hushed silence blanketed the congregation.

She started down the aisle.

Faces blurred before her, only a few, now and then, coming into focus as she stepped carefully along the petal-strewn white carpet.

There were Ana and John, holding hands.

Alec Anderson, the new art director of *Perfect Bride*, gave her a solemn thumbs-up.

On the aisle, Antonio pantomimed applause while Phil beamed approvingly at his side.

Seated next to Mimi Cohn, Henry Theogustus grinned broadly at her. Doesn't he look like the cat who swallowed the canary? she thought, and for a fleeting instant wondered why.

She caught Brian Michaelson's wink and Teri's glowing smile as they watched her glide by.

She spotted Eve and Andrew Leonetti seated near the front of the cathedral and was struck by how right they looked together.

The heady scent of crushed rose petals filled her senses. Colors and faces rushed by with dizzying confusion. She was almost at the altar.

Richard. Her breath caught in her throat as their eyes met. He looked spectacular in his black tux. Tall, suavely handsome, and commanding. A smile trembled on her lips as he stepped forward, elbow crooked, to escort her those final few steps. She took one last deep breath, and slipped her arm through his. Time journeyed on, surreal, as Linda relieved her of her bouquet, fluffed her veil, and the ceremony began.

"We are gathered here today as witnesses to the holy sacrament of matrimony. If there is anyone here present who has knowledge of any reason whatsoever to prevent the joining in holy matrimony of Monique Lisette D'Arcy and Richard Charles Ives, come forward at this time, or forever remain silent. . . ."

Only Richard could manage to get an annulment after so many years of marriage, Monique reflected dazedly, and then Richard's nephew, Paul, was holding out the lace-trimmed pillow cradling the wedding rings.

"Richard Charles Ives, do you take this woman, Monique Lisette D'Arcy, to be your lawfully wedded wife?" The bishop's words echoed through the cathedral as Richard gazed piercingly into her eyes. Monique saw his lips form the words "I do," but her mind was spinning so fast, she barely heard them.

"Monique Lisette D'Arcy, do you take this man, Richard Charles Ives, to be your lawfully wedded husband in sickness and in health . . ."

She didn't hear the rest.

"No."

The bishop paused, his pointed face startled. He peered at Monique as if he hadn't quite heard properly. Moistening his lips, he continued more loudly, ". . . from this day forward, until death do you part?"

"No."

Monique saw the bishop's eyes go wide. She turned to Richard, who was regarding her with an arctically frozen smile.

"Monique . . . what the *hell*?" he bit off with an intake of breath that was no less ferocious for all its softness. The video camera captured every nuance of his outraged expression.

Monique gave her veiled head a tiny shake. "No, Richard. I'm sorry. I can't."

A strange calm tingled over her like a halo of rosy

candlelight. She smiled her most generous smile, hoisted aside the skirts of her regal gown, and with head held high, strolled back up the aisle. She exited as only Monique could, skimming lightly up that pristine carpet, through the vestibule, and out again into the wilting heat and the waiting limo.

She yanked her gown in behind her and paid no heed to the driver's stunned expression.

"Take the Merritt Parkway. We're going to Connecticut."

Monique was soaked through to her satin bra as she scrambled down the path to the carriage house, catching her gown on every damned rosebush along the way as she tried to hurry.

The gown was now as wrinkled as elephant hide anyway. And her shoes were ruined. But all she cared about was that she wouldn't be too late.

She banged on the carriage-house door.

Pressed on the bell.

Shouted.

No answer.

A fly buzzed through her spray-scented hair and then lazily looped away through the garden. All around her, the peaceful, dreamy scent of roses, daisies, and oleander permeated the overbearing July air.

Monique bit back a sob of frustration. *You can't have gone yet. You just can't.*

She tore off toward the big house. Maybe the new owners knew where he'd gone. Music wafted from one of the upstairs windows, and her throat tightened. Pavarotti . . . she was certain. If it weren't so ironic, she'd have cried.

She leaned on the doorbell with relentless determination. She hammered with the handsome brass knocker, and was at last rewarded by the muffled sound of approaching footsteps.

"Can you tell me where—"

Holding a half-eaten slice of pizza, Pete Lambert stared incredulously at her.

"Where what?"

Monique's heart began to pound like a jackhammer. She closed her eyes and quickly reopened them.

"What are you doing here? I thought you moved."

"What are you doing here? I thought you were getting married."

She glared at him. "I asked you first."

That slow, lazy, infuriating grin spread across his face. "So you did, Comtesse." He took her arm and led her inside.

Even when it was stark naked but freshly painted, the house had been a dream, but with toast and caramel suede furniture, handmade fluffy rugs adorning the highly buffed floors, and Asian and African accents, it was incredible.

Monique, however, hadn't come here to admire the decor. She fixed a steely gaze on Pete and challenged him again, "I thought you moved."

"I did. Like my new digs?"

"*Your* new digs? In your dreams, maybe."

He laughed out loud, tossed his pizza into the Bertino's carton on the coffee table, and wiped his hands on a napkin while Monique wondered if she had fallen into some strange Dali dream. But Pete wasn't surreal, and he wasn't a dream. He was real and solid and gazing at her with a guilty gleam in his eye.

"I have a confession to make. This is my house. Has been from the start."

"How . . . what . . . ?"

"No. You've had your question, Comtesse. It's my turn." He caught her left hand and held it up. "I see you're not wearing a wedding band. What happened?"

Monique stuck her mud-streaked ankle out from beneath the limp folds of the gown. "I'm not wearing a diamond-studded ball and chain either," she retorted.

"Just heard a fashion update that those are passé this year."

He said nothing, but regarded her with an unwavering stare.

She sighed, muttered "What the hell," and plunged ahead. "I left Richard at the altar. For you. If you still . . . that is . . . unless . . ."

Pete seized her so roughly, she gasped. His mouth crushed hers. His arms captured her in a viselike embrace. Monique clutched him, kissing him with the long-pent-up passion she had futilely tried to deny.

"Dammit, Monique." He came up for air. "You went right down to the wire, didn't you?"

"Don't remind me," she begged, pressing kisses against the open V of his T-shirt and sliding her hands across the sinewed muscles of his back. "I was a fool. But if you don't tell me the truth about you and this house right now, I'm going to have to beat it out of you."

"Promises, promises. Monique, let's sit down a minute." He led her to the sofa, pulled her close, and kissed her lips, her earlobes, her throat. He yearned to rip her out of that wedding dress and taste every inch of her, but he forced himself to wait. It was time to explain, time for her to know the whole truth.

He clasped her hands in his and met her searching gaze directly. "All kidding aside, Monique, I really, truly, own this house. I own lots of houses, actually." He laughed at her astonished expression. "I like to buy them and fix them up myself. Some I sell, others I live in—like the one in Palm Beach, or the old castle outside London."

Monique gaped at him. "Who are you?"

"Pete Lambert. Actually, my birth certificate says Peter Ambrose Lambertino. My father made a fortune in the frozen-food business and left my brother, Ted, and me with enough capital apiece to buy a couple of small countries. Add in the stock options, the trust fund, *and* the interest that's accumulated—well, I don't have to worry too much about where my next meal is coming from."

"You're a millionaire?" she gasped, struggling to take in this startling revelation, trying to picture the rugged carpenter in sweat clothes and baseball cap as the heir to a fortune.

"Several times over," he replied solemnly. "I think my father would have liked me to join Ted in running the family business, but I never was much of a corporate type. I've always preferred working with my hands. My father understood that, bless his soul. He was a pretty down-to-earth guy, started out as a baker. So now Ted runs the company solo—I just pop into board meetings on a semiregular basis. It beats wearing the old suit and tie every day."

Monique jabbed her fist into his forearm. "And you never told me any of this? What the hell were you saving it for?"

"I've been burned, Monique—more than once. You struggled your way to the top, I was born there." A shadow crossed his face. "It's a strange perspective. All my life I've contended with women whose interest in me seemed to have more to do with what I had than who I was. It's a weird feeling, always wondering if someone loves you, hell, even *likes* you, just for yourself, without all the trappings. There were moments when I almost told you, when I wanted to compete with Richard Ives on his own terms, but I didn't want my money to be the impetus for your decision—or even a factor. If it had, I'd have lost more than if you'd chosen to spend your life with Richard."

"You idiot, you insecure, infuriating idiot, I do love you for yourself only." Monique grabbed him by the neck of his T-shirt and tugged in time to her words. "Dammit, I walked out on Richard Ives in front of four hundred of our nearest and dearest. I left him at the altar of St. Patrick's, I turned my back on a fortune, a job, and a honeymoon in the Greek islands, all for my needling, aggravating, stubborn, charming, and impossibly sexy dance partner. Do you understand what I'm saying?"

Pete kissed the tip of her nose. "Does this mean we're in love?"

"Is that a proposal?" Monique countered, tossing his baseball cap aside so that she could slide her fingers through the thickness of his hair. Her eyes were soft as she awaited his reply.

"Damned right it is . . . speaking of which . . ."

From his pocket, impossibly, came a small velvet box. "I've been carrying this around for days. It's wearing a hole in my pocket. Thought I'd be taking it back to the jeweler's on Monday." He flipped the lid open and held out the box, watching her face.

Monique could only stare, bewitched. A six-carat blue diamond ring glittered in its bed of black velvet.

"I've never seen *anything* as beautiful," she whispered.

"I have," Pete said softly. "And I'll take that as a yes," he added, and kissed her again.

"By the way," Monique murmured as he flung the headpiece to the floor and began toying with the satin rosette fastenings down her back. "What kind of food business did you say your father was in?"

"Pizza. Bertino's pizza."

"What?" Monique glanced wildly at the cardboard box on the table. *"You're* Bertino's pizza?"

"I told you it was an old family recipe," he reminded her. And before she knew it, he had swept her up into his arms and was carrying her toward the staircase.

As they neared the skylit landing, Monique lifted her head from his shoulder and murmured, "I'll have to design a brand-new dress for our wedding. *Maman* will help, I'm sure—something completely different . . . oh, I can hardly wait." She suddenly exclaimed, "You know, I had the best time designing this dress . . . bringing my own ideas from paper to something real, something beautiful . . . why couldn't I start my own design studio? I'm certainly not going back to *Perfect Bride.*" Her voice quickened with excitement. "I can see it now, a whole designer line of couture evening clothes and wedding gowns . . . the Comtesse line . . . I could work right from here, you could redo the carriage house as a studio . . . and we could go over every day and have lunch with *Maman.* . . ."

Pete dumped her on the bed. "Do you think we could wait an hour or so to get started on the carriage house? There's something else I'd really like to do right now."

Monique grinned at him as she drew him down beside her on the bed. "Oh, yeah?" She began tugging at his sweat shorts, eyes agleam. "What else have you got hidden inside here for me?"

Pete had her out of the wedding dress—the dress that took three women half an hour to button her into —in five minutes flat. "God, do I love you, Monique." He tossed the rumpled gown to the floor and covered her long, naked body with his own. "Something old, something new, I've always been in love with you," he grinned, and began nibbling a path toward the hard, rosy peak of her breast.

"And I love you, Pete Lambert." Monique smiled with intoxicating happiness and breathed in the scent of his hair. "Guaranteed."

ABOUT THE AUTHOR

JILLIAN KARR is the pseudonym of two writers collaborating on a novel for the first time. JAN GREENBERG is better known as Jill Gregory, the author of the *New York Times* bestseller *The Wayward Heart* and the 1992 Dell bestseller *Cherished.* She has previously collaborated with KAREN A. KATZ on a nonfiction book, *What Does Being Jewish Mean?* Both authors live in Michigan.

The Very Best in Contemporary Women's Fiction

Sandra Brown

_____	28951-9 TEXAS! LUCKY	$5.99/6.99 in Canada
_____	28990-X TEXAS! CHASE	$5.99/6.99
_____	29500-4 TEXAS! SAGE	$5.99/6.99
_____	29085-1 22 INDIGO PLACE	$5.99/6.99
_____	29783-X A WHOLE NEW LIGHT	$5.99/6.99
_____	56045-X TEMPERATURES RISING	$5.99/6.99
_____	56274-6 FANTA C	$4.99/5.99
_____	56278-9 LONG TIME COMING	$4.99/5.99

Tami Hoag

_____	29534-9 LUCKY'S LADY	$4.99/5.99
_____	29053-3 MAGIC	$4.99/5.99
_____	56050-6 SARAH'S SIN	$4.50/5.50
_____	29272-2 STILL WATERS	$4.99/5.99
_____	56160-X CRY WOLF	$5.50/6.50
_____	56161-8 DARK PARADISE	$5.99/7.50

Nora Roberts

_____	29078-9 GENUINE LIES	$5.99/6.99
_____	28578-5 PUBLIC SECRETS	$5.99/6.99
_____	26461-3 HOT ICE	$5.99/6.99
_____	26574-1 SACRED SINS	$5.99/6.99
_____	27859-2 SWEET REVENGE	$5.99/6.99
_____	27283-7 BRAZEN VIRTUE	$5.99/6.99
_____	29597-7 CARNAL INNOCENCE	$5.50/6.50
_____	29490-3 DIVINE EVIL	$5.99/6.99

Deborah Smith

_____	29107-6 MIRACLE	$4.50/5.50
_____	29092-4 FOLLOW THE SUN	$4.99/5.99
_____	28759-1 THE BELOVED WOMAN	$4.50/5.50
_____	29690-6 BLUE WILLOW	$5.50/6.50
_____	29689-2 SILK AND STONE	$5.99/6.99

Theresa Weir

_____	56092-1 LAST SUMMER	$4.99/5.99
_____	56378-5 ONE FINE DAY	$4.99/5.99

Ask for these titles at your bookstore or use this page to order.

Please send me the books I have checked above. I am enclosing $ _____ (add $2.50 to
cover postage and handling). Send check or money order, no cash or C. O. D.'s please.

Mr./ Ms. _____

Address _____

City/ State/ Zip _____

Send order to: Bantam Books, Dept. FN 24, 2451 S. Wolf Road, Des Plaines, IL 60018
Please allow four to six weeks for delivery.
Prices and availability subject to change without notice.

FN 24 4/94